More Praise for *A Short Move*

"*A Short Move* is an expansive and beautifully written novel. Through the story of star linebacker Mitch Wilkins, Katherine Hill explores the sacrifices men make to become legends, and the toll their fame takes on everyone close to them. This book is about more than just the complicated and contradictory life of a football star who wishes he were a better man; it is a profound depiction of masculinity, obsession, power, and the unexpected beauty we find even in our darkest hours."
—**Tom McAllister**, author of *How to Be Safe*

"I submit that there is nothing you can't get to about American culture through sports, and I further submit, as evidence, Exhibit A: *A Short Move*, Katherine Hill's splendidly written and smartly observed second novel."
—**David Shields**, director of *Marshawn Lynch: A History* and author of *Black Planet: Facing Race During an NBA Season*

"Fans of sweeping family epics will enjoy this dissection of fame, sports, and the drive for connection."—*Publishers Weekly*

A

SHORT

MOVE

A
SHORT
MOVE

A Novel

KATHERINE HILL

PUBLISHING
New York, NY

Printed in the United States of America

10 9 8 7 6 5 4 3 2 1

No part of this book may be used or reproduced in any manner without written permission of the publisher. Please direct inquires to:

Ig Publishing
Box 2547
New York, NY 10163

www.igpub.com

ISBN: 978-1-632461-03-2 (paperback)

The following chapters have been previously published, in different form: Chapter 6 as "Draft Day" in *The Common* and Chapter 10 as "The Finest Milled Cotton" in *n+1*.

For Matt

"To be alive meant to continually collide with the existence of others and to be collided with, the results being at times good-natured, at others aggressive, then again good-natured." —Elena Ferrante

1. JOE, 1971

Eight months before the legendary linebacker Mitch Wilkins was born, his father Joe stood at the edge of the Briarwood College pasture, gazing at a huddle of black-and-white cows. Joe had left his jacket at his girlfriend Cindy's, and he was cold, though apparently the cows, those living radiators, were not. Even from his distance, he thought he could see the heat rising from their backs. He whistled a little, trying to get their attention. When the right one looked at him—say, the near one in perfect silhouette—he'd go to Cindy, explain about the ring, and ask her if she'd have him anyway. He didn't know what he'd do if one of the other cows looked—the ones with their bony butts to him, or the ones already kind of facing his way. Try again, maybe, with a different cow?

He whistled again, louder this time, and the next thing he knew, the cows were all stock-still, but in slightly different positions, a head here, a belly there. He registered some noses, and above each, a pair of big, bored eyes, and yet it was impossible to say if any of these faces belonged to his original cow. He'd blacked out, missed the crucial shift, perhaps he'd even missed it twice, and with this realization he found himself seized with panic. He was nineteen and staring at cows. He had no jacket, no engagement ring, and no idea how he'd messed up so bad.

Part of him wanted to blame his brothers. Rob: the oldest, with the chin scar and the hippo hands. Tim: the veiny one, younger by a year, shorter by an inch, and true to all lazy assumptions more pugnacious by a mile. They'd always been a trio with him, the Wild Williams Boys, but then, out of nowhere, the older two broke ranks, voluntarily deploying to Vietnam when Joe was still in high school. Everything fell apart after that. His dad seemed to be drunk more often, even in the mornings, and his mom slowed down, then simply stopped cleaning the house. Next thing Joe knew, she had breast cancer and a forecast of six months to live. He coped by throwing himself into his final season of Monacan County High School football and Monacan County High School parties. His dad coped by trying to get Joe a college scholarship, a scheme that involved a lot of loud, beer-battered phone calls and one sideline chat with a suit-wearing "scout," whose gospel Joe actually allowed himself to believe. In the end, despite a solid senior season, Joe graduated with zero scholarship offers. Then his mom died, leaving him all alone with an increasingly belligerent dad, and no brothers around to tell him what to do.

He really could've used them in his present situation, especially Robbie, who didn't get mad like Tim. The present situation was that Cindy was pregnant. Cindy, who was so new to Joe she'd never even met his mom, and so studious and respectable she'd barely met his friends, though they'd all gone to school together all their lives, and she'd even played volleyball, walking the halls in her shorts and high socks. He'd noticed her then, how could he not notice an extravagantly tall and pigtailed creature like Cindy Wilkins, but he'd been too hamstrung by stereotypes—she was a good girl, he was a degenerate—that he mostly pretended to ignore her. All that went out the window after his mom died, and he was feeling raw and open to anything, especially to women who seemed healthy and good, and it was in this frame of mind that he ran into Cindy at a bonfire, and she turned out to be exactly his type, confident in herself and surprisingly eager to fool around. Just like that, she forced him to re-evaluate his understanding of goodness and by extension his understanding of himself. Maybe he didn't have to be a degenerate. Maybe he could be his own type.

But then came her pregnancy, and with it another re-evaluation. You're gonna run now, she said, aren't you. Stung, he promised to marry her that very night, while she, in all her decency, tried to talk him out of it, saying don't be hasty, marriage isn't a game, I'm not telling you to pressure you, maybe you're not done being wild. But what the hell else was he supposed to do with such serious information? He rushed home, which was by now a genuine junk box of a living situation, cluttered with his old man's empty beer bottles and half-eaten containers of food, not to mention towers of unread newspapers, used tissues and suspiciously smeared man briefs, to claim the one thing his mother had left him, her engagement ring. His dad was in his usual spot, passed out on the couch, which gave Joe a clear lane to the stairs. What wasn't choked with dust was sticky and crawling with fruit flies, and the entire house smelled tuberish, a mixture of exfoliated skin and fart and the sour tang of days-old booze. But amid the master bedroom mess, his mom's ring was still there in its faded velvet box: gold band, diamond crown, a tiny piece of indestructibility. He held it in his hand and thought maybe everything would be all right.

It was a short-lived happiness, because the next thing he knew his father was awake and before him, already ranting, demanding to know what the hell was going on. In recent months he'd been harder on Joe than ever, though Joe had never shown more direction, hauling peat, planting shrubs, clearing branches, and generally disposing of the natural debris that menaced the prim grounds of Briarwood College, where his dad ran the physical plant. He loved the sweat, the muscle groups firing, the little-kid thrill of sticking his hands into dirt, and he loved bringing home milk from the dairy. What he didn't love was coming home to his father, who devoted his down time to heavy drinking, ruthless criticism, and goading Joe into useless fights. The old man was spry for a congenital alcoholic, could get a good grip, every now and then wriggle out of a hold, but Joe's reflexes were sharper, his balance better, his brain not made of mush. He pinned his father every time, lightly held him down kicking and yelling until the old man just ran out of gas, which was exactly what happened again that night, when he came upstairs to find Joe, "taking priceless things without asking," except this time Joe was so buzzed on his sudden new future, so certain the ring was rightfully his, and so finally fed up with his father's distortions, the catastrophe of his inflated belly, the aftershock of his blood-shot eyes, his empty speechifying and his human smell, all the beers he drank while his wife lay dying, all the petty and regular ways he had of making Joe feel stupid and small, that he might've overdone it, thrown a real punch or two, and finished off with some personal accusations that reduced the old man to tears. And to top it off, after Joe finally disentangled himself and got the hell out of that miserable house, he discovered, driving in darkness back to Cindy's, digging into his pocket with one hand, the other loosely guiding the wheel, that he hadn't even managed to hold onto the ring. That he'd sought it and fought for it and won it—but then he'd lost it, slipped from his hand in the scuffle maybe, or dropped in the grass on the long way out.

"Come on," he called to the college pasture, where he'd finally pulled over around one a.m., too disgusted with himself to face Cindy just yet, and where he'd awoken that morning in his car, his neck bent almost to his chest, his body rigid from trying to clench in its heat. He leaned into the fencepost, desperate for a decision. The one on the middle-left, in perfect profile. That was his new magic cow.

He knew he ought to quit playing and just go to Cindy. What did she care about the ring? He'd buy her a better one later, and while he saved up for it, they could live with her parents, a sort of helpless but honorable pair, Mrs. Wilkins on disability from arthritis, Mr. Wilkins without an arm from World War II. It wouldn't be so bad. Her bedroom even had a private entrance.

But the problem, he was beginning to understand, was bigger than the ring. Say he married her and they had a son. Say he spent every day in a tidy house, teaching that kid how to treat people—didn't even make him play football, but didn't stop him either, if that's what the kid wanted to do. Say his brothers came home and raised families of their own, and in the meantime Joe completely turned himself around, got a million degrees and became a doctor or something. Even then, there'd be blind spots, gaps in coverage, things he plainly couldn't control. And whatever his situation, he'd still be himself, the degenerate son of his own failed father. Try as he might, he couldn't reason his way out of that one.

A cow was approaching him now with surprising velocity, like a time-lapse film of the cow's whole day. She stood before him, a woolly tank with a nose like a giant rubber pad and ears that fired straight from her head. Finally. It was almost uncanny, after all that time she'd spent standing around. He placed a hand on her neck, and she tolerated it, even seemed to authorize a transfer of warmth. In that moment of weird skin-to-skin contact, he had a memory of being a kid on his dad's shoulders, back when his dad was muscular and fast. Together, they were the Monacan Maniac, the strongest man that ever lived. They tore through the yard like that, stalking Joe's terrorized brothers, especially Tim, the spiteful middle one, who always made a point of pinning Joe. He remembered his legs hugging his father's neck, his father's hands cupping his ankles, so that Joe could be the big one for a change, so that Joe could sense in the grown man beneath him all the power his body would one day contain. His father had done his best for him, he could see that, but it hadn't made much difference.

Because how much bigger was he now, and how much better, if he could stand there as long as he had touching the cow, the one he supposedly sought, the one that meant it was time to go to Cindy, and already know that Cindy had been right, that he was scared and he wasn't going to marry her, because he barely knew her and he'd rather be wild, because the main thing his body contained, and would no doubt contain for the rest of his life, was nothing but an urgent and genetic need to punish his child, to be like his father, to be like his brothers, to ruin the good things, to run?

2. MITCH, 1977

Mitch Wilkins did not remember his first ball. He did not even remember the first one he remembered. It was too constant, simply part of the this that was everywhere and had always been with him: ball, grass, feet, sky, ball, hands, grass. His mother tossing it to him in his grandparents' backyard. His grandparents cheering from their plastic chairs.

There was one particular time, though, when his Uncle Tim, who he'd just met, held out a ball, an object Mitch saw by then as his own organ, and said, "All right, kid, let's see what you got."

Mitch was five and about to start school, and Tim was in jeans and a t-shirt, hucking the ball his way: shoulder, chest, elbow, wrist. Mitch had a grandpa with one arm and he didn't have a dad, but now, all of a sudden, he had an uncle, his dad's brother: a man with two arms in his own endless backyard, where he and his mom had just moved.

He caught the ball, reset himself, hucked it back. A movement so short and fast he immediately wanted to do it again.

Mitch had waited his whole life for kindergarten—significance began, it seemed, with school, with the sequence of one grade after another—and now he was finally there, one of the bigger kids, at the end of the alphabet, almost six. He wanted it to be the great event he'd always heard about, so he was frustrated when Miss B told him he had trouble paying attention, especially since he knew that the opposite was true. When he wanted something, his focus was fierce. He would be seized as if by a hand in the head, squeezing from his brain all other thoughts until he had the thing, and the squeezing at last released. He wanted the ball and he wanted to be good at school, and what he wanted most for his sixth birthday was a set of Rock'Em Sock'Em Robots. One was blue and one was red, and they stood in a square yellow boxing ring.

"Aren't you a bit young?" his mom said, when he told her. And when he insisted, she got even stricter: "I don't like these violent games."

"It's not violent, it's robots!"

"What if I got you one like this?" she asked, showing him a picture of a blocky silver figure with owl eyes and senseless dials on his belly. "It looks more like a real robot."

He was in agony. He could not explain to her that it was the shape of Rock'Em Sock'Em Robots that he liked. The dukes up, the bent knees, the way they were positioned across from each other so that every punch landed, because that's what Rock'Em Sock'Em Robots were built and meant to do. It wasn't about knocking the head off, though that was how you won. It was about the heads themselves, which were covered in bolts and bent forward, and came to a neat V at the back. It was about the upper arms and legs that were rounded at the joint, like giant drumsticks, almost human. As far as he was concerned, Rock'Em Sock'Em Robots were the real thing; any other toy robot was fake.

But she must've understood, she was smart, because she got it for him, and for many days after his birthday he was late to dinner because he was busy manipulating the triggers, trying to figure out how to play both sides, get both heads to pop at once. Sometimes Tim was red and he was blue, and then they were late together.

She also got him a dog, a puppy from a stray litter the neighbors had discovered under their deck, and this was smart too, because he hadn't even realized he wanted a dog until she put it in his lap, at which point he wanted it so much he thought his own head might pop. The puppy was mostly black with a head that was mostly white and a butt that was tough and a mouth that was often open and pink as raw meat inside. She would train him if Mitch would feed and walk him. That had to be the deal. Mitch called him Spike, and he did feed him, most of the time, and when he didn't, she yelled, and he knew he couldn't complain. He also chased Spike around the yard and threw him sticks that the dog only sometimes brought back. For his part, Spike liked to sit at Mitch's feet while he ate, but wasn't too fond of his bed. Every time Mitch put him there, he took off, his black eyes completely fixed on something urgent and invisible. He got into things, too. Garbage, stuff in the woods, certain pairs of his mom's nice shoes.

One day Mitch was in the yard with his mom and Tim and Spike, and Tim and his mom were hugging each other nonstop, and his mom was in such a beautiful mood she said why don't we all get ice cream after dinner, even though it was no longer summer. Mitch in his excitement started jumping up and down, and apparently it was too much excitement for Spike, because out of nowhere he let out a growl and leapt at Mitch's leg. It hurt, but that was not as scary as the blood, which came rushing up from some dark, endless place inside of him, soaking through his jeans, and it was not as scary as the look on his mom's face when she came rushing over to help. The endlessness was scary because he thought he was contained, but so was the thought of running out, because once you were out of blood, you were dead, even from your leg, even he knew that.

He got two stitches from the doctor, and in the end everything was fine. His grandpa, though, was furious. He threatened to shoot the dog. Mitch screamed and cried and begged him not to and his mom flung her hands and said, "No one's shooting anybody" and "Jesus, Dad, why do you talk like that?"

Spike ran away soon after that anyway. He'd never been too good at staying where Mitch tried to put him, and he'd been acting guilty ever since the bite. They'd only had him a few weeks. A little later Tim got him another dog, a smaller, cuter one called Daisy who didn't like to wrestle so much. But Daisy wouldn't stay in the yard. Where she went was a mystery to all of them, and eventually she ran away, too.

There were other mysteries, for instance Grandpa's arm, which was missing, and Uncle Tim, who was at the house now as often as Grandma and Grandpa, and who leaned into doorframes and folded his arms over his chest before he came all the way into the room. When he showed up, it was usually with something in his hands: a ladder to get the leaves out of the gutter, or a bag of green army men, or a big bunch of flowers for Mitch's mom.

When Mitch asked him what he did all day, he replied that he was fixing up his family's house and he was thinking about going to school, "Just like you."

Mitch laughed at this; it was preposterous. His uncle had played football in California. He'd been a soldier in Vietnam. He could not hang his jacket in a cubby and keep his pencils inside a desk.

Grandpa had also been a soldier, and though that had been a long time ago, he sometimes talked about it with Mitch.

"The war took it," he always said about his arm, which didn't exactly make sense.

"But where did it go?" Mitch finally asked him one day. "Where is it right now?"

"You planning a trip, son? Hoping to pay it a visit? Tell it hello for me, will you? It's been a while."

Mitch laughed. His grandpa was quiet, a solo smoker, not much of a comedian with anyone else. He saved all his cigarettes for his private time and he saved all his jokes for Mitch. "Okay, but where? Be serious, Grandpa." A thing his mother often used on him.

At this his grandpa resumed his standard gaze, filled with hard experience. His empty sleeve hung from his shoulder like a napkin as his remaining arm felt in his pocket for his pack. "Some of it's in a field in France, where it went back into the earth. The doctors took the rest to save my life."

"They took it?"

"I let them. I wanted to live. I wanted to meet your mom and you."

This hardly made sense, since he and his mom did not at that point exist, but Mitch knew he had to stay on track. "And where," he asked, "did they put it?"

"Tell you the truth, son, I don't know. Somewhere safe, I'm sure."

Later, after Grandpa came in from his break, bringing with him the faintest trace of smoke, Mitch heard him talking to his mom. "He's a special one, that son of yours. Most kids want to know why. Not Mitch. All he asks is where, where, where."

"Good for him. He's going places."

"Well, aren't you funny."

"It's just a word, Daddy. I wouldn't read too much into it."

Even so, Mitch thought she sounded pleased.

Mom was less of a mystery, having never in her life left Virginia, having always been with him. Her name was Cindy and she made him bologna sandwiches with mustard on white for lunch and fish sticks with peas for dinner, both of which he liked. Other kids' moms wrote notes on their paper napkins, which at first seemed strange to Mitch, whose own lunchbox came with a sandwich and a folded paper towel, and sometimes a cookie, but that was it. He mentioned to her once that Jeff's mom had written him a knock-knock joke to go with his orange, and for the next several days he got oranges in his lunch as well. He liked oranges, and was happy to eat them, but what he'd really wanted was the note. He wanted to see what she would write.

"Why don't you ever put a note in my lunch?" he demanded one afternoon.

She'd been hollering at him for sneaking cookies before dinner, a thing he knew was wrong, but not that wrong, and his counterattack had caught her off guard. "A note?" she asked, as though she didn't know the word.

"On the napkin. The other moms write notes."

She chewed her lip. "You want a note from me? That doesn't embarrass you?"

"No."

"Well, sure, sweetie. I'll write you a note."

She might not have always understood him right, but she was always true to her word, so the next day, he was not surprised when he opened his Superman lunchbox to find the usual sandwich and orange, along with a folded paper towel.

When he unfolded it, he saw that she had written, in thin, light pen marks that nevertheless punctured the towel on the opening "D,"

> *Dear Mitch*
> *You are always in my heart*
> *Love*
> *Mom*

He didn't know what he had expected, but he spent the better part of the lunch period examining her letters, which, puncture marks aside, were otherwise crisp and very straight. *You are always in my heart.* He felt hot, pictured himself very small inside her body. When he was done with his orange, he wiped his chin, and *Mom* nearly vanished in the juice.

"Did you get my note?" she asked him at dinner.

"Yes."

"Was it what you wanted?"

He told her it was. "You tore the napkin though."

"Tough customer," Tim laughed. Now that his mom was working overnight shifts, Tim was eating dinner with them almost every evening and sleeping in her bedroom so he could look after Mitch. He seemed happy with himself, and with both of them, and this made Mitch feel good about their house. He was growing up in a family. His mom had set it up just right.

She made a kissy-face at Tim. "See? He notices everything."

"Also Jeff's mom writes him jokes," Mitch said.

Tim threw up his hands. "You're killing me, kid. Give her a break."

But she stood, drew her finger along Tim's ear and neck in a way that made his face go mushy, and took her reminder pad off the hook by the phone. "A joke," she said, writing it down. "Yes, sir. Will there be anything else?"

A couple times they helped Tim organize things at his own house, Tim and his mom in jeans and yellow cleaning gloves, while Mitch poked around in the yard. There were always great sticks at Tim's—which was big and old and surrounded by trees, not like Mitch's house, which was boxy and new and out in the bright open—and plenty of pine cones he could bring to his mom.

The first time they went it began to rain and Mitch dutifully came inside. He found his mother in the second bathroom.

"If you think this is bad," she said. "You should see how it looked before."

It hadn't occurred to Mitch that Tim's house was anything to complain about, but now that she'd suggested it, the horror of the bathroom presented itself. There was a window, but it was so covered in its own grime that hardly any light filtered through. Beside that was a buried commode, stacked high with old beauty magazines and catalogs, which started on the floor and reached almost as high as the wall-mounted tank. The sink faucet and handles were bright orange with rust and the free-standing tub was completely filled, not with water, but with objects that Mitch's mom was sorting: small dusty bottles of personal cream, sets of hot rollers, wigs, several heating pads, two baby dolls with broken eyes, clothes hangers, curtain rods, bars of soap so old they weren't clean anymore, their wrappings rimmed with rings of brown. Mitch's mom explained that most of these things had belonged to Tim's mother and that Tim's dad hadn't known what to do with them, Tim's dad who had died from drinking and left the mess to Tim. The rest were just things he was saving for a future that never came to pass: burnt-out light bulbs, alkaline batteries coated on the ends with furry crystals, a dusty red Coca-Cola crate with twenty-four unopened bottles, a tin of chocolate bars that crumbled pinkishly when he unwrapped one to check it out.

"Can I have a Coke?" Mitch asked after they tossed the chocolate. She pulled out a bottle and peered up through the foggy bottom and told him she didn't think he should.

After the rain let up he went back into the yard and pretended he still had Spike. He threw a few sticks as far as he could and fake-threw the rest because it took some energy to gather them up again, and while he was doing this and thinking of Spike it occurred to him that Spike was probably dead, like Tim's parents, and that it was possible he hadn't even run away, but was shot by his grandpa after all, and that maybe Daisy had been, too, maybe even with his mom's consent. He stood there thinking about this, and about his leg that had healed except for a few dark marks, and he was proud of himself for not feeling sad about the fate of the dogs. He didn't even feel wronged. He felt pleased he'd gotten smart enough to see through the plots of adults.

When their work was done for the day, they made a pile of black garbage bags that Tim would drive to the dump. Several additional boxes were filled with items to take to Goodwill.

Tim said, "Never give up on a house with strong bones," a rule that obviously did not apply to dogs.

On a later visit, Mitch fell out of a tree he was trying to climb. Like the house, his bones were strong, so nothing broke, but his mom was furious all the same. She said he'd been at least two stories high. From then on, she made him help her in the house, where she could watch him. It was still full of things, but the bathroom, at least, was usable. He himself had tested the toilet, aiming at the orange oval at the bottom of the bowl. He didn't manage to vanquish it but he could feel the possibility as it faded slightly with the flush. When he ran the tub faucet the water now came out clear.

His mom might've bossed him, and covered up dog deaths, but she was careful with him, much more careful than he ever was with himself. One day she made him noodles with butter and cheese, and as he twirled them on his fork she told him calmly, like it wasn't anything to get excited about, that his father wanted to speak with him.

"Where?" he asked, thinking he might have to go someplace, someplace he might not want to go. He knew by then that his father was Tim's younger brother. He'd grown up in the garbage house with Tim, but now lived far away. He also knew their third brother had died in Vietnam, which his mom had warned him never to bring up with Tim.

"On the phone. But only if you want to."

He chewed and swallowed, then said, "Okay."

"You sure? Understand you don't have to. This is only a request he's made. It's entirely up to you."

Mitch thought for a moment because that was what she seemed to want. "I'll do it," he said, after what seemed like a decent interval.

"Do you have any questions?" she persisted. "Why now? What's he been up to?"

Mitch looked at her. She was doing such a good job. Even he could tell that. She really thought about things, his mom. Though he understood now that she'd been talking with this person—Tim's brother, his dad—and he wasn't quite sure how he felt about that.

"I guess I'll just ask him," Mitch said, and she let the subject rest.

It was a few days later that they actually spoke, after school at a pre-arranged time. "I'll just be in the other room if you need me," his mom said when she handed him the phone.

He'd seen photos of his dad—a school portrait with focused eyes, a snapshot with his mom in a parking lot—so he had a mental picture of the voice he was about to hear. But the voice didn't quite match the picture. It was rusty, as though he hadn't used it in a really long time, more like the house where he'd grown up than the face in the photos. At first, they didn't say much. But then his dad asked him how his mother was doing, what she got up to every day, and they coasted along on that subject for a while, Mitch telling him her work schedule at the hospital, the hours she was on and the hours she was off, and what she gave him to eat and what he wished she gave him instead, and his dad laughed and said, "All right," like he was really enjoying himself.

"She get you ice cream every now and again?"

Mitch told him she did.

"Good. You gotta have ice cream." And Mitch said that he agreed.

His dad told him a few stories about his life. How he'd lived all over the place, in New Orleans and Houston and Santa Fe and Denver, and how everywhere he'd gone, even the roughest places, and even at times when he didn't especially like himself, he'd always found good people. Good women, he said, in particular. They lived everywhere he'd ever been. Now he'd finally found his home in Montana, where he was working construction on a brand new road. He had read a book that had changed his life, and had bought a motorcycle he was learning to fix. It was about speed as a way of slowing down, he said, and it was about quality, a notion Mitch recognized but didn't really grasp. "I'm no maniac," he said at one point. "I'm making better choices." And later, about Tim, "Tell that maniac I say hello." It seemed to be one of his words.

As the conversation drew to a close, he gave Mitch his number if he ever wanted to call. Mitch thanked him and said he would, even though he knew he wouldn't. It wasn't that he disliked him. He'd liked the sound of his dad's voice once it got flowing, and he liked the idea of him on a motorcycle out west. It was just that he didn't call anyone, and anyway he figured they'd already talked.

"Hello, Maniac," Mitch said that evening, when Tim appeared in his doorway as usual.

"Hello yourself," Tim said. He came over to where Mitch was positioning a battalion of green army men in defense of the Rock'Em Sock'Em ring.

"That's from your brother," Mitch told him. "He said tell that maniac hello."

Tim stood over him for a moment, as though he were trying to remember what *brother* meant, as well as *maniac*, and maybe even *hello*, and when he finally did, he tore off, looking for Mitch's mom.

"So that's it? You just let Mitch talk to him? Just like that?" Mitch heard him say. He couldn't hear the exact words of his mom's response, but he could tell from her tone that they were strong. He rushed out of his room and found them facing one another in the hall. Tim was looking hard at her, so hard he actually seemed to be looking at himself. His mom was wearing her scrubs and had her hair up.

"I had to do it," she was saying. "I mean I had to. He's

already six years old."

"I could kill him," Tim said. "I could kill him." His hands were swinging at his sides.

"Tim, please."

"I could."

His mom said, "Honestly, I should've done it a long time ago. When Robbie died"—she tripped on the word—"I should've tracked him down."

"That was *his* job," Tim growled. "That was his job to show up for Robbie."

"I know it was, but you know what, maybe the time's finally right. I'm over it, and he's cleaned himself up. He's a Buddhist now."

"I told you, you can't trust anything he says," Tim said. "He's a shirker. He's no good."

"Forgiveness, Tim. What about that? You said yourself he always had a good heart."

Tim was pacing now, his hands clenching, then unclenching, then gripping the cap of his head. "So he's coming back, then?" he asked. "Is that what this is?"

"He lives in Montana," Mitch explained, and they both looked at him.

"Believe me," Tim said. "I know."

His mom gave him a look that was love, then turned a similar look on Tim. "It's just a visit."

"You shouldn't have gone on without telling me," Tim was saying. "Everything was going so good here with us."

"He's Mitch's father," she said. "Don't you understand that?"

Tim flinched, resisting her. Mitch himself often resisted her when she tried to force something on him, and he wondered what it was about this moment that was forcing itself on Tim.

Her voice was so soft it was practically holding them, and she was merely stating facts. There was no trace of the short, snappish tone, or the universe of impossible requests that usually set off Mitch.

"Tim?" she said. She was nearly begging. "It'll be good for all of us. Mitch. You. You and me. It really won't do any harm."

Nights she was home, Mitch sometimes went into her bedroom, even though he was a big boy now. Her grown-up stuff was everywhere, nothing like the disaster of Tim's house, but maybe on its way there: clothes thrown over chairs, her spiral planner at the bedside, bowls of pine cones she'd collected in the woods decorating the top of her dresser. They were extensions of her, these bedroom objects, things he'd sense on her in the light, as she went about her day. But for now, they stood back, respecting his specialness. He fought her so hard during the day sometimes, when frustration possessed him, when she made him do something, or when he demanded something that she had the gall to refuse. At night they got along better. He would look at her clock radio—two o'clock, it often said—and feel himself living an opposite life. He would cuddle up against her in her warm, white night gown and she would tell him he was her little man. "No matter what happens, we're together. It'll always be you and me."

"Joe's riding out here," his mom said a little while later, when it was almost Christmas. "It'll be good for you to meet him."

Mitch knew this was coming, but it troubled him all the same. "What are we going to do?" he asked. It was hard to imagine Joe in person. He pictured himself in an empty room, talking to an intercom.

"Get to know each other, toss the ball around, I don't know. Whatever y'all want."

He felt hyper. He needed more information. "Is he coming for Christmas? Where's he going to sleep?"

"At Tim's, don't worry. Not here. And, no, he's coming before Christmas. We'll still have Christmas our way." She spoke like his mother, like she had it all under control.

But when the day arrived she couldn't stop looking down the street, even before Mitch's father—Joe—was late, and when he finally did show up, two hours late at two o'clock, on the noisy motorcycle he'd told Mitch about, she acted almost surprised.

"Well, hello, stranger," she said, joining Mitch in the yard, where he'd been messing around all afternoon. Joe kicked the bike off and came up the path in his jeans and a heavy jean jacket. He looked like the man from the photographs—but realer, not black-and-white. He was definitely older, too. The skin on his face was tough and red. He squatted down in front of Mitch, looking confused, like maybe he didn't have the right family. Mitch was about to introduce himself, but when he glanced at his mother on the step, everything about her posture told him that Joe was supposed to speak first.

They got through it, somehow, Joe uttering something like an apology, Mitch shrugging it was no big deal. He felt grateful to be in his own front yard, no phones, no intercoms, everyone speaking through their own real bodies. Then the ball came out, and they threw it back and forth, and pretty soon everything was fine. It stayed fine when Tim pulled up with Mitch's grandparents. He walked over from his truck rubbing his hands together. Tim and Joe punched each other on the arm, called each other Maniac. Joe kissed his grandma's cheek and shook his grandpa's hand. Then everyone turned their attentions to Mitch. If it was not one of them throwing him the ball, it was another: Tim, Mom, Grandpa, Mom, Joe, Tim, Joe. He ran to the farthest points of the yard, diving for touchdown passes.

"You can't catch me!" he said, after one really excellent catch, and took off running down the street. It was a mistake, but an exhilarating one, because the brothers soon came pounding down the asphalt behind him, two pairs of grown man legs running loud as a motorcycle in his brain. He heard them approaching, and that's when he made his second mistake: He looked over his shoulder and saw their straining necks and chests, and the next thing he knew they had passed him on either side, neither one of them even tagging him, and then they were in front of him and he was looking at their heels kicking up dust, and again it didn't matter, because they were his and they were fast and that meant that he was fast, it was just that he was young.

They got to some endpoint and stopped. He had also stopped and he could see them in the distance, down by the Boatwrights' mailbox. They were bent over with their hands on their knees and talking, then standing upright, then walking back, Tim flapping his arm at Joe, who was a couple of paces behind. Pretty soon Tim broke into a trot.

"Come on!" he called. Tim came up to where Mitch had stopped, still clutching the football, and Mitch could sense that the game had changed; it wasn't going to be about him catching passes anymore. "We're having a do-over and we need you to officiate. You'll stand out there and hold your arms out. The winner's the one who tags you first."

"Who won that time?"

"That's what's in dispute!"

"Come on, Tim," Joe said, coming up behind him. "We don't need to do this."

Tim panted like an actual maniac. "You're so sure you won the first time. Don't think you can do it again?"

"I did win. Any fool could've seen it."

"So you won't mind racing again for the ref."

"*I* want to race!" Mitch cried.

Joe laughed. "You'll lose, kid."

"I get a head start! I want to race!" The brothers looked at each other and he could feel them working something out between them.

"All right, fine," Tim said. "You can race. Cindy!" He called to her through cupped hands. "Come ref!"

She came over, not as quickly as Mitch would've liked, her arms folded in front of her chest. Once the terms of the contest were negotiated, Mitch tossed the ball to the side of the road and went back to the starting point with his father and uncle, where he lined up between them and a little ways ahead, to wait for his mother's count.

This time, they seemed to overtake him immediately. He didn't care, though, he kept going, and for a moment or two he could feel himself closing the gap, pumped forward by some power deep inside him, which he'd never before had the need to use. He was chasing them and they were men, and the power he felt was the man already within him, telling him his time would come.

"Tim!" his mom shouted as the brothers slapped her hands. Tim let out a whoop and ran on, weaving back and forth across the road, then looping back toward the finish with his arms out. Mitch was there by then and he got to see up close as Tim flung his arms around Mitch's mom and kissed her on the mouth. When she stepped away, her face looked smudged, like she was trying to erase it.

Joe was nearby, hunched and gasping, looking more like the used-up voice Mitch remembered from the phone. He wondered if she'd been rooting for him. After himself, he didn't know who he'd been rooting for. He guessed he'd been rooting for them both. He went up to Joe and put his own hands on his knees and panted along beside him.

"We lost," Mitch said.

Joe looked at him.

"That's right, baby!" Tim crowed, punching air.

"No way," Joe managed, shaking his head. He looked at Mitch's mom and shook his head again. "No way."

She shrugged. "Fair's fair."

"That's what you get for drinking your youth away!" Tim said. He came up behind Joe and shook him by the shoulders, then offered him his hand. "Great race," he said, and Joe took it. Mitch went to his mom and hugged her and her face kicked its blankness away. Then they all walked back to the house where it was almost time to eat.

For a while after that everyone got along fine. Mitch showed Joe his army men and a few other things he liked in the house. While Tim stood by, Joe showed Mitch his bike, how to start it with the key, all the different ways he could turn it off. He told Mitch a bike was a good thing to have when you'd traveled as much as he had, lived as many different lives with as many different people, and even though he was settled now, he thought for sure he was settled in Montana, the bike was still a good thing. A bike gave a man the world. It gave him a chance to be free. Then Mitch's mom called them in and they all sat down together at the kitchen table while his mom and grandma brought out the food.

"Who wants a beer?" his mom asked from the fridge.

His grandpa nodded, and Joe said, "I'll take one," and then she looked at Tim. But Tim wasn't looking at her. He was looking at Joe and he was smiling. Only it wasn't his usual smile, the one that made Mitch feel better about pretty much everything. This one made him feel worse.

"You sure about that?" Tim asked Joe.

"Come on, Tim," his mom said. "It's just a beer."

"Not to him it's not."

"Maybe today it is," Joe said.

"I'd be surprised if 'today' was a concept that had any meaning to you."

"I'm here, aren't I?" Joe said. "The ref says you beat me, right? Let me have my beer."

"So now it's your beer."

"Easy, man. Easy."

"I'm not the one making it hard."

"Just take it easy, Tim," Mitch's grandpa said.

"I'm straight, aren't I?" Joe said, starting to sound like a maniac, too. "I got myself in order and I came out here to meet the kid. Like she wanted. And so I'm here, and now she's offering, and so, thank you, I'll take my beer."

It all happened so fast after that. Tim was out of his chair and the chair was on the ground and so were several forks and spoons. He slugged Joe in the face and dragged him into the yard and everyone shouted to stop it but none of it did any good. The brothers wrestled for as long as they could keep their grips before Mitch's mom and grandpa got in there to pull them apart, which only worked for a minute before they escaped and went at it again. While it was happening it was awful. It felt like something final, like they all might disappear into their own violence, leaving nothing but the yard and the house. But once it was over and no one seemed to have won, Mitch found himself feeling the way he always did when things happened to him too fast.

He wanted to do it again. Do it better. A great tightness gripped his head.

He wanted Joe to get a better shot at the beginning, and not just take it until Tim had him on the ground and had basically forced him to fight. He wanted Tim to say what he really meant and not, "You want a beer, do you? You want a goddamn beer?" which were the words he used, but which had to mean something else, because a beer was only a grown-up drink, and Tim had them himself all the time. He wanted a more decisive ending. He wanted Tim to win, for sure this time he wanted Tim to win, but he wanted Joe to show a little life, and he wanted them both to be fighting for him.

Most of all he wanted his mom to repeat her strange moment of power, when she had hair in her mouth, and her face was anything but blank, and she said, "You can't have it both ways, Tim! You can't be your own man *and* be the man of this house!"

When she said, "I am the man of this house, do you hear me? I am the man."

The church floor was hardwood, laid out in long planks running from entrance to altar. They went most Sundays and every Christmas Eve to remind themselves of God, and this Christmas seemed especially important for reasons having to do with Tim. He hadn't been to their house since the fight. Mitch missed him, and though a part of him wanted to ask why Tim wasn't allowed to come over anymore, another part understood that it wasn't really about what wasn't allowed. His mom had been quieter, like she was studying for something. If he didn't know better, he'd even say that she'd been sad.

Tim was joining them for the candlelight services though, and this was a relief to Mitch. He had so many questions. "You really don't like your brother, do you?" he asked as they filed into their pew.

"Shh," Tim said. "Your timing's terrible."

Mitch ducked his head and looked at the floorboards. In services he mostly looked down, so that he appeared to anyone glancing about to be praying, or at least in deep contemplation of the Lord. But really he was living in his mind, which was an increasingly elastic place. Today that place included the floorboards, which he counted as far as he could see.

Once they'd been sitting a few moments listening to the organ, Tim leaned over and whispered something else.

"It's not really about liking him or not liking him," he said as Mitch stretched his mind to include Tim's face. "He's made a lot of mistakes. I'm trying to forgive him for that."

Mitch took in the glowing heads of the altar candles and he thought his timing was actually just right. "I want to do that, too," he said.

"Sure," Tim said. "That's good. But you have to remember, he's still a shirker. He's not someone you need to know."

He thought about his father losing to Tim in the rematch race and getting pummeled by Tim at dinner. Joe had closed his eyes at one point, when Tim had him by the neck, and this seemed to Mitch like an effort to escape, to somehow disappear. Was that shirking? He wasn't sure. What he was sure of was that Tim was his favorite person after his mom. He had a way of saying things that made Mitch want to move, and now Tim was saying he didn't need to know his dad.

That seemed right. It seemed like something that would please his mom, who was sitting to his left and tapping her finger to her lips, then tapping it to her ear.

He looked down again and tried to listen to the pastor, a serious man who told stories about God and television, or God and fishing, and in doing so repeated certain phrases like, *See, I am making all things new.*

This was another thing Mitch tended to hear: a repeated phrase. He'd key in on it, like it was his own name, and soon enough, it was repeating itself, indefinitely, in his head.

See, I am making all things new, the pastor said. *See, I am making all things new.*

The words themselves hardly registered except as sounds tapping within his veins. But they gave him a drumbeat, a tempo, and on this night of floorboards and forgiveness and the people he needed and the people he did not, he came to think of that tempo as God's rhythm. For it had a rightness to it, a sense of purpose—onward and upward, and here we go—a rhythm some other being was setting for him, a rhythm that was himself.

3. TIM, 1983

His third season as coach of the Pee Wee Monacan Jets, Tim
Williams started carrying a calendar.

"Well, Tim," Cindy said when she saw it. "Guess you're a
grown up now."

She was his ex, and had reason to doubt him, but about this,
he was dead serious. He was thirty-two now, with responsibilities.
He had to mold the characters of twenty young boys, her own
son Mitch included, and he needed to see the weeks laid out in
order, to make sure he did his job.

Mornings he worked at the college, the other family business,
mowing lawns and carrying ladders, to cover the classes he
took there at night. He was what they called a non-traditional
student, the first man the little women's college had ever made
an exception to enroll, though in every other way, he was proud
to say, he was thoroughly traditional. A homeowner, a surrogate
father to Cindy's kid, his promising nephew Mitch. He hadn't
gotten married yet, but that would come: everything in its time.
For now, he was focused on being Coach.

Pee Wee was ages nine to twelve, those yeasty, carefree years
before your nose was sharp enough to know you smelled. When
Tim was that age, they'd been the Little Warriors, after the high
school team, which everyone hated, though they'd worshipped
the high school guys. Sometime while he was away there'd been
a petty revolt, and now they were the Jets, for the NFL team.

Also known as the Flyboys, which was different from "little," because even men were often called boys, especially when they were doing something serious, like tagging cattle or dropping bombs.

Flyboys. Well. Their minds were flying anyway.

"This is common sense," he told them in practice. "This is not rocket science." They easily won their first two games. At the end of the second, Ricky Franklin did a front flip to score the final touchdown, sealing it, 28-0. Good form, bad decision. The boy needed guidance.

"Get over here," Tim shouted after the game.

"What's up, Coach?"

"Don't be risking your neck like that. I need you to be smart."

"Aw, I was just celebrating, Coach!"

"Celebrate after. Go to La Pizzeria with your friends or whatever the hell it is that you do."

Ricky bounced on the balls of his feet, lit by the manliness of Tim's casual *hell*. "I ain't got time for La Pizzeria, Coach!" He danced away, laughing, and Tim tried to keep from laughing, too.

I ain't got time was something Ricky often said when he was feeling bored or just plain defiant, and like almost everything else that came out of his mouth, it couldn't have been further from the truth. Tim had driven by his house, seen him loafing about with the assortment of kids and adults who came and went from his mom's double-wide, drinking tasty desperations that were either made of sugar or made of alcohol, depending on if you were a kid or an adult. Kid had nothing *but* time, and no clue how to use it.

They were all idiots, nine- to twelve-year-olds, his nephew included, but the black kids seemed to give him the most trouble.

They were the ones who fought. He wanted to treat every kid equal, but that was easier said than done. The truth was, by the time kids were ten and eleven, the world had already decided who was who. Tim had had a drunk dad. He'd been to Vietnam for fuck's sake. He could understand why you might be angry. But you had to control yourself. You had to look around and notice it wasn't much fun for anyone else either, yet everyone else was mostly making do. Really he was thinking of Ricky. Jason Booker was a good kid, quick. An obvious talent. He'd make it to college anyway. Ricky was the one who looked at the world like a plate of food he could only have if he stole it.

Tim was a believer in systems. His hero was Paul Brown, of the Cleveland Browns, the first to time his players in the forty-yard dash, to enforce team dinners and curfews the night before a game, to make his players actually write down their plays. This season, in tribute, he made his Flyboys do the same.

He was tough on them because he knew what they were like. He'd been an idiot himself when he was young, and he'd let it go too far. Summer of '69, he and Robbie had joined up together, two brothers with low numbers and a hostile father at home. They were draft bait, no one would hire them, so they figured they may as well enlist, choose their own deployments, maybe in Europe or the palm-rimmed Caribbean. Why they thought they'd have this option was a mystery to him now, one of many in the world, and in his own being, that he'd been made aware of since. They were separated immediately, Robbie to Fort Jackson, Tim to Fort Dix, then shipped to Nam in different divisions, on different days even, seeing each other only once in the course of their twelve-month tours, when they were flown home together with PanAm stewardesses to attend their mother's funeral.

That was hard. Even harder was when Robbie died. Tim got himself transferred to Germany after that, where he worked a meaningless desk until his tour was up. After his discharge, he couldn't come home. Not when his dad was the only one left, and nastier than ever by the sound of it, Joe having split for who knew where. So Tim went to L.A., where he played semi-pro with a guy he knew from Da Nang. Between games, during which he felt, if not good, then at least all right, he did odd jobs, sat on the gritty beach, and hated himself for having no good reason to live.

He wanted to save these kids that kind of pain, scare the stupidity out of them, set goals for them, make them into men without anyone having to get killed. There were probably a lot of ways to go about this in the world, but he was a Virginia boy and a former receiver, and football was the way he knew best.

Fortunately, the kids took to it, craved it, even in practice gripping their collars with pride. They'd come up the hill from the elementary school y'alling and nuh-uhing, shepherded by a handful of overeager dads. The Warriors had zero tolerance for dads at practice, but these were children, they needed rides. As long as the dads respected his style, he didn't mind if they watched. Practice always started with stretches and jogging so the boys could warm themselves up. Then they reviewed and ran their plays and coverages, each one in sequence until it was right. No wind sprints. No crushing leg-raises. No drills just to prove he was Coach. He knew who he was and so did they, and drills only wore players out.

Still, he liked to talk. He had his coachisms, his general coachiness. He appreciated a little theater, a little religion. "What's going on in your head?" he liked to demand, tapping his knuckles on someone's hat, never actually wanting an answer.

"Devote yourselves," he also said.

And, "It's all about the fundamentals."

"It's our year," one of the dads said at Smokey's after another Friday night victory for the Warriors. His own son would win again that weekend under Tim's watchful eye, because Tim understood the fundamentals and knew how to plan for a game, but no one cared about that just now, not over beers on a Friday night.

"These Warriors are playing Texas-level," said another dad.

"Fuck Texas," Coach said. "I am so sick of Texas."

The dads nodded studiously. "You been there?"

"Hell no, but it ain't any better." Tim clicked his jaw out and back. "California football. Florida football. Everyone says it. Well, you know what? This is Virginia football. And you know what else? It's football." He was starting to bore himself, but decided to put forth one final *football* just to bring the conversation to a close. "Football's football," he said, and everyone said, "Yup," and "That's true."

There wasn't a better way to spend your life, which was a fragile thing, he knew that now, than on a playing field in a warm Virginia September executing the perfect game plan. It was an orderly game, football, it progressed in an orderly fashion, and it was because of democracy that he was free to make his plans, his perfect dreams, a series of plays for kids in motion, which it would benefit the kids to learn, and make them feel a sense of purpose, a sense of accomplishment, at having actually executed the thing he had dreamed.

He told them as much when he gathered them for practice the following week, the Tuesday after their third consecutive win. Twenty boys, one Coach: the perfect ratio, forget insubordinate assistants. Jason was nodding, a serious little man with a Band-

Aid on his finger. So were Jeff and Rusty and Ricky. Such a crew they were, those sixth graders, with their preponderance of J- and R- names. Caleb didn't exactly fit the pattern, but he didn't tend to fit anywhere, the fattest of the bunch, just barely made the Pee Wee weight limit, who if he had to be fat, figured he'd also be the fool. He was good at cracking jokes, at shaking his gut like a Slinky. The tallest was Rusty, the six-foot sixth grader, whose poor overgrown dome was so massive they had to borrow a helmet from the Warriors. He was the only Flyboy with a maroon hat in the season opener, and he was a starter, so he was out there all the time, abnormal, unmatching. The helmet was a muddy pine now, spray-painted under the shop teacher's supervision, not quite the bright emerald of the rest of the team, but at least it was some kind of green.

Mitch's name stood out, too, and so did Mitch himself, if Tim was being honest, though it was possible this thing he called honesty was just an expression of family pride. His nephew didn't yet have the build, but he was fast and he had good hands, plus he was smart, and old for his grade. He had desire and self-awareness but not self-consciousness, and he worked hard but thankfully not too hard: the factors all added up. It was this promising mix that Tim was sure of, the right combination that people sought, if not for football, then for something else. Football wasn't everything. But it was definitely on the road there.

"This one's all about the blocking," Tim told them, introducing a new short-yardage play. "This one's all about the blocking. This one's all about the blocking."

Jason's Band-Aided hand was up. His quarterback, a good kid, always raised his hand. "We gonna learn more passing plays, Coach?"

Tim held his mouth in its straight-line Coach formation but gave him the warm, smiling eyes. Authority you can trust. "Not this week, son. We're a running team. We run the ball."

"I just think I got the arm, is all."

Tim chewed his teeth, sensing a teaching moment. He put his hands on his hips. "Now listen, I know you want to throw the ball. And I know the rest of you think you can catch it." He could feel himself revving, his twang growing twangier and more truthful, his words piling up on each other, pleasurably and familiarly, forming a speech that sounded just like a speech, in the way a house was built to look just like a house, but with his own insight that was just now coming to him, ushered in with the words as he spoke them, and surrounding them all with a system of truth. "But there's something you gotta understand," he said. "That's your future. Being a team that throws the ball is your future. I'm just trying to get you there. You're gonna have to trust me on that one. And to get there, we gotta cover all the territory that comes before. You understand what I'm saying?" Some of them had begun to nod their heads, as was customary when Coach was talking. "This new formation? This isn't Redskin ball. It's not college ball. It's not even Warrior ball. Those are all still in the future. This is Flyboy ball. This is now. This is a play run at Yale in 1900."

He paused. He looked at them gravely, let the weight of the past sink in.

"1900?"

"Coach!"

"That's *old*."

So they weren't exactly converted, but they did line up on his whistle. They got to work positioning their feet, and angling their blocks to the left. And when Ricky Franklin jogged up at the water break and asked if they could practice something else, "Something more exciting," Tim widened his eyes to act surprised. It was important to feign surprise when a kid dared make a request. That was part of establishing authority, make it scary to make a request.

"Blocking's *boring*," Ricky said.

"Thanks for your perspective."

"It is though! I want to catch the ball!"

"Go on, son."

"Instead I'm just giving his ass a push, running right. I barely get to move!"

"I'll give your ass a push, son."

It was clear Ricky wasn't happy, but football practice wasn't about being happy, and as usual there was nothing to do but drop it and get back to work. Ricky dropped it. He practiced his blocks. Tim coached. And when time was up, they clapped, barked "JETS," and dispersed.

So he was genuinely surprised, Tim had to admit, when, after another Sunday win and then a long Monday shift at the college in which he'd been called in to deal with a flooded dormitory basement where the students stored their old rich-girl obsessions—cellos and camping tents that were so inviting to the now-drowned mice—he was genuinely surprised when he returned home to find his sixth graders, the Rs and the Js, Ricky and Rusty and Jason and Jeff, along with Caleb and even Mitch, in his drive beside a tangle of bikes.

"Boys."

"We was hoping to talk to you, Coach," Jason said. The poorest of the bunch, but the quarterback, the undisputed leader.

"What's up? Unsatisfied with the win?"

"No, sir. Well, yes sir. In a way. We was hoping"—he tilted

his head toward the rest of them—"if you think it can work, to have a little more fun out there. Try some more long passes, open it up a little, give everybody a chance to move." Tim looked at Ricky, who was nodding seriously. "Since we seem to be beating everybody so easy with the run."

He'd been wrong to use the word unsatisfied. He saw that now. Tim frowned and continued to say nothing, because nothing Jason had said really warranted a lecture. The boys stood together with their hands in their pockets, a gesture new to them, a gesture demonstrated and suggested by the dads and other men, and they looked very much like a group, a team, some kind of warm and willing collective. He looked at them: Rusty's pimply head, Caleb's gut, Ricky's mouth. Someone needed a shower. He looked at Mitch, his nephew.

"So…?" Jason finally asked.

"Who put y'all up to this?"

The question seemed to startle Jason, who wiped his palms on the legs of his jeans, his finger healed, the Band-Aid gone. "No one. Us. It was our idea."

"Your idea?"

"Yessir."

They had ideas. In those warm young bodies of theirs, sweating spontaneously in ways they didn't understand, they were somehow cooking up ideas.

"I'll take it under advisement," Tim said.

"Okay, but like—"

"I said I'll take it under advisement." Repetition, he was finding, was not boring. Repetition was his friend.

There was some standing, and a waft of ripe manure smell so common to his part of the world, and after a time, the boys seemed to understand that this was the end of the conversation, and so as a unit they picked up their bikes and peddled off down the long gravel drive, having done what they came to do, and Tim went into his house and opened himself a beer, his intention being to forget.

But Tim could not forget. They had talked about him when he wasn't around. He knew that, of course. Hoped for it, even. But they had talked about him and decided to band together.

"Mitch!" he called at the next practice when the boy appeared at the top of the field. His nephew jogged over.

"Yessir," Mitch said. He was such a ragged lawn rake of a kid, not yet grown into his bones.

"How're your boys doing?"

"All right, I guess. Ready to play," he added, hopefully.

"They still talking about those long passes?"

Mitch looked at the end of the field, where the elusive long pass might drop. He waited a considerable length of time before answering, "I dunno," as if hoping Tim and his question might grow impatient and disappear.

"Well, you let me know if they do, will you." He clapped his nephew on the back and sent him along to stretch.

He had dreamed a perfect dream, and play by play, and win by win, the boys were making his dream a reality. Four consecutive wins now. Again and again, they had won. How could they not see the beauty of that? The rarity.

He ran them through their newest formation, watched as Ricky's cheeks puffed with rancor when he gave his lineman a nudge, watched their heads come together in the huddle, Mitch's hand on Jason's back, Mitch patting Ricky's crown.

Second half of practice, he made some adjustments.

"Mitch!" he called. "You're under center."

Jason stepped back from his crouch, a good kid, silent even in disappointment. He didn't have to talk, because Ricky always would.

"That's a QB run play, Coach!" Ricky said through his mask.

"Are you suggesting Mitch can't run?"

"I'm just saying why would you take out Jason?"

"I don't have time for these questions, son! Wilkins is QB. End of discussion."

After practice, he watched them pick up cones, the blue afternoon zipping toward autumn, his brow buzzing toward a change-of-seasons headache. He would have to blow the whistle less. He'd have to run them with a little less whistle.

Mitch was the last to bring in his cones. One bendy, extra-tall stack, neatly done, orange rubber snout into orange rubber snout, just a slight puff in the middle where one had nosed in askew. Tim loved his nephew for this: careful, but not too careful, a boy built for systems with a little flair. The rest of the team was already halfway down the hill as he loaded them into the back of Tim's truck.

"Uncle Tim," Mitch said when he was through. "Coach. I'm not sure I should play QB."

Tim grinned. "Sure you should, son. You've got the potential to play any position you want."

"I mean, yeah, I know I'm good enough to do it. But it's Jason's job. Ain't it?" He squinted in the sun, which gave him the impression of looking craftier, and more suspicious than he was. "I mean, if I can be anything, why can't I be something that doesn't already belong to somebody else?"

His innocent nephew. Tim placed a hand on his young head. "Some roles are better than others, and there's only so many to go around."

"But Jason's good."

Tim withdrew the hand to his hip. "Look, you won't get anywhere turning down opportunities. Know that."

It was because of Mitch that he even coached this team. Hell, it was basically because of Mitch that he'd stayed in Virginia, reclaimed the old house from squalor, got himself into school. If his no-show degenerate brother couldn't make more than the occasional phone call, couldn't suck it up and be a man for this boy, he himself sure as hell would.

"But if it makes you feel better," Tim went on, "I'm planning on splitting the job between you. Trade-off. So both of you can learn. All right?"

His nephew opened his mouth, closed it.

"What's that?"

"Nothing."

"Come on, out with it."

"It's just." He stroked the red clay with his toe. "I don't know. Maybe you could just teach me at home. That way Jason can QB the Jets."

"Damn it, Mitch, always the same conversation! Did you not hear me before about opportunities? Did you not hear that?"

"No," Mitch said, backing away. "I heard it."

They needed stories was what they needed. He paged through the football histories, hunting for tales of valor and loyalty: Johnny Unitas throwing a game-winning touchdown while blood gushed from his broken nose.

"Y'all just keep winning," Cindy said the last time he paid her a visit. He had his books out and Mitch was with them in the kitchen, leaning over his shoulder, eating a Snickers.

"Don't poison yourself now," Tim told him, trying not to see the smears of chocolate at the corners of his mouth. "We gotta keep it up."

"Go, fight, win," Mitch said, through caramel, sounding just like his sarcastic mom.

Tim closed his book. "Are we going to the playoffs?"

"Yeah we are."

"I can't hear you. I said are we going to the playoffs?"

"Sir, yes, sir!" He mock-saluted. "You know Ricky eats like ten of these a day."

"Let him, if that's what he wants to do. Any kid can eat a Snickers."

Mitch nodded, swallowed his final bite, and tossed the wrapper in the trash. They never quite fought—Mitch respected him too much for that—but occasionally these days, they came close. These days, it was a relief to Tim every time Mitch held himself in line. The kid was getting his own ideas. Who knew how long his deference would last.

"I know you don't want to be just any kid," Tim said.

"Nope. I wanna be the best. I want to keep winning."

"Attaboy."

"What must that feel like?" Cindy asked, after Mitch had wandered out of the room. "To never lose?" She offered the question like a piece of nature, one of those pine cones she collected that had no purpose but was somehow worth contemplating. Tim was grateful to still have her friendship after all the drama they put each other through.

"Good," he said. "It feels good."

She gave him one of her looks, and he felt a pang that he'd accomplished just about everything except being a husband to her. She had never really been his type—too strong-willed, and too emotional, loving him hungrily, but also shutting him out, especially when it came to Mitch. But he'd only noticed that after they'd rushed into romance, around the same time he noticed she still carried a torch for Joe. Even so he knew he hadn't given her his best effort; that was his biggest regret.

It was his biggest regret about Vietnam, too. When he'd shipped out, he'd harbored a vague hope for greatness, but by the time he arrived, even before Robbie died, the mood had soured. It was a hopeless war, and a boring war, and so why try, why be a hero? He ended up in the rear, fixing trucks, and only did what he had to do. In hindsight, he'd lost whole years of his life to that attitude, the great undertow of not trying hard.

His little brother was losing them still. They'd gotten together his first Christmas in California and at that point it had been a few years, both of them having severed all ties with their dad, which made it a challenge to track each other down. Joe had hitchhiked all the way from Houston and he was a wreck. He'd missed Robbie's funeral because no one knew where he was, and now, more than a year later, his surviving brother exemption secured, he was still bawling about it, convulsing on Tim's shoulder before they'd even said hello. The kid looked totaled, greasy hair to his shoulders, bags like an old man's, practically purple, under his eyes, all kinds of buttons missing from his shirt. He said he was sorry many times. He told Tim about Cindy and Mitch.

"A one-year-old son?" Tim couldn't believe his ears. "What're you doing out here?"

"I don't know. Getting something out of my system, I guess." Joe slumped in the booth, ready for nothing. He didn't even have an address. "I'm gonna go back there. I want to meet him."

He didn't though. He got hammered that night, tried to steal a motorcycle outside the bar while Tim was in the head—*You die on it, you buy it,* read the sign over the unisex toilet—and it was only by some miracle that Tim overtook him, halfway down the road, and managed to pry him off and roll the bike back to where Joe had found it. He spent the rest of the night chasing and physically restraining his brother, eventually hauling him back to his apartment where he force-fed him whiskey, just to get him to pass out and be still. In the morning, Joe was gone, and so was the rest of Tim's booze, plus the hundred dollars he had saved in a coffee tin.

Joe called again a few months later, having relocated, not to Virginia, but to Santa Fe, apologizing, saying things were different. Again, they met up, this time on Joe's turf, but things were not different, they could not have been more the same: Joe blubbering in a bar, the picture of weakness, getting drunk, then getting violent, punching a man he'd introduced as a friend. Tim got punched in the scuffle that ensued, by whose fist he wasn't even sure, but whoever's it was he was one hundred percent sure it was all his brother's fault.

Same thing the next time, more or less, and then the next time, and at a certain point you had to acknowledge that these weren't flukes, they were the pattern. As kids they'd invented the Monacan Maniac, a lurching, irrational monster who took over the bodies of innocent boys, a figure that, in hindsight, probably had something to do with their dad. They took turns playing and slaying him, depending on their mood, and somehow this Maniac was exactly what Joe had become. He did not know how to drink and he did not know how to live and he didn't know the first damn thing about being a decent man.

More than a decade later, Joe claimed to be clean, but still, he hadn't been there for the kid. He lived in Montana instead, a shirker, and the one sorry time he made an effort completely fit the pattern of destruction. It was after the old man had died, in that hectic year when Tim had come back to deal with the house, and fallen in love, somehow, with Cindy, and decided he might as well stay, and Cindy, in all her well-intentioned intensity, had basically forced Joe to show his face, belatedly high on the idea of family. He'd shown up at last, he'd played with the kid, and then there'd been another fight, right there in Cindy's little kitchen, in front of her parents and Mitch. Tim couldn't even recall who started it, because fighting with Joe was no longer a decision, just the language the two brothers spoke. What a catastrophe, what a mistake everything to do with Joe had been.

Except for Mitch, of course. Now, having salvaged his family house, if not his family, Tim didn't want any more mistakes, especially when it came to Mitch, who he could hardly believe had not been ruined, and who Tim would see to it now was not. He just had to keep at it: his third season coaching, his second-to-last semester of college. If he kept at it, if word got around, maybe the Warriors would even hire him up.

The fifth win was a beauty. Jason kicked his first field goal and returned a pick for six. Everyone worked together to clear a lane for Mitch's twenty-yard touchdown run in the second half. Even Ricky was happy. He did a back flip as the clock ran out and Tim didn't chastise him. He'd heard it said that the pain of losing was far more intense than the joy of winning ever was. But whoever said that could not have lost much, not in the listless way he had before football saved his life. To Tim, winning had never not felt intense. It relocated him every time. He felt amazed with the world, its comedy, its colors. He'd stand there and watch the Flyboys smiling elfishly, swinging their emerald helmets over the grass like the pendulums of eternal clocks. Winning was intense in the way that living was. It was a job he loved, the cure itself.

Next practice, it all fell apart. Twenty pre-adolescent noses, twenty foreheads, twenty haircuts. Twenty boys in practice gear, their helmets on the grass.

"We ain't playing," Jason said. It was the Wednesday before the last game of the year. "We ain't gonna practice unless you let us throw the ball."

"This is our chance to go undefeated," Tim shouted back. It killed him how young they were. How young, and how wrong. They'd been born into a better world, on this point everyone agreed, but it was clear to Tim that this was actually a problem. Might even ruin them if he didn't intervene. "Come on, now," he shouted, "where are your heads?"

They merely looked at him, defiant, overconfident from their wins.

"This Sunday at three o'clock," he tried again, "you've got a shot at the playoffs. The four best teams in the state. Don't you want that?"

"Not if it ain't no fun," Caleb said.

Didn't they understand he was trying to save them? Look at his father, look at Joe. When you stopped caring about succeeding, that was when you started to die.

"You're lucky I'm the coach," he said. "You think you can go to high school and pull this shit? You think they put up with this in college? Hell, no."

"Let us throw it!" Ricky said. "Let Jason throw me the ball!"

Mitch still hadn't spoken, and here Tim had his chance.

"Mitch!" he called. "Get over here."

His nephew flinched, and Tim took that opportunity to look at him hard, to look his message right into the boy's spiraling soul. *These fools are lost*, is what that message said. *Only one you can save is yourself.* Mitch, for his part, did not flinch again. He looked at his comrades, then at the dads in the bleachers, then back again at Tim. Then the fatherless boy who had no one in the stands came forward to stand by his uncle. His helmet he left behind, on the grass with his team.

"Are we going to the playoffs?" Tim prompted him, hoping to God he wouldn't fail him now.

Mitch squinted. There were murmurs from the team.

"Yes, sir," his nephew finally said.

"I can't hear you. I said, are we going to the playoffs?"

"Yes, *sir!*"

"Damn right, we are. And will you tell these boys how we're getting there?"

"Win Sunday, Coach." Mitch's face was as hard as a book.

"What's that?"

"WIN!"

"And how're we gonna win, son? How have we always won?"

He was very close to Mitch now, his lip almost brushing his nephew's cheek in his intense need to make these boys into men.

"What's our game? How do Flyboys fly?"

Mitch's eyes settled on his uncle's and a sober knowledge filled his face. It was almost as though he had been there that day in California before Tim was Coach, and the lawyer had called, and told him that he, Timothy Williams, had been designated next of kin. His father had been found. He'd been near the sofa. That was all they would say, so he knew it had been much worse. He pictured the old man as he'd last seen him at Robbie's funeral, his skin stretched tight over bloated cheeks and chest and belly, his arms the same arms he'd thrown with, his legs the same legs that were always driving to town for beer. In the end, his father had been found to be his father. At long last, there'd be no more mistakes. But no corrections either.

There on the practice field, Mitch's twelve-year-old eyes seemed to know all this. Like a calendar, he had it all worked out.

What he said was, "We run the ball, Coach." Then he paused and added, "We always win when we run."

That was the thing about saving yourself. Realistically, you probably couldn't do it until you recognized all else was lost, until you understood that in the end, there's nothing good that comes of fun. Tim almost wept. He and his nephew, the sole survivors. They saw the same limits, the same cruelties, the same victory awaiting them on Sunday at three p.m.

4. MITCH, 1990

By now Mitch's mom knew how to treat his gear. There, on his bed, next to the team duffel the U's athletic director had sent as a high school graduation gift—orange and green, for Miami, factory fresh, basically bulletproof—sat his white senior season pants, folded and ready to go. His new game day pants would be waiting for him in Coral Gables, along with all the swampy weather practice gear he could ever possibly need, but for now it was nice to hang on to his retired favorites. For luck. For old times' sake.

She used to just ball them up like socks after she washed them. He would find them in the plastic basket totally humiliated, all tangled and sticking to themselves. At first he let it go, but then sometime in the middle of his junior year, around the time the college letters started stuffing up the mailbox, he realized he'd had it with her sloppiness. She balked when he lit into her—she had no idea it mattered—but pretty quickly got with the program, each week laying his pants out flat along the seam, then folding them in thirds like a wallet.

He wasn't ready to pack them just yet. They needed to go on top, and there were probably other things still lying around that had to fit in the bag. Better to save them for last, after he'd stopped by the school, after he'd met up with the girl.

On his desk was the corner-stapled paper—his final obligation to Monacan County High—well overdue and probably riddled with errors. But it was five pages, printed cleanly yesterday at the library where he'd written it, hunched at the computer in a monastic four-hour bender, starved for food and music and female company of any kind, the day so bright only the nerdiest kids were at the library, and even they had to interrupt him in a shy little group, to ask him to sign a crappy ball. The paper had at least one paragraph break per page, and every sentence started with a capital letter and ended with a period. So from a distance, it probably didn't even look that different from any of the on-time A-papers Mrs. Murray red-checked her way through each year. Maybe she'd do him one last favor and grade it on appearance alone.

His mom was sprawled on the couch in nursing scrubs and a flower-patterned top, staring down a mahogany dining set on "The Price Is Right."

"I'm gonna buy you one of those," he told her.

"I'll take it," she said, blinking heavily, halfway down the slide to sleep. She'd worked an extra overnight shift in the NICU so she could drive with him to Florida tomorrow.

"Turning in this paper first."

"Atta boy. Burgers tonight. Don't forget, everyone's coming," Meaning his grandparents and Tim and Tracy. "One last family dinner."

"Don't sound so morbid, nobody's died." And before she could respond, he'd burst out the door to his Bridgestoned pick-up, his tall-man's ride, his ship. She'd bought it for him last year, and it was gorgeous, half the size of the house, parked there with its tail hitched like a truck in a commercial, like he'd pulled the key in the middle of a donut and just sauntered on inside. The late summer sun beat down on him, bleaching the trampled grass of his lawn and the chewed-up cow pasture across the road, the sky itself, everything. Under his massive arms and along his hairline, he felt himself already beginning to sweat.

As he bounced along the road to town, he thought about the local talent his buddy Jeff had scouted on his behalf. Her name was Caryn Fletcher; she lived in Charlottesville and she was also going to college at the U. They could've waited until they got there to meet. But Mitch had her number up here, and it made him feel almost psychic to call up a beautiful stranger who shared a future with him. They were Virginians, going to Miami. So, actually, they shared a past, too.

As a kid, he'd never been the biggest, still well under six feet in eighth grade, but in other departments there were plenty of clues: his tall mom, his gorilla hands, his feet that kept outgrowing his sneakers. He played football because everyone did, and he was quick, but it wasn't until ninth grade, when all of a sudden he was huge, and no slower, that he realized he had a special kind of power. Wasn't that hard, people always had to ask him, playing football without a dad? He couldn't understand the question. It never occurred to them that when you had gifts like he had, you didn't need a father. Certainly you didn't need some Montana hippie who talked in circles about the simplest things. You needed a coach, sure, and a mother to cook you mega-tons of ziti and meatballs, six-egg omelets with brick-thick stacks of toast, or whatever it took to keep you from eating shelves of Twinkies just to tame the hungry beast in your gut. But from Tim on up, he'd had no shortage of coaches. No shortage of ziti either.

He was approaching the end of the straightaway now, where the prefab brick boxes got older and closer together as Spring Road curled into 29. He was hoping, as he always did, for open road, because whipping his truck around that bend, hopping the newer asphalt ledge and spraying gravel in his wake was one of the chief pleasures of his commute, and getting to do it on his final drive to school seemed lucky. Sure enough, the coast was clear, nothing but sky and trees and the old green interchange sign to scold him. He downshifted and gunned it until he felt the ass end start to break free, then rode out the drift until he was straight and responsible and a credit to his community once again.

The high school reclined on a ridge overlooking the highway, the one place in town that would never go out of business, even when its business got stale. The first door he tried, by the gym, was locked. So was the second, by the auditorium. Finally, he made his way around to the front, where a banner stretched between two redbrick pillars reminded everyone that the Monacan County High School Warriors were the Division 4A State Runners-Up in Football. He averted his eyes from that damn tarp every time he drove by, and thanks to the placement of the student lots in back, he could generally avoid it on foot as well. But now here it was, almost a year old already, still cruelly commemorating the last time he'd donned the Warrior Red, all amped up and vibrating on the biggest stage, raring to smash guys in front of the hometown fans who'd driven the hundred miles to Blacksburg for State. He'd come away from that game puking in the locker room shower, tasting not the sweetness of a Gatorade-drenched championship, but bile. Straight, nasty, loser bile, spiced with a bitterness so concentrated, it seemed to predate his own beat-up body. The single worst loss of his life.

He found a door that worked and went inside. His halls. Except, somehow, they weren't. He'd roamed them empty after practice a hundred times, but this was different, and it took him a moment to register why: the doorframes had been repainted red instead of whatever color they'd been before. Gone, too, was the smell of sour mud on linoleum, the trash cans full of half-empty milk cartons and lukewarm fish sticks, odors he'd never thought he'd miss. Everything was clean and orderly and unoccupied. He'd entered a brand new school. Gripping his paper, he followed his feet to Mrs. Murray's room, which faced the athletic fields, where he liked to imagine her watching football practice from her desk.

Thankfully, that was where he found her now. She was bent over a giant spiral-bound planner, making notations in her tiny hand. Her husband was a professor at Briarwood, and Mitch spent much of his summer stint on the grounds crew avoiding jobs that would bring him near her house. What a relief to be done with that. He lingered in the doorway and rapped his knuckles against the frame.

She looked up, and there was an uncomfortable moment, her bespectacled face on the verge of full expression, as though it had been many years since she'd seen him and she was trying to recall who he was. But then a smile broke free, and she stood.

"Mitch," she said, rubbing her hands together gamely. "What a nice surprise!"

He staggered into the room wielding the paper, which had grown sodden and loose in his hand. "Last day of July, you said. Man of my word."

She wasn't especially pretty, or even young. Her chin was sort of long, witchy even, and she had pale, reddish skin that grew redder when she got excited about a book. Her hair was either light brown or dirty blond or maybe more accurately just beige, and she always wore it in a braid that draped over one shoulder, with loose strands escaping near her face. What she did have was confidence. Whenever someone questioned the quality of a book, as some jackass always did, Mrs. Murray would fold her arms across her chest and level him with her stare. "J.D. Salinger *created* the teenage voice," she would say. "What, Mr. Campbell, have you done?" Until her class, he wasn't even sure he knew that books were written by actual people.

She took the paper and flipped through it purposefully, as though hunting for specific words.

"It's about *The Great Gatsby*," he said. "Want me to just sit here while you grade it?"

She turned back to the first page. "I'm impressed. You didn't have to do this."

He shrugged. "You said the only way you'd pass me was if I brought you my paper by the end of summer."

"But Mitch. Graduation was over a month ago. You got your D. You walked. There would be nothing I could do about that now even if you didn't keep your promise."

He didn't know what to say to that. He looked at the chalkless blackboard, cleaner than he'd ever seen it, as though it had been born in the factory that day. "Is that new?" he asked. The question seemed to confuse her, so he just plowed right on ahead. "So, wait a minute, you're saying it didn't matter?"

"I took you at your word. I gave you the benefit of the doubt even though it meant giving up all my authority. Or so I thought. I have to tell you I'm glad you were still scared enough to do the right thing."

He held his hands out, feeling equally stupid and proud. "What can I say: you're a scary lady. You know I worked at Briarwood all summer? But I hid every time I saw you coming."

This pleased her. She threw her head back and gave a short, loud slap of a laugh, an odd sound from a woman, but the sort of noise guys made in the locker room all the time. Then again, she was an odd woman. She had protested nuclear arms in New York City, and in the books they read for class, she was always pointing out the sex. He'd had more than a few dreams about her, which he felt was entirely her fault.

"Do you want me to read it?" she asked.

"Only if you want to. It's pretty awful."

"I'm sure it is."

"Hey, thanks!"

They were laughing together now, which was unusual, but not unpleasant. She perched on her desk, allowing one leg to ride up while the other remained planted on the floor. He noticed for the first time that she was wearing shorts. "Let me have a look," she said.

He took his place in the front corner seat, his thighs bulging up into the gummy underside of the desk. That much, at least, hadn't changed. "It's just about how Nick is jealous of everyone for being good at sports."

"Do you think that's true?"

"I don't know, I thought it said something like that. Is that wrong?"

"No, it's interesting. Do you think people are jealous of you?"

"It's pretty obvious, isn't it?" He stretched his legs out, away from the gum, which pulled at the hairs on his quads. There wasn't a person at the school who didn't envy him. Three years on varsity, playing every side of the ball: tight end, linebacker, sometimes he'd even punt. Every year, he dated the prettiest sophomore, and in those short, in-between periods he had every other girl attacking him with blowjobs and cake. Nerds ripped on each other in public just to make him laugh. They all wanted to feel his power, to taste how it felt to be him.

"Though I bet you can get jealous of them, too."

"Huh?"

"Their freedom, maybe? Outside of school, most of them can do whatever they want whenever they want. You've been following orders for a long time."

"I don't know, Mrs. Murray. I don't think about it that way. That's just how football works."

She smiled from her perch. "You can call me Laura now."

"Laura," he repeated, trying out the word. He knew it was her name; he'd heard other teachers slip and use it. Laura Murray. It had seemed right enough then, as a name, had seemed enough like her. But now, in his own dry mouth, he wasn't so sure. Laura was a completely different person, a chick at a bonfire. A girl who might bake him cake. He shrugged bashfully. "I don't know if I can."

"Give it time," she said. Then she exhaled as though he'd said something funny. She waved his paper in front of her air conditioner. "Must be hot out there. This feels like it just came out of the wash."

He looked at the slackened pages, drooping in her hand, then looked at his own palm, moistened and pink with heat. Half-disgustedly, he rubbed it on his leg.

"So," she said. "Miami. You ready?"

He bucked his head forward and back. "I leave tomorrow."

She made a brainy noise and set off from her desk toward the windows, where she kept a series of black plastic organizers marshaled together on the sill. He tried to think of her as Laura. Laura whose job was teaching, just as his was playing football. Laura who used black plastic organizers.

"Well," she said, turning back to him, having deposited the paper in its slot. "Don't forget us."

She'd always had plenty to say in class, so he waited now for her to offer some further piece of wisdom. Maybe a quote from a famous writer or something, to really gather up the moment.

But she just smiled and escorted him toward the door the way a teacher did, herding him, following him to make sure he didn't veer from his course. She held out one hand and, with the other, touched him lightly on the back. For some reason, probably because she was Laura now and not Mrs. Murray, he became aware that she was doing all of this with her body. Like a player actually, like an athlete, claiming a position that would force his body into a particular position of its own. And for some reason, probably because he was an athlete, and on his way to playing at a higher level than he'd ever played before, he found himself wanting to resist her. No guy on the field who ever tried anything could avoid having to answer to Mitch. That was his signature. On defense he'd fly over to wherever the action was, and he'd blow that action up. Like a time bomb, just stop it in its tracks.

In the doorway, he cut back, and because she was such a dogged herder, there she was right behind him, her witchy hair and chin hovering just inches from his chest.

He had a reflex then to swoop down at her and catch her in his mouth. Which, being a creature of reflex, he did. He felt her tender lip inflate against his teeth, her dense know-it-all breath pushing back. He held her there in place against him, and yeah! It felt exactly right.

When he stepped back she was still smiling in her superior way, and he saw now that she'd been kissed by plenty of men, not just her husband, maybe even by a student or two. In fact she seemed almost bored. As if she'd expected it. As if she'd known from the moment he'd turned up at her door that he was going to hand her his pointless paper, and sit in a gummy desk, and kiss her with sudden possession on the way out. Which meant that everything she'd done in the interim—the questions she'd asked him, the way she'd dangled her leg off her desk, the business with the black plastic organizers—was merely her way of resigning herself to the inevitable. The thing even he hadn't known he would do. He felt himself deflate a little, felt his shoulders hang a little more heavily. Even now, about this, she was smarter than he'd ever be.

"Come back and see us sometime," she said, still holding her line at the door.

Back in his truck, he flung into gear to an explosion of Lynyrd Skynyrd. He left the lot in a fury, suddenly starving, and instinctively turned towards home.

It was barely two o'clock; he wasn't due to meet Caryn until four. She'd picked the place, a diner in Buckingham County, about an hour from his house. "Best root beer floats in all of Central Virginia," she'd told him when they made their plans on the phone. He'd lain there in his bed with the window open wondering how the hell this girl knew a thing like that. If it had been up to him, he would've said Hardee's, because that was where he always went.

He headed there now, and as he drove, the mountains stayed with him in the rearview, blue bodies, the pastures tagging along underneath. People always said Monacan County was beautiful. Some even went so far as to call it the most beautiful place in the world. And to them maybe it was. Just not to Mitch. To him it was all the same. Green trees, green grass. Blue sky sometimes, sometimes not. Whatever the weather, the cows, those standing rectangles, staying put. It depressed him that nature was all there ever was, nature and brick boxes with attached carports made of the same material they used for Coke. Who could love a place with nothing interesting in it, not even a crappy little place that could claim the best root beer floats in all of Central Virginia?

But as the road discarded itself behind him, the natural world began to look a little better, and the beast in his stomach began to settle down. It wasn't like Mrs. Murray had broken his heart. He'd taken his kiss, hadn't he? When you got right down to it, that was pretty fucking bold. He *was* bold. He was a monster. Fuck, he was headed to the U! The Hurricanes, the outlaws! The fucking National Champs! He pressed the gas a little more, feeling better every second.

And then, suddenly, there was Hardee's, floating red and yellow on its little curve at the intersection of Lakeview Drive. He sailed under the light, and pulled into the lot, at the last minute whipping around to the drive-thru lane, where he ordered a double quarter pounder with cheese and an extra-large Coke and fries. The pimply black guy at the window was new, nobody he recognized from countless drive-thrus—though sure enough, the kid recognized him. "Yo, Wilkins!" he said, passing him his bag, no charge. "You the man!" Mitch saluted and pulled over to the side of the lot where he ate his burger out of its waxy wrapper and watched through the glass windows of the restaurant as people came in, balanced their trays of icy drinks, threw wrappers at each other's heads, and left.

His next thought was that the burger was gone. He was now only vaguely aware of it doubling and tripling itself to pin down the beast in his stomach. He had a memory of the taste though, a flush of warmed salt and fat, a drip of cheese, a breath of bread, a shadow of something on his lips. He licked them and thought again of Mrs. Murray, more fondly now than ever. He closed his eyes and let the sun pound his face through the windshield. He sat there feeling completely still, happy to be himself, and barely there, until the smell of his empty wrapper caught up with him, already growing rancid in the heat. If he didn't book it he'd be late for his date.

He drove east to the girl and the root beer floats, coming back to himself in specks the way he sometimes did on the field after a bell-ringer hit. The world would glide by softly as it did now, his path warm and quiet, the sharpness filling in drop by drop, until all at once, he rocketed forth, into the noise and the air and the wilting flank of the target who would know damn right not to dare ring *his* bell again. He popped half a roll of breath mints in his mouth and at lights flashed his teeth in the mirror, saw his veins on alert in his neck.

At the diner he stood for a moment in the doorway, evaluating the space, testing it for signs of opposition. He'd hardly registered the music, the counter, the scattered heads of old guys in green-cushioned booths, when his eyes keyed into a welcome sight on the far wall of frames: the familiar arrangement of figures and lettering that was this year's Warrior team photo. He was co-captain, the brown-haired Caucasian smudge in the front row, right of center, which he could see without even seeing it.

So he'd preceded himself. Good. They knew him here already.

Caryn hadn't arrived yet, which was unfortunate, because he particularly hated to wait. He felt a little panicked as he turned to choose his booth, but when he did the diner opened up to him and a second aisle revealed itself around the curve of the central counter. She was in that aisle in a booth by the emergency exit, behind a giant, frosted red cup of water. He recognized her immediately. Her hair was big and brown, beauty queen style. She probably *was* a beauty queen for all he knew. She looked expensive enough to be one.

"Hey," she said, before he could.

"Hey." He slid in and she smiled, nestling into the booth a little further. He filled his side, his knees bruising up into the table, his arms with nowhere to go but along the back of the bench.

"You made it."

"I'm good for something I guess."

"Good for a lot of things, from what I hear."

"Oh, yeah?" he said. "How do you know Jeff anyway?"

She flapped her hand as though Jeff were beside the point. "My mother's cousin. You play with him, right?"

"I let him hang around." She laughed and he found himself continuing. "Naw, he's my boy. I'd trust him with my life. Just maybe not on the field, you know."

"I was gonna say, I bet he's not exactly a starter." She held her straw wrapper on its end and let it go, tsking as it toppled. He laughed. It looked just like Jeff. He could relax now, stretching his legs out on either side of her, wide enough that she wouldn't know. Expensive or not, she was making this easy on him, and he liked an easy girl. Not sexy-easy, though that was fine, too, but easy with life, not having to make everything a fight or a game. He had plenty of that as it was.

When the waitress came they ordered the famous root beer floats, and after she left Caryn went right on talking and generally having a good time. He hardly had to do a thing, just sit back and let her tell him about her family, her ballet classes, and all the stuff she'd do in Miami. The dance team she'd join, the clubs she'd hit.

The more she talked, the more he understood that she was

advanced. She'd thought about the world beyond the one where they were sitting; she'd made reservations, planned the trip. She spoke quickly and her eyes were blue and extremely bright, as though they were capable of seeing more and seeing it clearly. She was like Mrs. Murray, maybe, but the difference was that she was including him. She was taking him along on her ride.

"I'm in Stanford. The freshman towers," she was saying. "You're in Foster, right?" She gestured at the booth behind her, as though Foster had temporarily installed itself there and was plowing through a BLT. He wished he had a map. He'd barely glanced at the one that came with his orientation packet. They took care of you at the U, was his impression. His mom had talked to his advisor herself. When he got there, the advisor assured her, he'd always know where he'd have to be.

"Anyway, you probably are," she went on. "Mine's this kind of new thing they call a residential college. For regular students. But Foster's where all the football players live."

She really was in deep with Miami, a whole new world of people and places he hadn't even begun to plumb. He'd been in deep with Monacan County and the Warriors, benching three-fifteen to the rafters, and thinking it was the world. But it wasn't. At least not anymore. It was already fading. All the small-town trophies, all the small-town girls. A bigger, badder world, harder and hotter, was coming to push them aside.

"So come on," he said, now that the root beer was singing in his nose and he was growing ever more comfortable in the presence of this fancy babe. "Tell me. I gotta know. What'd Jeff say about me?"

"What do you mean?"

"I don't get the impression you have root beer floats with

every guy who calls you up. There wouldn't be time. He must've said something."

She liked this characterization of herself, and she savored it as she took a sip of her float, which she also savored, if not quite as much.

"No, you're right." She swiveled to look him in the eye. "Well, if you want to know the truth, he said you were going to be a star. And not just at Miami."

He'd heard this before, of course. From Tim and Coach Long and all the die-hard, gator-lipped fans who hung around the bench after games and after practice, and from the scouts and Erickson and his many khaki-wearing assistants with their binders and gas puddle shades. Every time it felt great, a thump of air in his chest, a shock of light in his brain—better than any drug. From Caryn though, it was magic. It was as though everything all those other guys had promised was now finally coming to pass. You no longer had to know him to know how good he was. You didn't have to be an expert either. Pretty girls knew it. Pretty girls from miles away. People weren't hedging anymore. They were confidently spreading the word.

"You know what," he said. "I think I am."

"Well, that's good. Hey—how tall are you anyway?"

"Tall enough."

"No, really. How tall?"

"Just six three."

There were bigger dudes, even in Monacan, but she was small, and probably didn't know much about sports, so the number alone seemed to impress her. "Show me."

"You saw me walk in."

"Yeah, but I was sitting."

"You're sitting now!"

He liked it when women bossed him around, and maybe that was something she could tell. She leaned back in the booth like someone at the beach and looked up, waiting for him to rise. "Well, show me again."

He did it every day just getting around in a too-small world, unfolding, unrolling, extending himself. He could do it this once for her. He sighed for show and shuffled his foot out to the edge of the booth, slid after it, and dragged his left foot behind. Up came his knees, his ass, his back, his chest, his shoulders, his arms, his head. He straightened himself, growing taller still in his legs, in his spine, and in his neck, a lifetime of growth replayed in mere seconds. Something cracked in his back—a good crack— the kind that meant his body was finally approaching its God-given size. He had always believed in God, and even more, he believed in what he'd been given.

He stood there reborn, perfect, a moment worth preserving forever, except there really wasn't any need. It was only his own body. He'd have it all his life.

"Yep," she said. "You're definitely gonna play football when you grow up."

"Oh, yeah, and how about you?" He gathered himself over her like a storm.

She touched her hair and lifted her small, bare knee to her chest. "That's easy. I'll be a football player's wife."

Hours later he hardly knew what had happened. He drove home magnetized, with Caryn's Glamour Shot in his wallet, drawing everything in. It was like after a punishing pre-season practice, the kind where you learn to play the game again, where you leave your body for a bit, and escape with just your breath. He couldn't recall the last time he'd eaten, couldn't imagine ever requiring food again. It was night and the universe was made of movements and dark shapes. The mountains came to him as shadows, the road as a never-ending tongue, flicking this way and that way in pale yellow blinks.

He knew time better than most people. He'd been raised on the game clock, the stern ticking away of seconds from twelve minutes at the start of a quarter, to eleven minutes and fifty-nine seconds and right on down to the constant white-lit double zero, some stretches lasting an eternity, others lost in blackout pops. However fast or slow the time passed, and however often it was stopped or adjusted, the clock could not be denied. Everything you were going to do you had to do before time was up. It was just that simple. He wasn't like some people: lazy, dragging themselves through life without a drop of urgency. He knew the clock in his bones. The best habit of his career.

But somehow today, he'd let it get away from him. He'd kept his family waiting, and on this, his last night at home. He crept up the three steps to the door.

"Hello?" he called, sucking back his volume even as the word left his lips.

The front room was dark and smelled of burgers. He'd forgotten all about that. He found them in the kitchen—Tim, his pregnant wife Tracy, his grandparents, and his mom, all gathered around the coated-cloth-covered table, their dishes already in the sink.

"We thought you left," his mom said.

"Sorry, I was catching up with some of the guys."

She blinked. She was fierce. She had to be to have brought him up: she the lone woman, he the freak monster son. "Well, nice of you to join us. Your grandparents came all the way out."

No one asked her to give him a break. He looked at his

grandfather, whose lungs were doing poorly, and at his grandmother, who squeezed her eyes shut as if to conquer a sudden pain. He pulled his chair up between them and took their wrinkly old hands, catching Tim's glance across the table. Tim flicked his eyes at the ceiling as if to tell him he better watch out.

"You all packed?" his grandma prompted, helpfully.

He told her he was, told her about the photos and keepsakes he was taking with him, to remind him of them and of home.

"You want to take a burger, too?" his mom asked. "You're liable to get hungry on the road."

He was confused. "I figured we'd stop someplace. Tomorrow."

"Oh *we* will, huh? Sure you don't want to do this on your own, too?"

"Come on, Mama. We have to fight now? Don't do this. I've had a long day."

"It's settled then. To be honest, I could use the sleep."

"Mama."

"Just call me when you get there. That's all I ask."

It was her same, sorry, pity-me bullshit. He'd heard it now a million times, as often and as phony as a drinking boast from Jeff. She'd never abandon him. She could carry on all she wanted, act the prissy, offended queen. When he needed her, she'd be there.

But today was different, wasn't it? All kinds of things were coming to an end. He looked at Tracy's crowning belly, which seemed to carry a replacement for him. Without warning the back of his skull surged as though he'd stepped wrong, and his brain remembered it's bound to stop. The panic overtook him and shoved him to his mother's side.

"You gotta come with me," he said, crouching at her knees. "I'll die. I'll die if you don't come with." He really meant it. He meant it so much he might have died right there while she sat calmly on her kitchen throne.

She looked at him now with her own athlete's face: a mixture of victory and pain. The shrewdest of all his bosses, the one who made his world. She put a hand on the back of his neck. "'Course I'm coming. I already bought my plane ticket home. Now get yourself fed before you upset me all over again."

He released his grip on her seat and somehow found her burgers in the fridge. They were bulging with inner pink and blackened on the edges, fogging the Tupperware with their expiring breath. At the table, his family resumed their drowsy chit-chat while he found the tomatoes she'd sliced, and the lettuce and cheese, the buns in their clear plastic bag. She had to do a lot on her own, and she usually missed something, the house a permanent mess, the tag of her shirt sticking up. It embarrassed him sometimes that she had to do the job of two people, a hardship visible to anyone who looked. But more often than not he was proud of her. His mother, the superhuman, who routinely acted like it was no big deal. That night while he was out, she'd hauled herself up from the couch, changed her clothes, gotten everyone together, and even found the time to make his favorite home-cooked food. The least he could do was eat it. He found a grill pan, clicked on a burner, and got ready to enjoy burger #2.

5. MITCH, 1990-1992

He didn't practice the first day; he fought. One offensive player after another: fuming in pads and helmets, gnashing mouth guards in his face. He'd tangle with one, get separated, and then before he knew it, he'd be shoving and swinging at someone new. Guys hadn't even introduced themselves, except to say, "Fuck you, freshman. Think you're hot shit?" His implicit answer being, "Fuck yeah, and fuck you, too." He didn't know them but he knew he had to step up.

This was Miami. You did not fuck around. He'd heard stories, but he figured it ended with practice; as a team you had to leave it on the field. He sat by his locker after, freshly showered, clean undies, picking at a scab on his knuckle.

A fellow mastodon approached and flicked him with a towel. "Looking forward to a good night's sleep, Rook?" It was Gaines, a glistening defensive end, with three inches and forty pounds on Mitch, a trophy case of muscles that actually worked. He was naked but he was smiling. The least Mitch could do was smile back.

"You know it," he said.

"That's great. I hope you enjoy it." He slapped him on the back with a foot-long hand. "I'm gonna stab you in your sleep."

No one stabbed him, but it felt like someone could. It felt possible at Miami, where, per pregame tradition, they'd all come to do three motherfucking things.

"Hit! Stick! And bust dick!"
"And what else?"
"Talk shit!"

In the beginning, he called his mom every day and lied to her while his roommate Mike Garrison mimed a blow-job from his bed. Mitch told her people were nice, they were treating him well, he was learning. The last part was true enough, but not because anyone was nice.

There was a way of being black here that was new to him, not like the mildness of Monacan, the yes-sir blackness that just wanted to live. This blackness was furious. He'd expected that, of course. He wasn't a fool, he knew about the U. But expectation and experience were different things, and in his experience it was about ownership here. Owning yourself, owning the game, and humiliating anyone who tried to take it from you. *That* was how to play, it was obvious to him, and even though he was white, he was lucky, because he got to own it, too.

He learned other things. How to claw guys' necks above their pads, where to vomit inconspicuously in the facility and in his dorm, which professors would be like Mrs. Murray, passing him along without the work.

In Miami, the trees never lost their color, except when they were sick. Forget Virginia pines, palm trees were the true evergreen. He got rowdy one night and tried to pull one straight from the earth. He had clobbered it, he had it in his arms, and he was giving it all his strength, but it was eternal, it wouldn't budge, and the guys were hooting "Oh, shit!" and "Nooo, dude!" so he took out his humiliation on a bench. A gift from Linus Peabody, '51, it was toast, merely bolted with metal into concrete. Impermanent, manmade, unable to withstand the wrath of Mitch.

The trees, they were beautiful. The girls, too. Miami made looking beautiful seem like the easiest thing in the world. Hard to say how many of them actually *were* beautiful, as in really, underneath the hair and makeup. But like the trees they knew just how to plant themselves: tits high, eyes lined, legs tan. Like the trees they landscaped his life and were for the most part a lot easier to pick up. He was a white guy on a black team on a white campus, an extremely favorable situation.

"You asshole," Caryn told him, the first time she found out about a girl, which was not the first time, just the first time she found out. "You're so hard now. Miami's made you so hard. It's turned your heart to fucking stone."

She was angry but she was crying, and the mix of those emotions on her face did something devastating to him. It made him panic. It made him grab her.

So did her choice of word: *hard*. When she said it, he *got* hard, the same way he did pretty much every time she entered a room, even the times he wasn't looking. His crazy dick was like some kind of Caryn sensor, alerting him every time she was near.

She was worth the panic, though. If anyone was, she was. She wasn't like so many local girls, who grew small on the college stage. Caryn could compete. He lifted her and she came right off the ground, and he told her how sorry he was, because in that moment, he *was* sorry, and nothing he'd done or would ever do could change a single thing about how he felt.

In high school, he only hooked up between girlfriends. This, he was pretty sure, made him a monogamist—fundamentally, at heart.

But college had taught him something about fucking,

namely that it didn't change the world. The cock went in, and he felt everything, even terror, even weakness. The cock came out, and he reset, still himself, still evergreen. The whole experience was so detached from his mind and body, it was hard not to think of it as a hallucination, some trick of chemistry or light.

He considered trying to explain this to Caryn, but managed to laugh himself out of it before he could even finish the thought. She would want to know if he really thought she was that stupid, when actually what he was hoping was that she might somehow be that smart. So he had to keep her from finding out, keep her from crying the way she did at all costs. It was just his cock, after all, not his heart. Everything that happened in there, he instantly forgot.

It was not that way with other parts of his body. Things experienced in the feet stayed in the feet, same with the shoulder and the hamstring, and, especially in his case, the knee.

He'd fought with Caryn that week, about another girl, another nothing that evaporated the moment it was over, but apparently not fast enough, because Caryn had seen the gum in the trash and smelled the freesia body mist when she dropped by a few hours later with his latest problem set. She'd called him a little boy. She'd asked him if he was doing it for Gaines and Mike and Devon, if he actually thought they'd respect him more if he fucked every woman who chewed gum. She'd asked him if he knew his balls had a spot on them that looked like the state of Vermont.

He knew about the spot, of course, but he didn't know how the gum had given him away. Because it was pink? Because only girls chewed pink gum? She kept her distance a couple of days, which was fine. After all, he had to focus on his game.

And then that Saturday, he blew out his knee. He knew

it was final the moment it happened, because he immediately wanted to take the motion back. Rewind the tape, get a better jump, and re-meet the runner straight on. Enforce his will. Walk away the same as he came.

Instead, the guy burst into the hole, caught him off-balance, and yanked him around beyond the root of his feet. Reynolds, from BC—a pretty average back on a pretty average team. But quality had nothing to do with it, not when the pop in his knee was the sound of his sophomore season evaporating, faster than any girl who chewed gum. Mitch was livid. That moment was everything. It stayed in his knee where it remade the world. And Reynolds, that fucking insect, crawled back over to say he was sorry, and if Mitch could've moved, he would've killed him, that fucking flat-footed bug.

What followed was surgery and weeks of rehabilitation, the long, hard, boring work of reclaiming something he'd always had.

Recovery meant more time to brood. He spent a lot of it on the couch and on the phone while Mike was out at practice or lifting or generally using his body the way he was supposed to be using it. He called his mom more. He called his dad once, and it went well enough, he guessed.

The desire for a Cuban sandwich could give shape to an entire day. He'd be lying there on the couch, needing it, his tongue drying up and shrinking him from the inside because he wasn't already eating those layers of roast pork and ham. He would call Caryn over and over, ten, fifteen, twenty times if need be until she came back from wherever she'd been, and when she answered she was always breathing fast and annoyed, like she was holding weights in addition to the phone, and he'd feel righteous, he'd give her hell, and she'd tell him to chill out give her a second she was coming, and then eventually she'd be there to collect him and drive him in his own truck to La Carretta. The moments they were sitting before the food arrived were torture, toasty buttery plates passing them constantly on their way to other people's mouths, Caryn's arms folded and boosting her chest, taunting him and making him hard. It was hard to look at her sometimes and not think this was all her fault.

He called Joe a few more times, closing his eyes while the guy just talked. His voice was from a time before all this: the knee, Miami, Caryn, himself.

At a party that season, he found himself talking to a blonde girl in cut-offs who was majoring in English. "The punts," she kept saying. "They're so *poignant*. I didn't know a man could kick a ball so high. And then they just hang there. And then they fall. It's agony." She made an arc with the hand that was holding her beer, some of which sloshed over the side.

It was idiotic. The punts. Some people had no idea.

He saw her again later that night, and again she asked about the punter.

"You have to introduce me," she said, hanging onto his arm, almost knocking him off his crutches. She spoke at an embarrassing volume, like a man, though she was a girl with slim thighs and glitter on her eyelashes.

"Gaines!" he finally shouted, calling for backup. "Help me set this girl straight. The punter's shit."

"What's his name—Chris?" Gaines boomed, asserting himself on the conversation.

"You can't hit him. He doesn't even train with us. He's only out there because the offense fucked up!"

"Sounds like you got this." Gaines winked and roamed away.

"He's cute, though," the girl said.

"Gaines?"

"No—*Chris.*"

"He's barely a football player! I got a whole team of guys I can introduce you to, starting with the King. That's Gaines. Or are you allergic to chocolate?"

This offended her, and sometimes good offense was good defense. Maybe now she would leave him alone. "Fuck you, I've fucked a black guy."

"Give the woman a prize!"

She shook her head. "I don't understand where this hate is coming from. Do you want to fuck me? Is that it?"

"You want to fuck Chris."

"One does not preclude the other."

He freed a hand to stroke her ass. "Have fun. I hear he's very precise."

He fucked her, of course, and Chris didn't. Injured or healthy, the job still had its perks. Because that's what it was now, a job. Anyone who told you otherwise was fooling himself.

He didn't get paid in the normal way, with checks, the way he would eventually. But he got cash in white envelopes in his locker, at breakfast, and in the student lot. Fast, clever stuff, meant to disappear into clubs and bottles and plates and joyrides, which then disappeared themselves.

By his junior season, he had healed, was better than ever, once again evergreen. And yet it was clear by now that college itself was not eternal. It, too, was fast and clever, like sex, like money, disconnected from everything past and future, unless you went out of your way to pin it down.

Back from injury, he was seeking his titles while Caryn clung steadfastly to hers. His: All-American, National Champion. Hers: Caryn Fletcher, Wilk's Girl. She'd come in with him, and she put up with him, so she got to wear the crown.

They liked laying out in the sun together, whenever they could steal the time, he shirtless and in whatever shorts he was wearing, she in a bikini no bigger than two pairs of coasters, two up top and two below.

It was in one such stolen moment, five o'clock by his watch, that she rolled onto her elbow and looked at him, smug with something he didn't yet know. She'd been sick the past few weeks, but that afternoon she seemed to be feeling better, at least as far as her mood was concerned, her suit a wet pink to match the inside of her lip.

"Mitch," she told him. "I have news."

He looked at her body. It ran from the top of her head, down to her shoulder, across her stomach and through her legs to her toes. He took a long look. Was it already getting ahead of them? He imagined himself with that body for life.

He wouldn't get his national championship, but he did make All-American, and he won 48-0 over Temple in his final home game at the Orange Bowl. In three years, he'd never lost there, and though he had always liked oranges—they reminded him of the lunch bags his mom used to pack—he now considered them a sacred fruit. That thick, breakaway peel, crackling with mist, spritzing him with sweet victory juice.

"Yo," he told the guys that night. "Caryn's pregnant."

It was nearing five a.m. and they had driven in a caravan to South Beach, where they'd hit the club and were now dug into the sand with a couple of joints, no chicks, in the shadow of a posh white hotel. His lungs buzzed and he popped up into the sky, which glittered with distant cold. His last joint for a good long while; he would declare for the draft the next week. He'd be a monogamist again. His fast times were coming to a close.

"First it's like tar or something," Marcellus was trying to tell him, "but then it gets all carmel-y. Almost orange." Marcellus was already a dad.

"Man, that's disgusting," someone said. "I gotta eat later."

"He talking about diapers? He actually talking about poop right now?"

"I'm just trying to help the man out," Marcellus insisted. "He gotta know what he's in for, you know?"

"Psssssh."

"For real."

"Orange baby poop."

"Listen, y'all," Mitch announced. They were going to like this one. He was sure they were going to like this one. "If I'm never gonna play here again, I'm gonna have to get some orange shoes."

Laughter came from everywhere: that magic sound.

"Poop orange, baby?" said Devon, a strong safety, who loved to hear Mitch go on.

"Naw, Dev, orange orange." Mitch got to his feet before the group and swam his arms in a beastly hula. They were his boys. He was doing it for them. "I want shoes made of peels from the fruit."

"The fuck?!"

"You hear me, y'all? I'm talking Florida superhero, I'm talking breakfast of champions, I'm talking healthy, get-your-vitamins shoes!"

He'd never have a senior year, but that didn't matter. He'd

done college as well as anyone could.

"Man, you buggin'!"

"You trying to be OJ now?"

Mitch laughed. He hadn't thought of OJ. "Nah, man," he said. "The fruit was mine before all this. I'm just being me."

6. CINDY, 1993

"Hey. Hey, y'all! It's Jimmy Johnson."

The first time Caleb said it, Mitch vaulted the arm of the couch and was on the telephone in an instant, faster even than he cut on the field. Cindy remembered when her son moved purely for the joy of movement. Not today. Today it was all about the draft. How high he would go, where he would go, and how much money he would get. Cindy watched him listening, bug-eyed, the receiver to his ear, and thought to herself, *Dallas, okay yes I could live in Dallas.* They'd just won the Super Bowl.

But it was not Jimmy Johnson, the shellacked Cowboys coach who'd led Miami before Mitch's time. It wasn't anyone, just some automated recording Caleb had dialed when no one was looking. Come to think of it no one had heard the phone ring; they all just assumed that it had. Because this was one of those off-kilter, dream-come-true days when even unreasonable, vaguely magical things had to be taken seriously because everything that was happening was so different from anything that had ever happened before. And Caleb Campbell was preying on that; he was capitalizing on everyone's innocence and hopes. He burst into hysterics—this was a boy who laughed like a little furry forest animal even though he was three hundred pounds and shorn—and Mitch slammed down the phone and hurled himself back on the couch.

"Not funny," he said. He'd washed his chin-length hair

with some fragrant, feminine product of Caryn's, and as it dried his whole dark mane had fanned out, soft as cat fur, a massive imitation of his wife. But it was too much hair, even for him, so he'd pulled it back with his usual elastic. All day he'd been patting the top of his head, trying to help it settle.

"You shoulda seen yourself," Caleb gasped, clutching his turbo-tread gut, once a force to be reckoned with on the Warrior O-line, now an extra weight he lugged to construction jobsites. "*Oh! Jimmy!* They ain't picking till the second round, dumb nut."

"Think I don't know that?" Mitch asked. Other people were laughing now, too, mostly out of relief. Cousins, supposed friends, even Caryn was smiling coquettishly.

"Cut it out, Caleb," she said. "I'm sure the Cowboys would love to have Mitch. It's just too bad for them he's not lasting that long." She sat next to Mitch with her feet on a special ottoman, perimeters of white on each toenail in a style she'd casually proclaimed was French. When Caryn had left for the salon that morning, Cindy had promised herself she'd admire her daughter-in-law's nails no matter what color she chose. She was prepared for something audacious—Miami orange with sparkles or Barbie pink with polka dots—so when this muted arrangement of European piping returned, a style so classy Cindy hadn't even known it existed, she didn't quite know what to say. "Matchy," she'd finally managed, neutrally, looking from fingers to toes.

Caryn hadn't cared. She had so much confidence, it didn't matter what Cindy thought. Her daughter-in-law. Mitch's nine-month pregnant wife and hair twin, married in a hasty, family-only ceremony at Christmas, with talk of a real wedding to come. She'd taken a leave of absence from Miami and they were home now because of her, because her doctors had advised her not to travel at this stage and because Mitch had refused to go to New York without her. He would've gone without Cindy—she was pretty sure of that—but this was not the time to make comparisons. It was different with the wife, the mother of your child. It ought to be anyway. In the end, they'd all go wherever they were going together. The only question was where that would be.

Washington, Houston, Green Bay. Niners, Steelers, Rams. The last few months it was like some kind of hundred-year pollen had spread through town, making everyone sneeze out the names of cities and teams. Mitch was their first pro since Scooter Hartless had gotten the call from the Saints in '82, the first ever who stood a fair chance of being a star. People were just obsessed, and the itch intensified, was practically hives, whenever Cindy was around. They crowded her pew in church and carried grocery bags to her car just for a clipping of the latest news. How was his forty, how was his bench, had he heard from the Cowboys, the Redskins, the Cowboys? "April 25," she kept telling everyone. "That's the draft. That's when we'll know." She'd never repeated a date so many times in her life.

By the time she flipped the kitchen calendar to April, the date had taken on a personality of its own. Circled in red, it bloomed with all the exhibitionism of spring, the first of their many football Sundays—football Fridays and football Saturdays now consigned to Hall of Fames past. She could feel it pulsing at her when she turned her back to wash dishes in the sink, felt her eyes drawn to it every time she talked to him on the phone. It even appeared in her dreams, that red-circled date, whirling its arms the way Mitch would do when he managed to turn an interception into an end zone dance.

The intensity had grown and grown—at a certain point

she would've taken a coma if it meant the day would get there sooner—and now it had reached its limit on the afternoon of the draft. The party was her way of appeasing the masses, and of distracting herself from all the disaster scenarios that were too painful to contemplate. From Sam's Club, she'd ordered fifteen gourmet hoagie platters with an assortment of roast beef, turkey and ham; ten party-sized chicken Caesar salads with dressing on the side; five party-sized seven-layer dips with accompanying Tostitos; five plastic gallons each of pretzels, Goldfish, Cheez Doodles, and Mitch's favorite, Peanut M&Ms; two full-sized sheet cakes in the style of football fields; twenty-five two-liter soft drinks ranging from Coke and Dr. Pepper to A&W Root Beer and Sprite; and two full kegs of Bud Light for the yard. She'd puzzled over the cakes, thinking it might be nice to customize them the moment they learned where he would go, but that would involve ordering plastic decals for all twenty-eight teams, and more frighteningly, invited Disaster Scenario #1: No One Picks Him At All. In the end, she decided it was safer to stick with a generic green frosting field sectioned off with fine white piping, and in the end zones, his good, proud name MITCH, stenciled in his high school colors on one cake and in his college colors on the other. Whatever happened today, he'd played football all his life.

People came. Oh, they came. They brought jumbo pots of mac and cheese and bonus-sized bottles of champagne and Hennessy, cigars they tucked into the inside pockets of their windbreakers and kept flashing expectantly throughout the day. They brought Betty Crocker fudge brownies and confetti cakes they'd baked from boxes, plus extra Styrofoam cups and the stray bag of ice, in case she happened to run out. They helped her spread tablecloths and fan cocktail napkins, reach bowls and unfold chairs—even more solicitous than when her father had died, and two years later, her mother—but mostly they just took up space in her living room. Mitch's coach and teammates from Monacan, Donna from the hospital, people from church and the newspaper, even Pastor Ron dropped by, not to mention Caryn's parents and sister and two of her big-haired friends. And Tim and Tracy, of course, with their daughter Megan. All of them hooting and slapping Mitch on the back, crowding onto couches, hunkering down on the floor by the coffee table, filling doorways and laps and lounging beachily on the stairs. As the day went on, they proliferated and concentrated, hugging together before the television in an ever tighter and ever more desperate mass, a drink in every hand, all other needs for the moment met, until the draft officially began.

Some thoughtful person had saved her a seat on the central couch next to Mitch, which was only right, but she was grateful anyway. As the clock ticked down to the first pick, she wiggled her fingers up against his leg. His thigh was swampy. Poor boy, he was sweating already in his big khaki shorts, and he all but knew he wouldn't go first.

"The first selection will be made by the New England Patriots," the commissioner was saying, a fatherly man who did his best to hide his obscene wealth beneath the front of a bland black suit. Camera flashes quick-silvered his face and the beige wall behind him, and the moment seemed to accelerate as the television sucked them all in.

Drew Bledsoe, quarterback, Washington State University.

There was a collective sigh as everyone flexed their knuckles and relaxed their shoulders and generally settled in. It was real, it was happening, and it wasn't over yet. Though no one would've begrudged Mitch if he'd somehow gone first—on the contrary, that meant more money, which they probably hoped to share—she knew they'd been waiting for this moment too long. The speculation, and the sense of power and significance that came with it, had sustained them for so many months in their otherwise, let's face it, slow and fallow lives, that it almost would've killed them to see it whiz by so soon.

"They been saying it'd be a QB first," Ricky Franklin said above the murmur. Ricky was another ex-Warrior—a wiry corner—and current shift man at Frito Lay.

"Yeah." Mitch was massaging his jaw with his hand. "I knew it'd be Drew."

"Friend of yours?" someone hooted.

"He'll know me soon enough."

This drew a chorus of familiar hollers—"Yeah, Wilk!" "Look out, Drew!" "Gonna get a Wilking!"—which Mitch just ducked and accepted. She wasn't sure he even heard his own cheers anymore, not from these folks, whom he'd known his entire life. He was hungry for the unheard; she could sense the desire warming there in his muggy leg. He'd been on the biggest college stage in Miami. Where else to go but up? He wanted the cheers of New York, Chicago, San Diego. The nation really, in all its countless anonymity. The people who knew you were no longer quite enough.

"What, no suit?"

"Can't the boy dress?" The room exploded into guffaws at Bledsoe's plain red work shirt and jeans, as though he'd taken a break from chopping wood to accept his millions.

Cindy moved her hand to Mitch's knee and gave it a squeeze. His left knee. The only part of him that had ever been seriously injured. When he was first becoming great at football, some long-ago time in high school now impossible to locate, she had feared all kinds of damage, yet found it ecstatic to watch him play. She'd been a volleyball captain herself, but had never cared much for his sport. Football boys were unreliable. That had been her experience anyway. But then came her son and he was a natural, even better than his dad. He flexed his shoulders, he butterflied his arms, he seemed to grow an inch each game. She would stand in her lucky middle-aisle spot in the third row of the home-side bleachers and she would hold herself across the waist, wondering how on earth he could do these things with his body, things she herself had never done.

On the other side of Mitch, Caryn flexed her toes. Cindy saw why he liked her. She was tiny, and well-made, like a very special doll. She could almost fit in his pocket, where he kept his wallet and keys and everything else he cared about most. Yet she had the bearing of a much larger person. When she made any kind of declaration, even something as harmless as "I want a milkshake," Cindy often found herself feeling shrimpy—Cindy, who was six feet tall!—and truthfully, she didn't like feeling that way around another woman. Truthfully, she didn't like Caryn much at all. There was something about her shiny dark hair and her stacked little shoes that reminded Cindy of a China cabinet, as though she'd only allow herself to be set out for the finest occasions. Compared to Donald Trump, her accountant father wasn't rich, but compared to Cindy, he was, and Cindy was quickly discovering that the money of the person just a few steps above you was the only money that had any value.

Of course now all their fortunes would rise: Mitch's and Caryn's and Cindy's together. She had to hand it to her; Caryn had played her cards exactly right. Nine months pregnant on draft day.

Bledsoe was done shaking hands with the commissioner

and stiffly brandishing his new jersey and now the Seattle Seahawks were making their pick. Rick Mirer, Notre Dame, another quarterback.

"Standard," Mitch said, taking Caryn's hand. "This is all standard."

"How're you feeling, Mitch?" Gary, the reporter from the local paper, shouted from the corner by the standing lamp. He wore a yellow paisley tie, even in summer, and a shirtfront pocket full of pens. Cindy had known him since high school; his kids were several years younger than Mitch.

"Like a million bucks," Mitch said. "Maybe more than a million." He gave a media-savvy wink as Caryn kissed his cheek.

The next few picks sped by slowly, like trains in dreams she couldn't run fast enough to catch. Cardinals, Jets, Bengals, Bucs. One massive son after another, putting on a brand-new hat. The Jets had taken a linebacker; she'd talked to the coach of the Bucs herself. Now she was starting to worry.

"Y'all! It's Jimmy Johnson!" Caleb cried, cupping the receiver of the phone.

"Man, shut up, Caleb," Mitch said.

"Mitch," she couldn't help herself. "You don't think they've forgotten about you?"

That was a mistake.

He shot his eyes at her. "How's that?"

"Cause you're not there? In New York."

He gave a grunt. "They know where I am."

"Yeah!" came the ever-ready choir. She'd forgotten everyone could hear. "They know him!" "Forget Mitch?" "Don't you worry about it, Ms. Wilkins. Don't you worry." But their brio was escaping with every breath, and by the time the last voice died down the room was unmistakably deflated, their collective confidence hanging back like a kid who can't swim without his wings.

Cindy wanted to wring every one of their necks.

Whoever was sitting on her left had gotten up, but it wasn't long before Pastor Ron had come to take the empty place. He was pale with wire-rimmed glasses and a chin as pillowy as any pastor's, a mild, well-meaning man who relished his small-town authority.

"This must be hard on you," he said.

"I'll be glad when it's over, that's for sure."

He nodded and gave a little moan of empathy. "What you have to remember is that this isn't like kids picking teams. If all they wanted was the best, Mitch would be gone already. These are businessmen, and it's about more than talent at this level. They've got budgets they have to consider, growth plans. Not to mention regulations."

At one time, she thought he was the smartest man she'd ever meet. He'd gone to seminary at Duke and repaired cars as a hobby. He played the stock market, subscribed to the Wall Street Journal. He was too smart and probably too earthly for the ministry; their church had really lucked out. But now she was beginning to sense the limits of his knowledge, how far he'd gotten reading the newspaper in a town where everyone else watched TV. She was doing her own reading now, privately, and she'd spoken to all kinds of people she'd never had an opportunity to speak with before—agents, reporters, endless NFL representatives. She was starting to get a handle on the wider world: who had power, who didn't. Very often it was the people who explained things who had the least influence—the lackies and doormen and cheerful tour guides who had the time to talk. The people you spoke to the least, the ones who grinned and clasped your hand and said a flattering thing or two—those were the people who were actually in charge. People like Mitch's agent, Phil Holtzman, whose liquidy suits looked almost supernatural. People like Al Thorndike, the general manager of the Redskins, and Bill Braden of the 49ers, and Orin Phelps (Seahawks), and Bruce Walper (Patriots), and Greg Romeika (Buccaneers), each of whom she'd spoken to for a brief, buttery moment on the phone before he, the important man, was urgently called away. Pastor Ron, on the other hand, had never not had time for her. He proffered advice eagerly, often before she asked. He held it up with boyish pride, like an A on a grade school exam. She pitied him that he'd already shrunk so much in her estimation.

The draft lurched on. More players were taken, every one of them clomping up on stage in person, just about all of them black.

At the commercial break the phone was ringing; she heard it this time for sure. Caleb backed away with his hands up. *The Cowboys*, went her brain. *Let him be right, letimbe right, lettimbeeright.*

"Uh-huh," Mitch was saying. "Yeah." She could hear the cheerful munching of Phil Holtzman on the line.

"Well?"

"Come on, what'd he say?"

Ricky was leaning in theatrically, his torso bent in a freeze-frame of a factory man at his machine.

"Lotta teams still interested," Mitch told the room when he sat down. "Washington, Niners, Bucs. He said Green Bay this time, too."

Washington, a short move.

"I'm still rooting for Washington," Caryn said, as though

reading her mind. "I have always wanted to live there."

Cindy got up from the couch and motioned for people to pass her their trash. She took the stack of plates and napkins to the plus-sized garbage bag she'd tied to the handle of her louvered pantry door, then stepped out back for a moment to get some air. She stood on the concrete step and watched the blue-green world recline under moving clouds and settle into its clothes, the fields and trees zipping up to the low distant mountains, ringed at the base by their collar of trees. The insect orchestra was tuning a high drone. You couldn't live in Virginia without smelling bugs and dirt. She was a Southern woman, used to Southern light and Southern smells. She did not want to live in Wisconsin.

The draft was back and they were calling her inside where the house reeked of salt—from the bodies, from the food. She fanned her nose, feeling a little salty herself, and squeezed into her spot on the couch, this time next to Donna from the NICU. The murky glow of Caryn's engagement ring wafted from her hand like cigarette smoke.

"Cindy," Caryn said, but Cindy just turned to Donna to remark about a patient, an adorable little caterpillar named Keyshawn who'd been admitted earlier that week.

"He's just so beautiful," she said.

"That's how you know he'll be fine," Donna agreed. "They're never that cute at twenty-eight weeks. But Keyshawn's mom—have you seen her? Well, she could be a model, her skin's so smooth and everything. You see where he gets it from." Donna was a big-bodied woman who loved holding babies; she liked to joke that she was the backup generator, there to warm the preemies if the unit ever lost power. Cindy felt hot sitting beside her now, but grateful for the excuse to ignore Caryn. Donna had worked the NICU forever and for some reason liked Cindy even more than Cindy liked herself. "You know she's from North Carolina originally," Donna went on. "Mountain town not far from Danville if I could only remember the name. But then she went to Charlotte when she finished high school, got a job at USAir, which has got to be one of the best jobs in Charlotte. Every flight out of Lynchburg goes to Charlotte. She was in for kangaroo care this morning, and she said it really was an exciting place. I asked her why she was here then, and she said the opportunities. Which of course made me laugh, but she said nonono she was serious. When they opened the new airport here, there were jobs. That was a promotion for her." Cindy hummed in response and nodded, picturing Keyshawn's mom holding the boy to her chest as all around them the isolettes glowed like airplanes idling on the new Lynchburg tarmac. Cindy guessed she'd fly out of there soon enough, via Charlotte, to wherever they were told.

"And how about you?" Donna was saying. "You keeping calm?"

"I'm surviving," Cindy managed as another team selected another player.

"What round're they on?" someone asked.

"Still the first!" people shouted, disdainfully, to which Pastor Ron, standing against the back wall like a sentry, added serenely: "That was only number thirteen."

"Poor sucker!"

"Dodged a bullet there, Mitch!"

"*Fourteen*, though," Ricky said. "That's lucky." He tugged his shirt with pride.

Mitch expectorated a laugh. "I'd rather go last than be picked by your sorry-ass number." High-fives were exchanged over the back of the couch.

"Hey, there's always 'American Gladiators,'" Ricky said, grinning toothily. "Juice it up and off you go."

Fourteen came and went.

So did fifteen, the Green Bay Packers, who took a linebacker.

"Wayne who? I never even heard of that guy!" This was Mitch's buddy and Caryn's cousin Jeff, who'd kept his cool until now. Veins pulsed in his forehead below the box-top cut of his hair. "Where'd he play? *Clemson?* Never heard of him!" He punched himself on the thigh.

So the Wisconsin threat was over, but what did that leave? She tried to remember the selection order Phil had given them but the names of all those distant cities kept running together in her mind. She tried not to think about the money, how much they were losing with every pick. She was watching a fantasy, no different from "The Price Is Right." Win a car on TV, play football on TV. The odds were probably about the same.

The next hour passed with crushing slowness. Gary wrote in his little notebook with one of his many retractable pens. Caryn's mother yawned. Ricky tossed a fresh baseball to Caleb, and Caleb tossed it back, but the whole exchange was so limp and idle that Cindy didn't even shout her usual, "Not in my house!" Time extended itself, unlooping hidden coils she hadn't known she'd always skipped. The rest of the world was racing into the future while they in their little brick tract house sat suspended, blinking, examining their cuticles and scabby elbows, adjusting their butts in their seats.

Caryn had stopped trying to get Cindy's attention. She sank deeper under the cask of her pregnant belly, which only now had begun to look huge. Her painted toes gripped the edge of the ottoman. A rectangle shone on her forehead like a bike reflector, and she had taken to depositing Cheez Doodles one by one down the tubing of her mouth, a ring of atomic flavor dust glittering on her lips.

"Why don't you boys go outside?" Cindy offered. "Shoot some hoops."

Mitch's friends looked at each other, reluctant to take the suggestion. "The minute we walk out that door'll be the minute Mitch gets the call," Caleb said. "You know how it is."

The phone rang and again it was Phil. Mitch's conference with him consisted largely of Phil talking while Mitch nodded and offered the occasional "Okay."

When he sat down, they had to pry it out of him. "He says sit tight. He says it's almost over." But she could tell he had his doubts.

Time had been rough enough with her already—the wiry grays, the baby seals swimming permanently on the undersides of her arms—but this was an utter clobbering. The excitement and glamour of being chosen had eroded to a state of captivity. All around the living room, people wore the surly, arrogant expressions of kids in detention after school.

"Lighten up, y'all," Tim said. He coached JV now, and had grown into a classic coach: hoarse, yet loud, face pocked like pigskin from years of afternoon practice. "It's not contagious."

"He's getting drafted," Caryn snapped.

"I know he is," Tim said.

"It's still the first round."

"That's what I'm saying, people need to have some faith."

"You said 'contagious,' like maybe he wasn't getting picked." No one ever spoke to Tim this way. He was the testy one, the one who talked. Everyone else was supposed to listen and then go out and embody his words.

Cindy looked at Caryn's parents, who just sat there like

figurines. Her own mother was like that by the end, but she actually had an excuse: doped up on speech-slurring pain medications, her mind abandoned, her smile was her best social tool. Cindy missed her, would've preferred her demented company to the non-company of Caryn's folks.

"Look I hate waiting as much as the next guy," Tim was saying. "I hate it more. Tracy does everything involving lines. I don't have the patience. But this is the NFL. You do it their way. You don't question."

"I'm not questioning," Caryn said.

Cindy evacuated to her room, where she lay on the bed watching the broad brown planks of the ceiling fan as they made their fragile rounds. She wasn't sure she'd ever seen a machine move so slowly without finally coming to a stop. The window shades were up and if she tilted her head she could see Gary taking a cigarette break in the yard. He single-handedly ran a weekly paper that rarely had much news. She wondered if he was disappointed he never got to leave; he'd been valedictorian, talked of excitedly, a scholarship to UVA. If only he were a Methodist and not a Baptist, he might've befriended Pastor Ron. He stooped to see inside and gave her a tentative wave, which she ignored, pretending she was resting her eyes. In the living room she could hear Tim booming hoarsely about the 3-4 defense, which teams had it, which teams should.

The answer was all of them, if you asked her. The 3-4 used more linebackers, and she wanted the best for her boy. The most chances. Over on the nightstand the old rotary telephone sat like a prop in a play. She'd last used it to talk to Phil Holtzman, on a day she was home sick from work. She rarely got sick, and before this year, she'd rarely used the bedroom phone, preferring to conduct her business in the kitchen on the push button. But the draft had made her more private, and maybe it had also made her sick. She recalled his glossy voice on the line. "It's an exceptional market," he'd said. "He really picked the right year to do it." He'd phoned her, as he always did. Whenever she called, he wasn't there.

She didn't know what to do. She called him. She couldn't believe it when he picked up the phone. "Cindy Wilkins. What a day, huh?"

She collected herself. "You said it would be exceptional."

"And it will be," he said. "It will." She heard the murmurs of nearby rooms and pictured him in a corridor somewhere, outside a wild party of agents, coaches, and journalists, tonguing cigars, playing dice with people's lives. "We've been talking to people all day and I think we're zeroing in on a good opportunity. A couple, actually. But one I think you'll really like."

"I thought he was supposed to go top ten. This is killing him, Phil. I can tell it's just killing him."

Phil sighed. "I said top ten was a possibility. But by no means guaranteed. Hell, nothing's guaranteed. What I've always thought was really reasonable was sometime in the mid-to-late first round. And—off-the-record here—I think we'll get that yet."

"First round's almost over."

"Like I said, mid-to-late."

She was feeling emboldened. "Do you think it's because he's not there? I told him he should go but he wouldn't listen. Had to stay down here with her."

"Wouldn'tve made a difference," Phil said. "If you want to know the truth—and I just told this to Mitch myself—it's mostly about his knee."

"His knee?" She couldn't believe her ears.

"Left knee, sophomore year?"

"But he was fine after that. He played his entire junior season. Big East sack leader. All-American, Phil! He could've played at Miami another year!" She was starting to wish he'd stayed in school. Caryn, too. How had she ever let them get so confident?

"I know, I know, but there's still some scar tissue and these are big bucks. Teams figure they can get him for less. They still want him. You'd better believe whoever ends up with him will be weeping tears of joy. They're just trying to hedge the best they can, maximize their draft."

"You're telling me this is all over some little scar tissue? He's strong, Phil. You've seen him."

"I know he is. You'll be hearing from me soon."

She sat holding the dead call in her hand and saw that Mitch and his friends had stepped outside. Gary was gone and the Warriors had taken his place, shoving each other in scattered arcs across the flossy grass. After a pop to the chest that sent Caleb to the ground, Mitch took off. She leaped to the grimy window to see him approach the fence line in a full sprint, then slalom back at a ferocious angle, as if he were riding skis. She rarely saw him run without his helmet and uniform, and she'd forgotten how miraculous he was as himself, just an exotic animal in shorts and a t-shirt, his calves bulging like sacks of flour, his rump an engine, his brown hair streaming behind him like a tail. Charging back towards the house, he seemed to have discarded his stigmatized scar tissue, ripped it out and transplanted it somewhere beyond the yard.

"Command central?"

She looked up to see Tim at the door, scratching his chest in his coachy way. He'd grown that coach's belly, married the music teacher from the elementary school, had a daughter they dressed in pink. It was hard to believe she'd ever been in love with him.

"It'll be over soon," Cindy told him, as though he were the one who needed reassurance.

"You know what's nice about the second round?"

"What?"

"It still gets you to the NFL. I'm serious! Lots of greats came from the second round—or, Christ, later. I wouldn't make too much of it."

"Well, he wants to go in the first, and I want him to have what he wants."

"Sure you do. But these people have their own agendas."

She had no idea why he still condescended to her, even now, after all these years. Did he assume she was suffering because she didn't have a man to tell her things? He knew the choices she'd made: Mitch above herself, Mitch above all. "You broke it off with me," he'd always teased her, which wasn't strictly true, but it was the lie that they'd agreed on. "No way was I ever gonna be good enough for you. Hell, I'm not good enough for Tracy, either, but God bless her, she doesn't seem to know."

"Sorry, Tim, but what do you know about their agendas?" she asked him now.

He gritted his teeth, seized up in the neck. She knew it stung him to have been excluded from the negotiations, but didn't care. She'd wanted to make a point of doing this part herself.

She tilted her head back and shut her eyes. "I'm sorry. I'm being mean. It's just that I've talked to these people and I know they have agendas and I hate them and I'm just so damn tired." She peered at him over the ghost of her nose. "You hear me, Tim? I'm sorry."

He settled back into his stolid body. He'd coach JV until

he retired, and when he was finished, JV would probably be finished, too. The county was losing people every year. There was no sense in spiting a man who lived in so narrow a world. "I hear you," he said. "I'm sorry, too. I was just trying to help."

She could forgive Tim for trying to help, as she forgave him for everything else, but she couldn't forgive him his timing. Before the sentence was even out of his mouth, the phone had rung again. Just once.

Cindy froze, straining to hear. First there was silence, then a murmur of movement, and then all the voices in the house came jouncing alive at once. These were happy noises, victory cheers, the kind she was used to hearing for Mitch. "New England!" Caryn squealed, and in that instant every one of them was free. The hours of waiting dispersed, the old uncertainty now unimaginable. Cindy pushed past Tim to the living room, where arms were alternately raised to the ceiling and clasping bodies together. The Warriors were jumping in a huddle. Even Caryn's parents were exhibiting some emotion, her mother crying, her father securing her tight around the shoulder as they crouched in closer to the television.

In the center of it all Mitch stood with his hair down, having for some reason shaken out his ponytail. He was holding one hand to the sky, in a fist, and offering Caryn his other. Grinning madly, she gripped him like a branch across white water, and hauled herself to her feet. It was the first time Cindy had seen her upright since the telecast began, and she was almost as wide across as she was tall, a beach ball on balsa wood stakes. Still Mitch devoured her. He lifted her onto the couch, her knees lightly bouncing like a child's, and kissed her, two shaggy brown-haired trees meshing into a single creature in the forest canopy.

"New England," Caryn's dad repeated, approvingly, and

Cindy looked at the television where Mitch's name, face, and measurements were emblazoned on the screen. They had footage of him clawing for a tackle for Miami, dragging down running backs as if they were meat. Then back to his face, neck wide as his jaw, fox eyes smiling though his mouth was not. His mouth meant business. She didn't know when she'd started to cry.

"I just love this pick for the Patriots," the jumpy commentator was saying, barely able to stay in his chair. "First and last picks of the first round, offense and defense, both of them All-Americans. You can't do much better than that."

The first round was over. He had made it just under the wire.

She stood watching as everyone had someone to hold, aware of Tim and Tracy and little Megan behind her, Tim who she definitely didn't want to hug. A minute sooner and she might've been by Mitch's side. She couldn't have stopped them from kissing, a big man and his little wife celebrating their future, but she might've at least received a kiss of her own. She picked her way around the coffee table, tears streaming, and still they went on necking, fully curtained by their hair. She stood by. She waited, and when she could stand and wait no more, she lurched into them, wrapping an arm around each of their shoulders, making a huddle of their hug.

"Come here," Mitch laughed, adjusting his arm to include her.

The phone was ringing and she felt someone answer it, felt a buzzing in Caryn's belly, and fronds of hair—she didn't know whose—swishing at her eye.

"I'm so proud of you," she cried into her son's concrete neck.

"Hey, Mitch!" shouted Gary. "Jimmy Johnson's on the phone!"

"Tell him, fuck him!" Mitch said.

"Yeah, FUCK HIM!" Caryn echoed with the venom of victory.

"Language!" Cindy said, reflexively.

It wasn't Jimmy Johnson, of course. That was the thing: it never was. But it was Phil and he was ecstatic. "Best," she heard him say through the phone. Mitch smiled with every muscle, and Cindy stood there and watched.

"Contract.... result... deal..." Phil went on, longer than anyone expected, and the strangest thing happened: the moment became difficult to hold. People's arms drooped off each other's shoulders. Their eyes began to wander around the room. Cindy listened to Mitch listen to his value, and on subsequent calls, thank his general manager, his owner, his coach. He was still Mitch standing there before them, still dressed in his own casual clothes. But he was doing business now, which was vaguely embarrassing. For the first time it seemed possible to intrude.

Cindy brought out the first cake and cut it in mismatched blocks, her hand unregulated with nerves, her motions light and loose. The cake itself was airy and yellow, the green color from the frosting faintly seeping into its pores. Soon everyone had green lips, reviving the festive mood.

"FUCK JIMMY JOHNSON!" Caryn shouted again, semi-deranged.

More people came by to offer their congratulations, and before Cindy knew it, the house was packed. Tracy took over the food service, so Cindy could try to enjoy the moment, which was her moment, too, everyone insisted. Champagne was uncorked, the phone rang and rang. Other Miami teammates were getting drafted. Plans were forming for a massive convergence. The talk in every room was of money. How good it felt, how much it could do for them.

At some point, Joe called, and she watched Mitch talk to him, unfazed. "Thank you, sir, that means a lot," he said. They talked from time to time, she knew, but not, exactly, how often.

Around six o'clock, after everyone had gone home—Tim and Tracy and Megan back to the old recovered house, Caryn's parents back to Charlottesville, Mitch and Caryn off to a party somewhere without adults—she stood in her living room amid all the evidence of feeding and felt that her life had changed. She was living in a redundant moment, the first of her lame-duck days. Her current surroundings, so unremarkable and inevitable to her now, would soon be memory, or not even memory. Forgotten.

She went back into the bedroom and this time, she dialed Joe.

"What a day," he said. "What a pleasure."

These days, she only talked to him a couple of times a year, and she knew, vaguely, that the habit would only fade. Mitch was grown; she'd seen him off. It seemed less important to keep Joe in the loop.

"How'd he sound to you?" she asked him now.

"Relieved," he said, from his house in Montana she'd never seen. "Content. But don't ask me. You know him best."

In one of life's cruel ironies, Joe seemed to have gotten better with age. He was reasonable. Better yet, he was thoughtful; he actually seemed to enjoy thinking about the world. She half-admired him, though she hadn't seen his face in years. She wouldn't allow herself that. But every now and then, she had these calls, and in a way they were better. People were always at arm's length in the flesh. On the phone, she had his voice in her head.

"You ready for Boston?" he asked her. "You'll have to buy a better coat."

"To tell you the truth, I'm scared. He's got his little woman now. What's he need me for?"

"Help with the baby, for starters. From everything you've told me about Caryn, she's not up to the task."

"Oh, she'll be fine. Women always are."

"You were. That's not the same thing."

It was true. On the day he'd basically proposed, which was how she'd come to think of that day—the basic proposal, the pretty-much promise, since he then immediately left town—she'd told him she was pregnant. She hadn't wanted to tell him. She hadn't wanted the baby to be the reason he did anything; she wanted it to be her. But she was an honest person, and she couldn't help but confess. She felt he deserved to have all the information, even if it chased him away. Now twenty years had passed and he was living a meaningful life, not too different from the life they might have had. He was married. Her name was Tammy. He was a landscaper at Montana State.

Joe and Tammy. Tim and Tracy, who ended up with their mother's ring. But no one had married her. It felt so unfair sometimes when she thought about it.

"You know you don't have to go with him," he said, when she failed to respond. "You can live your own life now."

She didn't have to go with him. She'd thought of that. There were plenty of things to hate about moving for the NFL. But with her parents gone, the truth was that there was nothing left for her here. Just the things she'd been biding her time with. And wherever Mitch was, there was excitement: a baby, tickets to every home game, a better place to live. She looked around at her shabby little bedroom, so much cleaner now that Mitch was grown, but still with the water damaged ceiling, the old phone receiver in her hand, and she knew she wouldn't miss it. The keys to her rusted Ford, which she drove ticking to work each day, sat on the dresser—a car she'd no longer have to keep for a job she'd no longer need. She would miss the dim hum of the NICU, all those separate transparent cylinders jump-starting precious lives. But she wouldn't miss her own isolation; that, she could leave behind.

Months later, when Mitch was basically living in his locker at the practice facility, she knew she'd made the right choice. For herself, but also for Caryn, whose pain suddenly reached her in New England, overwhelming and all too familiar.

Radiant in pregnancy, Caryn grew tattered in the post-partum gale, her lustrous hair diminishing and falling out, a loge of darkness filling in beneath each eye. She wore her nursing bra like a harness, her jeans like surgical scrubs.

"Come on," Cindy found herself cajoling her. "Let's go out."

She'd drive her to the mall, where Caryn would creep among racks of onesies with diamonds in her ears and Alyssa strapped to her chest like a bomb. Under a skylight in the brand-new café, they'd order smoothies because Caryn's teeth had grown sensitive and Cindy wanted to show her support.

"People here are pretty awful," Caryn said one time, watching a woman in pearls and a quilted jacket cup her tea in two delicate hands.

"Amen," Cindy said, happily bouncing Alyssa.

"They just aren't—*nice*," she said, finally.

"They say please and thank you, don't they?"

"I've heard it."

"I'm with you. I'm just trying to put my finger on it."

"Eye contact," Caryn said, looking at her own hands. "They don't make it."

"That's it. You're right. Eye contact."

They had become friends. Which, for some reason, was thrilling.

"You've met nice people, though," Cindy mused. "The other wives?" For a moment, she felt like she was back at her job, that trippy, long-ago thing, like a half-forgotten bender, counseling a NICU mom.

Caryn shrugged. "They're not from here, though. They're all, like, Pennsylvania and California and Georgia. And Vicki's the only one who likes me."

"Who wouldn't like you?" Cindy balked, but Caryn just narrowed her eyes. "I mean, once they got to know you." Cindy kissed the hot cap of Alyssa's head.

Without warning, Caryn's eyes filled, and she blinked furiously, tossing her thinned-out hair from her face, the youngest and most dangerous she'd looked in months. "I'm not really that good at keeping people."

"Sure you are," Cindy protested feebly. It was hard to look tears in the eye, but she made herself. She was not one of these Yankee bitches.

"People always have other things that are more important. And they are important. I mean, the NFL is important!"

"It'll be different after the first year," Cindy insisted, not even believing it herself. "Once he learns the ropes." After the first year, it would only be more permanent. All those play calls, all those other personalities. Already, there was a defensive lineman named Hardy, Vicki's husband, who behaved as though he'd known Mitch all his life.

"But my parents," Caryn said, "what're they doing? What's their excuse?"

Cindy tried to recall a single thing Caryn's mother had ever said. She was one of those meek people who hid behind her smile, thinking maybe no one would murder her if she kept on looking nice. The dad wasn't much more outgoing. Oh, they were agreeable, all right. But Cindy could see why Caryn might yearn for something thicker.

"They haven't even come to visit yet," Caryn went on. "They just call every now and then to say how great they think my life is. They're so nice, but I feel like they're done with me. Sometimes I feel like *I'm* done."

For years Cindy had wanted to deface Caryn, and now here she was under a skylight in Massachusetts, doing all the vandalism herself. Well. People changed. Cindy certainly had. Over the years, she'd trained herself to hold back the heavy, complicated sea of herself, a lesson she'd half-learned from Joe, and then all over again from Tim. But something told her she no longer had to do that with Caryn. She sat there with her a moment longer, letting her not-cry, letting her regain her composure, before asking her, "Caryn? Do you want to know something about me?"

And then she told her about Mitch's dad. How they'd collided after their senior year, a desperate time, when she'd felt ready to topple off a cliff. How he'd wander over every other night or so—she left the sliding door unlocked—but they otherwise had separate routines. Life had gone from public—school, games, parking lots—to something so private she didn't have the vocabulary to describe it. *Boyfriend* was a sugar candy word, a lollipop for little girls. She was in nursing school, stacking her brain with information. Cold, hard facts, a great contrast to the jellyfish she felt like with him. He came to her smelling of earth and pine mulch, marked by the loss of a mother, and in another way, a father, wounds he could not put into words.

It wasn't clear they had a future, but it was clear he felt safe in her bedroom, with the portable record player and the poster of Robert Redford over the bed. Sometimes, Joe was so physically present, she thought she might explode, the boundaries that held her together releasing themselves into him. Sometimes, she thought he was just another Redford, because she never saw either one of them anywhere else but in her room.

The erotic confession embarrassed neither of them. Caryn nodded and scratched her neck with the hand she wore her rings on. She was wearing them again, her fingers returned to their original size. Weight was never Caryn's problem.

She hadn't been able to keep him, but she loved him; Cindy wanted Caryn to know. She loved him in a way you can love only one person, the one you're with when you discover you are boundless, that however you look standing around a bonfire and whatever name you happen to go by, you contain within you all your past and future selves, your current phase, and all your potential. He'd taken a lot from her, but he'd also given her something, more than just a son she adored.

"You are not done," she told Caryn. "You are just starting. You are taking off right this very minute."

Caryn snorted at Cindy's hyperbole, but then something remade her face. She understood. She grasped the use of it. She wiped her eyes and met Cindy's gaze dead-on.

NAME

One Wednesday early in his first NFL season, Mitch neglected his most important rookie duty: picking up lunch for the veterans. He spent that afternoon bandaged to the goal post in New England's crumbling stadium, wearing nothing but a jock strap and a helmet. It was already getting cold in late September, and after a few minutes of useless wiggling, followed by tingles that quickly penetrated his bones, and the understanding that even Hardy wasn't coming to cut him loose, his mind landed on a sort of meditation. *Wilkins, LB, 59.* That was how he appeared on the roster: name, position, number. The phrase circled back to him, and it calmed him down, helping him to endure the involuntary shaking, and the hair he was, with every lurching adjustment, forcibly ripping from his skin until he was free. *Wilkins, LB, 59.* He called it up pretty regularly after that, in the midst of another agonizing loss, in between another pair of legs that weren't Caryn's, pretty much any time he needed a little assistance quieting his body or his mind. *Wilkins, LB, 59.* An entire season, an entire life's ambition, condensed into a guiding mantra: the pleasing, reassuring sound of his own, successful name.

7. CARYN, 1997

When they talked about the game, which was not often now, Mitch liked to remind her that it didn't matter how smart you were, what kind of strength or instincts you had. If you'd only done something once, you probably hadn't done it right. You had to do it a hundred times, a thousand. Lift, drill, study, react. The movement had to slip through your veins so chemically, you weren't even making a decision; it had to be automatic.

It was with this gospel in mind that Caryn Wilkins was making her second rep at the Koalani Resort on Oahu, a cruise ship beached in postcard paradise, every window capturing cut-outs of the Pacific. Each year the NFL rented out the whole place for the post-post-season Pro Bowl, and when she arrived with Mitch, their daughter Alyssa, and Mitch's mother Cindy, it was once again crawling with board shorts, shot-put calves, and all the other regular pageantry of football families on vacation. The printed sarongs over titantic boobs, the thousand three-year-olds in water wings, everything just as she'd left it on her first rep—and what a funny thought that was, her *first rep*, the very concept implying a second, a third, and then, eventually, one that fails.

This time, she would improve. This time, she was nearly done with her two hundred hours of yoga teacher training, and as a corollary she was making a concerted effort to live in the moment, in her body.

Her body was in the hotel. It had come from the car past the koi ponds and through the glass entrance so harmonious with nature it didn't even need a door. She heard rustling and the sound of birds, taking a moment to register what she already knew, that the rear of the lobby had no walls. She recalled this sensation from last year, the breezy warmth of being outdoors even when you were inside, though this time it was a bit duller, the novelty slightly worn down. A good feeling nonetheless. With Mitch by her side, she stepped one foot forward, then the other. She spread her collarbone and checked in with her pelvis, leveling it as they crossed the tiled atrium lobby to registration.

"Wilk!" Jordan Cash was approaching, the Jets quarterback Mitch sacked at least once a year. Mitch turned to clasp his hand in a micro man-hug. "Good to see you, man," Jordan said, tugging Mitch's signature ponytail. "What room they have you in?"

Mitch laughed in that forced way of his. "Don't even try that shit with me. Ain't you found a rookie yet?"

"I swear, I don't know where these guys are hiding! I got a happy hour to bill!" Jordan leaned toward Caryn now, a Georgia boy with instinctive manners and a fat gold wedding band he wore ostentatiously during games. "Looking lovely as always, Mrs. Wilk." Caryn received his kiss on her cheek. "Pam'll be happy to see you."

"You too, Jordan."

"Where's your entourage?"

She pointed at the imperial couches by the coffee bar, where Cindy sat with Alyssa collapsed into her chest. The single tiny thing she could control: her own family. Every other power sat with the almighty League. "Just Mitch's mom and Alyssa this time. We're trying to make it a family trip. First week for them, second week for us."

Jordan heaved forth a laugh. "Good luck! You know how this place is! Camp Koalani!"

She did know. Mitch had brought his protector Hardy Mulligan and two other New England teammates to the previous Pro Bowl, leaving Caryn in the pool all week with the female element. Mothers, daughters, sisters, wives. Alyssa, then a few months shy of the ubiquitous three, bobbed in glittered wings, scooping water from her left into the water on her right. "It's all the same water," Caryn had tried to explain. But Alyssa hadn't cared, didn't even seem to notice her efforts were futile; for her, too, it was about the repeated movement.

She'd made some friends last time. Noelle DiMassi of Denver, Carmen Jackson of Pittsburgh. And of course she had her old New England standby, Vicki Mulligan, who came with Hardy as a package deal. But the best was when they'd been with their men, everyone wearing leis, drunk with their feet in the surf of their private NFL-only lagoon, raising Mai Tais and beers to the endless ocean beyond the breakers. It was possible, then, to believe that life did not get more beautiful than this. At last a rest. At last a vacation. On an island made for vacations.

Hardy had made the Pro Bowl on his own this year, so Vicki and the kids were back, and it was all lining up to be the perfect do-over, because this time, Caryn had some new beliefs. One: that she was valuable. Cindy had taught her that. It had taken some time, but she got it now. Two: that she deserved the truth.

"Camp hell," Mitch said. "I'm here to win my wife a convertible. Then she's dragging me to Kauai."

"You, the Pro Bowl MVP?" Jordan hooted. "I'd like to see that!"

"I know you would. Don't worry, you'll get your forty g's. Gonna need it if you can't find a rookie to take your sorry-ass tab."

They explained things to each other, these men did, things all of them already knew. It was part of being in the club, having something to say that had often been said before, the more often, it seemed, the better.

"Don't you dare try to put it on our room," she said, succumbing to the habit herself. "We haven't even checked in!"

The room—707, a number she would guard all week with her life—had an immaculate bed and sliding shutter doors that opened onto a lanai overlooking the ocean. She watched Mitch push them open with a resignation that seemed new to his body even in the last few minutes, the energy he'd whipped up for Jordan having thoroughly leached away. She picked up the phone, dialed Cindy and Alyssa next door to tell them she'd meet them at the pool. When she turned back, Mitch was settled in an armchair, as much as he was capable of settling, his leg canted at its big boy angle, jiggling vaguely in the direction of the sun.

It had not been a good year for them. She swore up and down that she would leave him if he didn't pull himself together soon, but she'd sworn it only to herself, so how was he to know? Tactically, she'd made many other mistakes, mostly involving her temper. The time she'd accused him of sleeping with the redheaded publicist was one she'd particularly like to have back. Of course he was sleeping with her; she kept calling, and she was so condescending to Caryn on the phone. But Caryn had timed it wrong, waiting up for him on a Sunday night early in the season. Mitch could be downright self-righteous after a loss, his temper much louder than hers, even more so at 0-2. She threw vodka cranberry in his face. He dragged her to the couch by her hair and punched a hole in the wall. A terrible start to the '96 season. No one knew they'd end up in the Super Bowl.

The Super Bowl was bad, too, and even two nights in the French Quarter were not enough to get over a loss like that. She'd handled him delicately ever since, a tiny, simpering shadow ready with Tums and Advil and water if he asked. He never did, keeping his eyes behind caramelized sunglasses throughout the ten-hour flight.

So there was never a good time. Really, that was the trouble. There was no such thing as a good time to ask a 255-pound man who made a million dollars a year when he planned to stop fooling around. Even now, alone in a room with a water view and nothing to do for the rest of the day.

The important thing, then, was to be in the moment, to let go of everything that didn't serve her, beginning with her travel clothes. She began stripping them off, a stretchy t-shirt and jeans that were now limp and vaguely stale after their half-day in recycled air. She felt something fresh attend her skin as she flicked them into a corner under the desk. She would put on one of the new suits she'd bought; she'd take Alyssa in the water. She was determined to feel relaxed.

Then, just when she'd forgotten to worry about him, his voice came ripping across the room. "What are you doing?" he asked.

It was not a neutral question, or even, she felt, a literal one. He seemed to be accusing her of something far outside the physical moment. She stood over her suitcase, naked, Brazilian waxed, with a pink bikini bunched in one hand and an aqua one in the other. They were both from Newberry Street and still had their safety-pinned tags.

"Going to the pool?" she said, which immediately sounded like the wrong answer.

"With the window wide open like that?" He was standing

now before the lanai, setting his arms out like a protective fence.

She laughed nervously. "Who could see me?" she asked. "The dolphins? I don't mean the kind from Miami."

He twisted his mouth trying to decide if he would laugh at her lame joke, his eyes lazing as if threatening at every minute to fall asleep. He must be tired. He'd been a machine for twenty-two weeks.

She hurried into the pink bottoms and tied the pink triangles over her boobs. "There," she said superfluously. "All better. Do you want to come? I mean—you don't have to. Just, if you want to. Maybe you'd rather nap. Whatever you want to do is fine." She couldn't believe how difficult it had become to ask him a simple question.

He shook his head, at which part she wasn't sure, then sluggishly waved her on her way, at least no longer annoyed. She grabbed her sunglasses and her key card and made her escape. Alone in the elevator, with the card in her mouth and the sunglasses on her head, she unpinned the tags from her side boob and butt crack. She wasn't sure why she was so scared. It wasn't as though he'd ever hit her, not really, not anything that she would count.

She made her way out to the pool, and there was Vicki, accepting a Mai Tai off a tray from her lounger. They'd suffered the long season together, all the way through to the flight from New Orleans, but the sight of her here in her fuchsia lei and fishnet sarong seemed to erase all that post-season misery. It was the post-post-season now, and had maybe always been, the eternal Pro Bowl, the endless vacation.

Vicki was her confidant from day one in New England, when the Mulligans cooked them their very first dinner, steaks and corn on their big back deck. She was like a homecoming queen out there, smiling constantly and at the same time constantly on the verge of tears, which might've been from the grill smoke, but in any case made Caryn feel at home. The old Caryn would've rolled her eyes in embarrassment and found another caustic girl to laugh with, but the new Caryn was a mother and had cried every day since Alyssa's birth. She felt grateful to have her hand in Vicki's as Vicki told her, "These men, you know, they'll test us. We wives have to stick together."

Caryn had been tested a hundred times already. They'd had, what, six months together, before Mitch started cheating? When they were babies still, in college, and the discovery came as a genuine shock. She'd cried, assumed it was over, but he'd done the strangest thing: he'd apologized. Eventually she came to realize that apologies did not equal change. She could smell it in his hair, all those other girls' perfumes. She could see in his ears how they occupied his mind. Occasionally, someone even told her. She put up with it because they were young, because he just had to get it out of his system. And because he stayed, unlike everyone else. For some reason, he didn't want to leave her.

Vicki was a good confidant. With her big blonde hair and her joy in baking, she'd been destined to marry a football player; she knew them inside and out. Caryn doubted her brain even registered other males, certainly not the noodly guitar players Caryn had concerned herself with before Mitch. At fourteen and fifteen, she had given herself to one warbling Romeo after another. Each time it began like a movie in which she at last found herself in the arms of a worthy boy, one she could actually love. Yet each time something went wrong. They were fickle, those skinny boys, they quickly lost interest, a slouched back retreating to a junky car outside her house, a phone call that never came. Those deceptive boys! They were skinny and pale and full of deep thoughts, and by all rights ought to be tender. Humiliated, she withdrew. She took more dance classes; she read. She seemed to have overvalued the best thing she had to offer, which was only everything, herself.

But as high school yawned on, she found herself inadvertently, almost without her own consent, catching other eyes: boys in Umbro shorts and Nikes, carrying cleats and various balls. Athletes. They looked at her with confidence, and not only in themselves. They seemed to see her, and judge her favorably. They asked her out loudly, publicly, in front of their equally vigorous, popular friends in the hall. It was strange that boys with their power should seem to want, or need, something from her.

Anyway, she went out with them, and she liked them. The way they held doors for her and gratuitously offered her their varsity jackets, even when it wasn't cold. The way they laughed at their own jokes, which invited her to laugh, too. She'd become a girl the athletes liked, a development that required a few adjustments to her erratic sense of self, but to which, once made, she gratefully adhered.

Her school being of the preppy, university-town variety, soccer players were her gateway drug. Next came the lacrosse players, one prima donna attacker in particular, who, if you liked menacing Nordic blonds, was far and away the best-looking boy at school. Contra his cheekbones and playing style, Dirk turned out to be a nice boy, with intriguing ties to Washington DC, and although she wasn't flinging herself into romance the way she'd done with the tortured artists, she was at the very least beginning to relax into it, allowing herself to have sex with him, and afterwards resting the side of her face on his chest, cooing over the corsage he'd bought to match her dress for prom, befriending the high school Vickis, even regarding them as comrades-in-arms. She could see where things were going, and it all seemed too easy, this gentle drive into magazine life.

But Dirk proved fickle, too, breaking it off when he went to Dartmouth, leaving her feeling abandoned and personality-less at the start of her senior year.

"Pull it together," her sister Ellen told her bitterly, when she came home from college to wash her clothes. "The guy wasn't exactly destined for the NFL."

"You're heartless, you know that?" Caryn wailed. Ellen hated sports so it wasn't a surprise she didn't know which one Dirk played, not to mention that he was actually very good, recruited by the Ivy League. Her sister was a mousy, incorrigible cynic, thumbing her nose at popularity and money whenever she got the chance, and never wasting an opportunity to make Caryn feel guilty for wanting something nice. She was still pining for tortured artists herself, and Caryn could tell it wasn't exactly lifting her up.

And yet, somewhere, beneath her disdain, Ellen sort of had a point. The football players at her school were not destined for the NFL either—unlike the lacrosse boys, they routinely lost most of their games—but they did walk with a lumbering swagger that suggested a certain importance. She knew them through Dirk and the rest of the athletic cabal, and in a generous moment, she let one of them take her to Homecoming. By spring, she had cast her eye a few miles farther, to the University of Virginia, where Ellen was enrolled. There the football players were a different breed, stacked to the shoulders and round in the leg, even in the off-season, stalking the campus paths and hangouts she'd begun to brave with a few of her friends. There were whispers of pro scouts and signing bonuses, a different breed for sure. Yet they looked at her with the same encouraging, flirtatious smiles she'd won from the high school boys. Some of them even chatted her up.

She didn't know what she was looking for exactly. She was observing, taking notes she'd take with her to Miami, a university she'd picked for all the reasons an eighteen-year-old picks a beach with performing arts. It was in the midst of this epoch, this period of great uncertainty, that Caryn's parents threw her a backyard graduation party, a gathering of friends and family from across the Old Dominion, where she got to talking with her scrawny cousin Jeff about his good friend Mitch.

Mitch, the linebacker, who was going to play at Miami.

How quickly it all happened after that, like fate, though after the Romeos she'd stopped believing in that sort of thing. By the second week of college, they were dating, and fickle he was not. He was an animal on the field and with his friends, but in private he clung to her, even when he wasn't faithful. Her big, thuggish baby, full of needs only she could meet.

And now, here she was, a Hawaii regular, best friends with Vicki Mulligan. For four years now they'd been inseparable, inviting lesbian jokes and questions regarding Vicki's whereabouts, the few times they weren't standing side by side. If her marriage to Mitch was tanking at least her marriage to Vicki still bloomed.

She settled into the adjacent lounger with a Mai Tai of her own. She didn't even like Mai Tais—too sweet—but she felt ungrateful ordering anything else. "You think I'm a bitch for taking an extra week without them?" She nodded at Cindy and Alyssa in the pool. They'd head home together at the end of the week, while Caryn and Mitch went on to Kauai.

Vicki's head snapped her way. "Are you kidding, you're an inspiration! If I could figure out how to ditch my gang, I'd do it."

"Mitch says it's mean. He doesn't see Alyssa much during the season. He's missed her."

"Sure."

"And she's missed him."

Vicki sipped meditatively, releasing her straw when she'd drawn enough juice to speak wisdom. "She'll miss him forever if you don't fix your marriage. You are definitely doing the right thing."

Caryn appreciated Vicki's confidence in her decision, but it was only the confidence of a friend, who didn't have to face her life as she did. "Mitch has to do his part, though," Caryn said. "Takes two to tango."

"Amen." Vicki clasped her hand. "You know I'm here for you. But tell me: Cindy really doesn't mind?"

Caryn returned the squeeze and glanced at Cindy half-submerged in the pool, with Alyssa clinging to her back. "She might. But I have to go by what she says, and she told me a week in Hawaii was long enough for her. I think she really just wants us to work things out. I mean, I haven't told her everything, but she knows. She's at the house every day. She's not blind."

"A saint! Should've married the mother instead of the son."

"Or finished college instead." She'd been just two semesters short when Alyssa was born, and there were days when she felt bitter about that. But Caryn no longer felt bitter. Hawaii, with its freshly squeezed drinks and lotion-scented air, had a way of washing stale bitterness away. Even her worries seemed to have drunk themselves down to indifference. She and Mitch might not make it to another Pro Bowl, but what did that matter when she was at the Pro Bowl now? She was by the pool now, releasing

Vicki's hand. She was watching the sunset now with Alyssa. She was awaking in the middle of the night now to find Mitch upon her like an incubus, inside her now, crushing her with his own breath, blind together now in tropic darkness.

The next day the network cameras were rolling as the men headed off to practice. Caryn and Vicki took their brood to Waikiki, scoping out cheap jewelry and Magnum P.I. shirts trimmed with certificates of authenticity. With the memory of Mitch's body still on her like a weight, Caryn bought a shell string necklace for Alyssa, while Vicki, being the corny person that she was, bought the one her daughter Brittany wanted, and the grown-up version for herself.

Back at the hotel, they moved along the curving stone paths bisecting the saltwater ponds where manta rays and small hammerheads circled separately. She received a kiss from Mitch's coach, caught up with Gaines, from Miami, now in Tampa. Two famous quarterbacks conferenced at the bar as though they were the only two people in the world who understood whatever it was they understood. They were not much older than Mitch, but with their thinning hair and thickened necks, they already looked middle-aged.

At the luau dinner, everyone was in good spirits, including Mitch, who finally seemed to have forgotten about the Super Bowl. He swung Alyssa toward a tiki torch and she shrieked with fearful joy, her small braided head flopped back in a way that reminded Caryn of the happy trust of pregnancy. How safe it had made her feel, how connected to the world in all sorts of ways she even hadn't known she'd been missing.

Had he really latched onto her the night before? She had the memory, but it was fading, flickering out now with dim uncertainty, and there was no way to tell from his public behavior. There was no way to tell if anything in the past was real. All she had was the present moment. And so she waited for the next one with him. When it came, again, that very night, she grasped it. She gave it her full attention.

"Listen," Vicki said. They were standing to their waists with their kids in the pool. The men were having media day at the practice field. "Here's what we're gonna do. We're gonna go to the spa tomorrow."

Two nights in a row now he'd come after her, and though it was dark both times and she'd hardly seen him, she'd felt the intensity of their engagement for sure. The force. How could he still be doing it with the publicity girl if he was doing it so desperately with her? She looked over at Cindy, who was reclining on one of the blue-padded loungers with a mystery novel, her long feet hanging over the edge. A plane flew in low overhead, descending for the airport.

"Six!" cried Alyssa, who'd been counting them.

"We'll get treatment after treatment," Vicki was saying. "They'll strip us clean. We won't have muscles any more. Or skin."

Caryn smiled. "I like this idea."

"I know you do." Vicki took a big sister approach to friendship. She was the one who made their plans, who knew where things were, what they should do. For the most part, this suited Caryn, a little sister, who was happy to just go along. "And we're not charging it to a rookie's room, either. We're charging it to our very own husbands, who are the reason we need it in the first place." She glided away from the wall to give Brittany room to jump.

Cindy was conferring now with one of the waitresses, a girl in a visor and khaki shorts. She looked at Caryn eagerly as the girl bent down and gestured with her hands.

"Seven!" Alyssa announced, as another plane swept low.

"What's going on?" Caryn called through cupped hands.

"Alyssa!" Cindy cried. "Brittany! You want to see a baby seal?"

In flip-flops and towels they all clambered down the short stony path to the second lagoon, which was not a part of the hotel property, and sternly marked as such, Vicki hoisting eighteen-month-old Mason on her hip, Caryn and Cindy holding the hands of the girls. This lagoon was shelved with lava rocks of varying degrees of natural roughness, and to the edge of a particularly angular outcropping camped a smoother, darker mass, nearly edgeless, and demurely ringed by a set of white protective flags. This was the seal calf.

It snoozed on its side, a blubbery bulk drying in the sand. They stood watching, trying to make sense of its apparent shapelessness. Only when a wave lapped its tail, and it gave a wild, jiggly shudder several feet up the beach, did its face emerge, squinty, whiskered, and puckered like a kiss. Yet after this brief, ecstatic motion, it fell still again, and lay as it had lain before, neckless, its top flipper tucked like a cocktail napkin on a linebacker eating ribs.

"That's a baby?" Alyssa breathed.

"More like a kid, probably," Caryn said. "A special one. See these signs? 'The Hawaiian monk seal is an endangered species protected under Federal and State Law.' We have to respect him."

Vicki was busying herself in her beach bag, having set Mason down in the sand. "Come on," she said, scooping him up again. "Let's get a picture. Would you mind?" She handed her camera to Cindy and beckoned for Brittany to join them. "Brittany loves seals. They're your favorite, aren't they, sweetie?"

Brittany came, but her doubtful face suggested more fear than love. "Are you sure he's not dead?"

"Oh, sweetie, no, he's sleeping! That's why they're guarding him!" She crouched down and pointed to a woman in a black visor and inscrutable sunglasses who was sitting near one of the signs. Then she swiveled back to Cindy. "Can you get it?"

"Hold on." Cindy adjusted her knees to crouch down, too. "I just want to make sure I get the whole thing." She squinted exaggeratedly through the viewfinder. "It looks pretty blobby from this angle. I'm not sure you can tell it's a seal."

"You'll know," Caryn said. Alyssa had gone closer to the shore get a better look at his face. "Stay back, Alyssa!" Caryn called. She shielded her face against the brightening sun.

"I am! I'm on the rock!"

"Well, I got a few," Cindy said, straightening up. "I'm sure one of them will come out."

Vicki looked over at the woman they all presumed by now was some sort of government official. "What if we just—?" She made some gestures of harmless advancement.

"Come on, Vicki," Caryn said. "It's enough."

"Okay?" Vicki persisted, waving, looking directly at the woman, who stared back, all sunglasses. After a moment she looked the other way, which Vicki took as her hoped-for cue. She scuttled back several feet, pulling the kids with her.

Cindy sighed and crouched down again with the camera.

"Cheese," Vicki said. She flashed her practiced smile, and Brittany and Mason, in their way, followed suit. Vicki's hair billowed spongily as she tilted her head towards her daughter's, and Caryn could feel how much Vicki wanted this, a magical moment she could relive and embellish with her kids for years to come. *Remember that time in Hawaii when we saw the baby seal?*

"Hey! Hey you!" The visored woman was marching toward them now. "You think these signs aren't for you?" Vicki stood as Alyssa jumped down from the rock and came running to Caryn's side.

"I thought you said—"

"This is an endangered species!" She stood purposefully outside the perimeter, like a heckler at a boxing match. Inside the ring, Vicki froze, her children padding her sides.

"I know, but—"

"Get OUT!"

Vicki bolted for the nearest sign, pulling Brittany and kicking up sand in their wake. Mason let out a troubled yelp. Behind them, the seal dozed on, unfazed. His defender met Vicki at the perimeter. "He is a *native Hawaiian*," the woman said. "And he's endangered because of people like you."

"I know and I'm sorry, but we didn't touch him. We were being very respectful."

"You think other people don't want a better picture, too?" She pointed at the smattering of people with cameras who were obediently standing back. "This is not just your vacation. This is his *home*." She was extremely short and extremely terrifying. Caryn found herself holding her breath.

"I know," Vicki said. "I'm sorry. I just thought you said it was okay."

"I don't know you. When did I say that?"

"When I called out to you. Just now."

The woman stared and it was impossible to know what she was thinking. "Observe the signs. And you." She turned to

Cindy. "You shouldn't encourage her."

Cindy, who was rarely the object of rebuke, bowed her head. "I'm truly sorry," she said to her chest.

"Now you know why I have to sit here." With that, the woman about-faced and reinstated herself at her post.

Back at the hotel, Vicki was all wound up, burning with humiliation. "Didn't she sort of nod, though?" She tossed their beach towels in the bathroom and began settling Mason in his seat for lunch. The maid had been through while they were out, snapping covers at perhaps the very same moment the seal's guardian had been snapping at them, and already the crisp white order she'd created was being undone and Mulliganized. Vicki was a perfect slob on vacation; it was difficult to be in her room.

"You're sure you don't just want to eat at the bar with Cindy?" Caryn asked.

"Positive. What if that woman tracks us down? She did sort of give me permission, though, right? I mean, God, I knew it was *technically* against the rules, but we weren't hurting him, were we?"

"I would never hurt a seal," Brittany vowed solemnly.

"I'm just so mortified. I always do the right thing. Okay, most of the time, don't I?"

"Of course you do. Listen, I feel bad about Cindy. I'm going back down there. You'll be okay, right?"

"Oh, don't worry about me. Just don't tell people, okay? It's too embarrassing." She was close to crying, her homecoming cheeks bright pink. "I can't believe I was so stupid."

That evening, everyone gathered for yet another luau, on the lawn just above the lagoon. People were reporting that the baby seal had moved on, safely back to sea.

"I heard y'all saw him?" Jordan Cash's wife Pam was asking.

"Yeah, he was real cute," Caryn affirmed. "Just a big old blob of mammal."

"Did you get pictures?"

"Some. I hope they turn out." For the first time, Caryn found herself sad she hadn't snapped a few of her own. There would be no photos without Vicki in them.

Vicki, for her part, was feeling better. Even after a hard day, it generally didn't take much festivity to get her in a pixie mood, introducing people, winking, giving her opinions and holding court. She wasn't drunk. Vicki rarely got drunk. She just got talky. Caryn should've known she would talk about the seal.

"There are only a thousand of them. That's all! It was a totally special moment." She'd drawn a crowd that included Jordan and Pam Cash, and everyone was nodding and shifting their drinks around.

"So I call to the woman who's in charge of the whole thing, like, 'Is this okay?' You know. I'll be real careful. And she's like, 'Sure, whatever.' Like *she* doesn't care about the line per se; she just doesn't want anyone to kill it. So I take the kids up close, and it's just the cutest, smushiest thing. And we're good. We don't touch it or anything. I mean, it could've been *much worse*. Next thing I know the woman's tearing over, *screaming*, telling me to get my ass off the beach. Mason's crying. *I'm* almost crying. Like, seriously, what a trap! You ask permission and still they get you? She must hate tourists. That's all I can think. You know: it wasn't about me. It was about her and her mother. Her and the traffic. Whatever!"

Faintly disturbed by Vicki's about-face performance, Caryn pulled herself away. She found Cindy in a gaggle with several other moms.

"She's telling the story," Caryn said.

"Of course she is."

"I thought she was 'so embarrassed.'"

Cindy shrugged. "Guess she's still working it out for herself."

The fact was, people liked it. They kept demanding it. "Heard y'all saw the baby seal!" they'd greet her, and she'd be narrating all over again.

Sometimes she offered a bit of self-doubt, but that only made it worse. "To be honest, I really shouldn't have pushed," Caryn heard her tell one group.

"Don't be so hard on yourself!" they cried.

"An opportunity like that?"

Later, after all the kids had gone to bed, Caryn and Vicki walked down to the private lagoon, where Caryn tried to distract her from the endless seal drama by shifting the subject to herself. They were holding their shoes and kicking sand and Caryn was telling Vicki about her hopes for the coming week, how she planned to enjoy herself but also to stand up for herself, finally demand Mitch's respect.

"He has to be better," Vicki agreed.

"He really does."

"The thing with Hardy," Vicki said, by way of comparison, "is he needs his recuperation time. Mondays we don't talk. He gets under the covers and I just leave him there. But that means he's with me on Tuesday. One hundred and ten percent."

"And you really think he's never had other girls?" This had long been the chief difference between them, the reality they'd often tried to puzzle out.

"Hardy?" Vicki paused, choosing her words. "No. I honestly

don't. Not because he wouldn't like it. I just don't think he's willing to take the risk. He might steal a kiss or two, sure, same as any man. But real cheating? No. He's too scared for that. In a way it's better when they're scared."

Caryn stood listening to Vicki and the unseen water lapping the shore. It was very dark on the beach. "Sometimes I think they cheat because they're scared."

"Sure, some. But Hardy knows which side his bread is buttered. I was with him before he got rich. And I'll be with him when his body breaks down."

Caryn had always liked Hardy. He had a gentleness common to the big men on the line, a care in his real-world movements because he knew how dangerous his body could be. He was Brittany's preferred hair brusher, the kind of man who didn't leave drawers open. She had always liked talking to Vicki about him. But she had a sense, now, that they weren't really talking about Hardy. They were talking, again, about Mitch, and how he wasn't Hardy's equal.

The men showed up then with extra leis and beers, and soon after they were doing their late-night beach thing at the Pro Bowl, a tradition two years running.

"*Sayyyy, my love*—" Mitch brayed at Caryn, looping his mitts about her waist.

"Ugh, your *voice!*" Vicki protested.

It was true that no one sang worse than Mitch, but Caryn didn't care. She reveled in the attention, delighted he was doing Dave Matthews, whose music had become a kind of private language between them, because the band was, like Caryn, from Charlottesville, and rising simultaneously with Mitch.

"I'll tell you what I'm seeking," Vicki said, in response to Mitch's continued growling. "A little respect for my eardrums."

Caryn looked in Vicki's direction, and saw, with sudden, perfect clarity in the dark, that her friend could barely tolerate her husband. That she would never, if not for Hardy, who loved Mitch like a brother, choose to spend time in his company. How, in their countless mall quests and pollen-infused play-dates, had Caryn missed Vicki's judgment before? She'd thought of her friend as a genuine person—a true straight-talker in a maze of phoniness, who never let herself get lost—but it was clear now that even Vicki had her blind spots. And what a violence that one of them was Mitch.

As this revelation turned itself over in her mind, Caryn found, to her surprise, that she did not feel especially wounded by it, though, certainly, she could not excuse it. Nor ignore it. When faced with opposition from outsiders, Caryn grew loyal. She clung, triumphantly, to her own.

Turning to her husband, she belted the chorus about celebrating life and climbing two-by-two. Hooking an arm around his neck, and a leg around his waist, she literally climbed his body to the words. Mitch, who loved everything hammy and obvious, from Adam Sandler to deli meat to, most of all, himself, joined her for the final lines, their voices crashing in happy disharmony.

"Oh my god," Vicki protested, covering her ears.

They made out messily and began the next verse, which was even sexier, about mouths and hearts and wine and minds.

"That's it," Hardy said, taking Vicki's hand. "We're out of here. You two deserve each other."

"God, finally," Mitch said, once their friends were out of earshot. "You get sick of people after a while, you know?" Caryn wanted to be pregnant with him she loved him so much.

They made their way to the other end of the beach to lie

down. "You wouldn't have done what she did, would you?" she asked. "With the seal, I mean."

"I'd get as close as I could. Once-in-a-lifetime opportunity." Heat emanated from his body, every organ inside him working, and just like that, they were back together. Perched halfway onto his chest, she could hardly recall her separate self.

"I'm not even sure it's that rare," she said. "I talked to the concierge. I think it happens more than we think. Every week maybe. But, I mean, you wouldn't have crossed the line."

"There were lines?" He traced one down her arm.

"That was the whole point. A clear boundary with signs and everything. And still Vicki had to cross it. Had to have her picture."

He thought for a moment, his throat moving, and she rested her chin on his meaty shoulder and watched it. "Wow. No. Absolutely not. Rules are rules. We have them for a reason."

"Absolutely!" she cried, hugging him closer, draping her little leg over his large one. It boggled the mind, how their past problems were just—gone. As though they hadn't even happened. Their cycle of long absences and strange returns was not normal. She knew this from her yoga friends, the few people she spoke to outside the NFL, who knew her not for her husband, but for her Uddiyana Bandha, her Ardha Candrasana, and perhaps also for her flattering pants. These were scarf-wearing women with henna tattoos who seemed to be in conversation with their own husbands at all times. They admired her poses and traded alignment tips, but they could not exactly empathize. That was why she had Vicki. It was why they all had Vickis. Only other football wives understood. Yet at moments like this—real, live in-the-moment moments—she felt exquisitely normal. Connected, content. And so who cared? She was only here and now.

"I keep thinking," she said. "If people like Vicki can decide for themselves what's safe and fair, what's the point of having rules at all?"

"Some rules are dumb," he conceded, palming the flesh of her butt.

"Not that one though. For the protection of the seals?"

"No, that's just common sense. Stop messing with nature. Stop the killing. They're endangered, right?"

"Yeah."

"Yeah."

"Vicki thinks she's good. She thinks she's incapable of harm."

"Everyone thinks that," Mitch said with sudden intensity, jostling her head. "But they're wrong."

Caryn exhaled, delighting in their agreement. She'd been afraid she'd been too ungenerous. He'd often called her on it— and he was often right, because when she was angry with him during the season, she'd been known to name pieces of dinner garbage after him, and run them through the disposal in his presence.

"We're not like that," she said.

"No way." He held her so tightly against him. "We know we're a total mess."

Mitch was already gone when Caryn opened her eyes the next morning, and as she stirred to wakefulness in the light, the crossing of palms and planes through open doors, the smell of lotion everywhere like balm, she realized she no longer wanted to punish him with an extravagant day at the spa. And yet she'd already promised Vicki. Vicki who worshipped control, who didn't like to change her plans.

"Ready?" Vicki asked her when she answered the bedside phone. "Our day of severe relaxation awaits."

Caryn yawned and stretched under the white duvet. "I can't wait for my massage."

"Don't forget your mani-pedi. And your seawater jet massage. And customized detox wrap."

"Actually if it's all right with you, I think I'll skip the detox and the jets."

"Oh, come on, girl! Don't get shy on me now."

Caryn mellowed her voice, like it was nothing personal, no big deal either way. "I don't know. I just woke up this morning and felt like I didn't need them."

"But I already booked everything," Vicki blurted. "I mean." She stopped, fumbled for the right thing to say. "I thought you wanted to go all out."

The door clicked and Alyssa bounded onto the bed. "Supreme Empress of the Universe!" she cried, kicking her leg in salute.

"Shh." Cindy came in behind her. "Mommy's on the phone."

"Don't let me stop you!" Caryn said, dragging Alyssa under the covers for a snuggle. "You should totally get the works. Treat yourself. I'm just not feeling it for some reason. You crazy monkey," she said to Alyssa.

"It's about the money?" Vicki asked, her voice lurching over the uncomfortable word.

"Of course not! You know we're fine." Mitch was younger than Hardy, and a first round pick. "I was calling Alyssa a monkey. Because she *is*." She bulged her upper lip with her tongue, eliciting a gleeful shriek from her daughter.

"Well, what then?"

"Look, if you want to spend the day there, you should. You'll love it. I'll be there with you in the beginning and by the time I leave, you'll be feeling so blissful you won't care if I'm there or not."

"I just thought you wanted to. You love this stuff."

Caryn sighed. Vicki always needed everyone to love the things she loved. "Sometimes I do. But if *you* love it *you* should do it. What I think doesn't matter."

"I do love it."

"There you go." Caryn wrestled Alyssa back under the covers.

"Can I come?" Alyssa asked into her chest once the phone was back in its cradle.

"I wish, baby. I'd have a lot more fun with you there."

It was a tense morning at the spa, which was elegant but connected to the parking garage, not what either Caryn or Vicki would have wished. Vicki couldn't stop thanking the native woman who crouched over the basin of steaming water at her feet, and she couldn't stop sharing snippets of the book she was reading about Jackie Kennedy Onassis. "Listen to this," she kept saying to Caryn as they had their toenails painted. Or, "Look at this photo. It's stunning." When the massage therapist came to collect Caryn from the nail dryers, she was relieved to be heading to a dark, quiet room.

She drank in the peace through her face cradle, tasting eucalyptus and meditative woodwinds, as the therapist worked her hands down her back. When it was over she oozed herself down to the beach, where Cindy and Alyssa were hard at work on a sprawling sand metropolis. She lay in a cabana for a while and watched them dribble water and pack walls, absorbing the sun in her shins, letting it fill them until they could take no more and seemed ready to melt away. For two and a half years in

Miami, this had been an almost daily ritual, but now she was a New England wife and mother, quickly anxious and overheated in the sun. She headed for the lagoon, which was surprisingly cool, and swam the length of it, emerging almost shivering on the other side where she had lain with Mitch the night before. Looking back, the Koalani looked small, less intimidating, like a folded paper hat. She knew everyone inside and she felt in her spine a fresh afterglow from her massage, perfectly cool and calm.

Before long it was game day, and then it was Monday again, and they were riding to the airport in a town car. Caryn watched stone apartment towers float before cloud-cloaked mountains, green with jungles. Hawaii was still the most foreign place she'd ever been, and after her week in nature perfected she found herself longing for everything else. The smudged pedestrian overpasses, the crowded city living, the traffic. This was the part of America that was most like another world. What America might look like if it was the world, or the world if it was America. It was like China maybe, or Mars. She half-expected to see a flying disc, passing between the towers. She wished now that they'd stayed in town. She and Alyssa could've gone exploring. She and Vicki could've avoided their awkwardness. "I'll call you," was all she'd said when they'd parted, meaning when she got back to Massachusetts. And she would, she was sure of it. But for now, she needed space.

Saying good-bye to Alyssa was much harder, a horrible scene at the airport as Cindy had to carry her, hiccupping, to the overseas terminal while Caryn felt like a criminal for going on to Kauai.

"It's fine," Mitch kept saying. "She'll be fine."

The flight to Kauai was a joke. They went up, they received juice, they came down, the fastest flight of her life. Moments later, it seemed, they had picked up their rented convertible and checked into the Princeville Hotel, looking west over a smooth curving bay. The AFC had won the game and with it came that extra cash, though Mitch was not the MVP, so there would be no additional car. Again she had the feeling that he was exhausted, that there was something about walking into a splendid hotel room with her that took every drop of energy he had. Again she went to the pool alone.

By happy hour he was unpacked and ready, as though he'd found himself among his clothes.

"Let's watch the sunset," he said. He took her hand awkwardly and she followed him down the hall, hearing their door click shut behind them. She watched his back work together with his legs.

Piano music filled the lobby and intensified as they approached the baby grand in the bar. They flagged down a server to order drinks and made their way out to the lanai. An older couple was sitting on the end in a pair of cushioned armchairs.

"Here," the man said, moving to the chair on the other side of his wife. "Now you can sit together."

"Thank you." Caryn settled herself into the chair on the end and stared straight out at the sun, which was hovering like a flaming basketball over the western coast. "Bali Hai," she said.

"That's it," the man confirmed. "You folks doing the coastal trail?"

"No, sir," Mitch said, in that folksy friendly manner he was sometimes capable of throwing on. "I'm not here to exercise." His knees jiggled, as if daring them to recognize him, which people seldom did without the helmet and pads.

Their drinks came and the older man had more advice. "Drive down there, even if you don't do the hike. Ke'e Beach is something to see, and there's a botanical garden just before you get there with two preserves. They have thousands of species there that the natives have been growing for centuries. They farmed them on terraces built from lava beds." He reached for his wife's hand. "We've been coming here twenty-five years, and I told her, when I die, that's where my soul is going. I told her she can come find me there."

By now half-blind from the orange sun, Caryn turned toward the man to show her respect for his soul, and to allow her vision to restore itself. They were Midwestern people, she could tell, round, unguardedly pleasant, and somewhat genderless in that way older people can become. They even had the same haircut. But he was the one making recommendations, so you knew he was the man. And she was the one with the large sparkling diamond: plainly a late-in-life gem. Caryn tried to imagine growing old with Mitch. She would never let herself get that fat, and she would never cut her hair that short, but that was not the point, was it, she was always skirting the point, failing to stay in the moment. The point was she couldn't see it. She couldn't see herself old and sad, visiting his soul in an ancient garden. He simply wouldn't be there. Mitch would go someplace gleaming. She saw his soul instead in the future, blazing new frontiers, in space probably, or something like it, not hanging around for her in some earthly terrace. Not ditching her, exactly, but definitely not hanging around.

"Thanks," Mitch said to the man. "How about Queen's Bath?"

"Now that's a sight. But it's too risky in the winter. The waves come right over the edge."

"You don't want to swim in it," his wife added.

"Some people say you don't even want to get near it," the man went on, excitedly. "Especially at high tide. The waves can get pretty powerful, sweep you right off the ledge. People have died."

"What's that?" Caryn asked.

"Queen's Bath," Mitch repeated. "I told you, remember?" She didn't.

"You've never seen anything like it. It's this perfect tidal pool in the rocks," the man went on, pointing, eager to share more information. "Just down the road in Princeville. In the summer it's big and calm enough to swim in. You can even snorkel. But not this time of year. Low tide maybe. But even then."

"We'll have to check it out."

"Mitch," Caryn said. "I don't want to die."

"Smart woman," the man laughed.

"You won't die. If it's too dangerous we won't go in."

"But he said it was dangerous even to look at it. Is that true?" she asked the older man. "You can't even get near it?"

"Some people say that. I haven't been in a while." His voice dropped off. "You'd probably be okay at low tide."

"Mitch—" Caryn began, but she heard in the stillness that had taken hold of the group that their chit-chat had come to an end. The sun was pressing into the ridge of the coast as cameras flashed mutely all along the lanai. She looked at the older couple, who were still holding puffy hands, and wondered why she hadn't moved her chair closer to Mitch's so that they might do the same. It would break the mood now to stand and scoot over, even to reach for his sleeve. Of course he hadn't moved his chair either, or reached his arm toward her, but that wasn't how he thought. He'd thought to find their first Kauai sunset and share it; she was one who wanted to be touched. Her fault, then, as usual. As penance she sat very still in her chair. Inwardly, she turned away from the moment, as she often did when moments became too real, and waited for it to be over.

"Well," he said, once twilight had fallen. "Seven o'clock. What do you say we get something to eat?"

Vacation Mitch was still an early riser, conditioned by a long season of early meetings, so the next morning, after allowing Alyssa to describe, on speaker, the cookies she was baking with Cindy back east, they drove into town for the first surfing lesson of the day, he in his aloha-patterned board shorts, she in the one bikini she had yet to debut on this trip: a block-striped rainbow set with white piping and strings, which seemed to her very surfer girl, and which she'd been saving, vaguely, for last. They signed waivers and received long-sleeved black shirts called rash guards and were given directions for finding their instructor at the pier.

"You done this before?" the girl asked Mitch as she swiped his credit card.

"Couple times."

Why he lied, she could not understand, or perhaps he was not lying; perhaps he had done it before with the publicity girl, or one of his bits in Miami, or, or, or. "First time for me," Caryn blurted, banishing his lie with her truth, and feeling superior for it.

"When did you surf?" she asked as they drove the few blocks to the pier.

"When—? Oh, never. I just told her what she wanted to hear."

"I really don't think she cared."

He shrugged. "Why does anybody do what they do?"

The instructor met them at his black GMC truck as promised. His name was Kai, and he was a lean, deeply tanned native Hawaiian, with buoyant, hairless pecs. His brother Palani, who would be helping with the lesson, was just as cute. Finally, something for Caryn.

"I can't believe I'm finally doing this," she told them. She was committed now to telling the truth. The whole truth. As much as anyone could stand.

"Oh, you picked a great day," Kai said. "Looks like we're gonna get some pretty nice waves today." His was not the tone of someone trying to manage her expectations, or sell her on something that would only benefit someone more powerful, which was the tone she'd grown accustomed to as a supernumerary in the NFL. Of course, he had sold *her* something, she'd already bought it, or Mitch had, but unlike all the other salespeople she'd encountered in recent years, Kai genuinely seemed to know what was good for her. It was the same thing that had been good for him—sun and sea and only a drizzle of clothing—and he was unselfish enough to share it. She felt her spirits lift with the air in his vowels.

On the overcast beach, Kai positioned Caryn and Mitch on their boards, facing each other. They found their centers. They bent their knees and kept their backs straight.

"I teach yoga," Caryn said. "Is that going to help?"

"Oh, yeah!" Kai brightened even more, which she hadn't thought possible. "Just remember Warrior Two."

They practiced lying on their bellies, their collarbones aligned with the centers of their boards, and pushing with their hands to all fours. "Cobra," Caryn said. "Cat-Cow. Warrior Two."

"Exactly!" Kai exclaimed.

"It's so helpful. See, Mitch?"

"Yeah, I got it." She watched him press himself up, planting one Sasquatch foot at a time. He was normally so sure of his movements, diving to the turf, popping back up, but here he seemed unbalanced, as though afraid he would drown in the sand.

"I bet it'll be easier out there," Caryn said. "More natural."

"Oh yeah," Kai said. "No substitute for feeling a wave."

"I told myself I'll be proud if I stand up once."

Kai looked at her. "Oh, you'll do it," he said, and she felt buoyed by his faith.

With their boards Velcroed to their ankles, they paddled out as a group, and it seemed they went a long way, the first wave rocking her back a bit as she figured out how to maneuver herself over it, the second following just after, and then the third, a ceaseless cycle that was now her ether. Kai and Mitch were pulling ahead of her, as always seemed to happen on outings with Mitch. She had no idea where Palani was. "Wait up!" she wanted to shout, but she knew how weak it would sound. How soft. And if there was one thing Mitch valued, it was toughness.

She approached them at last where they'd stopped to wait for the waves. They were talking and laughing like old friends, and she felt a pang when Kai gave her the signal to wait as he explained something seriously to Mitch. Just like that, in the short time it had taken her to catch them, they'd chosen each other over her. From her distance, she rocked on her board, surveying her liquid surroundings. There was the horizon, pumping forth fresh waves, which broke for the first time at the lip of the bay, where the real surfers had their fun. There was the hotel, cascading down the Princeville promontory, a spoiled only child on the cliff. She thought of Alyssa in Massachusetts, mashing chips into dough with Cindy, Alyssa who she desperately hoped would grow up to be independent and kind. There was the shore, largely empty at this hour save a few older couples out for their morning constitutionals, and there just in front of her was Kai giving Mitch a push and a shout. Mitch had started paddling in advance of an approaching wave that had somehow slipped underneath her, undetected, but would, she realized now, unfurl itself for him. He flung his arms one after the other, and as the surf crested over him she saw his ponytailed head rise and fall, his body crouched for an instant like a hiding giant before it tossed itself from the board. He hadn't stood. Hadn't even come close. She felt a twinge in her neck from looking so urgently, and along with it, a twinge of satisfaction that he'd failed, that this might not be so easy for Mitch.

It was her turn now and Kai was beckoning, smiling at her in his breezy, tender way, his shoulders smooth and glistening. She paddled over to where he was standing—so far out, and still, he could stand—and it occurred to her for the first time that he was not just youthful but also literally younger than them both.

"I'm nervous," she told him, sticking to her vow of honesty. Why it suddenly meant so much to her she couldn't say, but it calmed her to think of herself unmasked, faking nothing, pure. She was twenty-four and she felt ancient.

"Aw, don't be nervous!" he cheered. "Just let the wave take you in."

"You've been doing this your whole life?" she asked, for additional reassurance.

"Since I was a keiki. I grew up right over there." He pointed at an improbably gorgeous curve of shore. "So I'm a natural. But you'll be a natural, too."

They bobbed there for another minute or so watching for

waves that wouldn't come, and then before she knew it, he'd picked her one, and she was paddling, paddling, paddling for the shore. She heard him calling to her, and on his order she dragged herself to her knees, thinking, *now stand*, a simple thought that was far less simple an action. She was literally being rushed, the force coming from somewhere beneath and behind her too fast for her to grip. She seized up, saw her spa-painted fingernails, and between them one foot of painted toes, and before she could wonder about the other foot and how it would get here from wherever she had left it, the blue board under her hands shot free, and she was in the water.

It was a soft landing, at least, the sandy bed of the bay like something padded safe for children, and as evidence there were now a few of them in the water around her, sleek as seals in their rash guards, tethered to boards of their own. How she hadn't scattered them like duckpins she didn't know. "Sorry," she said to the nearest boy, who looked at her in that appraising way of children, forgetting she could see him, too.

She hauled in her board and somehow made it to the outbound lane. As she made the turn she caught sight of Mitch toppling into a loose curl of foam, having clearly failed again. She dug harder with her hands, gripping the board with the tops of her toes. After an age, she reached Kai.

"Well," she gasped. "At least I'm over that fear."

"Huh!" He was smiling at the horizon, gauging future swells.

"The first fall was nothing. Nothing left to fear."

He didn't try to relate, having perhaps never known such a fear, just gave her a breath of encouragement and shoved her off again.

This time she would stay in the moment—her first rule, so nearly forgotten. On his command, she rose to her knees, stepped to one foot, then the other, and felt herself become weightless. It was only an instant—less—but it was all the suggestion she needed.

She made it back to Kai in no time, having wiped out close to the break. "I'm so close," she told him. "I can feel it."

He chose her another wave and once again she was off, paddling, pressing up, stepping, and, in a little bit of unconscious magic, abruptly standing on her strong yogi feet. The big toe mounds, the little toe mounds, the inner and outer heels. The moment she found herself in was already long, and still she hadn't wobbled. She was on her feet and her board was as sturdy as a boat and it seemed she could continue on like this forever if not for the suddenly terrible inconvenience that the ocean was about to end.

She threw herself from the board and it was not graceful, knees knocking, arms torquing as if to avoid an invisible wall. But it was joyful. Her rules were working together now. Stay in the moment. Tell the truth. Tell the truth in the moment and in that way keep right on telling the truth every moment of your life.

She bounced up pumping a fist. "Did you see that?" she shouted, looking around for the person she was addressing, which, she realized the moment she saw him, was Mitch.

He was standing in the broken surf like a newborn gorilla, holding his board under one arm, clear out of the water, and she could tell by the pride on his face that he'd seen.

"You did it!" he shouted. "You did it you did it you did it!"

"I did it!" she whooped back, tossing foam with her fingertips.

"Now I'm gonna do it!"

"You're gonna do it!" she affirmed.

"I'm going back out!"

"I'm gonna watch you! No, I'm coming with you!" She had to keep saying words even though none of the words she'd come up with thus far could convey any of what she felt, which was a convergence so natural and annihilating it seemed impossible it ever eluded her. Psychedelic was a surfer word. She understood that now. Though it, too, was inadequate. So was every word in the world.

She chased after him, scooting over waves that were nothing now, no more challenging than air.

"I'm watching!" she called. "I'm watching!"

"You did it!" Palani was with her, having been working with Mitch before. "That was awesome! Is this your first time?"

"Yes!" Her entire body spoke the word.

"No wonder you're so excited! Let's get you back out there."

"I think Mitch is—" she said, but he'd already given her a push and was shouting at her to paddle, so she had no choice but to do as she was told. She stood, so easily she might've skipped a step, and in the calm above her wave she dared to look up for some glimpse of her husband. She'd been watching him for years in his anonymous armor and was by now hawk-like in her ability to pick him out in motion on the field, even when she couldn't see his number, even when she'd somehow missed the snap. She knew his stance, his stride, the nano units of time it would take for him to reach a man and cut him down, and how the man would fall into the earth as if buried beneath the heavy stone of Mitch. She'd been there herself, in that grave, if not very often during the season.

But the season was over now, and with it that televised distance. Virtually the same moment she realized she couldn't see him was the moment she felt him at her back, on the very same wave she rode. She saw him now over her shoulder, his back to her back, because she was a lefty and therefore "goofy-footed" as Kai had teased her all those centuries ago that morning when they'd practiced together on the sand. Mitch was beside her and he was standing. Her giant.

"Yes!" she cried, bailing to meet him in the water, and what a honeymoon moment it was: a high-five and a chest bump, and Mitch lifting her up and making her feel tiny, their boards clapping like hands near the shore.

She was giddy the rest of the morning, though the skin on her hands and the tops of her thighs and feet was rubbed raw from the countless Cobras. On the porch of the café where they collapsed for lunch she held her Mai Tai in her lap, soothing her victorious burn.

"You were better than me," Mitch said. He was straddling the table, outer leg jiggling. He was giddy, too.

"I'm just better conditioned."

"A natural."

"Aren't you the one who's always saying there's no such thing?"

"Yeah, but I don't believe it. We're naturals, you and me."

"Shh," she whispered, "someone might hear you."

He whispered back, "I think we're safe."

"Mm. Maybe I'm the Mitch Wilkins of surfing."

He hooted. "I'd like to see you shoot the curl in Cohasset."

"It's wicked hahd," she offered in her best Boston brogue. "It's hahd ahnless yah from Bahston."

"That's good!" he exclaimed.

"It's just hahd. You gotta say hahd a lot."

"Hod," he tried. "Hod."

"*Hahd.*"

"Hod." He looked hungry for her.

Then their food came.

"We get along, you and me," she said, as he brought his unwieldy pork sandwich to his mouth.

He paused before taking a bite. "Course we do."

"But I mean, I like being with you better than any other person. Like last week for instance? Vicki drove me crazy. My best friend. But she gets so mental on vacation. I just wanted to get out of her way."

"Mm."

"Did I tell you the other day I brought all these snacks to the beach for Alyssa? Carrot sticks and grapes and stuff like that. Vicki's got no snacks. But of course Brittany and Mason get hungry. So guess who ends up eating Alyssa's snacks?"

"Alyssa didn't get any?"

"She got some. She was fine. But the point is, like, get your own, you know? Don't count on me to carry you."

"Sounds like it worked out okay." He was arguing with her a little, which was a thing he did, which was fine. Actually, she sort of liked it, because it meant that he was with her.

"I mean, of course I'm happy to share with them," she went on excitedly. She loved talking to Mitch. She loved to have him there, listening. "But Vicki *never* shares. It just doesn't occur to her. She thinks she's working so hard just to take care of her own, and then she forgets when other people bail her out."

"She's never bailed you out? What about when we first showed up in New England—didn't she take you around?"

"And I'm grateful! But I'm talking since then. I can't spend the rest of my life repaying her for that one big kindness. At some point it's got to stop."

"Well, I'd rather be the one to bail someone out."

"Even if they're always taking advantage of you?"

Mitch blinked. "No one takes advantage of me."

She sat back again with her Mai Tai, and held it against her leg. "I know, you always win, don't you?"

"So do you. You just have to look at it right."

She held her hand up to her forehead. "I'm looking. I don't know why, but I still don't see my new car."

He heaved one of his lung-emptying sighs. "Next year, babe."

She felt silly. "I was kidding. I don't care about the car. This is enough. I mean it, babe. It's enough."

After lunch they drove back to Princeville but instead of heading straight down the boulevard to the hotel, he turned into a residential neighborhood.

"We're just about at low tide," he said. "Let's check it out."

Before them was the sign for Queen's Bath. Instantly, she felt old again, and trapped. "Oh no, Mitch. Are you sure?"

"If it's dangerous we'll just come back." He was always saying flippant things like that: matter-of-fact answers to an apocalypse, as though he could snap his fingers and start from scratch. "They have signs. How bad can it be?"

More than Vicki, more than Alyssa even, he was the one person she couldn't resist, especially when he was excited about something. So, with towels over their shoulders, they made their way down a muddy lane to a rushing creek, beyond which lay a shelf of snakes. She stood there, petrified for a moment, before she understood they were only tree roots and it was fine to walk across. They abandoned their flip-flops on the other side, at the slick boulders leading down to the oceanfront. "We'll get 'em on the way back," Mitch said. "Or we'll get new ones. Who cares?"

Caryn clung to the first boulder, stretching to reach the

next one down, half-hoping Mitch would just come and pluck her off it, if they were really going to do this. But Mitch was already several boulder-jumps away, on a vast shelf of darker rock overlooking the ocean. She found her footing and made her way over, the wind catching her towel and whipping it into her face until she managed to bat it down and stuff it into a ball she wedged underneath her arm. It really bellowed, that wind. No way Mitch could hear her from where he stood.

Waves slammed against the rock shelf, shooting spray well above their heads. She felt moisture on her skin and watched water trickle among the crevices under her feet, from the ocean or the recent rain, she couldn't say, nor could she bear to contemplate it, since she had no choice, since she was here. Again, she was chasing him, but this time, he paused often enough to check out the surroundings, which gave her a chance to catch up.

"Don't stand so close to the edge!" she called, approaching.

"This is intense!" he shouted back.

They stood on adjacent rocks looking out. In a cove below them the ocean rose and fell precipitously, slamming itself against the ledge.

"I don't think we're going swimming," she said, relieved. She was still wearing the rainbow bikini, which she now considered good luck.

"This isn't it," he said. "See how it opens to the ocean? Queen's Bath is enclosed. It's a pool."

"It's probably not here."

"I think it's just around this bend," he said, pointing. "See those people?"

There were indeed people filing back among the rocks, having come from somewhere with towels. She looked at their hair—was it dry enough?—looking for something, anything, to bail her out. "They don't look like they've been swimming."

"Which way?" Mitch called, and they pointed.

Off they went again, overlooking more tumultuous coves, some of them rounder and more bath-like than others, all of them violent. Alone now on the rock shelf with no one to guide the way, they peered at one cove, then another, then back at the first.

"It's this," he said. "It has to be."

"But it's so shallow. And all that water is rushing in."

"That's the point."

"No, I mean." She shook her head, understanding perfectly but unable to explain herself to him. What were the words she needed? "In the summer no water rushes in," she managed. "But it still has to be deep enough to swim in."

"It's this," he insisted. They stood together looking at it. "We're here. Let's sit."

They found a spot that seemed connected enough with the heaving hollow below them to be considered a part of Queen's Bath. They were there now, if this was there. She thought again about the moment. Though what a moment was, exactly, she was no longer able to say. This was, and this. She struggled to think without words.

"Ricky's in a bind," Mitch said, suddenly, meaning his buddy from high school. "He lost his job at Frito Lay. He needs a loan to tide him over for a while."

This was abrupt, but it was always that way with Mitch: a piece of grown-up information brought home, already worked through and decided.

She sighed. "So what are we giving him?"

"Ten grand."

"Ten *grand*?!"

"How much that bikini cost?" he asked.

"Not ten grand!"

"I'm saying we have enough money to buy you a thousand bikinis. The way I see it, we have enough to help Ricky, too."

"I didn't buy a thousand; I bought three," she snapped, knowing she was answering the wrong question. "But of course we'll help Ricky. Of course. What happened? Layoffs?"

Mitch nodded absently.

She sighed again, thinking of Ricky, a wiry guy who'd stayed fit, much younger looking than Mitch, which made her feel old to even notice. "I hope he gets another job. We can't keep rescuing him."

"This is the first time!"

"I'm just saying you know how hard it is down there. And you know Ricky doesn't exactly love to work. We have to think about Alyssa."

Mitch flicked his hand scornfully as though her sense of responsibility were just another irritating gnat. "Alyssa will be fine. She has everything. We can share a little with the folks who got us here." No wonder he'd acted so Christian before, when they were talking about Vicki and the snacks.

"I thought you were a natural," she said, bitterly. "I thought you did it all on your own."

He hoisted himself to his feet. "All the more reason to be generous. I'm going down there."

"No!" she cried, but he was already moving, feeling his way closer to the rim of the bath. She scooted over to watch him descend, as profligate with his body as he was with his money. How could she ever feel safe with someone who distributed himself so widely, to friends and football and other women, as though he were some endless natural resource and not a man with a bank account, and a child, and bones? She had to tell him at some point. She had to say, palms out: this is it. This is all I can stand.

He was looking up at her and his mouth was moving. She could never hear him when he went ahead like that. He was only a few rocks away from the edge of the pool, and the water was all worked up behind him, a frothing secondary poised to crush the developing play. "Don't look at me!" she shouted. "Look at the ocean!" She pictured a wave leaping out to seize him, and bashing him into the hard, black rocks. She pictured herself beside him. Would it be so bad to die here with Mitch, she asked herself, crushed together into the natural world? The question answered itself the moment she'd asked it: yes, yes, it would.

He hurtled back up to her, laughing. "Look at you!" he said. "You're freaking out!" He loved to scare her, put the fear in her, he sometimes called it, when he was feeling especially Southern. He lunged at her, and she shrieked, pictured them toppling down into some deathly hidden crevice, a backdoor to the ocean, arms torn, hearts burst, brains dashed among the rocks. What the hell was he thinking? Nothing! He was thinking only of fun.

She had to tell him, but all season long he was overworked and in pain, and then after the season a wreck of another sort. Now he was feeling better and actually enjoying himself. And he was enjoying himself with her.

She tried to enjoy herself, too. She let him swallow her in his arms, and they didn't fall, they stayed upright, because Mitch knew the strength of his body, the resistance it encountered in space. He was as large as a planet, his force gravitational, his behavior outside the power of a mere woman to control, and she hated him for that, because hate was the one, sad weapon she had, and even it was totally useless.

"Stop it," she said. "Just stop." She stood pressing herself into the topography of his chest and understood that there was never a good time to talk to Mitch about her sadness. The time to bring it up was not now or soon or sometime later; the time for it was never.

PRIME

Mitch moved through his prime as he moved through everything, making it his event. Eyes, feet, hips. Caryn, woman, woman. Feet, hips, hands. Pats, Eagles, contact. Woman, woman, Lori. Hips, hands, head. Lori, baby, baby. Contact, contact, contact.

There was a saying in football about playing unconscious, and it was as true of Mitch in his prime as it was for anybody else. It wasn't literal. It didn't mean he actually blacked out, nor did it mean he wasn't keeping track. At any given moment in any given season, he could always tell you how many points his defense had allowed, how many tackles he had, how many picks, and which of those was the game-changer, and which was gritty but not pretty, and which was beautiful but too easy, and which was a helicopter and which was a derecho and which was a couple's dance.

But in the sense that he was deep inside all that, and in the sense that his body was always moving, both simultaneously, and in sequence, from Foxboro to Philly, from Caryn to Lori, from x to o, and x to o, and x to o, in that sense he really was unconscious, for the entire action of his prime.

8. D'ANTONIO, 2003

D'Antonio Mars has an eye for patterns, and he sees them everywhere his first year in the NFL. For starters, there's the dim, full-team auditorium where Kowalczyk, the head coach, lectures, which is just like the dim, full-team auditorium back in college at CSU. The cinderblock walls painted white with team color runners are just like the walls of his high school, only with different colors. The Purell dispensers are the same, the vending machines are the same, though here they have Coke instead of Pepsi. Even the janitors have the same rolling metal buckets, emitting the same artificial lemon fumes. A lot of individual things are nicer—there's more money here, of course things are nicer—but at the end of the day, the NFL still feels a lot like school. Just another, richer institution. And it occurs to D that this is how he's spent his entire life, parking in designated lots, prowling halls in a backpack and shorts, checked by trainers, talked at by men whose job it is to boss him.

They have every kind of football guy on their team. Big-smiling black guys who love to talk, who love God, and who love to talk about their love of God. Bearded white guys who put their stinky feet on the desk in team meetings. Long-haired white guys with tattoos. Dread-locked black guys without tattoos. Guys who like to fight. Guys who specifically like to fight guys from other races. Guys from California, guys from Georgia, guys from Iowa. Guys, like him, from Texas. Guys from Florida, Pennsylvania, Utah, Texas, Florida, and Texas.

They have nicknames, too. The rookie lineman, who's so big and nervous, they call him Muffin, for reasons no one can really explain. But that was only in training camp. He got his legs under him and he got his hands out, and now they call him by his name, which is Kohler. The QB is Rainman. The strong safety is Lucky. Informally, everyone is bro.

Mitch, who's from Virginia by way of Miami by way of New England, is just Wilk, short for Wilkins, but whenever anyone says it, it sounds like a whole lot more than that, like an animal you don't want to meet in the woods. He's the biggest, baddest middle linebacker in the league, and he shows up at minicamp with a beard, a fact D makes the mistake of pointing out. "Aw, I'm sorry," he says, after he steps backwards into Wilk at their first team meeting, their first meeting, period, ever. "I didn't recognize you with that beard."

"How would you recognize me when you don't know me?"

"Huh?"

"I said how would you recognize me when you don't know me?"

"It's just, um. I mean, you Mitch Wilkins. Like, I'd have to be under a rock not to know who you was."

"Yeah."

"And you still got that long hair but you got a beard now, too."

"Yeah, all right."

Technically, in camp, D's still working to make the team, but he's pretty sure he will. He's the only rookie linebacker and he knows he's been undervalued. Coming out of the tumbleweeds at Colorado State he only got looks from a few pro teams, but the scouts who worked him out were pleased. In the interviews they asked about his mouth. "It's the truth," he told them. "That's who I am on the field. I also work hard, and I'm skilled, and I have passion. The talk is part of the passion. It's also, to be honest, a skill." Eyebrows went up. Elbows appeared on the table. These coaches: he could read them like a book.

When the draft call came, he was deep inside Shawna, his former high school tutor who was bold enough to look him in the eye when he ran into her at Target, and even better, to let him look back. He couldn't just sit there at his mom's house with everyone pestering him nonstop. Better to try to get out of his own head. Better to fuck himself senseless with a baby-faced older woman, the kind who clearly had sense enough to spare. His brand new cell phone was in his shorts pocket on the floor and for some reason he didn't hear it even though they were doing their best to keep it down because Shawna's little sisters were home. Luckily it rang again a few minutes later, and the second time he was post-coital, and lucid, and he heard it loud and clear.

"D'Antonio Mars, where the hell have you been? Are you ready to be an Eagle?"

It was Eddie Hatchett, the legend, former running back turned Philly GM, calling him by his full legal name. D swallowed drily and told him that yes sir, he was. He absolutely was.

"Hold on then, it's going through. And next time answer your phone. I can't draft you if I think you're dead."

Hatchett was his first new boss, but soon enough came the head coach, Kowalczyk, and the president, Pastore, each of whom spoke stock encouragements to him on the phone.

Now he's also got Delahanty, defensive coordinator, and Schmidt, special teams coordinator, not to mention Tripp, the linebackers coach, and Woodson, the strength and sideline coach. And then, of course, there are all the veterans, who make him sing in the cafeteria, and bring them sandwiches whenever they feel like it, and the chief tyrant is none other than the bearded Wilk, who earns, like, ten times D's salary, and seems to think some significant fraction of his extra income is tied to bossing D.

"What was that, Mars?" Wilk likes to say. And, "Get it, Mars!" And, "Look at my feet, Mars!" And, "Mars!"

His last name is his real last name and fierce enough to stick. The Martian, Lucky sometimes calls him. Or, when he does something especially killer, Mission to Mars. His favorite is The God of War. "But that one's all me," he tells his mom on the phone. "No one wants to call a rookie God."

"They will, baby," she assures him, a church-going woman all her life. "Just you wait. They will."

There's a lot to learn in minicamp: a whole system of plays, and a whole language for calling them. D writes everything down, because that's what the coaches say to do, his hand cramping as he races to keep up. But when he reviews his notes later, the words only throb a bit, like the bruises that cover his body from all kinds of contact he can't recall. They mean something, he knows that much. He just has no idea what. And it isn't only the learning that has to be fast. They practice at top speed, too, so that the games will feel Matrix-time slow. "Look at the linemen's knuckles," Wilk says. "If they're leaning forward on them, it's a run, if they're lifting up, it's a pass." D looks; he tries to read the subtlest shifts of position. He hardly has time to talk, he's working so hard to keep pace.

"Give me a nice pause at the bottom," Woodson tells him in the weight room as D bows his head to work his neck. "Then control the motion back up to the top. We want clean reps. Eliminate that momentum." He works all four planes, bowing, looking to heaven, listening right, listening left. It's for his head that he's doing all this, building a cylinder of iron to keep it in place.

"Football," Kowalczyk tells him, "is a change-of-directions sport."

At least he's not a camp body. The other Texas rookie is, a safety named Brandon Stackhouse. D is at his locker, borrowing a wad of Kleenex, when they come for him. "Oh no," Brandon says, and then he walks out the door and D never sees him again. The Kleenex dampens in his hand, and it's as though Stackhouse has just evaporated, turned to sweat in D's own palm. He's a good man, Stackhouse. Liked to freestyle in the recovery pool after practice to keep everyone's mind off the iceberg cold. Good heart. Scary-looking quads. Just wasn't quite fast enough. The data did not add up.

D's data does. At the end of the preseason, when they cut the roster to the final fifty-three, he's on it, a back-up linebacker and a key player on special teams. "Every single one of you has earned your spot," Kowalczyk tells them in the auditorium, his soft voice belying the hardness of his words. "Some of you really busted your asses to get here. Some of you have been superstars from day one. But starting now that can't be anyone's mentality. Not if we're going to be successful." He taps the yellow cover of the business book he's given them. He's a man with vision, arctic eyes that see clear to the poles, and to the end of the winning season he's painstakingly constructed for this team. Week by week, he outlines the season that has, for him, already occurred. "An integrated team depends on every single individual doing his part. That means knowing your role on every possession. It means stepping up when guys go down. We all do our part, we go to the Super Bowl. It's that simple, gentlemen. We're in the Super Bowl because we all did our part."

D thumbs the cut edge of his book and looks around at all the blank meeting faces. If someone gets hurt, there's a chance that he could start. Someone will get hurt; someone always does. It's a future that's guaranteed.

Actually, Wilk says at their lockers, *everyone* gets hurt, it's just a question of how bad, and when. He's been there himself—torn a hamstring, broken a wrist—and still he says it nastily, like he's almost rooting for it to happen to D, which makes D want to get nasty right back. He's lucky Cam's locker is between them.

"Won't be me," D tells him in anger, an emotion he's spoken fluently for as long as he's known how to talk. "I ain't going down." D knows himself to be an exceptional specimen, a singular mind aligned with its singular body, a living letter *i*. *I am*, he thinks, and all the *i*-words apply: *integrated, intelligent, intimidating, intense.*

"That's what you think," Wilk says.

Of course it is. What the fuck? To think anything else would be death.

The first game of the season is on a Monday night, the first ever played in the state-of-the-art new stadium with its winged roof and its cup holders for all, and its blended grass-and-plastic turf. When D takes the field for eight o'clock warm-ups, half the city is already there, dressed in jerseys, just like him, like avenging ghosts from former teams. Back in the locker room for the laser show and fireworks, he can feel the entire structure quake. He pukes. He jumps, pulling his feet to shoulder height. He's happy to be on special teams. Come kickoff, he will detonate.

What goes down after that is pretty devastating. Four quarters, zero points: a shutout by the same corny team that ended their season the year before. In prime time, with all the league and nation watching. It's a perfect humiliation, even for D, who hadn't been there the last time, and has no personal need for revenge. Guys are angry. Stunned. Lucky is out with a broken finger, wideout Jennings has a hamstring tear. Carter, the special teams safety, is in all likelihood concussed. Kowalczyk's perfect future is rapidly dissolving; the post-game atmosphere is something more than tense.

All the following week D tries to feel integrated, as a part of the whole and as a whole in his own right. He thinks about his feet and his head and his hands, and he talks to keep himself up. He decides he isn't going to be a casualty. On Sunday, he joins the pregame chatter circle in the locker room, trading lines with all the churchy guys who dominate the talk.

"Live proud!" they shout.

"Live tall!"

"Live to fuck those motherfuckers up!" D adds, expletives being as godly as he gets.

He can tell it bothers Wilk. Wilk, who technically doesn't curse, but is vulgar all the same. He isn't especially racist. He's D-ist. He has something against him simply because he is D. It would be easy to be Wilk-ist in return. Wilk had messed around, wrecked his first marriage. It's something everyone knows. But then he went and married a new girl, and just like that: clean slate. A wife and two babies smiling in his locker in a wooden frame that boasts "I can do All things through Christ." Wilk attends Fellowship now and has no patience for immaturity. A natural leader: the kind of big-buck free agent who creates new realities everywhere he goes. Guys laugh for him when he jokes, and nod their heads when he speaks seriously. The kind of guy everyone silently agrees not to remind of his own immature past. And that seems a shame to D. If only they'd met when they were both young and wild, they would've gotten along fine.

It's hard enough after the first loss, but then they go and lose again, to Wilk's former team at home. Everything that can go wrong does, starting with injuries and ending with mental mistakes, a team loss, through and through. But all that seems to matter to Wilk is that D hasn't played his best. On the sidelines he'd been a goblin, hissing in his face and swinging his helmet to make his point, and when he arrives at the facility on Monday, his D-ism is ugly and overt.

"We're 0-2. Why are you smiling?"

"I ain't smiling."

"You won't be smiling this afternoon. That's for damn sure. Just wait 'til we run the film. Schmidt is gonna make an example out of you. He is gonna circle your ass and then he's gonna break your ego and you are just gonna have to sit there and take it."

"Man, why're you telling me this?"

"I'm telling you so you can be prepared."

Like prophecy, like the future he never wanted, every single thing Wilk says, right down to the laser pointer circle and the anguish of sitting there and taking it, comes to pass. D sits in his chair and pulls his shirt up over his face, trying not to see himself miss the tackle that results in a punt return for six. He is small on the screen, but so is his man, and when the camera swings right to follow the ball carrier down the field, D can be seen lying flat on his stomach, heels up, head down, before he completely disappears from view. Again and again, Schmidt rewinds to the moment D leaps, a step behind, at the back of Marshall, the sprinting returner. "You see this?" Schmidt screams. "I see it," D mutters. Again and again he slides off Marshall's hips and down his legs to the turf, as though no other outcome were possible. "You see your feet?" "I see 'em." "You see how they're doing exactly what I told you not to do?" "I see it." Leap, slip, fall, fail. Marshall streaking down the field, free. On film, it is foretold, it is unavoidable, it is all he is capable of doing. "Your body is my body!" Schmidt screams. "You make it move like I told you to move!" D watches himself get it wrong and thinks, *fuck no, no more of this*. He thinks about his feet and his eyes and his whole integrated body, and he thinks, *fuck no, next time, not this*.

The bye week comes early. He flies home, winless, to see his family and Shawna, who's paralegalling and studying for the LSAT and who chooses that dreary occasion to tell him that she'll be having his kid in the spring. He doesn't respond well at first, and she is hurt, which only makes him angrier. He feels himself glaring at her. He hears himself shouting. He'd been under the impression that she was on the pill! She is, she swears, she's not happy about this either. She says they should've been using condoms as backup. She says she told him that a million times. But he's always hated condoms, hates the way they dull sensation.

"Well, that looks pretty selfish and stupid now, doesn't it?" she tells him. "I can't believe I listened to you." He knows she's right but he can't hear it; his self needs every ounce of his attention right now.

"*Selfish* ain't all bad, you know! You could use a bit of it in you." She won't meet his eyes, and for the first time ever he feels older than her. "I thought you wanted to go to law school! I thought you wanted to do something with your life!"

That brings the eye contact, all right. "Wait a second, you think I'm pregnant *on purpose?*"

"I'm wondering."

She throws her prep book at him, literally. "Get the fuck out my house, you stupid, selfish dick."

The next week, they finally win. The week after that they win again. D gets his feet right, reads the knuckles right, and as a result he's getting more defensive snaps, the weakside "Will" linebacker to Wilk's middle "Mike." Dropping back into coverage, he's begun to think of his body as a vessel for Schmidt and Delahanty's plans, for their future that's already happened. Which is not to say that he's found God, or is looking forward to being a dad, but rather that, over the course of endless practices, he's simply begun to get it, just like in high school, and then in college, when each higher-level game demanded higher-level play. Piece by piece, in ways he can't even remember, he's mastered it, and everything his body is doing has become a little less new. Wilk hasn't stopped yelling at him, but D has stopped caring so much when he does. He's nearly skipping along; he's automatic. Even his voice has returned.

At Dallas, he sits in the tub, talking. It's pregame and he's just warming up his muscles and mouth. He's going to rip heads, eat children, yank tears from mothers' eyes. His own mother will be in the stands, along with his two oldest brothers and his aunt and nephew and niece. He's the Martian: he's here to cover your planet. The other guys in the tub with him are chuckling; they're wearing headphones, but he knows they can hear him, even the back-up RB who's studying his book. You try to beat him, he'll fuck you up, he'll run you down, he'll blow your ass to Mars.

He doesn't. He plays okay, a little too hard maybe. He'd wanted his mother to see him. He'd wanted her to see how useful his anger had become. "I know you mad," she used to tell him when he got thrown out of practice, or his middle brother got thrown in jail, or his cousin got shot on the ashy sidewalk in front of his cinderblock house. "But anger won't get you anywhere." He'd wanted her to witness his alchemy: how he's made something bad he didn't ask for into something gloriously good.

But the bad is persistent, still with him. They lose again, falling perilously to 2-3. He punches things in the cramped visitor's locker room: a wall, his pads, his head.

She's there to hug him after his shower, before he gets on the bus back to the airport. "I got to see you," she says. "That's all I care." She inches him to the side as they embrace so the other guys coming out can get by.

He doesn't cry, but he asks her a question. "How long you think I got?"

"You, baby? A whole career." She looks up at him. "But you know however long that is, it's short."

He likes this. He nods his head, working the words into his brain. "It is, though. The future's near."

"That's right, baby. It's just another one of our short moves."

He pictures the little house she lives in now, with its porch, a new construction palace he bought her with his signing bonus. She lived in two different houses when he was in college, and three in the high school days, all of them dark with permanent stains on the windows or ceilings or floors, most of them not even houses, but apartments. Each is less than an hour's drive from where they stand now, and each was a good decision at the time. She's still got some of his things at her new place, boxes of old trophies and construction paper drawings, tights so tiny it's hard to believe a living person could ever wear them. Short move is a good line; he's going to use it. Just about everything good he's got has been stamped on him by her.

The next week, in New York, he's talking in the tub once again.

"Man, shut up."

The voice is Wilk's, always lurking somewhere nearby.

"I'm a universe of pain," D says, pretending he hasn't heard. He can't respond to what he can't see. "I'm the Milky Way that's in your way, you best find another Earth."

"I said shut up, Mars." Now Wilk is in front of him, showered, naked, his towel bunched up in his hand. "Mars, I said shut up."

"It's my game, bro."

"And it's my house. In case you hadn't noticed, we keep a quiet one."

"Oh, it's your house is it?"

"You know it is."

"Last I checked we all on the roster." He looks at his tub-mates. "Y'all care if I talk?"

They mutter non-answers, shift in the water, the whole situation too expensive for them.

Wilk smiles, that nasty smile, the one that makes D want to kill him. "Now listen to me because I'm about to tell you something you need to hear. You know what the NFL stands for, don't you?"

"Please, like I never heard that before."

"Not for long," Wilk says anyway.

"Say it to yourself, old man. I'm doing me."

"You better stay in that tub. You better sit there. 'Cause when you get out I'm gonna cut off your tongue."

He doesn't do that, exactly. But he can't make false promises either. D goes about the rest of his pregame routine, getting taped, getting Toradol-injected, getting dressed, knowing the whole time that Wilk is waiting, gathering himself against him. During warm-up drills, they stand side by side in their position group, cock rock music blaring as they talk and occasionally knock heads, until the edge between them builds to a point so sharp, all D wants to do is bleed, and he'd bet his life that all Wilk wants to do is make him. Sure enough, back in the locker room, Wilk slams D into his locker and throws his chair at one of the laundry bins.

"You shut your mouth," he says. "You don't talk until you've got game."

And then he's off to the prayer circle, and D's picking up his seat and gathering himself in return. D-Mars is the greatest there ever was. He's gonna send someone's ass to the grave.

An hour later he's shouting into the ear hole of Matt Henshaw, a dude the broadcasters like to call a leader, which is just another way of saying that he is a quarterback, and he is white. "Get off the field!" D screams. "You're weak! Get off the field! You're weak!" Wilk sent everybody in on the blitz, but it was D who chopped past his lineman fastest on his way to toppling the king. Oh, he's a king all right, as in a mattress, a perfect cut of memory foam. "Remember me!" D insists. "Remember ME!" He pounds his chest and looks at the heavens and there he is on the Jumbotron, bringing his victim down to Earth again. All the rest of the game, whenever Henshaw's eyes pass his way, D sees something fidgeting in his expression: a flicker of doubt, a second guess, an adjustment he doesn't want to make. It's working its way inside him: the very weakness D suggested.

It's usually not until the postgame shower that his body begins to hurt, when the burns and cuts start to blister and the bruises bloom beneath the spray. Flower after flower of pain, like the bouquets he's been sending Shawna since the bye. This time, though, it's the good kind of hurt, the kind incurred from a banner game: six tackles, that devastating sack. His feet burst and bleed into the water, like packets of Russian dressing swirling over the tiles.

He begins to research his opponents. Where they're from, what kind of car they drive, little things he can tell them on the field.

"You're a smart player," Delahanty tells him. "Just keep on playing smart."

D knows smart goes beyond the body. Smart means reading, and reading others. It means converting every cold, dry piece of information into white-hot knowledge he can use.

"Speak up," he tells a taciturn running back, after he stuffs him at the line at Green Bay. "I know they taught you some words at A&M."

"Three-one-oh," he sings to E-Jacks, a pretty-boy slot receiver whose girlfriend's phone number was far too easy to find. "Nine-two-oh. Eight-seven, nine-seven."

"Knock it off, asshole," a Packer lineman tells him, defending his boy.

D sings the number again on the next possession.

"Don't you call her!" E-Jacks eventually screams. "Don'tyoudarecallmygirl! I'llfuckyouuup!"

"Now you did it," the lineman says. His name is Duckworth and he's got a mustache and trucker hair and pickle-shaped rolls under his titties, the perfect shelf for catching crumbs.

D asks him, "Where you live, bro—the seventies? Don't worry, I'll find your number there. Send you a pizza, double extra large."

"Ooh, boy, you're talking," D's mother says. "I see you out there on TV." They've been winning, three in a row now, and he can hear the relief in her voice. He likes that she pays such close attention.

"You always said I was born talking."

"We had a house full of loudmouths, yes we did. I think you knew you had to make yourself heard."

He'd grown up playing with his older, bigger brothers, getting shoved and tricked and angry before popping right back up for more. Again, he always told them, again, again, again. *That the best you got? That the best you can do?* For a long time, his mouth was his only weapon, and it stayed useful after his body found its form.

"You know, I'm thinking out there, too, Ma."

"That right?"

"I'm thinking about more shit to say! Naw, I'm just playing. I'm thinking about selling drugs. Naw naw naw, Mama, listen. I'm thinking about girls."

They are cracking up now, and it feels good.

"When my grandchild comes, boy, I am stealing him away. He is living in a world of proper grammar and conduct. None of your lip to mess him up."

Wilk plays in a tense crouch, like he's almost standing, like he's almost arthritic. Which maybe he is. But he's still got that odd tilting run that starts upright and ends horizontal as he brings down whoever has the ball. D watches tape in the meeting room after a Wednesday practice. He is supposed to be watching himself, then his opponents. But instead he finds his mind on Wilk. He knows how his own body looks when he works. The game, with its constant taping and reviewing, has ingrained that in him by now. But he hasn't scrutinized Wilk as much, though he's seen him play for years. He stands there in the middle, his ponytail peeking out of his helmet, his new beard visible behind his mask. He bounces a little, sensing, then torpedoes forward, his hips dropping almost imperceptibly as he lays out. It's like he's swimming at guys. He's a freak! D studies him on play after play, and before long his legs are sparking, he's feeling the ride in his own hips and feet.

Then he watches his opponents. When Wilk comes in, sits down to see how he's doing, he makes a game of it, calling the plays an instant before the snap. Seven out of ten, he gets.

"Pretty smart," Wilk says. He's eating from a carton of blueberries with his fingers, like a friendly animal in a book for kids. "But that's three plays you got your ass beat."

So Wilk. Always focused on the failures, even after a win.

"Practice makes perfect," D says.

"No. *Perfect* practice makes perfect." Wilk pops another pinch of berries into his mouth, his fingertips stained fuchsia. "Anything less, might as well go home."

"Psshhh."

"Your talking's helping, though," Wilk says after they watch a few more plays. "I hate to say it, but it is."

When Dallas comes to town, his whole family is there once again. He's flown them in just for the occasion because they get such a kick out of rooting against the home team. He gets them the best seats he can wrangle, paying for all but two out-of-pocket, which he tells no one, because who would believe a starter has to pay for his own family to watch a regular season game? On the field he knows where they are, in the end zone, a few rows up, feels the heat of their eyes every time he runs out.

Late in the fourth quarter he picks off a pass to author the end of the game. He won't even need to see the tape later. He sensed it all happening right there in coverage, saw the future in the quarterback's eyes: a crossing route, a drop-off spot in the open field. He got there well in advance, received the ball like a package he'd ordered and paid for himself. In the stands he pictures his family in ecstasy, jumping, shaking, a preview of the dance floor he'll encounter later that night at the club.

The NFL parties every Sunday, but it's always better after a win. He's got his brothers with him, and they're pointing at him every minute, marking him as their own. The club is darker than any house they ever lived in, but it's the kind of dark that makes everything beautiful, not the kind that makes things sad. Wilk hasn't come, though he'd grinned when D invited him. "Have fun, man, you earned it. Just don't do anything I wouldn't do."

Remembering this, D tries to act like a Christian. When a perfect ten approaches him, he's charitable, buys her drinks, praises her. She's got one of those forest animal necks, like a deer, and one of those asses, too. She's creamy coffee toned and smells like magic wrapped in rose petals with a smooth candy shell.

"Don't worry," she says, absolving him, light speckling across her skin. "I'm on Depo."

Even so he wears a condom. He's learning in this arena, too.

~

The next week, there he is in *Sports Illustrated*, screaming, holding his pick to heaven, while the quarterback sits on the ground behind him like a kid who doesn't want to go to sleep. "INT by 53!" was what he'd been saying, "I! N! T!" though there's nothing about that in the caption. He cuts out the page and tapes it in his locker.

"You see me?" he asks Wilk before practice, nodding at the photo.

Wilk gets funny all of a sudden. He puts his face up close to the image and peers at it, like he's an old man beyond the help of corrective lenses. "That isn't you," he finally says, pulling back and straightening up.

D emits a protective sizzle, a sound like water on a skillet. "Sure is."

"It is?" Wilk crouches down again, really studies the thing. He blinks. He's taking forever, and D starts to move around behind him, feeling weird.

"See, 53," he says.

"That's your number," Wilk agrees, as though this might not be a relevant fact.

"Bro, it's me. That's my face in there."

"It's a picture of you."

D shrieks. "Damn! Quit it! Same thing, right?"

"It's not the same. This"—he jabs D in the sternum—"is you. That"—he jabs D's sternum on the page—"is your picture. You. Your picture. You. Your picture. See what I'm saying?"

"Not really."

Wilk sighs. For the first time he seems not angry but genuinely disappointed. "Then I can't help you." His beard looks grave and fatherly in his disappointment, and D wonders if that's why he rides him, if he thinks they're somehow alike because neither one of them had a dad.

"All right, all right, I'm not my picture. That's deep. But look," he says, trying a different tack. "I'm gonna have a son. I can't wait to show him this."

And then, like he does, all of sudden, Wilk explodes. "So he can think his daddy's a football player, is that what you mean?" He swings around with his Gatorade, which he spikes, to stay sharp, with caffeine. "That's your *job*, bro. It's not your purpose. But you are so lost in the world you can't even see that. You can't even see how tiny you are. I know you think you're permanent, some kind of once and future king, but you're not. None of us are."

He's not sure he's ever heard Wilk say this many words in a row. "Chill, bro. Why you telling me this?"

"Why am I telling you? That's your problem, you don't listen! Not to God and definitely not to me."

"Jeez, I'm here. I'm listening to you."

"You're listening."

"Yeah."

"But do you hear me?"

"Yeah, bro."

"Then get rid of that corny picture."

D hears. He actually always hears Wilk, even when he makes no sense. He picks provisionally at the taped edge, but it's already adhered. Stalling, he turns around, making sure to block it with his body. "You really think that's my future? King Mars?"

Wilk flaps a gnarly hand, which means, I forgive you, but also, Don't push it.

The truth is it's something D thinks about more than he should. The future. Not Kowalczyk's or their opponents', but his own future, the world's. It's so invisible to him; that's what's scary. Nothing at all like an developing play. If he had to describe it, he'd say his future world would probably be a lot smaller and darker than the world he looks at now. Confined, somehow, like a photograph, instead of the boundless thing itself. Except when he sees kids; then he thinks differently.

"I mean, I hear what you're saying about the job," D says. "But I really don't think prayer's the answer for me. If that's what you're trying to say."

"That's because you haven't known adversity, bro. You've been so lucky this season. Everything you could hope for and more. And I'm telling you, that's the most dangerous feeling in the world. It's deceptive."

What Wilk is saying is so tone-deaf, D feels an obligation to correct him. "I haven't known adversity? Am I not a rookie? Am I not a black man in America? Come on, man, don't be ignorant. You went to the U." He turns back to the magazine page, tries to unpeel it as carefully as he can, but even so, the long edge rips. Whatever, he can always buy another.

When he turns back he notices Wilk sweating, a halo of perspiration ringing his forehead. "You know what I mean," Wilk says. "I just mean it's easy to be in the NFL and see nothing but the NFL."

D understands putting pictures of himself in his locker is weak, but he can't understand Wilk's edge. The man's thirty and at the top of his game. He's been in SI countless times. Even if the NFL were the only thing he saw, he'd have seen a lot more than most.

"Yeah, man," D says. "It's a short move no matter what. But that's true if you're a garbage man or playing garbage time." He isn't sure why he even has to say these things, what it is they're fighting about.

Wilk blinks wildly. "A short what?"

"A short move, baby." D takes a little step to the side. "From your mama's womb to your final tomb. Whatever your religion, that's the only truth there is."

Wilk shakes his head. "Wise man, all of a sudden. Kowalczyk should put that on one of his signs."

D pictures his mama's catch phrase next to STAY IN YOUR LANE and DO YOUR JOB over the door to the players' lot. Kowalczyk is the kind of coach Wilk believes in, inspirational signs and all. He's played for lots of coaches, guys who love the players too much, guys who hate the players too much. Kowalczyk's the autistic kind: out of shape but not quite fat, eight steps ahead, obsessive, clean. He has those permafrost eyes, and is actually pretty unlovable, but anything can be tolerated as long as you win. So Wilk says.

"IT'S A SHORT MOVE," D says, holding up the ripped magazine page as a stand-in for his imagined sign.

"It's also a long season," Wilk concedes. Another Kowalczyk line. "I don't know. He'd probably disagree."

By December, the cheerleaders are wearing Santa hats and muffs, and everybody on the team is worn down. It's just a physical condition, but it feels like one that's been with D always, as regular as hunger, as taking a shit, as sleep. Anyway, they continue to win, drinking chicken broth between drives on the sidelines. Wilk is right that the NFL has not been hard for him; with a few months' hindsight, D can see that now. All the advice he's been given—how to conduct himself, how to play smart, how to show respect—none of it has really mattered, because at the end of the day, he's had the athleticism and the willingness to develop the skills.

Somewhere along the way, despite their gap in age, he has

become Wilk's best friend. He isn't quite sure how that happened, or if he'd even grant Wilk the title in return, but he guesses he might, and he guesses it has something to do with the conversations they have, which often start with film, but easily move on to all sorts of other things, like Wilk's understanding of God as a coach who loves him, who he can talk to and laugh with in his mind, or how much they both hate Tom Brady, who only Wilk has met. He discovers a lot of surprising similarities in the course of these conversations, like how they both got bit by dogs growing up, which really shouldn't be a surprise, because every country kid has been bitten by a dog, because that's the ordinary violence of growing up in the boonies, a fact that's probably significant, because it's the same violence that conditioned them for this game. He enjoys these conversations, the way they don't really end when practice ends, but pick up again, elastically, back at Wilk's place, where they've taken to watching film on the giant L-shaped couch, and then the next day, back at practice, and then the next day, and then the next. He enjoys the way Wilk encourages him, increasingly, despite his old habit of bossing, to not be weak, to be a man, to speak his mind. And it occurs to him, when Wilk mentions a retired guy named Hardy for the fifth or sixth time, that Wilk has not played for this team much longer than he has, and it's possible all his real friends are elsewhere, and what a funny idea that is, a real friend, as though what they have right now is fake.

Even so, Wilk sometimes tells him to leave him alone. "We're just co-workers," he says one day when he decides he's not in the mood.

"Oh, I see," D says. He dusts himself with baby powder, half of it evaporating like the rookies from camp. "Now you ain't gonna talk to me."

He pretends to be a mage, casts some powder in Wilk's direction, which Wilk answers with a spell of his own. He just stares, and it is dark, and after all the brow-beating, and then all the commiseration, and all the conversation, and all the— honestly, there's no other word for it but—*love*, Wilk's stare threatens to black it all out.

It hurts at first. But D's lost scholarships and friends and relatives; he's used to love being withheld or withdrawn. He decides he does not care. He can stare right back. He, shirtless and black, in a room made for shirtlessness and blackness, can stand there, rubbing cayenne pepper into his arms for extra heat, and he can look murder straight into Wilk's mind.

You are outnumbered here, says his murdering look. You are not permanent. Your days are numbered, too.

Sometimes D thinks about how much all this football stuff costs. The shoes alone. They're complicated, and he gets a new pair just to practice in each week. He's lacing his latest, freshly barnacled with molded bottom spikes, and he's finally beginning to appreciate his solitude when Wilk comes around, fickle man, and invites him to his house again to study. Just like that.

"You know I don't watch film anymore," Wilk says under his inflated ceiling, the mahogany rafters peaking like a private church.

"How's that. What are we doing right now?"

"After ten years in this league, I've seen it all." He's drinking a shake Lori's made him, eating a sandwich he's made D buy. "There are only so many plays that can come out of any formation. It's instinctive. I just go to the ball."

"But what are we doing *in the present moment*, bro?" D gestures at the wall-mounted plasma. He wonders what it costs.

The rafters, too. "Ask yourself. Be honest."

"You're watching film. I'm just spending time with my rook, helping keep him on the straight and narrow." A sling of meat hangs off his lower lip. "Thanks for the sandwich, by the way."

"Not like I had a choice."

"I do, though. And I am choosing to say thanks."

"You've seen it all, huh."

Wilk licks his lip. "All of it and more. Stuff I'd rather just forget."

"How you mean?"

"I'll tell you how I mean." He gets fatherly again, leans forward over his knees. D thinks of Wilk's babies sleeping upstairs and tries his best to look serious.

"I've been in the game so long," Wilk says, "that when I look at guys now to size them up, I practically look inside them. I see the surgeries, the anti-inflammatories, all the weak parts."

As he talks, his expression fades from sober to nonexistent, and for a second D doesn't know if he's forgotten who he is or what.

"You go for those parts," Wilk goes on. "You don't want to admit it, but you do. You don't want to admit it because you're taped and sutured and gauzed up, too. Those are *your* weak parts. It's your body you're attacking. It's like cancer; it's, what's the word, it's self-defeating."

He gets quiet and once again D thinks he might have blacked out. He's on the verge of nudging him when Wilk resumes speaking, even more soberly than before.

"This is a zero-sum game," he says. "Everything you get, you take from somebody else. But you take it from your own self, too."

~

The zero-sum idea is a powerful one, and D enters the postseason thinking hard about football math. Week in and week out, it's did you win. For half the league, the answer is yes. For half the league, it's no. Then you get to the end, and suddenly there's only one team that gets to say yes. This is logical. This is something everyone knows. But it's a pretty fucking cruel piece of logic, because winning is also the norm, the thing everyone thinks they should be able to do. But one winner, thirty-one failures: what kind of norm is that?

They are on the cusp of their own failure when it happens—Packers, playoffs, and D has been talking all game. To Brett Favre. To various fat linemen he beats out to Favre. There's a ferocity to every communication, even the play calls, every one of them a threat of costly things to come. This kind of talk has substance. It congeals, forms a necessary future. On game day, D completely lives in that future, the one in which every play succeeds.

He is in it now, even now, down two TDs in the fourth, when, on the heated bench, Wilk tells him, "Keep talking. Keep it up."

He's been flying around, knocking receivers unconscious—not literally—and saying some unadvisable shit. He's been warned once already by the ref, for chatting down to a leveled receiver just a few moments too long. It wasn't his fault the guy just lay there on the ground, wincing. Wasn't his fault the guy figures heavily in Green Bay's game plan, and is small for his position, and a diva. He's Jackson, E-Jacks, the Cali kid with the girlfriend whose number D is proud to know by heart.

"It's getting to them," Wilk says. "I can see it."

Woodson, the strength coach, squirts water into D's open mouth. He swallows. "I'll get fined," D says.

"Fuck it." Wilk grins. "It's a short move."

D's so flabbergasted to hear Wilk swear that he hardly registers the rest. "What's that?"

"It's a short move, right?" Wilk says again, and D is filled with a warm memory of himself. "You can afford it."

D nods automatically. "You know what." He does the side step. "I can't *wait* to pay that fine."

So D keeps talking, and the Packers keeping stalling, and the wincing slot receiver, E-Jacks, keeps jabbing him with his needly elbow every time they intersect.

D talks to him again about his girlfriend. About his facial hair. About his bling.

"Imma take your hat off, Princess Ice," he says. "Imma steal those diamond studs."

But E-Jacks just looks past him, like there's something much more striking in the mesh of white lights and green jerseyed fans that encloses the playing field. He's not reacting like he did before. He's keeping his cool.

"You better *run*," D says.

"I'm running."

"Not for office," D says, liking this stroke of cleverness. "Not for office," he repeats. "This ain't no debate. You ain't got no podium to protect you, son."

"Pssh. I get all the votes."

"Fuck no!"

E-Jacks shrugs, flashes smug, Cali teeth behind his mask. D can almost see the diamonds through his ear holes. "I'm the hero, man. You the one they love to hate."

They head uphill to the line of scrimmage, which crowns, the field rising slightly in the middle to help it look flat on TV. E-Jacks' jersey is streaked with grass and paint and it appears to have been restitched at the sleeve. D pictures a Packers seamstress bent lovingly over the work, and the irritating thought of this makes him want to shove E-Jacks' face in the dirt. Jacks who? He ain't no president. D feels sharp on his feet.

The next down, E-Jacks cuts and the ball comes his way but D is right there to slap it with his hands. "Vote for this!" D screams. "Vote for this!" He gets shoved backing away, and whistles blow, but then he shoves back so the penalties offset. E-Jacks limps daintily to the sidelines, leaving the bellies of the offensive line to defend his honor. One of them, Duckworth, is the old mustachioed dude, the one D has never liked. He swings at D, calls him a thug, and probably goes on to say something even worse. D has no idea because every sense in his body is at that moment exploding as Wilk literally holds him back. "Naw, man, you the thug!" D shouts from Wilk's embrace. "E-Jacks ain't no president, he's a puppet!" Dancing back to the huddle, he mimes a marionette on strings.

It's soon after this that it happens. A run play, a run play that in hindsight, they might have called just for him. He's swooping, headed for the ball carrier unblocked, when out of nowhere one of those same offensive bellies bears down on him, and it's Duckworth, of course it is. He's ugly and yelling something about his precious baby E-Jacks, and he cuts D right at the knees.

Every hit is louder in the winter cold, but this one is so loud it practically silences his mind. He cannot even recall how it sounded before, because all he can hear is the tear in his knee.

"The fuck!" he shouts. "You can't go for my head like a man? *You can't go for my head like a MAN?*"

Then he screams, not in fear, but to cause it. He hopes that fat-ass can hear him. Hopes he knows his revenge will be worse.

When he gets him again. When he gets up. Though D's pain right now is no picnic. He screams again, pounds his fists on the ground, sees the concerned faces of Wilk and the medical staff above him, hears the guilty crowd look away, thinks *who the hell are these people*, thinks *Wilk, you motherfucker*, thinks *there are so many people, so many motherfuckers*, thinks he can see three fingers, thinks he's fucked.

He's calmer by the time they cart him out, maybe because he's actually in shock. His head is fuzzy from hitting the ground. Riding backwards into the tunnel, he aims the obligatory thumbs up at the ramp to the upper decks, which it's possible he's never really seen before. A whole season in this house and so much is still brand new. The ramp juts out like a kiddie roller coaster that makes up for its gentle grade by looking really hi-tech and mean, and there are men on both levels of it, waving at him, and he can't explain it exactly, but this is how he knows. He sees the future clearly, like he can when he's at his best. Surgery, restless rehab, thunderous workouts, the birth of a son. In week nine, screw the doctors, a triumphant, dominant return. You'd never guess he tore his ACL. He's playing unconscious; he's playing furious; he's better than ever before. On the whirring cart, D is surer of this than he's ever been of anything. A fury like his has to live.

9. MITCH, 2006

By Mitch's final season, it happened a couple times a game. That moment of gentle panic in which he felt he was faking football, while everyone else was playing for real. He was playing at playing, and the only way to avoid being caught inside himself was to stick to his assignment, stay in his lane.

He usually found his target, even under these questionable circumstances. A read. A gap. A surge. An *unh*. Then he and his man would get to their feet and the panic that had gripped his inside self would leave him with a shiver of withdrawal. Before he knew it, he'd be back in his body again, back in motion, back in play.

As for the panic, it tended to hang around. He could see it, sometimes, in his opponents' eyes, transferred there by the hit.

It was a look that said, "Oh God."

And, "Wow."

And, "None of this is real."

Day to day it was all too real. He awoke on Tuesday, Week 14, feeling like a man with a beating heart trapped inside a stone.

Wake up you peace of shit. A text from Hardy, Hardy who was done: out there somewhere, living. Hardy who had a Super Bowl ring.

Peace be with you you piece of s#!+, Mitch thumbed back.

He had just four more regular season games ahead of him.

Four more for the rest of his life. Though for the moment no one knew that but him and God. Not Kowalczyk, not his agent Phil, not even Lori or his mom. Even Mitch didn't know for sure. God changed his mind daily. In the middle of a game he sometimes felt he could go on another decade. The day after, as a rule, he was ready to call it quits.

A short week, in the home stretch, the players' lot was packed when he arrived. Technically, it was their day off, but everybody was in the building, getting food, getting looked at by the trainers. Through the double doors at the end of the hall, he could see Matt Rainey, the QB, pacing the practice field with his dogs.

When he arrived at his locker, D was already there, shirtless and fussing at his own spot, while Lowry and Griggs, both second-year defensive backs, and Moore, from the D-line, gathered around in their sweats.

"Sup, Wilk."

"So early," Mitch scolded him. "I know you're not injured." Since his rookie season ACL tear, D hadn't so much as lost an eyelash. He was more committed to maintaining his body than most women were to marriage. Though he turned out to be committed in that way, too. He and Shawna had finally tied the knot that summer—a confident move for a guy in his contract year—and he'd spent much of the preseason bragging to anyone who would listen about the beauty and brains of his black wife. Still hadn't found God, but that was fine, he would. In his heart he was a man of faith.

"Naw, naw," D said now. He aimed a small digital camera at Mitch. "Say hello to the fans, Wilk. You on TV."

"Is this media? You working for the enemy now?"

D rocked his head, grinning. "Undercover brother, reporting to another."

"Spying for the networks or the Redskins, which is it?"

"I don't know, Wilk," Griggs said, peering over D's shoulder at the screen. "You looking kinda tired. You know how they say the camera adds fifty pounds?"

Mitch swung his hand, "Man, get out of here," and Griggs made for the nearest pillar, giggling. "None of y'all even need to be here today."

"But you do, Wilk. Tell the people what you came in for." D refocused his gaze through the camera.

"That thing on?"

"You see the light, don't you? Come on, you ain't that old. You've seen a camera before."

"But I am old, is the point. I live in the training room because I'm old. Seriously, man, what's this all about?"

D hit stop and pulled the camera back. "Aight, so, last night I got to thinking. We just won a must-win game at home, on Monday night. Suddenly, we're 6-6. We make the playoffs if we win out. But that doesn't come fast, right? Remember last year, dog? People gotta want it. They gotta love each other." He'd been stroking his chest unthinkingly, but here he tapped his heart. "You feel me?"

D was right that they'd totally fallen apart the previous year, partly because of injuries, but mostly because everyone just hated each other. They'd cut a lot of the bad seeds, and this year had been better, if only because everyone was so much more relaxed. "So, what," Mitch asked, "you're gonna videotape the love?"

D laughed. "Don't get kinky now!"

"You're the one with the camera."

"I'm saying I'm gonna create a little fun for us. Give us a chance to reflect, player to player, on what this game means. Maybe also have some rap battles. Maybe upload it to my blog."

"Oh no, you got a blog now?"

"I got it all, baby. Now you ready for your interview or what?"

Mitch shook his head. "Come back to me later. I have to get looked at."

Days he felt pretty sure he was retiring, D was one of the few guys who could make him think twice. All he'd ever done was talk. From the moment Mitch met him in training camp, he was talking. It was awful at first. Grating, obscene, like Ricky Franklin in eighth grade. But over the years—this being their fourth—D's words had come to feel essential, even the obscenities. Because he didn't just talk trash. He talked the world to life. He explained things to the rookies, reported back on what everyone else was up to—in the cafeteria, in the laundry room—said hello to everyone he passed every single morning. He was the team's soundtrack, their constant narrator, and while it could still be annoying in the moments Mitch sought silence, for the most part, D's voice was something Mitch valued very much.

His go-to trainer, Steef, was busy working a wideout's hamstring when he came in, so Mitch sat on a table with his new phone and waited. It flipped open two ways, vertically for calls and horizontally for keyboard texting.

Excited for dinner Sat, he wrote Alyssa, who was probably at that moment in class. At Washington had become his favorite game of the season because it meant he got to see her. She was in eighth grade now, in Maryland.

"All right," Steef said, "what's your body saying?"

"How much time you got?" His body was saying never again, and at the same time, more more more. He ran through his areas of concern: the standard hands, wrists, knees, and right foot, which he'd broken about fourteen months back, as well as a new tightness that wouldn't let up in his back. Steef checked them, gave him a recovery pill and some advice, and then it was off to the whirlpools for rehab. Everyone who wasn't in the locker room was in the whirlpools, competing for the crown of worst-off. Not that you ever wanted sympathy. You just wanted to hurt the most, to win.

Sitting with his brothers in the cold tub, he was glad he'd stuck it out another season. He could've easily thrown in the towel after that '05 disaster, in which he'd sucked and the team had sucked, no coincidence his thirteenth year. But there weren't a lot of jobs where you could sit around shooting the shit with other men all day, and between last night's win and D's optimism, it was possible his fourteenth season might turn out lucky after all. He thought of Ricky Franklin, who would love to hear him think it. Old Ricky, the acrobat, lucky number fourteen.

"Okay, but say we'd gone on the road to Carolina," one of the O-linemen, Kohler, was saying. "Where would we be going? Charlotte, right? Which is in North Carolina. But they don't say that. They just say 'Carolina,' which has to mean both states. So aren't we kind of going to South Carolina, too? I don't know why no one talks about that."

"Man, you're an idiot." This was Hock, another guard.

"But it's the same thing with New England, right?" Kohler persisted, not that anyone wanted him to stop. You had to be talking in the cold tub; it was the only way to survive the chill. "How many states are in New England? Six?"

"Yeah, six," Mitch answered.

"Boston, Massachusetts, Connecticut," Kohler started counting. "I mean! Not Boston. Boston is *in* Massachusetts. Even I get confused when I talk about this. So it's Massachusetts, Connecticut, Rhode Island, Maine, New Hampshire, and Vermont."

"What's your point?" Mitch asked.

"I mean," Kohler laughed. He was always laughing at everything he said, because everything he said intrigued him, especially the stuff he knew was dumb. Hardy would've loved this guy. "When you're playing for New England, aren't you actually kind of in all those states?"

"No." Mitch scratched his beard. "You're in Massachusetts."

"So literal," Kohler said.

After five minutes, he was out. Five minutes a day bought you five extra years. That was the promise the trainers made when they first introduced the tubs, and it was a prescription he would continue to follow, even with only four games left. Guys were still yakking as he climbed over them towards the bubbling hot tub, where he'd sink up to his neck and die a little, productively. Their voices filled the room over the power sounds; water filled the tubs. It was so much better when people liked each other. You could stay anywhere longer—the cold tub, the weight room, the sideline, the league—as long as you liked the people.

He was half-dressed at his locker when Eddie Hatchett came to get him. "You got a minute?"

Most GMs left the players to their spaces, but Eddie was a former player—and not just a former player, a former great. He wore mesh shorts all year long, even in winter, and he was as comfortable as any player in the locker room.

Mitch threw on a shirt and went with him to the cafeteria, where they got a first lunch of smoothies to go. Back in his office, Eddie took control of the conversation, as only guys in management can. "We just wanted to get a sense of where you're at," he said. "You think you got another season in you?"

It wasn't customary to talk this way, GM-to-player, without an agent in the room, but Eddie and Mitch hadn't had a customary relationship for years. In his first year on the job, Eddie had recruited Mitch himself, with personal visits to New England and weekend meet-ups in Miami, where they both had ties as former Hurricanes. He'd even encouraged Mitch to buy property in his neighborhood, and their kids—Mitch's born early, Eddie's born late—attended the same New Jersey school. Mitch hadn't been much of an office guy in New England, but for his second team, it made sense to get closer to management, as though some portal were opening between their dimensions, giving him a glimpse of the afterlife. For his part, Eddie made it look good. His bowlegged stride was stiff but quick, and the ripples of bumps on his arms and legs were nothing too troubling, just a reminder that he'd made his name on the field, where it counted most to Mitch.

Even so, Mitch wasn't ready to take Eddie into his confidence. "Honestly, I can't say. I'm trying to focus on Washington. All I see is the week in front of me."

"Wilk," Eddie said. He leaned forward onto his elbows, demanding straight talk. "I'm not the media. You can tell me what you're really thinking."

Mitch shrugged. He appreciated candor, but that didn't mean he'd let Eddie rob him of his privacy. "I guess I'm choosing not to think. I'll play better now if I don't."

Eddie nodded, chewing his jaw. "If only everyone played like you. We'd win every week. A team of forty-five-year-old men would win every damn week."

"Quit taking more years from my life," Mitch said. "I've been taking them back in the tub."

"'Five minutes a day,'" Eddie recited. "So listen, no pressure, but I'll have Stu make you a tape. We're looking at linebackers and I want to hear what you think. When you can think."

"Foolish not to."

"That's what I'm saying." They stood, clasping hands. "And listen, don't tell all your secrets to D. He puts that stuff on the internet?" Eddie made an explosion with his mouth, made his eyes jolt up in recoil.

"How in the world do you know about that already?" Mitch laughed.

Eddie tapped his temple, cocky. "I see all. I know all."

It was so pleasant talking to Eddie, who had a way of including you in his thoughts, as though they were somehow your thoughts, too, that it wasn't until Mitch was back in the locker room, gathering his things, that he realized he was being pushed out.

Which he then immediately second-guessed, and then immediately rethought. Over the course of his career, he'd had so many between-the-lines conversations with bosses, and this one was not even that opaque.

Eddie wanted his view on the future; he'd called him forty-five.

"Ready for lunch?" D asked behind him, and Mitch shelved the future for the moment, grabbed his protein shaker, said sure.

You had to have superhuman willpower to tear yourself away from the facility, which had been built, ingeniously, to keep you. They would cut your hair here, do your laundry here, feed you. The young guys who didn't have wives lived for the unlimited food and the endless sitting around the tables with dessert, all the more so because they knew that even endlessness was fleeting. By Week 17 there would be printed reminders in all the meeting rooms: "Players and staff are responsible for buying their own meals during the off-season."

Mitch had a family, though, and a players' day off meant a family day on. There was no excuse for lingering, and he'd already hung around well past lunch. He drove back to Jersey, just beating the kids home from school. Madison was up from her nap and working on a block tower while Lori stood at the kitchen island with the laptop.

He hadn't intended to remarry so quickly. When he and Caryn called it quits, not long after that awful Super Bowl, it was sad, but it was also exhilarating. He was twenty-four and he could finally have some honest fun. The first thing he did was to end it with Angela in Patriots Publicity. That was too bad, because she was always down for fun, but he couldn't risk her thinking she might be the reason for his divorce. The second thing was to fly to Vegas to throw away some money, and shortly thereafter, to Miami, where every model and bottle was free. When he tired of freedom, he went back to Vegas; when Vegas maxed him out, Miami saved him a seat. It was on one of these cross-country relays that he dropped in on Joe, whom he hadn't seen since he was five. Mitch was living experimentally, down to try anything once, and going to stay at his hippie dad's Montana compound definitely qualified as an experiment. But Joe had an inviting bliss about him, and so did Tammy, his half-Asian wife. Their home was a collection of brightly painted huts and shacks clustered around a geodesic dome, all of which they'd built themselves. When it got dark, they sat around the fire pit with the dogs, smoking weed and trading stories about Monacan. Mitch spent the night on a camping cot in Joe's studio and left the next morning feeling higher on himself than ever—on his choices, his genetic strength, his great capacity for forgiveness. In Vegas he met up with Hardy and Gaines, and after a good night of blackjack, he rewarded them all with a charter jet to

France, fully stocked with cognac and stewardesses. Hardy just talked to his stewardess, so he said, but Mitch's kept leaning over him with her mouth half-open, and he felt so enormous he couldn't help himself; he begged her to let him do her in the ass. Her name was Celine. She complied.

It was barely a year of that life before he swung by a late-night Miami house party, summer of '98, and found Lori Taylor swimming with some of her friends. They were twenty-two and all of them had gotten their hair wet, which made it hard to tell who was the hottest, let alone who was brown-haired or blonde, but he singled out Lori for her tits, bobbing amply in the underwater lights, and her laugh, which had the soft, microphoned quality of a pop star's, pitched to capture the attention of crowds. He offered her a robe. She accepted it with a forthrightness that made him feel sorry for Angela, and for Celine, and for all the girls he'd nailed in Miami, a few of whom were at the party: Kim, the gymnast, who said she wanted to cut him, and who he fucked until she cried; Gina-or-Tina, who had been naked in a movie with Keanu Reeves; Nadia, a more successful actress and a klepto, weird stuff always disappearing from his possession whenever he was with her, not just cash but also CDs and personal products like deodorant, though he'd never been sober enough to catch her, so he didn't know for sure. Lori was different from all of them. She was a model, with shoulders like a luxury hanger, but he could tell instantly she wasn't a liar. He took her out for a Cuban sandwich that very night. Her hair turned out to be blonde.

Before he knew what he was doing, he was following her to church. He'd grown up Christian, so he was familiar with God, but only in the way he was familiar with guys who'd played the game before he was born. At Lori's church, people were casual, having coffee and doughnuts, coming in, going out, singing and praying together, yet on their own. During Worship, Lori liked to close her eyes and raise one long hand to heaven, resting the other one on her heart. She almost always cried, and it moved him, first, that she was so comfortable in the feeling, and second, that he felt no urge to tease her. The more he went, the more he realized how anxious he'd been, especially in that last year, when he'd lived so fast, without laws. All that time, there'd been a voice in his head, a gentle, worried noise just shy of audible that he'd always dismissed as an echo of his mom. But it wasn't her; he knew now that it was God. As for his head, it wasn't strictly *his*, but rather a place, like a playing field, where he could walk and talk with God. It wasn't all immediately apparent, but the more time he spent with Lori, the lighter he felt in his body, and the more skilled he became at hearing God, at discerning who was who. It was something, he realized in his conversion, he'd always known he'd have the power to do one day. Like beating Tim in a sprint, like making the pros. All he had to do was practice.

Lori had flirted with danger as a kid, sneaking out with her friends, letting older boys touch her between her legs in movie theaters, and generally not thinking too much of herself, until one night she lost her virginity like an extra hair tie, just put it down on a metal playground slide with an opportunist who gladly took it. She was fourteen, her testimony went, and as she sat up in her own bed the next morning, fully recognizing her sin, something inside her flicked on. She understood that she would destroy herself if she couldn't resist the darkness that was so attractive to her friends, that until that moment had been attractive to her, too. It was so easy to hide in darkness, to not have to look too closely at herself. But she understood then, tossing the covers aside to reveal her toes, that most of the easy things were bad, while the good things, starting with honesty before God, would always require work. Hard work, even. She looked at her hands, spread them gladly into the morning light, and then, falling to her knees by the bed, clasped them together in prayer. She was imperfect, she had sinned, but the same body that had sinned could work. That belief had saved her that very morning, and it served her well as a football wife.

"There's Daddy," she said to Madison now.

Mitch scooped up their daughter and puffed kisses into her neck, which she received with an obliging giggle. Maddie was the only one of his babies he'd actually known as a baby, having spent six weeks at home with a broken foot last season, right after she was born. He'd been changing her when her umbilical stump fell off, a little piece of burnt cheese on the blanket. He'd been tempted to taste it. He'd fed her breast milk from a bottle, which he did taste. Because of this he was more comfortable with her than he'd ever been with the others: Kaylie, the little general; Tyler, the problem child.

With Maddie on his hip, he went around the kitchen island to kiss his wife. "How are you feeling?" She cupped his beard in her hands.

People constantly asked him how he felt. It was one of football's biggest questions. How's the knee, how's the head, how's the body holding up? He always told the truth in some measure: some constructive, useful portion of the truth, the portion that would tape him up, keep him around a bit longer, allow him to keep wreaking havoc. But to Lori, as he had done to all the women in his life, he just surrendered. Every hit, every lost hour of sleep, caught up to him. He didn't know how he was still standing.

"I'm beat, baby," he told her, pulling her with Maddie and

him to the couch. "I quit."

Maddie cried out and wriggled free, back to her blocks.

"That's a lie," Lori said. "Don't even get my hopes up."

He considered telling her, and wasn't that a dumb idea. If she really was hoping, and he changed his mind, it would only break her heart.

His pocket buzzed. Alyssa, responding to his text. Good for her, she'd waited until school got out. Maybe that was a rule, the kind of thing he'd know if he'd been around enough to raise her.

Can we go to Osteria on Sat? Italian in Capitol Hill

He reread the text. It hadn't been that long since he'd seen her. Was she into classy restaurants now? She was only thirteen. But maybe that was what happened when you grew up in the city. He'd had Hardee's. She had Osteria.

Wherever you want, he texted back, *as long as I can eat meat*

Lori sat there next to him, chastely, her leg millimeters from his, her elbow on the couch back, propping up her head. She never invaded his space. She never demanded anything. The year Kaylie was born, in New England, she didn't even live with him, spiriting the baby away to Florida like some tribeswoman, returning to her village to nurse. He saw her as the end of the line, his final woman, the one he might not disappoint.

"You want to come to dinner Saturday?" he asked her.

"No, you go," she said. "She never sees you. I spoke to God today, and He left me feeling calm. I think He was saying, Let Alyssa have her dad to herself."

He nodded. That was settled, on to the next thing. "D brought in a video camera today." He didn't want to discuss Hatchett's request.

"Oh no."

"He wants to make a team movie. Celebrate us. I think it's

all right. Some guys'll love it. They're clowns. And the quiet ones will probably appreciate the attention."

"Sounds nice then."

It shamed him sometimes that there were so many things he didn't tell her, but he also knew his secrets helped make their marriage work. She knew he'd sinned before he met her, as she had, but she didn't know the extent of it, or how far back it went. With Lori he really was faithful, so he found it better not to shake her faith in him. Better to keep all that old baggage locked away, between himself and God.

DFW: Drug-Free Wednesday. He was sitting on the leg press where the taped note read "Reps 10" and D was aiming the Canon right at him.

"Come on, man, you know I hate the camera."

"It's me, though. How you feel about leg days, Wilk?"

Mitch took a breath, closed his lips, took his mind off his nagging back. Rather than talk, he started his set.

"Come on, man."

He had to focus on clean, timed reps, every bit of his detoxing body checked in for every count. But D's face was still there beyond his feet. He was making no demands, just the assumption that Mitch liked him enough to talk.

After his fifth rep, halfway there, he managed to offer him something. "I feel my legs." Then he waited for the next pause before spitting out a bit more. "Can't hate 'em. They hold you up. But some days they let you down."

"That's why we in here, though, right?"

"Recovery and maintenance," Mitch said.

"Tell the fans what you mean by that."

Mitch pressed out the set and sat back. "After a game," he

said, "your muscles are pretty beat up, so during the season it's important to get back in here and take care of them, get the blood flowing again."

"Buy yourself time."

"Always."

"How long you think you got, Wilk? People want to know." D was grinning, nothing serious.

"That's my secret," Mitch told him, grinning back. "You think I'd tell you?"

"If not me, then who?"

They'd talked about it, of course, in the off-season. Maybe this one will be my last, et cetera. Just a little experiment, just testing out the words. But nothing public, nothing ever on the record where it could hurt. "I'm not telling your camera anyway."

"My camera is my conscience. Come on, we'll do something funny. We'll bleep it out."

"Nope."

"Come on."

"Uh-uh."

This time, he made the grin vicious, and D, like a pro, took the hint.

"All right then, what're you doing to stay competitive? What's your secret? What's your voodoo?"

This, he liked. "Well, it's interesting," Mitch said. "I recently paid a visit to a healer and he gave me a little bottle of something. I think it started with an H. There was a G in there, too, and maybe another H. Gosh darn it if I remember. But, boy, I tell ya, it must've been some kind of magic. If I had to go by the way I feel right now—which is awesome—I'd say I probably have another fifty years of football in me."

D was letting his laughter escape through his teeth. "Your

wrinkled ass on the blitz?"

"That's what I'm saying, bro, there will be no wrinkles. I'll be elastic. A walking football uniform."

"You found the fountain of youth, dog."

"God's supplement."

"How has no one thought of this before?"

Mitch held a finger to his lips. "Shh. Don't go spreading it around. I don't need them bringing LT back to interview for my job."

They installed the game plan after lunch, walking through each new call, working it into their legs and brains, rubbing out the old patterns and plays. Mitch also tried to rub out his doubts. It was not a familiar state of being: doubt. But he kept seeing D's camera, with its stern recording light, and he kept hearing himself joke about HGH. He shouldn't have talked that way, even to D. He'd made it a rule never to talk much to reporters, because words could be used against you, none more harshly than your own. That had been his rule. Why had he let himself talk to D?

"You're dangerous," Mitch told him when they were back at their lockers. "Getting me to joke around like that."

"I love it," D said. "You're more honest when you joke."

"Just erase it," Mitch said. "I have to ask you to erase it."

D shook his head. "You say so."

"I mean permanently. For real. I can't have anyone thinking I use HGH."

"And I said all right," D said, abruptly, which put an end to the conversation, but not to Mitch's doubts.

Thursday's practice was in pads. "Missy Sixteen!" Delahanty

called, and they knocked it out, a middle blitz for his daughter's birthday.

"Gemini Zone!"

"Nickel Shake 1!"

"I should've had you make one for Alyssa," Mitch told him at the break.

"A's hard," Delahanty said. "But I can work on it. She coming to any more games?"

"Just this one that I know. But there's always playoffs."

"And next year." Delahanty's smile took up a considerable portion of his face. Mitch tried to decide if he was fishing for info, then figured, no, that was how he smiled, it was just how he was built.

"Hey—hey." D ran over, elated. "You see Force's new endorsement? It's some kind of fruit roll-up that's supposed to recharge your muscles and make your sweat taste like cherries. He's handing 'em out over there. 'Compliments of ReGrowth.'"

Mitch looked at Griggs, who D called Force. "Name could use some work. A little generic."

"Yeah, but get this. So he's giving them out, he's working on his spiel. And he gives me mine, and he looks at me."

"No no no," said Griggs, who had joined them, and was twitching like a sidewalk worm. "Don't tell Wilk."

"Oh, I got to tell Wilk."

"Yeah," Mitch said. "No turning back now."

"He says, 'This has camouflage so it won't hurt your stomach.'"

"*Camouflage?*"

"He means chamomile, dog!" D could not contain himself.

"I just thought that was, like, for my grandma," Griggs said. "She's got her glasses and her Sudoku and her chamomile. You can see how I got confused."

"But that's it, though!" D insisted. "It's, like, 'Here, eat this fruit roll-up. It tastes like gum on the bottom of your shoe, but it'll hide your injuries from yourself.'"

"You can't put that on camera, though," Griggs said. "I won't say it again."

"Not even if I pay you? Think about your brand."

"Ask Kohler about New England," Mitch told D, his way of saying he'd forgiven him. "Seriously, ask him." Just because he hated the camera didn't mean he didn't want to help. Kohler could talk enough for them all.

They had visitors on the sideline for the second half of practice: a well-dressed woman and three matching men, one of whom was the owner, Greg Goldman. In all the time that Mitch had been an Eagle, he'd found Goldman to be an admirably unobtrusive presence, an investor who left the football to the football people. He was not old, but bedecked with hair that was comfortably white, the kind of man you instinctively addressed as Mr., genial whenever he greeted the players at the official functions they were occasionally required to attend. He knew the names of all of Mitch's kids, and not in a creepy way.

At a water break, Mitch found himself standing beside him. They watched the offense put together an irritating little series of screens.

"Just have to chip away at them," Mr. Goldman said. His voice was crisp and dry, almost papery.

Mitch wasn't wild about screen passes. He considered them cheap college tricks, easy to execute, easy to stop. But he wasn't wild about tattling, either. "They really believe in this scheme," he said, neither a statement nor a question.

"Gives our receivers a chance to make some plays. They've

got the speed."

"Sure they do."

Mr. Goldman cleared his throat: a man used to winning arguments. Mitch recognized the assurance because he was the same type among players, the veteran who got the last word. There was a structure, and people organized themselves to maintain it. But an owner trumped a player any day. That was also part of the structure. It was in the org charts, right there in plain English, in the words they used for themselves every day. You played for him; he owned you.

"I think," Mr. Goldman said, "that everyone in this organization just wants to do his part to win." His face had a philosophical cast, like this was a truth he'd come to recently, after many hours of rigorous meditation. His tall spread collar was pulled close around his throat, which contributed both to his monkish demeanor and to his appearance of having something to hide. Was it possible it was just his neck?

He turned to Mitch and gave him a direct order. "'About time you and I had a meal together, don't you think?"

He'd phrased it as a question, but Mitch hadn't been a fool for some time. "Yes, sir, it is." His water break was up. He had plays to call in the next defensive set.

"How's tomorrow night for you and Lori?"

"She'd love to," Mitch said. "Absolutely."

Mitch lived on a nice street, each house with its own private drive, so you almost didn't realize you were on a street. Mitch's had ten acres and a three-car garage, and it wasn't even the biggest. Those belonged to the guys with real money: Goldman money, the kind you couldn't make on salary. Not that he'd seen them all. Every one of them was out there for the privacy, for the unspoken understanding that I will not ring your doorbell and you will not ring mine. He knew they wanted to; in New England, they did. But these guys, in this neighborhood, they had class. He'd seen them in their understated BMWs, their feminine haircuts. One guy, had to be at least sixty years old, jogged every morning at dawn. As the sun rose later, he rose later; when it jumped back, he did, too. He wore a wristwatch that tracked his strides per minute, and he would glance at it every now and then as Mitch drove past him into the city, an early riser himself. He often saluted Mitch in the rearview mirror, the mildest of acknowledgments. When it got cold, as it suddenly had that Friday, he wore an Eagles skullcap—just, Mitch liked to think, so he would see.

In the locker room there was every kind of feeling about the temperature, in the twenties for the first time that year.

"Oh no," Moore was saying. He was from Florida, and he was old like Mitch. "Oh, hell no."

"Are you kidding?" Griggs cried. "I can finally wear my worsted three-piece!"

"Your worst what?" D asked.

Griggs flicked his chin at D's camera, tugged the collar of his workout shirt. "My Italian wool, son. The *finest*."

"You sure you're not talking about your coverage?" Moore said.

"We gotta get Delly to do something with that," D said. "A Worsted Three-Piece for Force."

"Now just a minute." Moore again, always enforcing hierarchies. "Wilk's already got him working on a call for Alyssa. Force is gonna have to wait his turn."

"Tell the fans about your wardrobe," Mitch said to Griggs, feeling the charitable effects of his morning Naproxen.

"Suddenly I got a co-host!" D said. "Tell the fans."

"Aight, look." Griggs snapped into character. "As a rule, wide receivers get all the attention for fashion. But the Paris of this locker room is right here in the two-deep zone, number 24."

Kohler poked his crew cut into the frame. "I'll be naked in approximately five minutes. After that, I'll be wearing clothes."

"Worsted wool is finer and more durable than your everyday Walmart wool," Griggs continued, unfazed. "Not unlike yours truly."

"I'm a big guy," Kohler responded. "Walmart is the place for me."

"Tell me the last time you bought a suit at Walmart," D demanded.

"Well let's see..." Kohler's voice trailed off as he flicked through his fingers, performing an attempt to recall. "It had to be...never. What's wursted wool? Do you eat it with mustard?"

"Only in New England," Mitch said.

"I'm telling you," Kohler said, delighted to have come full circle on camera. "It's a whole geographical concept."

When Mitch turned around, Eddie Hatchett was behind him, waving a DVD. "As promised," he told Mitch, ruining his festive mood. "No hurry."

Because of the short week, and the cold, and the scent of playoffs, Friday practice was all business. No position group contests for better seats on the next day's train, no standing around any longer than anyone had to. Mitch inhaled the stinging air, clapped his hands coming out of the huddle. Sunday was supposed to get up past fifty, and that was fine, that was preferable. But part of him was hoping it wouldn't. In winter, hits sounded like hammers on steel, that was something he'd learned in New England, and he liked that, that the music he made just kept getting better the longer the season went on.

You never tackled in practice, but you did collide, and today Mitch couldn't help it, he had to plank a guy. Rookie on the practice squad, thought he could make an old man miss.

"Thanks for the love," the kid said, popping up in his Stormtrooper helmet.

"Just teaching you how to run," Mitch said. He still wore the old-school headgear, the kind they issued when he joined the league. He was proud of it, considered it a symbol of his wisdom. No helmet could save your head from a concussion if your head didn't know what to do.

After practice he and D popped into the D-line meeting room, looking for candy. They were animals, the D-line, they hid their Dum Dums and Jolly Ranchers in a garbage bin crusted with melted sugar. D dug around until he found a box of Junior Mints and a Werther's Original for old man Mitch. There was also a Twinkie rubber-banded with a hand-written note: *Do not eat me I belong to #79*. Moore. Mitch pocketed that one, too.

His phone was glowing with a new message at his locker. *Can mom and grandma come?* Alyssa had asked.

He waited until he was showered and walking to his car. *Sure*, he thumbed back. So much for one-on-one time.

Tyler and Kaylie were fighting when he got home. They were in some kind of phase now where they fought all the time, over food, over controllers, over who was where and who was what, his stubby fingers jabbing her neck, her princess foot crushing his toes. "Tell it to your father," Lori told him the minute he walked in. "I'm done." She was upstairs before he could refuse. No need to tell her he'd be seeing Caryn the next day.

He looked at his kids, six and five, a puddle of orange juice between them. "It's Friday!" he said. "Shouldn't you be happy?"

"She's always telling me what to do," Tyler whined.

"You spill something, you clean it up," Kaylie said. "That's just a rule."

Mitch tended to defend his only son, especially when the girls got after him for being a slob. He was a boy; boys were messy. But there was something too pitiful in Tyler's face. He was letting this get to him—a little orange juice on the floor?

"Paper towels," Mitch told him, swatting his head. "Get control of yourself."

"But I didn't do it!"

"Yes, he did," Kaylie insisted.

"You calling your sister a liar?" Mitch asked Tyler. "And you." He pointed at Kaylie. "Nobody likes a know-it-all."

Now they both protested, telling their separate, shouted narratives, and Mitch wouldn't have it, grabbing them, one, two, by their young, slow, tender arms and pulling them side by side. "If you give Grandma trouble tonight, you'll have trouble from me."

Kaylie returned a blank, submissive stare, but Tyler's eyes grew slick as hot oil, shimmering with rebellion. "I hate you," he said. "And I hate Grandma, too!"

He was spanked for this, of course, and hauled off to his room with orders to stay in there until he was ready to apologize.

Mitch was worried for a minute when his mom arrived and Tyler still hadn't emerged. Cindy was missing her poker night for this. But then Lori, in jewels and makeup, escorted Tyler, his face splattered red with psychological pressure, into the front room where Mitch stood with Cindy, and Tyler recited, to Mitch's feet, words generic and practiced enough to pass muster, and Cindy gave a little nod, and everything was forgotten. After that Tyler acted shy, like he was going on a date with Cindy, and Cindy, who was actually Tyler's favorite family member, had him peaceably in front of the TV with Kaylie by the time Mitch and Lori walked out the door.

"I mean I don't really care," Lori said in the car. "God help me, I'm a good soldier, always will be. I'm just surprised he was so last-minute. Aren't men like Greg Goldman usually booked solid?"

"I don't know."

"Do you think something's wrong?"

"What could be wrong?"

She laughed nervously. "Maybe he's going to make you an offer you can't refuse."

Now Mitch was laughing because what other choice did he have? Hatchett was making him tapes of younger guys; Goldman was cornering him for social engagements. In six seasons in Philadelphia, he'd eaten with the owner twice, and never just the two of them with their wives. He was picturing it now as an organized hit. Janie Goldman would lead Lori away by the elbow, on the pretense of showing her something on the grounds. Mr. Goldman would turn his hidden neck to Mitch and ask him an enigmatic question. Soon enough Mitch's brains would be all over the banquette, his eyes open like he'd never seen it coming. Lori would be spared, but she'd have to break the news to the kids, who would never forgive her for surviving.

He couldn't have those kids hate their mother. If Mr. Goldman started talking funny, he'd make some excuse and go home.

The restaurant was one of those out-of-the-way places on a farm that people drove to for miles just to eat food that came from right there exactly. It was a whole operation: valet parking, orchard tours, craft center during the day for kids. The perfect place for a hit.

Lori clung to Mitch's arm as they made their way up the lantern-lit path. He knew it was only because she was wearing stilettos, but it heightened the drama nonetheless.

He couldn't say he was relieved when he saw Dave Brewer, O-line, and Derrick Jennings, wideout, standing with their wives at the bar, but he was curious as to why they'd chosen this place, too, and why they were double dating. He looked at Natalie Brewer and Korenna Jennings, both wearing diamond jewelry, the similarities ending there. Then he looked at his teammates. These were two of the three most senior men after him, the third being Moore, the Twinkie eater and eternal child, who was only now walking through the doors, his five-foot fiancée Lisa hanging on his arm like a subway handrail.

Then, from the bowels of the restaurant came Mr. Goldman. "Everyone's here!" he said, and Mitch finally understood they were all attending this dinner together.

"You didn't tell me you were coming," he whispered to Moore as they made their way to the private dining room, where Janie Goldman was waiting to receive them. This wasn't her house, but she owned the place all the same. "Please," she said, indicating where everyone should sit. Her hair was cut short, like a man's.

Moore shrugged. "You didn't either."

The offense made sense; he didn't really interact with the offense. But Mitch and Moore talked every day. They held their ties down and performed what felt like decorum as they assisted their women with the high-backed chairs.

"This is good," Mr. Goldman said, once everyone was seated: five couples, no coaches, no Hatchett, nor anyone else from the front office. Just an intimate little dinner of ten. Everyone looked expectantly at the host, his tie knotted fat as a purse.

"My veterans," he said, unlooping his napkin and placing it in his lap, which seemed to be a signal to the rest of them. He spoke with possessive pride, and they couldn't help but beam. They understood, and their wives did, too, what a special thing it was to make a rich man happy.

"I'm sure you're all wondering, 'Why the hell did this guy invite me to dinner?'" He smiled, and they all laughed, disarmed by his honest *hell*.

Moore laughed the loudest. "I was like, is this some kind of forced retirement party?"

"Shh," Lisa said, instinctively, as though speaking it could make it true.

"He's just saying what we're all thinking," Mitch said.

Goldman made his face convey respect as servers brought out bowls of yellow soup the same shade as Tyler's spilled juice. Then, slowly, he began to explain. "We've got a new commissioner this year," he told them. "The league is evolving. Meanwhile, you guys are really turning it around on the field."

Everyone smiled, pleased with the praise.

"So I wanted to bring you guys in, get us all together and talk. Think of it as a show of appreciation, and a little focus group at the same time."

"Focus group?" Brewer repeated.

"What's working, what we could be doing better. Where are we now, where should we be next year. No one knows this stuff better than you guys."

There followed a period of clinking and slurping. Finally, when it was clear that Goldman was done speaking, and it was up to them to respond, they began to offer tentative platitudes, the same ones they'd been drilled on when they first entered the league. *We have to pull together. Every man does his job. I'm grateful for the opportunity. I just try to come in every day and play my game.*

"Aw, come on," Goldman said, conspiratorially. He seemed poised on the verge of a wink. "Not that stuff. We taught you that stuff. I mean your own observations."

It felt very much like a trick. The owner asking them to think for themselves? But when Mitch looked deep into Goldman's face, he found no trace of malice. It might've been there, once, when he was young and ravenous and amassing wealth, but along with the age lines that had also once been there, it had since been cleansed away. He was a beneficent magnate now, interested, adept at drawing men out. He didn't have to be, he could've been a tyrant, so why not give the man what he wanted? It was obvious from the way he regarded them that football players were his favorite people on the planet. And anyway, he was picking up the tab.

While Mitch sat thinking, Jennings had begun to speak, murmuring, like a voice from another room. "You know," he said, "where I come from, there wasn't a lot of opportunities for kids like me." He wore Timberlands, even now, with his suit, and unlike D and Griggs and Moore, he didn't hang out with white guys. In the locker room, he played cards with his small crew of receivers and backs, and if you didn't know better, you might mistake his seriousness for sullenness, because he rarely made eye contact, even with his friends. Actually, Mitch thought, he was shy.

"But I was lucky," he continued. "I was blessed by God. I had people around me saying if you work hard, I mean really hard, you might just get to use those hands and feet. I was lucky. I had friends that died. But I got the chance to work hard, and it paid off. That might not be an original story, but it's mine."

It was the most Mitch had ever heard Jennings say. They were all Christians here, he realized. Except excess-loving Moore, already done with his soup. And even he'd been raised in the Church.

"You have talent, too," Goldman said, generously, as though he'd been the one to give it to him.

"Yeah, but it can't just be about talent. If it was, it'd be a whole different league. I know the guys who'd be in it."

"Of course, absolutely, it's about hard work," Goldman said, emphatically, to dispel any dangerous confusion.

Mitch's mind floated to Jason Booker, the only other Monacan Warrior to play both sides of the ball with him. He could've gone to college on his talent. Instead he went to Iraq, twice. And not because he didn't work hard.

"What we want to do," Goldman was saying, "what Eddie Hatchett does every day, is cultivate the widest possible pool of talent. And that takes hard work, too. A tremendous amount."

Did Mitch flinch at the mention of Hatchett's name? He hoped not.

"I'll tell you what I love about football," Dave Brewer said. They were on to the main course by now; they'd grown used to the room, the chairs, the company, everything necessary to finally get real.

"I love that men can come together and lift each other up," Brewer said. "And it's not just about winning. It's about quality. It's about doing something really, really well." He looked at his wife.

"And hitting people," she said.

The men roared. Unused silverware rattled on the table.

"It's true!" Natalie Brewer said, her round face reddening

happily. "It's not even a secret. Y'all love hitting people. You say it all the time."

"That's also about quality," Dave said.

"Quality hit," Mitch agreed, thinking suddenly of his dad, who was obsessed with the concept of quality, and who owed him a call. Or maybe it was Mitch who owed Joe a call. It was hard to keep track of that stuff in-season.

Goldman sat back in his chair. He looked comfortable, even vigorous in his lumpy, unathletic body. "Hits feel good, don't they?"

"Not good," Mitch corrected. "They feel *great*." He didn't mind pulling rank in the moment. This was something he knew about. It was something Goldman did not.

On reflex, Goldman licked his lips. "What's a great hit feel like?" he asked, his appetite piqued.

The players looked at each other.

"Come on, you know I know, generally." There was that monkishness again, that deliberate slowness in his voice that somehow commanded respect. "I watch you thump your chests every week. But I want to know how *you* see it. Paint me a picture."

"Go on," Moore said.

Mitch shrugged. "It feels…" He closed his eyes, tried to visualize himself in that blinding moment, when you can't even see the guy you're hitting, but you know you've messed him up. "It feels like the most power you're ever going to have on this Earth."

"Yeah," Goldman said softly. Then, more emphatically, "*Yeah*. See, that's what I'm talking about. I've been attending these conferences. Leading minds from around the world talking about science, psychology, creativity—every subject you can imagine. And it's an important thing, that feeling of power. Comes up again and again. By accident, practically. Except it's no accident. Same thing happens over and over and pretty soon it's not an accident, right?"

"It's a pattern," Jennings murmured.

Goldman's eyes darkened, turned genius. "That's right. A pattern." He looked at his wife. "People want to feel powerful. They also want to feel safe. They want to feel loved. But they want to feel powerful.

"I ask myself, why do I care if the team wins? To be perfectly honest with you, I make money if the team is popular. The team wins, sure, that helps with popularity. But it's not the only factor. So why bother with winning? Why care?"

He looked at them. He seemed to want an actual answer.

"Because you don't care about money?" Korenna Jennings asked.

He laughed and the rest of the table fell in line. "Oh, bless you, sweetheart," he told her. "Are you that good? I'm not. No one's *that* good. But in a sense, of course, you're right. Because it's about more than money. It's about the city. It's about giving people something to believe in. That's true for the fans, and it's true for you guys, too."

"Like D's doing," Moore said. This time Mitch definitely flinched.

Goldman perked up. "What's that?"

"D—" Moore said, carefully, darting his eyes from Mitch to Goldman then back to his empty plate. "D'Antonio Mars? He's starting a little thing for the guys. Making videos of us in the locker room, just being ourselves."

"Yes." Goldman nodded himself into comprehension. "That's exactly right." He sat back in his chair. "You know, we are lucky in football, because we love it. Most people never get to do what they love. They might not even get a whiff of it. But I think every man here would play for free if I asked him to. If only politicians felt that way. If only teachers did. But they do get paid, and so do you and I. Which means we all lose a little something. It's not corrupted, necessarily, but it's a little less pure, right?

"You mentioned D'Antonio, and it's a funny thing, because I'm actually something of a filmmaker myself. I get it from my dad. He was a serious man, with rules for everything, which is how he got to be so successful. We were afraid of him, mostly. He would come home after we'd spent the whole afternoon arguing with our mother, trying to see what we could get away with, you know, my brother and my sister and I. And we would think we really had her nailed on something, some point of hypocrisy, like how come we have to go to college when she never did, that kind of thing. And she was always very calm about it. She'd look at us and say, 'We'll see what your father has to say about that.' And sure enough, all he really had to do was show up and we'd think, 'Never mind, okay, she's right.'

"But he had a soft side behind that authority. He loved movies, and when Eastman came out with the eight millimeter, he was first in line. This is before I was even born. We have a film of him leaving the synagogue with my mother on their wedding day. Someone else took that. There's also footage he took of me coming home from the hospital. You might say my entire life has been lived on film. In three-to-four-and-a-half minute pieces.

"Anyway, I got interested when I was a kid. I had to petition my dad to let me use the camera, and he would say, 'Write me a proposal,' which is a pretty good test for a kid to see how bad he wants something. Just about every film I ever made I had to summarize first and explain what I would do. He would review the application and then grant me film and license to use the camera for a stated period. But I wanted it, so I did it. I don't think I ever had an application turned down.

"I would make these little adventures. Hero stories, really. I would stage the whole scene in advance, get everything set up, and then make my brother or mother hold the camera while I performed. I always had to be the hero. Wasn't going to be my little brother. No way. I remember one film, the one I'm most proud of. I still have it. I was obsessed with space. Kennedy had said we were going to land a man on the moon and we were going to do it within ten years. My imagination was just on fire with this idea. Are you kidding me—the moon? That tiny dot?

"So one day in winter, I'm in my backyard. The grass is dead, no wind, and there's this feeling of total desolation, everything all flat and gray and small. But it gets me thinking: this is what the moon is like all the time, and how disappointing is *that* going to be? And suddenly I just have to make a movie. It can't wait. It can't get held up in the approvals process. Is my dad going to kill me? Probably. But I don't have time to worry about that. I have to work while the mood is right. So I just take the camera and get going on my moon story, which is going to be about the first man on the moon—me—and the civilization he builds against all odds.

"After that a few weeks go by, and somehow, I've forgotten about the film. Did I give it to my dad and apologize for breaching our protocol? Did I just leave it for him to find without owning up to what I'd done? I couldn't tell you. All I remember is being at school one day when the teacher wheels out the film projector and tells us she has a surprise for us. She dims the lights, and a feeling of destiny ripples through me. It had always been my favorite moment in a classroom: the lights dim and we all kind of settle into ourselves. Finally, we are not being watched. Finally, we can watch something interesting. So I have that usual feeling, but I also have an unusual one. I sense, the way we sometimes do, that *this is actually all about me.* It's my turn. I'm sure you all know what I'm talking about. It's such a powerful feeling that it's almost as though you've raced ahead of your body. That's the only way I can think to describe it. Because I knew, a moment or two before it began, that we were going to be watching my film. My film about the moon."

"It was like that at the draft!" Moore interjected. "I knew they was calling my name before they called it."

"The film runs," Goldman continued, unaffected, almost without pause. "And I hardly know what to think. It still seems good to me. It's basically what I envisioned: boy conquers moon, builds a world. But as the projector clicks, I become aware that there are so many different ways this moment could go, so many different meanings it could have. Am I being punished? Am I being celebrated? The teacher is smiling, but why? Is she happy because she's getting to teach me a lesson? Is she happy because I've done something good? The other kids' faces are hard to read, too, and I realize in those few minutes while the film is still rolling, that they're all waiting for things to be explained to them. Why this, why now. I realize, too, that I have the power to explain it."

Mitch looked at his teammates, whose expressions were open and tolerant. They were willing to be persuaded, waiting for explanations in the exact same way. The conversation had reached this point because Moore had mentioned D's videos, and Goldman was a man who liked to hold court, and yet, at the same time, it seemed possible that God had arranged the entire dinner because there was something specific he wanted Mitch to hear.

"So when it's over," Goldman said, "I stand up. The lights are still down, but as they're coming up, I take a bow. And what does the class do? They start applauding. The teacher may have led them, but it doesn't matter. What matters is that key moment when I decided I was proud of what I'd done, not embarrassed or scared. It was the pride that made it good. It made it something worth applauding, and it made me think, *I should do this again.*

"I went home that day still feeling strong, and that evening, when my dad asked me his standard question about what I had learned in school, finally, for the first time in my life, I had a really good answer. I told him what had happened, carefully, without in any way implying that he might've had something to do with it. He listened as I described the moment I decided to take my bow, and I still remember the look on his face. It was neutral, which, from my dad, was the closest thing to approval. So I got out the film reel that the teacher had given to me to keep, and I asked him if we could watch it. Again a neutral response: 'If you want.' I still remember those three short words. *If. You. Want.* Well, I did want him to see it, I always wanted him to see my films, so I loaded it up. We watched it, and he said, 'You're a filmmaker, son.' Again, that neutrality. But it was the greatest gift you can get in this country. Because neutrality, you see, means possibility. It means it's up to you to make your own destiny. He was telling me, in his way, that I had no barriers. I no longer had to follow his rules.

"My next film was even better. I worked harder on it. My skills improved. I didn't know it at the time, but that's what faith is." He ran his fingers up the scale of an invisible piano. "It's directing a certain kind of energy toward something good. For me, then, it was films. For us, now, it's football. We want this team to be a place where people can give everything they have. Where they can surprise themselves by being even better than they thought they could be. And I don't just mean you guys: the starters, the veterans. I don't just mean the rookies we're looking to see improve. I mean every last man. I mean special teams. I mean the practice squad. I mean the guys we cut next year in training camp. I want them to leave saying, 'Damn, I was a pro. I *made* it. For four weeks of my life, I flew.'"

Mitch felt himself getting hyped and sentimental all at once. He took Lori's hand under the table. Goldman sat back in his chair, his eyes almost levitating with his football faith. You could see how he'd gotten to where he was, why it was that he'd been so successful. He understood that it was a team, and that guys had to sacrifice for that, but he also wanted the best for every single person, the absolute maximum each man could do. Football sometimes felt a little wrong, tragic in ways Mitch could not explain, but when he listened to someone like Goldman, how could he argue? How could anyone? The team glorified the individual. The individual glorified the team. They were all doing what they loved and getting paid.

On the drive home Mitch let the dark Jersey fields slip by. It had been one of those electrifying nights, Goldman's words still sizzling in his brain. Neutrality was not a concept he'd thought about much before, but he could see now how it applied to his life. We are born, we are met with indifference, we go positive or negative, that's it. He'd gone positive, the only way forward. He didn't dwell on the things he couldn't change. He saw in the long stretches of countryside a good world, and he was one of the good guys in it.

He did not watch Eddie's scouting tape that night. It stayed where it was in an old Powerade bag in the backseat of his car.

"How was the boss man?" D asked, settling into his seat across the aisle from Mitch. "He fire you up?" The team had chartered an Amtrak for the game, and the train was big enough, and the men were big enough, that everyone got to have his own row.

"You know what," Mitch said. "He did."

Griggs scooted by in his worsted three-piece, which looked to Mitch like regular winter wool. More notable were the diamond earrings and purple pocket square. He and D weren't much for dressing sharp. Give them fleeces that fit, clean pairs of jeans. Look appropriate, look like you've been there before.

D pulled out his bright blue Nano, a tiny electronic ocean in his palm. He'd never liked the owner, never liked any owner. "Long as he's got you going towards victory."

"Sure, definitely, victory."

"I thought you said he fired you up!"

"But I don't just go towards victory. I go towards excellence."

Mitch said this almost without thinking, as though this were an old mantra of his, and now that the words were out of his mouth, echoing in the neutral air, he realized it basically was.

D narrowed his eyes, peering through the crack in Mitch's logic. "Excellence is code for victory, though."

Mitch conceded that it was. "In this game."

"In any game! Find me one that's just about going through the motions. Find me one people don't want to win!"

He thought about other games. Individual sports like tennis and golf. Long-distance running. Every one of those guys wanted to win. But maybe you could invent a sport that didn't care. He tried to imagine it. Something challenging everyone could work toward together, like climbing a mountain. Well, sure, like climbing a mountain, people did that already. He banished the thought in embarrassment, wiped his hand across his forehead, which was sweating, and reached up to adjust his nozzle for air.

"What about you?" he asked, needing to take his attention off himself. He could always get nice and quiet for a while if he could just get D to talk. "Don't you go towards anything else? Like action, maybe? Or anger?"

"Well, shit," D laughed, because they both knew his anger was historical. "Who doesn't? But anger's another step on the road to victory. Gotta have anger."

"Wouldn't be hitting people for a living if we didn't."

"No, sir, we would not."

Mitch felt a twitch in his leg, the good kind. The kind that whispered, Tomorrow.

"Offense might not have anger," D said. "Or not as much. They have to be sane, right? Calmly carry out the plan." He nodded his head toward the next car up, where the quarterbacks and running backs were sitting. "Rainman's too busy training dogs anyway. Oh! But you know what? If someone hurt one of those girls? That's when he'd lose his shit. I can one hundred percent guarantee it. So no matter what, calm as you are, offensive-minded as you are, you got to have that violent streak."

"Hey, Wilk!" The right guard Hock was passing through, gathering intelligence. "Who's the best ping-pong player?"

"Kohler."

"Thank you!" Kohler cried, pointing from other the end of the car.

"That manatee?" Hock laughed.

"Just—thank you, Wilk," Kohler said. He flapped his bloated arms. "See, Hock? You're the best driver; I'm the best ping-pong player. Rainey's the best at corn hole. Small's the best singer. Quinn's the best dancer. Everyone's got their thing and it's important to recognize that."

D leaned like a minister over his seat. "Go back to your pen, Kohler," he shouted, as Steef squeezed by with an ice pack. "This is a car for serious men."

"Who's the strongest?" Moore called, receiving the ice pack.

Kohler grew diplomatic. "That's a tough one."

"He don't even *need* to say best dresser," Griggs boasted. "We all know that."

"What am I the best at?" Mitch asked, unable to resist.

"Let's see," Kohler said, everyone in the car looking his way. "You're the grandfather, so you're probably the best at wisdom, right?"

Groans throughout. D whistled through his teeth. "Man! What does that even mean? The best at *wisdom?* That's not a skill. It's a general quality. 'This my friend Wilk: he's the best at excellence.'"

"Wisest, then?" Kohler giggled. "Most wise? What's the correct term? I'm actually asking. I was terrible at grammar."

"You definitely were, because you *are*," D retorted. "'Kohler *is* terrible at grammar.' *Was* and *is*, son. Present tense."

"Maybe I should revise that. Maybe you're the best at wisdom."

"Now, see, that's just what you don't understand," D said. "Grammar's practical shit. Like paying bills, but with words. Wisdom has a more spiritual component, and Wilk is definitely the wisest. I'm just better educated than you."

"D-Mars: best educated!"

D shook his head. "Oh, we got work to do."

"I'm not wise," Mitch said. He looked out the window at the

dim 30th Street platform. They still hadn't left the station. "Not in the past, present, or future."

"Come on." D's voice was dismissive in a way that was meant to pump him up.

"I'm not." He spoke from his power center, that self inside him that never went dark. "I'm just the all-time greatest."

Alyssa, Caryn, and Cindy were already seated by the time he arrived at Osteria, a clean little white tablecloth place with mirrors on the walls. This was life now, apparently: a ropes course from one fancy restaurant to another.

"The Princess in her palace," he said, taking the seat next to his daughter.

Alyssa gripped her menu board, hardly looking at him. Her nails were the color of a wet frog. "I could've said the Inn at Little Washington. It's like $500 a person there."

"Alyssa," Caryn said.

Mitch bent down, tried to hook his daughter's eye with his, but she was dug in. "Well," he said. "Lucky for me I have a meeting at nine." He looked at his mother, who was sitting across from him. "How was the train?"

"Fine." She beamed next to Caryn as though Alyssa's behavior were completely normal. Maybe it was. Or maybe she was just so happy to see her favorite daughter-in-law, she didn't care what else was going on. Cindy and Lori got along fine—there was no one who didn't get along with Lori—but Cindy and Caryn were the real comrades.

"You know y'all can call each other," he told them. "You don't need me for your excuse."

"We do," Cindy said, and a whole life he had no part in whistled through his mind. If that was the case, he wanted to ask, then why are you crashing my dinner with my kid? She could've come down the next day with the rest of them.

He looked at Caryn. She was wearing earrings that hung like fireworks. Her lips were lit with their own red light. The whole effort was perilously attractive. He felt grateful that most of their recent conversations, about the yoga studio she was preparing to open in Bethesda, and in which he was the chief investor, had happened over the phone.

He turned to Alyssa, who was still practically living inside her menu. "So what looks good?"

She shrugged.

"Come on, you were the one who wanted to eat here. What're you getting?"

She shrugged again. Such strange resistance, and no help from Caryn and Cindy, who were already locked in deep conversation. Maybe he needed them after all.

"How about the pork chop?"

Alyssa made a face.

"Are you kidding? It sounds delicious. Mashed potatoes and brussels sprouts?"

She twisted her mouth and shook her head.

"Well, if you don't want it, I'll get it. I'm sold."

A few more agonizing moments passed before she finally released him from her nervous hold. "You don't want the octopus salad?" she asked.

"I'm thinking pork chop."

"But—" She took a breath as though she had something terrible to confess. "I could have a bite."

"Then why don't you get it?"

"Because I'm getting the tomato tart."

"Get them both."

"But I want the fennel ravioli for my main."

Mitch looked at Caryn, who had snapped out of her conference with Cindy. "We have to talk."

"Can I help it if she's developing a palate?" Caryn asked.

"You sure you don't want the pork chop?" he asked Alyssa. Then to Caryn, "You sure she's mine?"

The menu talk went on for several more minutes, eventually involving the waiter, a skinny guy who sensed in their indecision a chance to sell more plates, and even though Mitch was hungry, and even though the waiter was maybe a bit too proud of himself, the delay was fine by him. There was normalcy when people argued about food, because everyone was just saying what they wanted. No stonewalling. No games.

When at last their negotiations concluded, and everything Alyssa mentioned had been ordered, they turned their attention to the next day's game.

"We beat 'em once, we can beat 'em again," Mitch said.

"You know I love watching you play," Cindy said, "but I still get scared. I just can't stop myself from imagining worst case scenarios."

"Mom, how many years have I been doing this?"

"I know," she said. "I know."

"And how many times have we had this conversation?"

"Tell him about your time," Caryn urged Alyssa.

"Huh?" Mitch asked. The repetition of his own word confused him.

"Whatever," Alyssa said. "I beat the boys. Nothing new."

At his perplexity she rolled her eyes and poured forth a torrent of words. "Remember last year I was the fastest, even faster than the boys? Everyone said they'd catch up, and they did, but now boys and girls run separately so you have to actually challenge someone if you want to know you can beat them."

"She beat them all," Caryn said.

"All but one."

"And that one is headed for the Olympics."

"That's just what they *say*," Alyssa said, exasperated. "Mostly the boys are slow."

"So you're gonna be a runner, huh?" Mitch asked.

Alyssa shrugged, her new favorite word. "I don't know. I have to pee." She went off to the bathroom with a shoulder hunch that only drew more attention to her womanly back. She seemed to have grown four inches in four weeks.

"It's been a rough year," Caryn explained. "The high school boys are circling, but she's not interested."

Mitch was shocked. "Good." Caryn leaned back to allow the waiter to set various special utensils. "What are they doing?" Mitch asked, when the waiter had gone away. "The high school boys."

"Nothing, really. It's still more about the girls. But she's so honest, you know? When she's upset, it's all right there on her face, practically begging people to hurt her. And they will. The queen bees will. I keep telling her she's gotta act a little. Not show them all her cards."

"*She's* the queen, though, right?"

"You would think." Caryn pursed her lips, trying to decide something. "She's in a cautious phase," she finally declared.

"That's normal," Cindy said. "Girls are mean. I hear these things from Alyssa and I'm just so grateful you were a boy."

He had been looking forward to this meal all week, but now that he was inside it, a prissy dining room with carefully set utensils, surrounded by fennel and the lives of girls, he found himself missing men. Where were the jokes? Caryn had been funny once. Where was that? Where was the meanness that wasn't mean—that was love? His felt his leg twitch and it wasn't the good kind of twitch, it was the kind that wanted the hell out. He looked at his leg. He loved his leg. He couldn't retire this year. Not possible. Give him a boss, give him hell, give him a mandatory meeting every morning of his life if only there were men in it.

He felt better once the food came. The pork chop slid down his throat; it calmed the self inside him. He looked at his girls: his. Well, Caryn was technically a was, not an is, but he felt the past belonged to him, too, especially when it continued to look so good, and to require his financial assistance. He ate his tiramisu while she updated him on the studio, which was scheduled to open in January. She was telling him about flooring and HVAC, and the wall system for bolsters and props.

He couldn't tell which was better, Caryn's confidence or the dessert. The tiramisu was rich, but Caryn was practically her former self. When she talked about spending his money, she reminded him of the entitled Glamour Shot he'd fallen for, the Virginia girl who'd seen the best in him. She'd gotten sidelined for a long stretch there in Miami and New England, first by football, then by motherhood, and truth be told, by his own ego, too, and that was unfortunate for them both, because Caryn did not thrive on the bench. By the time it was over, he was sick of dealing with the pleading, selfish thing that she'd become, both because he hated those qualities, and because he'd known it was half his fault. It had to be. She'd finished college in no time once they'd agreed upon a divorce.

"I'm really proud of you," he told her. He felt himself gathering for an apology, as he often had in recent years. "I never gave you enough credit."

The suggestion of their past seemed to embarrass her. "Water under the bridge, Mitch," she said.

"Well, I'm serious about this yoga thing as a gift," he said. "You don't have to pay me back."

He figured thanking him would have embarrassed her, too, and that was fine. When you gave something, you had to give it freely. But she smiled, and that made him feel good. Then she made him picture his breath circling around his heart, expanding across the width of his chest, rising to the top of his skull. "Try it before the game," she said. "This time actually do it."

After paying the bill, he stood outside with Alyssa while the women used the bathroom one more time. "You know Mom has a new boyfriend," Alyssa told him.

"No," he said, "I didn't."

"Well, she does."

She hugged herself in her coat while he opened his to let the air in. DC was so much cleaner than Philadelphia, like a hotel even out on the street. "This one treat her right?"

"She's not crying or anything. They go on real dates." She ducked into his armpit for warmth.

"What does 'real' mean?" He hated himself for asking follow-up questions, but Alyssa's evasiveness practically demanded it. Thirteen years old and already running the meeting. He gave her a little squeeze.

"Like plays and really nice dinners. He drives a BMW."

"Don't tell me: the Inn at Little Washington."

She grinned up from the cave of him, caught. "Yeah, they went last week."

"It's all coming together."

"He's old, though."

"I'm old."

Alyssa gave him a look like he'd just tried to take the fall for a crime she'd personally witnessed another guy commit. "He's, like, fifty," she said. "Don't say that."

He mimed zipping his lips. "Whatever you want," he said, and she huddled closer to suggest there were all sorts of things she still wanted, and he squeezed back to tell her, just ask.

He was back on time. He'd paid his share of bullshit fines: roughing the passer, low block, cell phone on the sidelines, unauthorized socks. Lately, he was squeaky clean, at least according to the official record. When you got old and distinguished, they wanted you to be a role model, which meant they touted you at least as often as they looked the other way. But it worked, that little lie of theirs. In his dotage, named one of the league's best men, he found himself following the rules.

Nine o'clock, and the defense was all crammed into their designated meeting room at the hotel. It was so much worse than the brand new classrooms of the facility, not enough chairs for everyone, and those who got them had to smush, shoulder to shoulder, thigh to thigh. A crinkled team banner more suited to a sports bar was strung along one wall. Tomorrow's locker room would also be worse, one of the many mind games of playing on the road. Not that Mitch's mind could be messed with at this point. He'd been a pro too long.

He stood in the back with Moore, who was still icing his elbow, while Delahanty reviewed every weakness in Washington's game. They were legion, most of them real and exploitable, some invented just to fire the guys up. The lead running back was indecisive. The second-year QB was soft. Number 8, remember him? We own him. He was built to take the sack.

"We're blitzing all day because they're vulnerable," Delahanty said. "Even when they know it's coming."

That was the best, getting guys who knew you were coming and still couldn't get out of your way. He would miss that. He would miss hitting guys in general, especially the smaller ones he could carry a few yards before they crashed. Like sweet little brides across the threshold. Welcome to your new home.

They reviewed everything they'd learned that week, everything they already knew. Football was a perfectionist's game, which meant it was a game of repetition. Look back. Plan ahead. Review, review, review.

He avoided Hatchett in the dining area, focusing his attention instead on the whirling blade that was making his strawberry banana smoothie. He watched the creamy liquid rise to fill the blender, pictured his breath rising to fill his lungs. Caryn would be proud, this was just what she was trying to get him to do. He headed to the elevator with half the D-line, Moore and Burgess and Smith, all three of them carrying gummy worms from the bottomless candy bowl and overflowing bags of buttered popcorn.

Back in his room, he called Lori, said I love you and yeah and me too and good night, then gave himself over to Pay-Per-View. He was a faithful man, but pre-game porn was practically on the official itinerary, in that conspicuously lengthy space between *9:45pm Snack* and *11:00pm Curfew and Bed Check*. What else was a man alone in a hotel full of men supposed to do? You didn't just want to rub one off, though, no way. Some guys did, but not Mitch. For him, there was power in the tease. It fueled him, filled him with a little extra juice, a little more aggression. He lay there, getting hard, sound on mute, as a bomb-chested brunette with maraschino red nails worked her tongue all over a faceless dick. He clenched his fists, thought of Caryn, clenched his ass. He felt everything necessary inside him tighten.

By the time the strength coaches knocked, he was breathing normally again, having bottled most of what he needed, his dick flying reverently at half-mast. "Yep!" he shouted, hearing the noise of protocol move on, already knocking at the next door down.

D called a few minutes later.

"MoJo's ready," he reported, meaning their star running back Morris Johnson, whom he'd spotted getting his usual stretch while everyone else was getting dessert. They rarely talked to MoJo, or any of the offense, but they watched them, D especially. He wanted to know what sort of conditions the defense would be playing under. "He was in his legs already," he told Mitch. "I'm telling you. I never seen the man so calm."

"Kid's got what it takes."

"He's a specimen," D said appreciatively.

"We just gotta do our part."

D took a breath and Mitch could almost hear his brain shifting into its philosophical register. Rhetorical questions were coming, metaphors for understanding victory, the subject of every conversation with D. It was one conversation, in a way the only one they'd ever had. Their positions had changed over the years—once it was Mitch who insisted D take everything seriously, now D drove the motivational car—and maybe that was why one conversation had sustained them so long, because no matter what, they were always in motion. No position was ever really fixed.

Still, D's angle this time took Mitch by surprise.

"I know we don't have you much longer, man—" He must've felt Mitch's resistance, because he stopped there, but without stopping. Instead he cleared his throat and restarted. "I just keep thinking how special it would be to do it for you this season. I think the guys could really rally around that."

Certain kinds of straight talk, Mitch liked. From certain people, at certain times. This wasn't any of those.

"Huh," he said, which seemed safe.

"You feel me, brother? Guys need motivation."

"Not me, though," Mitch muttered.

"Huh?"

"That's not me. Let 'em find that somewhere else." He wasn't sure these were the right words, exactly. But his tone, at least, was unmistakable.

"Aw, don't be like that," D said.

Now he was angry. His head was off the pillow. He could feel D's complacent body resting effortlessly through the phone. "You think because you're in your prime right now, it's never gonna happen to you?"

"Course not. I *know* it is—"

"I can still *do* this. I feel it. So I'd rather not think about anything else. Okay?"

They breathed together. Mitch looked at the heavy hotel curtains, drawn against the next morning's light.

"Just seems like we could do something to prepare ourselves." D's voice had grown less aggressive, but that didn't mean he was going to relent. "This job chews people up. Spits 'em out. Guys live for this job, and then it's 'Bye. See ya. Go live for something else.' But, like, imagine a different reality, where we prepare ourselves for that other thing, same as we prepare ourselves to play. Celebrate it, even. Turn it positive."

Why they were even talking about this, he had no idea. Had he asked D to bring it up? He had a semi for freak's sake and he was trying to make it count. He felt his back, which had been nagging him all week, but had he complained? He hadn't. He pushed it down into the mattress, felt the pillow top push back. He had power still inside him. He had stored up those extra years. He had no need right now for conversation.

"You prepare yourself however you want," he told him. "Let me take care of me."

Sunday morning appeared before him. He'd been asleep, now he was awake, a new day popping open like a fresh box of cereal. He got to his feet, ignoring every twinge, thinking only of breakfast. He threw open the curtains, threw on his sweats. In the dining area he walked from Smart Start to sausage, in the ballroom he walked through the defense one last time. The carpet below his feet was ivy-patterned; above him were three crystal chandeliers. The mood was light, guys joking like dads at a barbeque. And why shouldn't they joke? They played a game. Other people worked for a living; they were the jerk-offs who got to play.

Go Dad!!! Alyssa texted. *You've always been my hero. I'll be cheering for you so hard.*

She killed him sometimes with her love. It was more than he probably deserved. *Bet I won't be able to hear you*, he texted back. Maybe he'd get to spend more time with her once all this was through.

Ten push ups says you will

God bless you baby girl. Love you

Love you MORE

The most

You win

Then he texted Hardy. *Game day! What u up 2?*

And Hardy immediately replied, *Dont choke*

He took a hot frothy shower back in his room, a luxury each

week to rinse alone, then boarded the last bus to the stadium. In the locker room, at every spot, all the uniforms were set, like a hall of mirrors of uniforms, each jersey carefully stretched over its pads, shoes and helmets on each shelf, pants on hooks. Griggs, who was superstitious, was already out of his worsted wool, taped and head-phoned, and in his warm-ups, sitting with his chair facing in. He listened to the same handful of pregame songs in the same order each week, no skips, no substitutions. One of them, Mitch knew, was "Fuck tha Police." He wouldn't look at anyone until they were dressed, and then, just like that, at a moment known only to Griggs, he'd join the room. When he did that, you could see it in his eyes, he was with you, he was present.

Mitch wasn't that fussy, but he was old enough that he had to take care. A little time in the tub, another rinse, a little time stretching on the field on his own, the best he felt all week. His breath was good, too, almost mentholated. It filled his ribcage and puffed out toward the seats where a few early-access fans had already taken up their positions. Back inside he taped his foot and fingers, a promise ring between each knuckle. I will love, cherish, and honor you, I will help you get your best grip, I will pop you back when you get gnarly, forever and ever, 'til death do us part.

And then he was dressed and on the field again, stretching in line with the team, running show-off drills for the sideline crowds, and then he was in the training room, getting numbed and juiced, and then he was in the shower room, asking God for strength, and now they were all together in the locker room and everyone was absolutely dialed in. Kowalczyk gave his pregame sermon, which always invoked a war. This time it was World War II, a favorite. Something about a foxhole and a desert. His eyes grew bluer in their righteousness; his belly seemed to sit up straight. He was a quiet guy normally, he saved it all for Sundays when he had to send them to battle. And this Sunday was 6-6, division rival, on the road. This was the most excited he'd been all season. He spat half the words; he couldn't help it. Then he wiped his forehead and asked Mitch to lead the prayer.

He hadn't told him he was going to do this, which was uncharacteristic. The man famous for driving to work the most efficient possible route, who probably didn't even need a secretary he kept such meticulous files, who designed playbooks like they were lives—Kowalczyk didn't believe in surprises. Not when he could plan things in advance. Mitch looked at D, who was holding his camera. His fault. Had to be. He'd said something he had no right to say.

Though D talked nonstop in the pregame locker room, firing himself up, tapping guys on the hat, keeping the headphone-filled room safe from silence, Mitch hadn't really engaged with him since they'd hung up the night before. He'd been lost in his own routine that morning, his own body, his own mind. But now he remembered his anger. It had kept him awake longer than he'd wanted, staring first at the muted sex on his TV and then at the dull wall behind it.

Everyone knew you didn't talk about the end. Think about it in the off-season, maybe. Plan for it, sure. But you kept that discussion on the inside, and you did not let other people in. You had to keep moving forward, protect yourself from their doubts. Only D would have the nerve to try to get in Mitch's head and call that a good thing, something helpful. *A job*, he'd called what they did. Well, Mitch used to call it that, too. But it wasn't a job. It was heaven on earth.

"We are here because we are blessed," Mitch said, looking

at Jennings, who was already nodding along. "We were given talent, and we were given the opportunity to use it. A lot of people sacrificed for us along the way. We give thanks to them: the mothers and grandmothers and fathers and grandfathers who fed us and coached us and drove us so we could make it in this game and in this league. We wouldn't be here if not for them."

He looked at a few guys in turn—Kohler, Moore, Griggs. He looked at Hatchett, in the back, who was no more exempt then the rest of them, and the look he gave him said exactly that. Then he looked at D, who wasn't even being sneaky about it: he was recording the entire thing. He wasn't smiling like usual, though. His mouth was closed behind his little silver camera, and he might as well have been shaking his head, that was how obvious it was he disagreed. Well, fuck him, Mitch thought in D's own foul language. Fuck his philosophy. In your prime you can imagine whatever you fucking want, and still imagine you're going for the win. Mitch knew better. He knew football better and he knew God better, and he knew he couldn't out-think them.

Mitch looked straight into the lens. "We talk all the time about 'doing our job,'" he said. "We talk about 'getting to work.' But that's bull, and we know it. What your parents did was work. What your grandparents did was work. This is not work. This is a game. We give thanks that God lets us *play*. We give thanks that God lets us win. So let's get out there today and play. Let's win this game, amen."

"AMEN!"

"Eagles on three."

"Onetwothree EAGLES."

They pounded out into the tunnel, awaiting their entrance cue.

"You know it is though," D shouted through his facemask in the dark. "It is work." The tunnel clanged with all their bodies, D's growing more furious as the start of the game approached. But Mitch's brain was so charged with his own faith that even D's disagreement sounded to him like further proof. He felt his faith *in* him, which was how he knew it was right, like a straight line from the ground to God and on that line was his own honest body.

"Post *that* video!" Mitch told him. "'Bout time people heard the truth!"

In the first half, Rainey threw well, and MoJo ran as if through walls.

"That's it, Offense!" D shouted. "That's the way to do your job!"

"Post it!" Mitch shouted at D every time they took the field.

"Let's get to *work*!" D snarled back.

It was almost as if the Skins weren't there. They'd taken a hostile field and made it neutral and then they'd made it theirs. Mitch flew to every threat at his best, which in the moment was the only level he remembered. He heard D talking at guys the way he did, weakening them with his words. "Post it!" Mitch shouted, killing another drive. His inside self had logged off. He was all action now, all body. He lost his vision once on a hellacious hit, and it was exhilarating because it stopped the guy and it brought D's voice to his ear. "You're a beast, Wilk! You hear me? You're a motherfucking BEAST!"

But then the second half began, and the poles began to shift. The offense kept stalling, standing themselves up on date after date.

"Bunch of gay ponies out there," Moore muttered.

"Limp dicks," Griggs agreed, disgusted.

"Do your job, 44!" D screamed. "Offense! DO YOUR JOB!" He had on his insane look, his look of historic anger, with his eyes standing up as straight and tall as he could make them.

One plan fell through, then another. Rainey snapped his chinstrap in frustration. Coaches ran back and forth on the sideline, their clipboards like sandbags to hold off a flood. When, after Rainey finally completed a good pass that was brainlessly ruled incomplete, Kowalczyk threw the red challenge flag, his face nearly matching its hue. Some coaches tossed the flag the way gamblers tossed their bets. A formality, because they had to. But Kowalczyk threw it like a gauntlet, always ready for the duel.

It turned around after that. They won the challenge. They kicked a field goal. And on the final drive, they stopped the Skins, Mitch and D combining for a coffin-nailing sack. Mitch had the front and the primary leverage, and D arrived a split-second later at the back. When they went to the ground together, Mitch could feel D's wrath through 8's pads.

"Post it!" Mitch crowed the moment he got to his feet. He couldn't help it. He had the power like he'd always had it, and "Post it!" had become the thing he said. They brought their helmets together, and Mitch saw D's eyes up close. "You're an alien," Mitch told him, making peace. "You're out of this world, 53."

In the locker room, he was happy to talk to the media. More than happy: overjoyed. They found him on his way back from the showers, his fawning suitors, presenting him with their bouquet of microphones and tape recorders. He let his towel drop; he let himself be himself. Amanda from the *Inquirer* was there, working hard to keep her eyes up. But she was cool, Amanda, she got him, they were friends.

"Forgive me, y'all," he said, looking especially at her. "I just have to. I feel too *good* to wear clothes!"

They laughed collectively, and there wasn't any time to decipher if the laughter was genuine or nervous or good-natured or what, because the questions started coming immediately.

He was ready. He was born ready. He was certainly ready right now.

"Oh, that sack was a thing of beauty," he said.

He felt so real. He was in his body and it was a good thing. And here in this crappy visitor's locker room, cramped with tape and skin and stink, his own good thing met that other good thing that was the entire world.

"The Martian's my main man," he said. "We love coming together like that."

And, "It's a team game and that's what a team game's about."

And, "It's a beautiful game. Football's a perfect game. Honestly, we're just trying to match it. We're just trying to play at football's level."

And, "*Man*, this feels good!"

And, "I think about the past few weeks and all I can say is, I thank God. I thank God because we are blessed."

And, "We get to play a game for a living. We get to play a game and win."

Dressed, he found his women and children in the chilly family waiting area, where he gave his warm body to each of theirs, felt each of theirs in return. Tim was there, too, with Tracy. Caryn, naturally, was not.

"That last hit sounded like a tree falling!" Cindy panted.

"Pretty good, wasn't it?" he boasted, looking at Tim, who

clasped his hand, then clapped his back, then coughed in lieu of praise.

"Almost ready to compete with my boys," he said. Typical Tim. He looked thin. He coached varsity now in Nelson County.

"Come on," Mitch said, looking at Lori, who was bent sidewise to hold Maddie's hand. "Right?" Her smile was studiously neutral. She had to drive back with Cindy and the kids tonight, and she'd have to collect him when he was done. And when would that be, his self inside him asked God, when would that be?

"Right?" he asked the walls.

"Jeez, Dad, you were good," Alyssa capitulated.

He swung around. "Yeah?"

"*Yeah*," she swung back, flailed her arm at him. "You said you'd win and you won."

"That's belief," Mitch said to Kaylie and Tyler, who nodded to indicate they understood. He and his renewed faith were growing more attached by the minute.

"They ran the ball on you," Tim said. He was chewing his lip as he said it, as though the top half of him wanted the bottom half to shut up. "Give 'em a fifth quarter and they would've won."

Mitch laughed. Had to respect that: Tim had his own beliefs. "That's why there are only four, though! Gotta do it in four!"

On the train, Mitch tossed Moore his Twinkie. "Good one, Moore!"

"You motherfucker," Moore said, but he tore off the wrapper and ate it.

"I gotta be honest, man," Kohler was saying to D's camera. "I was worried there for a bit in the fourth. Like, 'Oh no, are we gonna blow it? Am I gonna get cut?'" I actually thought that in the huddle, 'What would happen if I got cut?'" He scratched his billowy chin. "I'd have more time to work on my other interests, that's for sure. Maybe I'd take up the violin—because that's what people say, right?" He looked for agreement. "You fail at something, try the violin. I've never given two shits about the violin. Why is it always the violin? I'm serious!"

D wasn't even trying to contain his laughter. He didn't care, he was so happy with himself and his teammates. Mitch collapsed into his seat, grateful for the camera and Kohler's foolishness. He'd been floating since the clock ran out, but was starting to feel his age again. His burning elbows. His lower back.

"That's honesty, man," D was saying. "Oh, shit, that is honesty." He held the camera on Mitch. "Honesty is one thing. Truth's another. Not to be confused. Don't you agree, Wilk?"

D smiled, so Mitch smiled, and now, again, he saw D's anger. It still lived in him, high and hard in his shoulders, low and tight in his hips. Of course it did. No matter how happy he was, no matter how much he laughed.

"Wilk," D prompted him. "Wilk."

Anger was useful, that was why, even when you had the love of God. Mitch used his own to punch down the scared self inside him. To punch down physical pain. When he got home he'd use it to punch Hatchett's tape in the trash. He'd watch it first, let those desperate young bodies rile him up a bit more, and when Hatchett circled back, he'd tell him he wanted a title and a guaranteed salary before he gave him any advice. Deputy Director of Player Engagement sounded about right. But that was for later. That was exactly what he had to punch down now. I got three more weeks and a post-season, he told his inside self. Don't tell anyone, not even me.

"Wilk!" D said again.

"All right, man," Mitch said. "You win! Honesty."

All this arguing over something that was fated, that was visible to anyone who looked. He looked at the camera and at D behind it, and he gathered himself to say something neutral that was also the thing they both already knew. His body. His time. It was the thing that made him angrier than anything else in this world, the thing he fought God on the hardest, and even so, he couldn't help it, he started laughing. He let the laughter close his eyes and he let the camera disappear, and for D he did the best he could.

"For real, though, man, no more words. Game over. We won. I'm done."

10. ALYSSA, 2012

Four days after Alyssa dropped out of college, she snagged a job at the preppy clothing retailer that made sumptuous cashmere in a rainbow of farmer's market hues. Persimmon. Morel. Sage. A friend's brother had worked there the previous summer and he put her in touch with the manager, Mark, a hair-geller in herringbone who sat her down in the chairs normally reserved for customers trying on loafers to ask her a few questions about herself.

"That's a good school," he said, looking at the resume she'd printed on a piece of her mother's linen paper. Light from the mall-front window filtered through the sheet, illuminating a watermark that vaguely resembled an anchor, tilted rakishly on its end. Or maybe it was a crab. Either way, it was the sort of thing this company might embroider on a pair of green chino pants, so she figured she was set.

"I'm taking some time off," she told him, hoping he wouldn't need a reason.

He leaned forward in the chair and looked her over, resting his eyes an extra moment on her thigh. "When can you start?"

Like most people with an ounce of talent, Mark had recognized hers right away. Alyssa was good-looking. Actually, she was better than good-looking. She was lucky. Her frame was symmetrical and not prone to weight gain, and she didn't even have to wash her face much; it was naturally, almost ghostly, clean.

Her mom was lucky in all the same ways, which made sense, genetically. But she'd been at it much longer than Alyssa and she had some tips for getting by. "You've just gotta fake it," she'd told Alyssa when she was little, and didn't want to go to school. "If you can make your teachers like you, pretty soon they'll let you do whatever you want." What Caryn had wanted was respect. Alyssa was born when her parents were still in college, and even though her mom had finished her degree first, her dad, the football pro, was the one who shaped the world. He had a whole new family by the time Alyssa was in second grade. Fortunately, his new wife, Lori, was all about charity. She wore a diamond cross around her neck, and anytime she went to a beach, which was often, she liked to march giant hearts into the sand. Alyssa still got presents from her dad all the time, and Caryn's life had actually gotten better. She'd moved them to DC, the city she'd always admired most. She had her own yoga studio. She had an even richer husband in Steve. So faking it, in Alyssa's mind, wasn't the worst way to live.

She faked it straight to college. The one she chose had a decent track team and a romantic bell tower on a fleecy green quad. She'd always enjoyed gazing at natural fields of color. Who was she? Who would she become? The historic quad, which had seen it all before, seemed to have the answers. Plus, the school was in Pennsylvania, where her dad had played, and several guidebooks had singled it out as having particularly good-looking students.

"How 'bout that?" Mitch said when she visited him that summer in Florida, where he did something involving beachfront condos and wore sunglasses even indoors. He'd retired several years earlier, after his fourteenth season, which she knew because she'd turned fourteen a few months later, and she'd always been the same age as his career. He was harder to keep track of now, out in the real world. He still had his trademark ponytail, and he was back to being clean-shaven, but his body was more massive than ever, reminding her, somehow, of a beached sea mammal. She worried about him, she knew he missed playing football, but he always managed to reassure her. In Florida, they looked at the ocean together feeling cheerful, and he told her the college she'd chosen sounded like the perfect school for her.

Only it wasn't. Nonsense assailed her from the start. Having to run the steps of every section of the stadium the first week of track practice. Having to write a business plan for a cookie company that would somehow empower the poor. Having her crotch prodded by shaggy prep school boys in moldering fraternity house rooms. Maybe it was just the girls who were supposed to be good-looking. "Your dad's going to kill me," her hook-ups always bragged, breathing festivals of bacteria in her face. "I can't believe you're real!" As though it even mattered what was real. She once found a girl crying in the laundry room because she couldn't remember a poem. She kept wiping her nose on a pair of cotton panties she'd just taken out of the dryer. Alyssa was disgusted. Wasn't she planning on wearing those later?

"Everyone tries so hard," she told her mother when she called to tell her she was quitting track. "It's kind of screwed up."

Caryn didn't tell her to fake it anymore. "Well, sweetheart," she said instead, "not everyone's as talented as you."

After a cleansing summer on the beach, Alyssa was ready to give sophomore year a chance—but the boys only got more barbaric, the girls needier and more competitive. How could Obama be losing ground to Romney while her classmates only cared about themselves? Freshmen elections were the final straw. Obnoxious signs polluted the quad with bubble letters and glitter, ruining the one lovely view on campus. "You Need A Nina!" "Badr Does It Better." They depressed her because they were as shallow and desperate as the signs from the year before. In fact, the year before, she was pretty sure that Heather Did It Better. Heather, who'd won, and aside from tritely blowing half the lacrosse team, hadn't done a thing.

In this context, it was a comfort to return to her childhood mall, which went out of its way to celebrate nature, but never tried to be something it was not. The drive encircling it was packed with stately, peeling-bark trees, the corridors inside with oversized potted ferns, and each wing was lined with all the familiar storefronts selling just what they purported to sell. Her first day on the job she was assigned to the women's section, where she was expected to hang things that had come unhung, fold things that had come unfolded, and use her cylindrical skeleton key to let customers into dressing rooms when they asked. She quickly found she loved folding the most. Each garment had a code: a series of faint creases she could follow to reshape it for display. The careless customers, those who left the trousers and cardigans they didn't want turned inside out on the dressing room floor, were in some ways her favorite, because they provided her the opportunity to restore order to a rumpled pile of cotton flannel, stretch merino, and heavy worsted serge. She would extend the hidden shelf on the cash wrap and set to work with a fresh stack of tissue paper, humming along with the airy store mix, and if, when she was done, the floor was quiet, she'd flip through the catalogs in the wooden tray, their fibrous fields and textured beaches quelling any feelings of uselessness that lingered from her time at school.

Her co-workers were exceptionally friendly. Nearly every shift brought new ones, both full-time personal shoppers and area college kids working for the discount, all of them eager to introduce themselves and welcome her aboard. Alyssa smiled and said hello, but sooner or later she knew they'd grow distant. People usually did. She'd seen it in their eyes a million times: something draining, like water from a bath grown cold.

"People are gonna hate you, kiddo," Mitch had told her as a child. "That's why you have to rise above." He was fond of pep talks. They'd kept him from losing it when things got tough: nagging injuries, blood-thirsty reporters, watching New England win Super Bowls without him. She used to love the way they fueled her, though she'd never been churchy like her dad. He was less churchy now, and paradoxically, also less helpful. "You can't let the haters distract you," he'd told her when she first complained about college. "You just gotta keep on being you." Often, in the last few months, she'd wanted to ask him who that was.

"I'm worried about you," her mother told her over dinner, after she'd been working at the mall a few weeks.

When she'd moved back home, Caryn had made Bellinis and presented her with a spa treatment to help her through her "sophomore slump." Her mom was smart, but sometimes she acted dumb.

Now she seemed out of ideas. She pressed her fingers to her temples, giving herself a momentary facelift. "Steve is right when he says it's important to plan." She nodded toward her husband who sat complacently, leaving the parenting to her. He'd already raised his kids. They were in their thirties, with respectable careers selected straight from the drop-down menu: finance (hedge fund), law (environmental). "People who don't have plans in this country just end up waiting around. Look at your Aunt Ellen."

Alyssa took a long, bored drink of water. Ellen was her mother's older sister, the humorless one who wore shoulder pads and fancied herself a poet and sent so many email forwards about computer viruses, she seemed infected herself. It was impossible to imagine becoming Ellen.

"Look," Alyssa said. "I have a job. I make $10 an hour and I love it. Haven't you always told me to do what I love?" She smirked. She couldn't help it. It was exhilarating to be so unambitious, to declare without shame that she loved folding clothes in a big, clean store that sold items not everyone could afford.

"Your father and I are just hoping you'll finish your degree. It was a lot harder for us to do it later. Him especially."

"Dad knows my reasons. He's cool." Which wasn't strictly true. She'd written him about her plan to take time off, somewhat disingenuously suggesting she might volunteer for Obama, but he'd never responded. A week later he passed through town on his way back from a meeting in Philadelphia, and it was clear he hadn't read the email. She knew he was skeptical of the President. And she knew he was busy planning a new business venture on the Jersey Shore, and that he'd recently thrown out his back. She knew all that. But still.

"Shoot," he said, when she reminded him. He smacked his forehead harder than necessary, his belly quivering from the reverberations of the blow. "Well, you know what I think, sweetheart." He squinted at her through his sunglasses. Lately he'd been squinting at everything, as though the entire visible world were getting farther and farther away. "Never let anyone tell you you can't do something."

But the folding, oh the folding—the turning in of sleeves, the flipping up of shirttails, the straightening of collars and cuffs. What did she care so long as she could fold? She thought of her dad's locker room, how they used to hang everyone's jerseys and pants every week, and she thought he'd appreciate what she was doing. There were no simulations here, just real pieces of fabric made right, several of which she bought so that she could wear them to work herself.

"Oh, you got the Bonnie," someone said one afternoon. She looked up from her pile of liquidy tees to see a ponytailed blonde standing before her, twirling a skeleton key.

Alyssa examined the sleeve of her olive green cardigan and shrugged. "It just seemed practical with the discount."

The ponytail nodded emphatically. "It's the best cardi. Michelle Obama has, like, five. Actually, I do, too. I'm Tory."

"Alyssa."

"Alyssa, nice. Good for you for not shortening it. Sometimes I want to shake my parents for nicknaming me before I was old enough to decide. I mean, seriously, Victoria is so much better than Tory."

"You can always change it."

Tory shook her head. "I tried once; didn't work. I never knew when people were talking to me. They'd literally be shouting my name in my face before I got it. Even my parents don't call me Victoria. Not even when they're mad."

Alyssa smiled, not knowing what to say next. She knew the mindlessness that so irritated her in other people was partially her fault. There was something limp and available about her that invited nonsense. Before people lost interest in her, they talked her ear off about awesome cardigans and disappointing nicknames. Some of them—and this Tory person was clearly one—even insisted on being her friend.

"So," Tory said, "I've seen you on a couple shifts now. You in school?"

Alyssa nodded and told her where. "But I'm taking a little time off."

"How come?"

"Uh, the classes were a joke and the people were creeps?"

She was still staring, so Alyssa elaborated. "It just wasn't for me. Not my thing."

Tory was wearing her college ring, like someone recruited to talk Alyssa into line. It was engraved with her class year—she was a senior—and dozens of other indecipherable abbreviations. In the center bezel, a red gem flashed like a radio tower light as she folded her arms across her chest. "You sound just like a guy," she finally said. "Don't you know girls don't drop out of college? Not unless they're bulimic or something. You're not bulimic, are you?"

It was Tory who told her pretty much everything about the store. How two employees had been fired for having sex in the shoe room, the only stock room you could lock from the inside, and they were so stupid they hadn't even thought to do that. How the company was unveiling a line of buttery leather handbags to compete with the high-end designer brands. How they were operating under a Loss Prevention Plan because they ranked among the top stores in the country for missing merchandise, especially men's accessories and shirts. Alyssa knew some of the idiots who'd taken those shirts—just layered them on, clipped the censors, and walked right out of the store. They were friends of her friend's brother, the one who'd gotten her the job.

And it was Tory, too, who told her about the big visit, ambushing her one Saturday the moment she stepped through the employee entrance.

"Are you working Tuesday?" she whispered, as Alyssa punched in. "If not, you have to switch."

"Okay, well I am. Why?"

Tory dragged her by the wrist into the empty manager's office. "Teddy Bailey's coming."

"Who's that?"

"Jesus, Alyssa, *who's that?* You really don't give a shit, do you?" Tory tapped her finger on the desk, as though pointing to treasure on a map. "Teddy Bailey is the CEO. He's coming to check on our progress, maybe give us an ass-whipping."

Just when she thought things were going well. "God, why would I want to be here for that?"

"Because he's supposed to be *inspiring*. He was just on the cover of *Bloomberg*. Do I have to spell it out for you? He's famous and influential." As nitwitty as Tory could be, her information was usually correct and her instincts rarely off. She wasn't the best dresser, sticking to a reliable cycle of black slacks and Bonnies, but she'd seen even before Alyssa that the new peacock pencil skirt would sell out in a matter of days. She'd been right about the election, too: Obama and the shifting demographics.

"Well, maybe I'll read the article," Alyssa said. "After all, I have time."

There were pictures to accompany the *Bloomberg* profile, which celebrated Teddy Bailey's intuition and communication style. He'd turned some little apparel store into a household name, then did it again for somebody else. Until she read the profile, Alyssa had no idea how much money her company made in a year, let alone how many other little companies it had in its back pocket. On each page, Teddy Bailey's lithe, bald form leaned against white columns and country mailboxes, smug in jeans and sweater vests. Yet Alyssa thought he looked rather kind, not the way she expected a CEO to look. He was fifty-four, born in New Hampshire to an auto mechanic and a nurse. He'd dropped out of college, too.

Driving into work the next morning, she looked at the cloud cover pinned like lambswool above the trees and thought about Teddy Bailey. She wondered what he'd think of her store. He, who now spent half his life on private jets, but probably used to save up his allowance to buy the one pair of shoes that every kid had to have. Would he notice that the bath store across the way gave off a fruit-cakey aroma that often clashed with the subtle blend of furniture polish and grass that her managers strove to maintain in their space? Would he care that their biggest competitor was located in a different wing?

On Monday night, she stood in front of her closet, mentally assembling an appropriate outfit for meeting the CEO. She assumed it ought to feature company merchandise, but not too heavily, lest she appear incapable of thinking for herself. She was wiggling into her skinniest non-company jeans when her mother knocked on her open door.

"Going somewhere?" Caryn asked. Her eyes were heavily charcoaled and she was dressed in yoga spandex under a fluttering woven wrap. It was the way she always looked, tiny biceps slightly bulging under tight sleeves, hair shining in triumphant disarray, a faint promise of fun in her eye.

"Just figuring things out for the morning," Alyssa said. "It's stupid."

"Thinking ahead. That's my girl."

Alyssa knew kids who were traumatized by their parents' charisma, but she took hers as an article of faith. Her father could lift enormous pieces of furniture and had frequently leveled quarterbacks on TV. Her mother was like a flowering plant, filling rooms with the scent of vacation. It didn't even matter that they weren't a couple. If anything they were more powerful apart, ruling their separate but vast domains, each of them a pledge that everything would work out okay.

Tuesday morning came and Alyssa showed up at the store ten minutes early, dressed in the skinny jeans, a jangly necklace, and a navy blazer over a white t-shirt that highlighted the twin peaks of her clavicles. To her relief, Teddy Bailey had not yet arrived. She deposited her handbag in the locker room and ran the lint roller down each arm before making her way to the floor.

The store opened to a surprisingly busy weekday morning. Alyssa was constantly in the dressing room, holding hangers and knocking gently on doors, since women startled easily when they weren't wearing tops. The armloads she brought out to fold contained nearly every piece in the store, giving her the sensation that anything was possible. She worked through lunch, barely pausing to chat with Tory when she arrived for the closing shift. There was pizza in the back, and she eventually ate a slice, then washed her hands in a full head of lather so that no trace of grease would threaten the clothes.

As her shift neared its end, at five o'clock, Teddy Bailey still hadn't arrived.

"Do you need me to stay?" she asked Mark, who never failed to give her extra hours when she wanted them. Over his shoulder, Tory twirled her key and winked.

The morning tide of housewives had given way to the usual evening trickle of after-school teenagers, who touched everything but bought nothing, and after-work professionals, who bought all kinds of things full-price. Closing was now minutes away and the registers were silent, the clerks murmuring languidly to one another as they rested their elbows on the cash wrap. Alyssa was crossing the floor with a pair of Mary Janes for a customer to try with the Cluny lace cocktail dress when she saw a man holding a feather-crystal brooch over the jewelry bin, as though trying to estimate its weight in his hand. Dressed in jeans and a navy v-neck sweater, he had the unhurried manner of someone who'd shown up early for an appointment. His shorn, balding head glistened under the display lights, and he would've been completely unremarkable had he not been Teddy Bailey.

Alyssa delivered the Mary Janes to her customer and returned to the floor, where the CEO continued to linger unnoticed. She wondered if he'd somehow been there all along, patiently examining each garment and accessory while a woman friend tested the customer service in the midst of an unexpectedly busy day. It was possible he'd sent the morning housewives there himself; possible, too, that one of them was *his* wife, or even somehow Teddy himself. She didn't think he had whole days to waste checking up on single stores, and yet what else did a CEO do? The magazine profile made it seem as though he spent a lot of time following his intuition, which after all was just what she had done, and it had led her here.

She approached the jewelry bin and began re-sorting the goods on the side opposite him, not daring to make eye contact. She had realigned all the sunglasses and nearly disentangled a wad of hair elastics before she worked up the courage to speak.

"Are you finding everything all right?" she finally asked, with a slight inflection, so that he would understand that even though she was asking what she asked every customer, she knew exactly who he was.

His pale blue eyes met hers as he seemed to consider her question on several levels. Something in his cheek twitched, betraying a possible lunacy, and she wondered for a moment if he was not Teddy Bailey after all. Then he smiled. "I think I'm fine for now," he said, fully articulating each word. "But thank you."

Bewildered, she continued with her lines. "Well, let me know if you need anything. We'll be closing in fifteen minutes." He nodded and returned his attention to the brooch, like a counterfeiter trying to commit it to memory.

Alyssa wandered back to the dressing room only to find that her customer had left without purchasing anything. The cocktail dress was suspended lightly on its hanger, the Mary Janes tucked together on the floor. She returned the items to their places and set about reordering a rack of cropped corduroys. She wasn't sure what she had been expecting, but it certainly wasn't this: this placid ordinariness, this feeling of not even having been tested. At the very least, when a powerful man paid a visit, it shouldn't feel like just another day.

The store music had stopped, and the last customer was escorted out, heels clicking, the double wooden doors double-locked in her wake, and just when Alyssa thought that this was all the day was going to be, Mark's voice came over the staticky loudspeaker. "Attention, everyone," he said, echoing across the ghost town of halted commerce. "I'd like to ask all staff to join me at the women's cash wrap for a special meeting."

Teddy Bailey stood before the counter like a professor, having solved whatever he'd been puzzling over in the brooch, which was no longer in his hand. Mark and the woman who'd asked for the Mary Janes stood beside him, and a few other managers had materialized as well. Alyssa gathered round with the rest of the staff, joining Tory by a display table covered with the casually draped mohair sleeves and rhinestone buttons of the must-have cardigan for fall. Who must have it? Alyssa wondered, fingering a hem. She preferred the summer's more basic iteration.

Mark introduced Teddy, and if anyone hadn't known who he was or how long he'd been observing them, they didn't let on, smiling as though meetings like this were some kind of regular reward.

"What do you think went well today?" Teddy asked neutrally. "Don't be shy."

"We had a lot of foot traffic," one of the college boys finally said. "More than usual for a weekday."

"Is that right?" Teddy mused.

Hearing this, the college boy seemed to lose an inch of confidence—not much, but a perceptible amount. "I mean," he said, sliding his hands into his pockets, "I think so."

Teddy nodded. "All right. What else?"

People volunteered anecdotes. Someone had sold a customer the jacket she came in for, and the matching skirt as well. Someone else had tracked down a size from another store and was having it shipped directly to the customer's home. They'd sold a few gift cards. A favorite regular had come in for a belt.

"And what do you think didn't go so well?"

Everyone looked at their feet. Alyssa tried to think of a weakness that was actually a strength, and failing that, tried to look like she was thinking at all.

"I have to tell you," Teddy said, "this is one our most under-performing stores, so I imagine a lot of things didn't go so well today. You know about the missing merchandise, of course. That's getting better. But you're still not keeping pace with other stores of this size. Why do you think that is?"

The ass-kicking was coming after all. Alyssa tried to catch Tory's eye, but she was staring intently at a display niche bearing a purple leather handbag.

"Could be a question of store placement," the college boy said. Evan—that was his name. He was clearly used to speaking first.

"Could be," Teddy replied. "We're looking into it. But I have to tell you, my gut says that's not it."

Alyssa was becoming aware of an ache cresting from her knees to her lower back. She had never worked twelve hours straight before, arriving at ten in the morning, still on the floor now at ten at night, and all that standing was finally beginning to test her stamina. She shifted her weight to one side, then the other, finally coming to rest against the table of mohair cardigans, cushioning her elbows on the many-layered pile.

"What do you think?" Teddy said. Mark whispered in his ear, and Teddy added, "Alyssa," and still it took her a moment to recognize that he was speaking to her.

"Well," she said, standing up straight again. "I think there are several issues."

"That's right," Teddy said. "And I think you know what they are. When we spoke earlier, you were a perfect model of customer service. Great tone. And your personal style is completely of the moment. Everyone look at Alyssa." A dozen groomed heads turned her way, their gazes even and appraising. "This is exactly how we want our sales associates to dress. So, then, from your perspective, what needs to change around here?"

No one had ever asked Alyssa such an important question before. Even the questions her college professors had posed from their faraway lecterns were clearly directed at someone else—someone who'd already obsessed over them or was looking online that very moment and would therefore have some kind of answer. Her professors knew better than to expect anything of her. But Teddy Bailey did not. Here he was, an incredibly rich man, a famous CEO who'd built his success on intuition, asking her what ought to be changed in his store. His face waited expectantly across the room, cool and bright as a refrigerator.

"For one thing," she said. "Most of us are part-time, and none of us work on commission. So I don't know how invested we are in actually making sales. And there are also issues with inventory and store layout." She grazed her hand over the pile of mohair sweaters. "These have been here over a month. No one buys them. Definitely not anyone cool."

Teddy's expression brightened further. "Why not?" he asked.

"Because they're too similar to a lot of other styles, but not nearly as versatile. Like, the Bonnie?" she pointed at Tory, who had on a pink one. "It's sexy and you could wear it every day. Michelle Obama pretty much does." She bit her lip, hoping she hadn't gone too far in calling the garment sexy.

"You know what?" he said. "You're absolutely right. I hate that sweater." Someone gasped. "I hate a few pieces every season. It's the nature of the business—some styles work, some don't. But this store should've recognized the mistake when they didn't sell and moved them out of their prime position. See how many are left?" His previously calm voice rose, almost precipitously. "You think the customer can't smell failure? Believe me, she can.

She can smell it the moment she walks in the store. It's like that one stinking stall in the food court. The frying oil, or whatever it is. It sticks to everything! It makes it all taste wrong!"

Teddy could've been a televangelist the way he ranted and flapped his arms. It was an ass-kicking all right, but she was somehow exempt. As he thundered about the cash wrap, he repeatedly singled her out for her perception and wit. Alyssa felt as though she'd been wrapped in a cashmere cloak of immunity. Other staffers were called upon to rethink their methods. The Mary Jane woman was called upon to make suggestions. And through it all Teddy kept looking her way. Alyssa could barely listen, feeling as good as the fall catalog cover girl looked, standing atop a seaside boulder in a brilliant red toggle coat while blue ocean and green sea grass vied for her attention below.

Less than two months on the job and already she was headed for better things. He shook her hand before he left and asked her to send him her resume. A few of his trusted stylists would be back to speak with her directly. She walked out to her car in the deserted garage feeling like an astronaut touching down on a brand new planet.

"Hey!" Tory's voice called out from behind her. Alyssa stopped and waited, one foot on either side of a white parking space line.

"Way to go," Tory said, as she drew nearer. "Way to throw the rest of us under the bus." Her forehead shone and she was panting a little, as though she'd been running to catch up.

Alyssa laughed and tossed her hand like it was no big deal, but Tory didn't seem in the mood to laugh. She zipped her coat as though striking a match.

"He was going to say all that anyway," Alyssa said. "Hey, I

used you as an example!"

"Everyone loves the Bonnie!" Tory said, not quite mad, not quite sarcastic. She looked tired. "Whatever. It's just a part-time job. I'm on again Friday. You?"

"I'm always on," Alyssa said, before she realized how it sounded.

Tory grinned. "Honestly, you're nuts. You should just go back to college already. How hard can it be for an NFL kid?"

Alyssa and Tory had taken plenty of breaks together, but they'd never talked about Alyssa's dad. When it came up, she just said he lived in Florida, and that she'd always lived with her mom. She looked at Tory. "Who told you that?"

"No secrets around here. Not for long. Anyway, if you're special enough for Teddy Bailey, you're probably special enough for college."

Alyssa thought about the girl with the panties in the dorm laundry room and the fraternity boys, some of whom, it was true, had forced things a little, pressing harder on her dry, unreceptive body while she let her mind turn off. But that wasn't the reason she left, not really. She always had a more general reason for doing whatever she did. She saw herself as a freshman, standing alone on the green that had been washed of color by weeks of winter and the lightless late afternoon, while everyone else— teammates, other students, professors, whoever—hurried about in pairs and trios, caressing their books, caressing their cell phones, absorbed in a game that had somehow started, and now continued, and probably would for years, without her. She saw that she'd been special once, and then she'd blacked out, and when she came to, she wasn't.

Except that now, again, she was.

~

When Alyssa got home, Caryn was in the great room, triangulated in downward dog. Alyssa flopped on the couch and watched her mother realign herself under the skylights, which hung, black and rectangular, like the eyes of a carnival mask.

"Long day!" Caryn exclaimed, once she was fully upright. "I was beginning to worry."

Her yoga mix swelled with woodwindish voices, making the room seem full of people rooting for Alyssa to win.

"The CEO came," she blurted. "He wants to see my resume."

"The *CEO?*" Caryn was instantly ecstatic. She pulled Alyssa to her feet and hugged her in the middle of the sticky purple mat. Her beautiful mother, smelling of eucalyptus and talc. She hadn't always given the best advice, but there was no one in the world who cared about her more, no one in the world more elegant.

Before Alyssa went to bed that night, she emailed her resume to Teddy Bailey.

> *Dear Mr. Bailey*, she wrote,
>
> *It was my great honor to meet and learn from you today at Democracy Mall. It was definitely the highlight of my year. You asked for my resume so I'm attaching it to this email. I look forward to speaking with you about my professional career and your theories of fashion success.*
>
> *Sincerely,*
>
> *Alyssa Wilkins*
>
> *P.S. I don't know if I should be telling you this, but I left college just like you because I didn't think the classroom could nurture my talents. Fashion is not about lectures and assigned reading. It's about knowing what makes people*

*look good and what makes them feel good about how they
look. You have to touch fabric every day to know those kinds
of things. I know I have so much to offer if you'll only give
me the chance.*

For a moment after she hit send, she regretted the line about
touching fabric. It was possible he didn't think about things
metaphorically as she did, or that he'd misconstrue it as a come-
on. But he didn't strike her as that kind of creep, and it really was
how she felt.

She checked her email first thing the next morning. There
was an alert from the college registrar and a sale announcement
from a rival retailer, plus a joke forward from a high school
friend with the subject "21 Clues You're Tanked." Nothing yet
from Teddy Bailey. She went to work and unpacked a shipment
of three dozen v-neck sweaters. For lunch she got a cup of
vegetarian minestrone, which she ate on a fern-flanked bench
by herself.

There were no emails from Teddy that night, or the next
day, or anytime that week. The next week, she helped her mom
organize a mostly vegan Thanksgiving. Caryn wouldn't shut
up about Teddy Bailey. "The CEO," she kept telling Ellen, as
though he were a new brand of organic yogurt she wanted
everyone to buy. Alyssa wore her blue Bonnie cardigan over the
new Donegal mini-dress, and tried not to feel humiliated. All
night long, she couldn't even look at Steve, who made his usual
dinner speech about gratitude. She felt genuinely grateful she
hadn't had a chance to tell her dad.

The days dragged on through Christmas, and into the New
Year, 2013. Alyssa bought a hooded parka with her discount and

every morning watched her breath disappear while she waited for the car to warm up. She went to work. She folded. She sold alpaca sweaters and gabardine trousers and calf-skin boots with buckles. She even sold a few mohair sweaters, now that they were on sale.

With time she recognized that nothing had happened—despite Obama, despite the promise in Teddy's handshake that he would take care of her, despite the energy he had directed her way. Even her mom had forgotten, back to sending her transfer applications to various colleges closer to home. She felt like a team snuffed out in the playoffs after a miraculous end-of-season run. Her dad had had seasons like that, in a way it had been the story of his life; it was certainly the story of his final season, in which he'd also suffered a herniated disc. Yet each time, after the initial disappointment, he'd told her it wasn't so bad. "I'm still going to work for the team," he'd said when he retired. "I'm still a lucky man." He didn't end up working for the team, and that, too, seemed to be a disappointment, but in the end, he said it was for the best, because real estate was a much better bet.

Designers from headquarters eventually paid a visit, and one morning when Alyssa came in all the displays had been rearranged. The jewelry case where Teddy had examined the brooch was gone, but in its place was a rack of petal-colored blouses that heralded the new season. In the center, a nylon tree plumed like an umbrella over a gathering of crop of waterproof galoshes. Alyssa stood beneath it in the quiet minutes before opening and felt almost exalted to see the branches disappear in the blazing lights above.

The cash wrap, of course, still stood, and during the slower periods of the day, she still liked to stand beside it, flipping the pages of the latest catalog, traveling with the models from a covered bridge in Vermont to a lavender field in Provence, from a Moroccan bazaar to a zesty peel of Pacific beach. These were real places she might go one day in any of her own real clothes. In the meantime, the pictures gave her comfort. They were landscapes like the finest milled cotton. She'd wear them onward into spring.

11. MITCH, 2019

In the end, Mitch came back to Monacan, where he could finally be himself. He had the right wife in Julie Matthews, and he had the house he'd always wanted, with Blue Ridge Mountain views. But Monacan turned out to be different without his mom living there, and it was even more different without Tim.

Less than a year before, Tim had been alive. More than alive, he'd been coaching, and having weekly dinners with Mitch. Then he'd shown up at Thanksgiving with a cough, and then he was dead by May. Lung cancer. It seemed unfair after the scare he'd given them the year Mitch retired: the sudden weight loss, the odd stomach pains that turned out to be nothing, just a manifestation of stress. But that, Mitch knew now, was not an escape. It was a warning. No one stays in your life forever.

He'd had to break the news to his father by phone. Joe took it with his usual mysticism, responding first with somber condolences, then with a YouTube of people hugging and crying while a British voice proclaimed death an honorable thing, because it made room in life for others. He took Joe's point but he was pretty sure Tim wouldn't have. Tim had fought the end until the end, lobbying the doctors for another round of chemo, literally gasping for his last hour of breath. Tim was only sixty-seven. He had wanted to live.

Mitch had offered to fly Joe and Tammy out for the funeral. Or even just Joe if Tammy felt she had to look after the dogs.

But Joe declined, said he couldn't leave Tammy alone with so many—they were fostering half a dozen that month, most of them crippled or old. Mitch knew his dad well enough to know he was bullshitting, but not well enough to call him on it. You could only get so far with occasional phone calls. To really know a person, you had to coexist. You had to spend at least a little time occupying the same space.

Anyway, he had his hands full as it was, being a rock for Tim's family, not to mention his mom, who took the loss especially hard. She'd had a romance with Tim long ago but he'd expected her to be over it by now, not calling him from Maryland every night to tell him she couldn't stop crying.

"Focus on helping Alyssa," he told her. "Focus on Journey." Cindy went where the babies were, and the newest baby was Alyssa's three-year-old in Bethesda, so for the first time in his entire life his mother was not just a shout away. Journey. Of course Alyssa had to pick something weird, as though a baby were a mantra and not a person.

"I'm trying," she said. "But every time I look at him, I just see you, and then I see Joe, and then I'm right back to thinking about Tim."

He could hear her gulping for air. "Jesus," Mitch said. He wasn't used to being the one to comfort her; it generally worked the other way around. But after all his years on the receiving end of her efforts, he guessed it couldn't hurt to try. "Do Journey a favor and just try to see him as him."

She sniffled, clearly piqued. "Well, aren't you the wise man all of a sudden? Parenting expert."

"Basically." He liked when she got feisty and called him on his crap. This was intimacy, even on the phone, earned in all those years they'd spent as a two-person unit, coexisting, sharing space. It was also a sign she was coming out of her funk.

"That's not funny," she said, but she was laughing. "Parenting is not a joke."

In his defense his life had never been easy. Not when he played, not even now. A part of him had always known he'd struggle after football, and not just because he'd miss being at the center of the action. Maybe his back would hurt. Or his foot. And they did hurt, both of them. But not as bad as his eyes, which fizzed all day and then refused to sleep at night. That was one consequence of playing that hadn't even crossed his mind.

His specialist called the daytime condition photophobia, which did not, he assured Mitch, actually mean that he was afraid, only that he was extremely sensitive to light. Mitch had gone all the way to Baltimore to see Dr. Heller, and though *afraid* was not a word he would ever use to describe himself, he was relieved it wasn't a brain tumor. He'd been squinting involuntarily for years, wearing sunglasses even indoors, but only in Monacan had the headaches become insane. In desperation, he'd signed away his brain to research. He thought what any rational person would think after three wives, four kids, and twentysome years of head-on collisions. He thought he was going to die.

But he wasn't. At least, not yet. Instead, he got remade. Heller fitted him with photochromic electrical stimulation goggles that gently shocked his supraorbital nerve. They were ingenious things. Combined with illicit weed, they really kept his headaches in check. And Heller's team had even better therapies in the pipeline, most excitingly a bionic stimulator, which they would actually implant inside his head. Mitch sort of liked his X-Man look—Ricky Franklin called him Cyclops and joked about avoiding his optic blasts—and he sort of liked the way certain shapes popped forward, making a 3-D movie out of life. But in the goggles, his world was always a little pink, and the straps a little too tight on his head. He looked forward to a full-color world. He looked forward to going bionic.

In the meantime, he did his best to keep busy. After the NFL, he'd finished his bachelor's online, then went back and got his MBA, and now he owned a couple of car dealerships that actually turned a profit. He spent his days walking the lots checking the stickers, then in parts checking random bins. He made sure he studied the daily operating control, and heard from his managers, and reviewed their processes, and took Ricky, whom he'd hired out of lifelong loyalty, to lunch. He took discreet hits from the vape when he needed it, and he took customers for test-drives himself. Since he was up all night anyway, he made himself useful then, too, bidding at auction while the competition slept. In his constant hustle, he was a little out of place in Monacan, where most people just sat in their plastic chairs, drinking sweet stuff from plastic cups, but it had to be that way to keep his mind off the pain. And it wasn't bad for business either.

Sundays he tried to take it easy. Go to church just to be there, play a round of golf just to walk the course. Then he'd come home to Julie, his little boss, and the house they'd custom-built for his oddities—the doorways wide, the windows affixed with heavy motorized shades, the television powered by organic light-emitting diodes specially designed to be gentle on his eyes. It was a steady place that was also a steady action, property guaranteed to appreciate, assuming he didn't let it rot.

Since Tim's passing he didn't have much stomach for football, but he had to make some exceptions. Tyler's freshman homecoming game, for one. At the end of September, he and Julie flew to Syracuse, then drove an hour to watch Tyler make a few decent D-III plays. It was good to see his son, the wide receiver, and over dinner at a Chinese restaurant, he made sure to praise his speed. He couldn't tell how much Tyler cared what he thought; the kid talked more about the party the team was hosting later that night, which featured an ice luge emblazoned with their founding father mascot. "Trust me," Julie had said. "He cares." Either way, Mitch came home the next day beat from the cramped, back-to-back connecting flights, and collapsed in his poolside recliner.

The hour was good, approaching dusk, when long shadows covered his lawn, and the sun was at an angle he could tolerate, even without his goggles. He took a hit from the vape, looking forward to the massage Julie would give him later. He felt a little bad about that sometimes. As punishment for falling in love with him, she'd had to give up her glamorous New Jersey client base, Eagles owner Greg Goldman included. She now worked lazy Virginia hours for even lazier Virginia rates, and on top of that took care of him for free. But she seemed to like it; she never complained. She'd use her best creams, her sharp elbow, and her tiny, deep-sensing hands that seemed to triple in size on his back. Then they'd lie in bed together smelling lavender until she fell asleep. Sometimes he'd watch her for a few minutes in her daily death, her body breathing, her naturally red lips puffed, her piercing blue eyes safely hidden beneath their lids. It could have bothered him how flagrantly she nodded off, but he had no resentment. He admired her for making it this long without letting life rough her up.

The secret was not having kids. Had to be. That was football for women. He'd seen the wear on his mom when he was a kid, and on Caryn and Lori, too. But Julie was thirty-five now. Wouldn't she want one soon? She swore she didn't, said she loved her freedom, said she wouldn't be able to take her time in the mornings or keep up her Taekwondo if she were always running around after kids, said her older siblings had the next generation covered, two nieces and three nephews being more than enough for her—but he didn't believe her. Every woman he'd ever known had wanted a baby, and he didn't know what he'd say when she inevitably changed her mind. He had kids already, four of them. He was almost fifty years old.

He put the vape down and heard an air horn, jolting him upright in the recliner. It sounded repeatedly, a sound of panic, and it seemed to be coming from inside his hip. He patted himself down, shifting and groping until his hand finally fell upon his phone.

Obviously his phone. He pressed the button and resumed reclining. Someone—meaning Tyler—must've switched the ringtone when he wasn't looking. As pranks went, kind of lame. D would've done something better.

That was his thought. It really was.

Which seemed so improbable a moment later when he actually looked at Hardy's text.

He lay there thinking maybe he'd gotten the order wrong. Even without weed it was sometimes hard to see things as happening in an order.

But, for sure, there it was, the text from Hardy. *Hey Man*, it said. *Did u hear?*

And then in the next bubble, *About D.*

They drove to Philadelphia for the funeral, past all the familiar horrors. Entering the city from the south was like entering

Mordor, the oil refinery belching smoke beyond the bridge, the bridge itself quaking and full of holes. He wished they were driving to Toms River, where the little murderer lived. A seventeen-year-old kid, they wouldn't even release his name. He'd grown up on the shore, had his boating license and everything. He probably loved the Giants, probably woke up that morning feeling superhuman and ready to jet ski, no idea his idiocy was about to end a great Eagle's life.

At dinner in Center City, where everything was a building instead of a tree, Mitch kept seeing D through the street-side window. But then it was always not D. It was a dark white guy, or a tall woman, or just a black guy with similar features. He felt grateful he lived in Virginia, where he knew everyone and wasn't likely to confuse them with someone that he knew was dead.

The service was held on the field at the Linc the next morning, with all the punishing extravagance of a halftime show. They'd erected a stage in the end zone and covered it with flowers like a parade float, two giant 53s made of roses doing their best to upstage the closed casket. There were too many people to clasp hands with: former coaches, former players, even Eddie Hatchett, who'd distinctly told Mitch he'd always be welcome in Philly, then met with him twice after he retired, but never offered him a job. "We miss you around here," Eddie said, same as ever. Easy for him to say; he was still GM. What was Mitch supposed to do? He looked in vain for Moore and Kohler, and the others from his team, but his eyes kept finding the current guys. Most were recent Super Bowl champs, an achievement that used to mellow guys out. Not anymore, if these kids were any gauge: brainwashed and jumpy as any college team, sweating anxiously without the weight of their headphones and cross-body duffels, young men with pimples and casual smears of facial hair, playing dress-up in their best black suits. Oh, who was he kidding—he was jealous. All he had to do was blink to see what everyone else saw: vigorous men, at the very center of life, no idea what lay ahead of them, even here, at a football funeral. They'd head straight from the service to Carolina to get ready for Sunday's game.

"There's Greg Goldman." Julie pointed at the owner in the front.

It was Goldman who'd first sent Mitch to Julie after he pulled his back in the owner's box. Possibly the most humiliating moment of his retirement, getting injured watching other guys play. He and Goldman had been working toward a friendship then; Mitch had even asked him for advice on a steakhouse venture that never quite got off the ground. But after Mitch found himself clinging to Goldman's liquid white sideboard, his spine snarling as Goldman smiled, almost paternal in his unworried compassion, they never managed to have another conversation that didn't leave Mitch feeling winded and cranky and sort of duped. Goldman was right about Julie's massages— the best in the region, right there in Jersey—but a lot of other things about him now seemed wrong.

"We can talk to him after," Mitch said. Avoiding Goldman's eye, he herded Julie into a row as a Skycam spidered overhead. People turned around, said hello. He shook their hands, pretended to know them. That was something he'd forgotten, all the people that came with football. Everywhere you went there were people. He spent so much of his time now on his own.

They waited an eternity, and while they waited he searched his messages for his most recent exchange with D. January 8, a cheerful New Year's update. It was less than a year ago, but it felt like ten. D had his hands full with the players' union and his charities. Shawna was lawyering for a community clinic. Donte and Serena were in high school; Damien was twelve, Tara ten. Mitch's own update had been entirely about the house—*We gotta have you guys down here*—which was strange, because early January was when Tim had started chemo, and it was hard to imagine himself thinking about anything else back then.

"Why is no one from the NFL speaking?" Julie whispered into her program.

Mitch shrugged. "Maybe the family didn't want them to." He looked up, saw a row of weapons casing the stadium. "The hell are those?" he panted.

"Wind turbines," Julie said, and he saw that they rotated, slightly.

Mitch felt himself sway in his folding seat, felt Julie clasp his knee to calm him down. He listened to the conversations around him to get himself up to speed. Donte was a senior now. He played football at Lower Merion. He'd been surfing with D when the jet ski hit him, was in the ambulance with him when he died. Mitch wanted to be angry that D would allow such a stupid accident to leave his kids without a father, but then, at long last, the music kicked up and the entire family walked in, looking healthy and almost honored to be there, and instead he just felt sad.

The sadness intensified when Donte rose to speak. "My dad was the strongest man I ever knew," he said. "And not just because of the way he played. Though, obviously, that was awesome." He paused at the podium to let everyone laugh. "He loved me and my brother and sisters. He told us every day. And I'm here to tell you that we felt that love. We still feel it."

People were sniffling throughout the crowd. Relatives, friends, reporters. But Donte Mars was completely composed.

He seemed to perfectly understand the occasion, and to not understand it at all.

"I also want to tell you something I told my dad just a few weeks ago. Something we agreed on. I will not be playing football in college. I have offers. Some of them are really good programs. But life is short. I know that more than ever now. And football isn't the opportunity for me that it was for my dad in his day. He gave me big dreams. He believed that if I studied and learned to work with people, I could actually change the world—which, I mean, I think we all know it needs some serious changing right now. I've had some great times on the field, and I'm playing tonight in his memory. But starting next year, I'm choosing a new life. For myself and also for him."

The gathering sprang to its feet. Football players, coaches, owners. Didn't they know they were applauding against themselves? After everything the NFL had been through in recent years, the favorite scapegoat of the pious media on one side, and the whiney president on the other? Mitch sat there, flabbergasted, looking at the backs of enormous legs, a mass sacrifice of big-and-tall suits.

"It's okay," Julie said, leaning down. "You don't have to stand."

Well, he could stand, for pete's sake. He hoisted himself up so as not to look like an asshole, though he felt like one inside. What did Donte's personal decisions have to do with anything? Wasn't this supposed to be a memorial service? He let his bitterness envelope him until, suddenly, it gave him hope, like maybe this was just another of D's jokes, a way of ribbing guys for their own mindlessness, a way of bringing them all together after too many years apart. Maybe he was lying in his casket, thinking, *Got 'em.* Thinking, *Yeah, I got 'em good.*

They took their seats again as the Jumbotron awoke with

thrashing highlights from D's career, his body flying, his body occupying space. And then, again, Mitch felt sad. That body had been brought down. It occupied the casket right there on the stage.

Then it was Shawna's turn. "It's been a hard week, y'all," she said. "The hardest week of my life. I have asked 'why' so many times I no longer know the meaning of the word. But today, I'm done with why. Starting today, I'm asking how. How can I keep him with me?

"Y'all know my husband was a talker," she said. "He talked about a lot of things. Himself, how great he was. His kids, how great *they* were. I bet in his smarter moments he even told some of y'all that I was pretty great, too. But the thing he actually talked about most wasn't greatness. It was justice. It was a thing he didn't get to see much of in his life. And it's a thing we're going to work for in his memory."

She was a goddamn superhuman, Shawna Mars. Had she always been this way? He remembered her mostly as young, herding kids around. But at some point she, too, had grown up. She'd let her hair go, stopped taming it. She was big into Black Lives Matter.

By the time the service wrapped up, with D's mother leading the entire gathering in "We Shall Overcome," Mitch felt like a bag of bricks. It was all he could do to make it to the bathroom, where he snuck several hits from his vape.

At the reception in the club lounge, he finally spotted Moore and Griggs by the windows. He forced himself to go to them, even though he knew it would be awkward. They were guys from another time, another life, though it appeared that for the two of them at least, their time together had continued. He checked them out as he approached. They were fatter. Good, so was he. He planted his feet and they turned, greeting him with deadened faces.

He was going to have to muster himself. He held up his phone like he was recording them. "'I'm an alien on Earth,'" he said. D's catchphrase. "'Can someone please explain this shit to me?'"

Shoulder to shoulder, they held him in suspense, maybe still deciding how they felt, maybe just wanting to be dicks. Stop being dicks, he thought at them, and apparently they heard, because after another beat, they caved, made their brotherly sounds, clasped his hand, thumped his back.

"You some kind of scientist now?" Moore laughed, batting Mitch's goggles.

"Cured my migraines, bro," Mitch said, which was met with appreciative noises. He wasn't the only one with headaches.

"They would've killed on 'The Martian,'" Moore said.

"They would've."

D's locker room interviews had gotten big on YouTube, at least among Eagles fans. By his last few seasons he was posting weekly episodes of "The Martian with D'Antonio Mars." Mitch had been back a few times as a guest, but never recently enough to show off his goggles. The premise was that football was a complicated life that most fans didn't understand. And that made sense, D insisted, because most players didn't understand it either. Neither did the coaches or the front office or the media. Especially not the media. "We were born into a system that completely shapes our life. It's complicated. And we are basically all Martians just trying to figure it out." That was D's belief. Eventually led to his work with the union.

It turned out Moore and Griggs didn't see much of each

other either. Moore was back in Florida, Griggs in Cali. Kohler had joined them, totally red-faced. He was back in Iowa most of the year, wintering in Arizona, like Hardy. Like a lot of guys, in fact.

They talked about the old days: Kohler's naked musings, Griggs's girl problems, Griggs's suits. Griggs had been a baby then but even he'd caught up. Now everyone was stiff as hell and grim and responsible and worried about their kids. They asked Mitch about his goggles, traded tips on supplements and patches and pills. It was easy to talk, like no time had passed, though every memory was a reminder that time had done nothing else.

"He was just *better* than the rest of us," Moore said, when the conversation finally came back to D. "Always was." They were all sitting around a table with plates of rib carcasses and crumpled up napkins and empties all over the place. The wait staff couldn't come fast enough. The women had come and gone.

"Fearless," Griggs agreed. "Team player."

"Come on, y'all, wake up," Mitch said, finally feeling comfortable enough to speak his mind. "The man died in the most senseless way possible. Let's stop pretending he was some kind of hero."

Moore and Griggs looked at each other.

"I mean, this funeral?" he went on, because no one else was talking. "'Donte's quitting football. Everyone work for justice.' No disrespect to the Marses, but it was crazy!"

Kohler leaned forward, and before he even spoke, Mitch could feel his condescension, like something physical. Which was odd, coming from Kohler. "Every death is senseless," he finally said. "People have to do what they can."

"Direct hit to the head," Griggs said. "Brother never had a chance."

"It's ironic." Moore was almost wistful. "We'll never know if he had CTE."

"They're saying he pushed Donte out the way," Griggs said. "Saved his life."

"I heard that, too," Kohler said.

"Obviously they're saying that." For some reason, Mitch was exasperated. "They always say stuff like that."

"Naw, man," Moore said. "Usually it's, 'That stupid black man, he had it coming, what a thug, don't he know black people don't surf?'"

"Come on, bro," Kohler said. "They don't say it like *that*."

"You right—it's worse! D knows."

"Knew," Mitch said.

"Whatever," Moore said. "He knows a lot of things now that we don't."

Mitch made a noise that was not quite supportive, not quite dismissive. "Since when did you get spiritual? And when did D learn to surf?" He thought of Caryn and it was almost too much.

"I guess he was learning. Since when did you throw in the towel?" He reached over and swatted Mitch's gut.

"Trust me." Mitch shook him off. "It's been worse."

"Seriously, though," Moore said. "Y'all were like this." He held up two banged-up fingers, pressed them together as tightly as he could, and still, there was a gap. "Why not call him a hero?"

January 8 flashed again in Mitch's mind. "I don't know. It's been a long day."

He stood. He needed Julie. He looked around until he found her little fighter's form, listening to someone who needed comfort. In movies women were always screaming and being useless, but in his experience it was not like that at all. A terrible thing happened and they sprang to action. They knew important phone numbers, and gave clear instructions, and had enormous emotional reserves. They needed reassurance, sure, but they also tended to come to the right conclusions. The ones he liked to think he would've come to had he been half as smart as them.

"We've got a long drive," Julie said, having made her way over to his table. She had those big eyes that saw the whole situation. "What do you say we head home?"

The next several weeks were fine, nothing out of the ordinary. He dove back into work, took Ricky out for lunch, closed out a decent September at both lots. But then one day shortly after his forty-eighth birthday, he felt dizzier than usual, and the next day was even worse, his head like a rowdy, overcrowded harbor, and when he had space to think about anything at all he couldn't help but think about the jet ski, crushing tissue as it banged through D's skull. He came home early, sacked out in his chair by the pool. He could almost feel his goggles working overtime. Tiny shock, tiny shock, tiny shock. He fired up the vape and took a hit. He tried so hard not to think about his headache that he wasn't thinking about anything else.

He tried praying, even though prayer had not done it for him for a long time, not since he'd left Lori. Or really, if he was being honest, not since he'd left the league. He hadn't lost his faith so much as he now recognized it for what it was: a tool for getting through football and marriage, which any neutral observer at the time could've seen. Even at his most outwardly devout, he'd talked to himself far more than he talked to God and was so tolerant of other creeds as to not even pray for those, like D, who held them. He was more honest with himself now and he felt pretty certain that this also meant he was being more honest with God.

Still, there was this problem with his panic, which was only intensifying. He tried getting in his Suburban, and going for meditative drives along the Blue Ridge Parkway, where the October leaves were just beginning to change. But all that produced was more vertigo, ears popping, the kudzu creatures advancing and falling towards him, the mountains shrinking into heaps beneath the double-speed clouds that raced through the infinite sky.

"Can we talk about therapy?" Julie asked him one night as he lay there clutching his head.

"But what if I'm really sick? What if I'm having a heart attack?"

"Are you short of breath? Do you have pain in your belly?"

No, he told her, and no. She pulled the blood pressure sleeve from the nightstand and slid it up his arm. "When did you last check it?" she asked over the device's inflating drone.

"I don't know," he whispered. Now his memory was dying. Surely he was dying, too. The sleeve released him with a sigh.

"It's fine," she said. "Your meds are working."

But she still looked at him with unsettling concern.

"I think you need to talk to someone," she said.

"We're talking."

"No," she said. "A professional."

He had to drive all the way to Charlottesville to see the doctor Julie had found, an older woman who spent most of their first session together asking him who he was and why he had come. He liked her well enough. Dr. Evans. She was deeply wrinkled, but pretty for an older lady, and she smiled a lot, which he always appreciated in a woman.

He started slow, told her who he was. Football, family,

basic stuff. He told her Julie had wanted him to come because she thought he was feeling down. He told her an old friend had died, so of course he was feeling sad, he'd been sad when his uncle died, too. He also told her he'd felt some dizziness lately, but he'd checked out fine at the doctor, so that, too, was probably just because he was sad. By the end of the hour, they had agreed: when people died, you got sad. If this was therapy, he'd be fine.

At the start of the second session, she asked him if he had any questions for her. He didn't, so she took a few minutes to explain her method. He listened, heard the main point about it being more like a practice than a cure, but found himself zeroing in on her mouth, the source of all her educated words.

"You know who you remind me of?" he asked her, suddenly. "My high school English teacher, Mrs. Murray." He remembered he was in Virginia. "Do you know her?"

"I don't think so," she said, plainly not thinking about it at all. "Why do I remind you of her?"

"It's not how you look. She was younger. It's something about the way you talk." He laughed, realizing what he was getting at. "You're both too smart for me." Caryn had also been too smart. Maybe he'd give her that little tidbit, see what she did with it. "But so are all women, aren't they."

"Is that what you think?"

"Don't you?" He was pretty pleased with himself for managing to turn the tables. Now he was the one asking questions.

But she was quick, this Dr. Evans. "It isn't about what I think. We're here to talk about you." And she was crafty, too. Before he knew it, he was filling her in on his childhood. He tried to tell it all from the beginning, in order, the way it happened: first his mother who raised him, then his father who didn't, but even this basic, straightforward chronology broke down pretty fast. He had to backtrack to cover his grandparents and Tim, and the one time his dad did visit, and the fight between the brothers. Then there were the couple of times he talked to Joe on the phone as a kid. Then all of a sudden he was in the present.

"We talk once or twice a year now," he told her. "It's been pretty normal for a while."

"How did that happen?" she asked.

"I think I just called him up one day. I wanted to see how he was doing."

"Do you remember what prompted that?"

He shrugged. "I was in college. There wasn't any need for bad blood."

"I see. And do you ever visit?"

"He won't. Doesn't even text."

"What do you mean 'won't'?"

"I mean he always has some excuse. He's got these dogs. I'll be honest with you, though, it's because he's broke. Always has been. I went out to see him once, after my first divorce. Stopped over on my way to Vegas. I could tell he was touched. He made up a bed for me. His wife made me dinner. It was nice, but it was weird, too. I forgot they don't drink, so I brought them this bottle of top-shelf tequila. It just sat there on the counter the whole time."

"Have you seen him since?"

"We're better on the phone."

"Has your mom seen him?"

"No way. I think she would if he turned up. But like I said, he doesn't travel, and she's not gonna go chasing him."

She nodded. "So when did you last talk?" She really was fixated. Who could remember the exact timing of one little thing when there were so many other things happening?

"I don't know," he said. She was exhausting him. "Recently."

"A few months ago, maybe," Julie said, when he put Dr. Evans's question to her. "Why?"

"Just wondering." He was glad she couldn't put her finger on it either. Very few important things escaped Julie's finger.

She gave one of her disciplined pauses, in which he imagined her resting inside her brain, preparing to kick him with high-impact words. "Does this mean you're liking therapy?"

Like was not the right word. For the moment he still found therapy pretty random—not like in the league, when you talked to the team psychologist specifically to improve your mental game. This Joe thing, for instance. Why was it even on his mind? He'd come to Dr. Evans because he was grieving, because he was dealing with Tim and D. Now he was annoyed at her for letting him get off-track.

The next week, he went in with a mission.

"We talked about my dad last week," he reminded Dr. Evans, feeling agitated the moment he sat down. "But that's not what I'm here for. I want to talk about my friend D, who got his brains bashed in by a jet ski."

He spoke to shock; he hadn't mentioned before that it was a violent death. But she was smart, she must've read the news, and she was ready with her neutral smile.

"We played together four years, the last four of my career," he said. "I was a mentor to him, showed him the ropes. And he was willful at first, but eventually we were friends. Then, a few weeks ago, he died."

"And how did you feel about that?" Dr. Evans asked him.

"Sad," he said. They'd covered that. "But also angry."

"Who were you angry with?"

"Just—God. That this happened. But also the kid who caused it. His parents. And D. And everyone at the funeral who was like, 'He was a hero.'"

She looked confused. "They said that?"

"Thank you!" Mitch cried, clapping his hands.

"Who said that?"

"The other guys, my teammates. Because he might've saved his son's life."

"Well, that is pretty heroic."

Mitch shrugged.

"You don't see it that way?"

"Absolutely not. If you listen to the witnesses, it's pretty clear the jet ski was never hitting Donte. People are just saying that because they don't want to believe it was meaningless."

"But you do?"

He looked at the poster on her wall, from a museum show in 1998. The central image was of a yellow house. "You know who else you remind me of?" he told her. He heard the edge in his voice. "The reporters. Always asking questions." Van Gogh, he thought proudly. He would've known it even without the label.

That smile again. "It's my job."

"I didn't mind them so much by the end, but only because we understood each other. I didn't like to talk much and they didn't push me. When they did, they knew they'd get nothing."

"You seem to like to talk."

"I do like to talk. I don't like answering questions."

"That's going to make this difficult. Questions are central to talk therapy."

"And why is that, though? Who decided that's the way it has to be?"

She shifted forward in her chair. "Who decided football has to have four downs? It's a practice that's evolved over time. No one is saying it's the only way to proceed, only that it's proven successful."

He grinned. So she knew her football. "And what if one day it's proven *not* successful?"

"Then I think we would adjust."

A word he respected. *Adjust.*

"But," she continued, "I don't think today's that day. Now, we were talking about D. Do you want to go back to that?"

He shifted in his seat, a partial concession.

"How's his family doing?"

"They're holding up." He wasn't an idiot. He knew what she wanted. She wanted him to admit he'd driven all the way to Philadelphia to honor D and pay his respects but hadn't managed to talk to the family at all. Just completely skipped the receiving line the way he used to skip class in high school. And why did he do it, she would ask if he told her this? Because he didn't know what to say, because he was angry with them for letting D die, because he was ashamed he'd been so out of touch with a man he'd claimed to call a friend, because he was scared to look Shawna and Donte and D's mother in the eye and tell them he was sorry for their loss. Because they might, in all their other-side wisdom, look back at him in a way that says *you're next.* And how weak that would make him feel to admit. Wasn't it enough that he was thinking it? What good would saying it do?

He had to give her something, though. He hadn't been looking at her—most of the time he spent in her office he didn't look at her—and now he looked at her aggressively. She was wearing loafers and plain tan slacks.

"I was just thinking about the other guys," he decided, finally. "It was all Eagles at the service."

"And where did you play before that?" she asked, even though he knew she knew.

"Before that, New England Patriots, before that Miami Hurricanes, before that Monacan Warriors. Before that Monacan Jets." He rattled them off on his fingers.

"That's a lot of teammates. Are you still in touch with any of them?"

He nodded as names and faces crowded his head. Hardy, Ricky, Caleb, Gaines. Though he hadn't really talked to Gaines. But he'd hired Ricky to sell cars, and he golfed with Caleb, because they both still lived in the area. He'd thought of this as a safe topic, just football, just guys, but it was almost wiping him out to recall.

That whole thing in New England—aside from Hardy, what was there to say? The Philly guys, too. They were lost. He remembered what Tim had said about Vietnam: "You only know guys in the moment. When it's over it's over and you have to live your life." Like high school, like college, the NFL was a moment. But it was a moment that had felt so permanent.

"It's hard to hold on to people," he confessed. "I'm doing the best I can."

Thanksgiving was a sorry showing. Another year, another turkey tied by Julie. Alyssa and Cindy came down with Journey and the five of them stuffed themselves on a meal better suited to fifteen. He couldn't remember the last time his crew had been so small. Without Tim, Tracy and the girls had decided to go to New York to shop and see some shows. They'd sent him a selfie from Times Square: three round Virginia faces nearly blocking out the lights. He used to have his other kids, too, but Kaylie and Tyler were both in college now, which made Lori more desperate to see them. She was taking back Thanksgiving this year, same as she'd done last year, and with Lori he always gave in. He'd get them for a couple days after Christmas, if he was lucky. They hadn't even begun to work that out.

At least he had Alyssa and Journey. Normally, they behaved like a whole ecosystem, every role in nature accounted for between the two of them. But at dinner this time, her phone kept lighting up, and she kept reading it, more focused on the screen than on Journey, who sat singing to himself under his wavy blond hair, which Alyssa seemed determined not to cut.

"You seeing someone?" Mitch asked.

Alyssa looked up. "Maybe."

"Uh-oh," Mitch teased.

"Don't get ahead of yourself." She tucked the phone away. She'd grown secretive as an adult, every new development in her life a shock to his sense of the world. First she dressed rich and went to a rich-kid school. Then she switched colleges. Then her hair was purple and she had a massive tattoo of a seal on her back. Then she was accidentally pregnant, no father, then having the kid with a midwife at home. The trick was to expect an about-face every six months or so, and that was exactly the kind of thing Mitch never could learn to expect. This fall she was a first-year law student—Alyssa, who was too smart for school.

He looked at Cindy for a clue but she just shrugged and offered him more turkey, which he accepted, because why not. He'd have to remember to interrogate her later. He tried to expect nothing, yet even as he chewed, he allowed himself to hope. A guy for Alyssa, someone he could golf with, another warm body in the room. He needed all the bodies he could get.

The next week, Mitch walked into Dr. Evans's office and collapsed on the couch.

"Can I just lie here?" he asked her.

"It's your time."

He closed his eyes and they were quiet, the sound of cars pulling into the parking lot slowly eating away at his head.

"Don't you even have one question?" he finally asked.

"What's troubling you?"

He tapped his head.

"Migraine?" she asked.

"Good guess."

"We haven't talked about that. Or about your goggles. They're pretty impressive."

"I really just want to be quiet."

"But you came in. That suggests you want to talk."

"I want to be in this office and not talk."

"It's your time," she said again, and for some reason he heard it as a warning.

"I know what you're up to," he said after they'd listened to a few more passing cars. "I've seen 'The Sopranos.'"

She made a noise that was nearly a laugh. "It's a good show," she said. "Psychotherapists love it."

He sat up. She was looking at him.

"So it's all my mother's fault, right? Or my dad who wasn't around."

"What do you think?"

"Always what I think! What do you think?"

"That's not important. We're working to understand what you think. And what you feel."

"I think I do better when I don't think about what I feel." He grunted and flopped back down.

"You know I have to ask: Why do you think that is?"

He looked at her ceiling, which was tiled with panels the exact color and texture of athletic tape, and he felt her smiling in her purposeful way, thinking the answer into his head, the answer she wanted him to give. It was like school again with Mrs. Murray, or football with its endless coaches. It was even like his old talks with God. He wasn't against those folks; they'd helped him along his entire life. But if there was anything to be gained from retirement, it ought to be freedom, the right to finally have a conversation that wasn't controlled by someone else.

He closed his eyes and went silent. And in that silence, he thought his answer back at her, thought it up the drab legs of her trousers, along the little canyons of her wrinkled cheeks, and in between the teeth of that satisfied smile, where it dissolved and got washed back into her gut. If she was half as smart as he thought she was, she'd know he could take it from here.

A few days later, he ran into Mrs. Murray, of all people, at CVS. He'd been standing behind her in the pharmacy line, wondering if he was imagining things, and it wasn't until she stepped forward to speak to the pharmacist that he was positive it was her. He'd know that voice anywhere. It still didn't belong in the South.

"Mitch Wilkins!" she said, when he gave her his name. She hadn't recognized him, but that was not her fault. "Those glasses!"

She cupped his fat elbow in her cool, thin hand, and pressed her cheek against his, which was not ever the way they'd greeted each other, not even that long-ago time when he found himself floating in her doorway, overdue paper in hand, halfway between one life and the next. They were both undeniably adults now. She still had that braided hippie hair, now fully gray, but remarkably, her face wasn't wrinkled. If anything, it boasted a dry sheen, like certain sweat-wicking fabrics.

They stood chatting for several minutes, every now and then having to step out of a new customer's way, and when it became clear that neither had anywhere to be, they went across the street to the gas station bar, where they ordered beers and fries, against their doctors' advice.

He found himself talking to her, well lubricated, the words just slipping out one after the other, about his life since the last time he'd seen her, which was his entire life, a life full of people she didn't know, but might as well have, since she'd known him when he was young. It was everything he'd told Dr. Evans, but sharper this time, more connected, as though that had only been practice for this. He didn't need Dr. Evans. He needed Mrs. Murray, someone who knew him, and knew where he came from, to whom he didn't have to explain about his parents, and who would let him talk the way he wished.

And then came her turn, and he found himself interested in a way that buzzed in his brain, earnestly wanting to know what her life had been like. "I actually retired this year," she told him, smiling, as if over a private joke. "We're moving to DC in January. So you're catching me just in time."

He felt gut-punched. "But that's crazy, you can't," he blurted. "I'd been thinking about you, and then all of a sudden, you're at CVS. You have to admit that's a sign."

She smiled again. "I'm flattered. Truly. But Gordon and I have always wanted a city life. And to be closer to our daughter."

This was news. Mrs. Murray was a mother? "I never knew

you had a kid."

"We had her late. Well, late for here. Her name is Sarah. She lives in New York." She held up her phone, where a young woman tilted her head: dirty blonde like her mom, bigger mouth, same unimpressed eyes.

"She a teacher, too?"

"She's a researcher. Studies proteins in the brain. I don't know where she gets it."

"Obviously from you!"

Mrs. Murray gave one of her masculine laughs, and Mitch felt that old, rare pleasure of pleasing her with an observation. "I don't know anything about what happens on a microscopic level," she said. "I only know about things I can see, hear, and feel."

"That makes two of us. And I'm not even that good at seeing anymore."

As if to check his claim, she snuck a glance at the clock behind the bar, but he caught that move clear as day, and she must have seen his panic, smart woman that she was. She must've known he wanted more, as she'd known all those years ago in her classroom. Only this time, she had nothing to lose, no boundaries to protect.

"Another round?" she asked, almost flirtatiously.

"On me!" He ordered and they went deeper. She told him about teaching in the same small place for almost forty years, which basically meant teaching whole families, first the parents, then their kids, and even, in one case, a grandkid of one of those first kids, which was how she knew it was time to quit. She talked, too, about her daughter, whom she worried about because she was single and always in pursuit of very particular and exacting forms of excellence, in her diet, in her vacation plans, and maybe also in her boyfriends. She worried this quality would work against her daughter in the end, a thought she repeated again a short while later, unwittingly showing her age. Mitch said he felt the same way about Alyssa, and Mrs. Murray—he still couldn't think of her as Laura—affirmed that it was natural to worry about their kids this way, but that if parents wanted to offer advice that might be taken, they had to wait until they were asked, excruciating though that might be. He was struck again at how much better this was than talking to Dr. Evans, precisely because it was not neutral, because Mrs. Murray was admitting that she was a parent, too. He found himself wanting her advice on other things, and in this way he allowed himself to venture a few uncertain words about his dad.

"Has Dr. Evans brought up medication at all?" Julie asked the next morning as he popped his breakfast pill.

"If she does," he said, "I'm not interested." He pointed at his weekly pillbox. "I take plenty of crap already."

His current daily regimen was relatively Spartan: one extended-release oxycodone, morning and night, with food, which he knew he was lucky to get. Plus an ACE-inhibitor for his blood pressure. And turmeric supplements. And his self-directed weed. He'd taken all kinds of candy in the league, especially after surgery, but since then he'd been vigilant, preferring to live with the known pain of his own broken body rather than risk an addiction that might turn out worse. Once, at Julie's suggestion, he'd tried sleeping pills, but they had messed him up bad. He'd had the tingling limbs, the shaking hands, the dizziness, you name it—virtually every nasty side effect the pharmacist could fit on the accompanying insert. Better to stay awake all his life. An implant was one thing. But he would not lose himself to pills.

"Honestly," he said. "I think therapy has done its job."

"Ha," Julie said.

"Yep. I think I'm done. Haven't felt dizzy in weeks." A lie. But he hadn't felt like he was dying. "That's gotta be proof of something."

"Proof you have to keep going."

"You'll see," he said. "You'll see."

He waited until his morning oxy had kicked in before he picked up the phone. By the time it had, he felt fine. He felt Mrs. Murray was definitely right: he needed to make this call.

"Listen, Joe," Mitch told his father when he answered, "I want you to come for Christmas."

"Oh, well, now," Joe deflected. He spouted his usual noise about the dogs, Tammy, the distance. Never the real issue, which was cash. Well, that was fine. Everyone had his limit. But Mitch would not let Joe's limit stop him from getting his way.

"I'll take care of it," he said. "I'll take care of everything. The fact is I'm in therapy now and I'm really trying to work through my issues. So just do me a favor and come."

They weren't magic words, but for a New Age hippie like Joe, they were close, so what if they were a few weeks out of date. When his dad called back, after talking it over with Tammy, he said yes. Tammy would stay with the dogs—someone had to— but he'd be glad to spend Christmas with his son.

At last, at last, a conversation he had controlled.

"You'll meet your grandkids," Mitch said, excitedly, not realizing until this moment that this was something he wanted to see.

The next few days he threw himself into organizing, calling Alyssa, Lori, Maddie, Kaylie, Tyler, Cindy, Tracy. Everyone sounded blindsided by his vigor; they weren't used to him making any plans, and they weren't used to plans being made so assertively. With little protest they all agreed. Kaylie, Tyler, Maddie, and Joe would fly in on the twenty-third. Alyssa, Journey, and Cindy would drive down on Christmas Eve. He got on the fare site and ordered everyone flights. He hauled out to Wal-Mart to pick up a tree, a beautiful evergreen thing, in every way different from all the other trees in the roped-off enclosure, and in every way the same.

When he called Mrs. Murray to tell her the good news, she told him how happy she was to hear it, what a nice Christmas he'd have with everyone together, and he told her he owed it all to her for putting the idea in his head. She laughed her gratifying laugh and said it was nothing, she was happy she could help.

"If that's your idea of 'nothing,'" he said, "I'd like see what 'something' looks like to you."

"It looks like a lazy football player handing in an English paper after he's already graduated." And they both had a good laugh at that.

A few days before Christmas Eve, Caryn called in the middle of the night. She had insomnia, too, he'd probably given it to her, and she also didn't beat around the bush. "Is it true Joe's coming?"

Mitch told her that it was.

"Then I'm coming, too."

"You can't," he blurted. "There's no room." He already had Cindy staying with Tracy. He no longer had to check himself from thinking, *and Tim.*

"That's fine, I got a hotel."

"Where?" There were only a few B&B's in the area, and a flea-bag motel below the Food Lion, next to the old county jail.

He could not see Caryn in that establishment. "You hate it here. You'd rather live in Bethesda with all your fancy stores."

"I never said I wouldn't visit! I'll be at that nice inn at the college."

"Well," he stalled, searching for other obstacles. "What about Steve? You're just going to abandon him on Christmas?"

She found this particularly hysterical. "He's Jewish! He'll be thrilled to do his old movie-and-Chinese-food thing. Anyway, we can handle a few nights apart. This is your *dad*. Alyssa's *grandfather*. You think I'm going to miss out on meeting him now that I finally have the chance?"

"I didn't know you cared."

"Well, I do."

He wasn't sure he was comfortable with that. "Alyssa's coming alone with Journey," he said.

"I know."

"I hope she hasn't broken up with her guy." Might as well fish, while he had her on the phone.

Her initial pause betrayed something much more complicated than her answer, which was "No."

"No, what?"

"No, they haven't broken up. But I guess it's time I told you. She asked me to. I was going to wait until the New Year, but you sort of forced everyone's hand with this whole Christmas thing."

"Tell me what?"

"Her guy is not a guy. She's a woman."

"A woman."

"Her name is Joan. She's a graphic designer."

He felt her waiting in her own dark, mid-life dream house, across the state line in Maryland. Back in New England, he would wake sometimes from a deep Monday sleep and feel her there warming his back. Even when he was mad at her for causing a fuss over some petty domestic thing, he never really minded her curling up into his body and breathing into the space between his shoulder blades. How else were they supposed to spend any time together in season? In the end, it was all their marriage was.

"You think it's a phase?" he asked.

Caryn sighed, and in his phone-heated ear, he felt an echo of that old animal warmth. "I have no idea. That's not for us to ask. It's our job to love and support her through this and everything else."

"Is that what the yogis say?"

"It's what *I* say. It's just what's right, Mitch." He hated when people said his name like that. It made him feel as though they weren't sure of him, as though without his name he might've been somebody, anybody, else.

"It's easy for you," he said. "You've known about this, obviously. You're with those liberals all the time."

"Mitch," she repeated, crushingly. "*I'm* liberal. For years I've been a liberal. How many times do I have to tell you that?"

"No wonder our daughter's gay."

She ignored this. She must've been able to tell he'd come around, whatever he was saying right now. "You'd be a liberal, too, if you just took the time to think about it. Didn't you vote for Obama, even?"

"That was different. That was about sending a message. But I was never voting for a Clinton. I don't care if she's a woman, or a man, or a transgender."

"So you went for a bigot instead!"

"Joan, huh? Kind of an old lady name."

"Trust me, she's young. And honestly? I don't even know why I called."

He let that one hang there. He was glad she had. No one called anymore; it was all just little blue puffs of data, pretending to be people, cluttering up his phone.

"Because you're trying to crash my Christmas," he said. If he couldn't control this conversation, he could at least try to have a little fun. And it was sort of fun to annoy her. He felt like the guy he'd been when he was with her, the guy at the Pro Bowl, in his prime.

"I am coming," she said.

"I know you are."

"Christmas Eve."

"See you then."

He sat in the airport waiting area with a handful of his fellow Virginians. Unfussy people in sweaters and hunting jackets, clothes they'd worn since the eighties, even the items that were technically new. In his playing days he'd never realized how many old people there were in this country, how many fat people, and how many of the nation's businesses catered expressly to their needs. His own business for instance. But he was one of them now, no longer deceptively-strong-and-fast-fat, just regular-old-American-fat, the perfect man to sell you a Tahoe.

At least he'd had a prime, a period he actually recognized when he was in it. He'd felt great for most of the years he played, but the entire time there were reminders it was fleeting. *Now or never*, guys said in the huddle. *Cherish this moment*, coaches told them after a win. Football was lucky like that, it carried with it a sense of its ending. Other people, the people on the benches all around him, hadn't necessarily had that sense. They clawed their way through life, going for someday, hoping their best was still to come, hoping it wasn't already behind them, at some humid high school party in a field. Football knew better. Football knew it was as good as it gets.

He got to his feet, looking for his dad in the small horde of people dragging rolling bags toward the carousel. It was a funny thing to look for a person he hadn't seen in twenty years, a face he didn't even know from Facebook. He watched one white-haired lady call out to another, watched college kids hug their parents. Before long an older man came into focus, a man with a ponytail in a denim jacket who was not exactly short, but gave the impression of someone who'd once been taller. He was standing by a potted plant and his face was turned away from Mitch, toward the window, displaying the back of his head. Mitch stared just long enough to give himself the creeps. It was his own private horror movie: the steady back of an old man's head.

When it turned, the face was not bloody, or crawling with maggots, or lacking an eye or a nose. It was just the ordinary horror of Mitch's own face, and Mitch's own ponytail, twenty years, give or take, down the line.

They walked toward each other, propelled by some genetic, magnetic force. They knew each other, even though they didn't.

"In the flesh," Joe said, and Mitch felt better. He did know that voice.

"With some assistance," Mitch said, indicating his goggles, so Joe wouldn't have to ask.

"Those are really something," Joe said. "You like them?"

"They do their job. They're part of me now."

Joe's blue eyes brightened and he nodded, some word of Mitch's chiming with a word he already had in his head. "That's good," he said. "That's the best way to see it."

They retrieved Joe's pack from the carousel and went to get

a coffee while they waited for the kids, who would arrive all together within the hour. Joe's flight had involved two stops, including an overnight in Charlotte, and it was clear that he was tired. There were many moments of silence. Mitch found it most comfortable to look at the coffee counter and the various territories not occupied by Joe. A guilty feeling crept over him. What had he wanted—closure? The whole stupid thing had been his idea.

But then the kids arrived and Mitch introduced them, which meant having to claim everyone. These are my kids; this is your grandfather. Your grandkids. My dad. It helped.

Kaylie was sweet; Lori and Cindy had brought her up well. She hugged Joe without hesitation, said, "It's so nice to meet you!" Even if it was all premeditated, rehearsed exactly this way in her mind, Mitch was grateful. Sometimes the only way to convince yourself was to act as if you already believed—and why not, when the intentions were good? She was nineteen and blonde, just as she was supposed to be, a sophomore at his own school, Miami. He liked visiting her there in her clean, well-lighted dorm, liked taking her out to the original La Carreta. She was an earnest Christian, like her mom, and she always dressed like she was going to be seen, hair brushed, clothes ironed. She'd never had a rebellious phase.

Tyler was more suspicious. "Hi," he said as Joe patted him on the back. He smiled, but there was something missing in his tone that put Mitch slightly on edge. Tyler had grown wild in adolescence, wrecking cars and neighborhood mailboxes, shoplifting the stupidest, most obvious bottles of malt liquor, and nearly flunking out of his freshman year of high school. Football and Aderall were his only salvation. He seemed happy enough now at his little D-III hinterland, even if it meant he wouldn't go pro. But that no longer mattered to Mitch. What mattered was that Tyler stayed alive, passed his classes, got a job: a new, more modest set of hopes that looked increasingly achievable each month. Tyler had normal brown college hair, not long, not short, but in the presence of Joe and Mitch's ponytails, it suddenly felt like a declaration of independence.

And then, of course, there was Maddie, Mitch's baby, his favorite person, with dark hair just like his. She'd gotten into horses and there'd been talk of her coming to live with him and train with the college girls, until her mom found a stable in Florida and the whole plan fell apart. "I wish I could live with *both* of you," Maddie had told him, so mature, already, at fourteen. "But if I left now it would break Mom's heart." She walked ahead of him to the car in her tall boots and backpack, a stuffed penguin charm clipped to the zipper. Sometime this week he would have to ask her why it was a penguin and not a horse.

"How's your foot speed holding up?" Mitch asked Tyler, who seemed to be lagging alongside him.

In his backpack, Tyler faked a cut in front of him. "Race me and find out."

"Easy kid," Mitch said, coming to a stop. Why, on the few occasions he wasn't totally tuned out, did Tyler always have to try so hard?

"That a Yes?"

"It's a Never Going to Happen." Mitch clicked the car open. "Now get in there."

They organized themselves in the Suburban, Kaylie and Maddie in the middle, Joe up front, Tyler sprawled in back with his headphones. Mitch had gotten the car as a practical measure. Like every vehicle he'd ever owned, it was built for a driver his size. And it had room for his entire family, for just these rare occasions. Growing up alone with Cindy, he never felt he was missing anything, but looking back, he probably had been, since he was so obviously compensating now.

"When was the last time you were in Monacan, Grandpa?" Kaylie asked as they pulled into traffic. He had to hand it to her; she'd managed to absorb some family lore. But who had told her—Cindy? Cindy talked about that stuff?

"Oh, it's been years," Joe said. "Many years."

At the light, Mitch glanced in the review mirror, trying to determine if they harbored any grievances. Maddie met his eyes immediately and smiled, sitting up straighter, like a puppy, proud of herself for being good. Kaylie appeared to be readying her next interview question while Tyler was lost in his music. What did they care about Joe? He was a novelty, never promised, never lost. Their grievances, if they had them, would only be with Mitch. He'd left them at vulnerable ages: thirteen, twelve, eight. Well, not them. He'd left their mom.

"Has it changed much?" Kaylie asked.

"More built up now, that's for sure. Used to be you could drive for miles without hitting a light. Now it looks like nothing *but* lights."

He'd still be with Lori if he hadn't met Julie. That was the hard truth. And would that have been so bad? She'd believed in him, put her faith in him, and faith was no trifle to Lori. But her tireless sympathy had worn him down. In the years after football, when he'd been so lost—fat and useless and moody, and stupidly trusting expensive suits with his money—she wouldn't even call him on it. "But you've always been big," she'd say. And "He was an NFL-approved advisor—how could you know he'd rip us off?" And "God loves you no matter what."

She excused every damn one of his failures, even as she raised their kids to succeed. He had to be hard on himself, because she wasn't. Even when he'd started sneaking away to see Julie, muttering falsehoods about investment opportunities back in Philly, spouting developer nonsense about "a real will to build," he was the one who called himself a failure. Never her. "I just wanted you to be happy," she'd wept, when it all came out at the end.

He was happy to see Julie when they got home, Julie who was also good, but not too good, who had in fact basically beat him up the first time she met him and then accused him (rightly) of not taking care of himself. What he needed was not God's love. He needed someone to yell at him about therapy. He needed an elbow cutting into his back, big blue eyes like a kick to the chest.

She hugged them all, including Joe. Kaylie had brought chocolates, which she presented to Julie like an award.

"I just remember you said you had to give up sweets because they were too tempting for Dad," Kaylie said. "So these are just for you."

"Oh my God," Julie exclaimed. "Come here." Nobody was better than Julie when it came to receiving gifts, and when people discovered this about her, they tended to fall all over themselves to give her stuff. She made them feel generous, potentially psychic. Even Kaylie, who was supposed to hate her, who *did* hate her for a few years in the beginning, was no longer immune to her charms.

"What are your favorites?" Julie asked, peering at the key.

"Probably mint," Kaylie said. "Or anything with dark chocolate."

"Okay, you take the mint. I'm having espresso. Ooh, and the coconut."

~

Joe hung back most of the evening, even when they went out for pizza and he was seated in the middle, with Mitch and Kaylie on either side. Conversation happened around him—went through him even—while he just sat there, eating, his ponytail caught in his collar, evidently not itching his neck.

Maddie was reminding everyone about the snowstorm the year before, which coincided with their December visit to Virginia. "And we were having a snowball fight and Tyler got Dad in the face and his goggles got all fogged up and he couldn't see," she babbled, working herself back into the moment. "And Tim called him a maniac. Remember? He said, 'The Monacan Maniac's on the loose!' And then I jumped on his back and Dad said—he said—he said—he said—" Her giggles conquered her, cutting off her breath. She put her pizza down and tried to swallow a hiccup.

"He was like, 'Where? Who?'" Tyler took over, closing his eyes, whipping his head around like a prehistoric beast.

"Because he couldn't see!" Maddie finally managed.

"He thought Maddie was the maniac, an actual crazy person," Tyler explained to Joe.

The restaurant volume was squeezing Mitch's head, and most of the noise seemed to be his own kids. What had he done to make them want to tell his father this story, a story that made him look weak? "I knew it was Maddie," he said. "I was playing along."

"You were scared, though," Tyler said. He had that old anarchy in his eyes, the element inside him that wanted to break things, especially, it seemed, his dad.

"You almost bucked Maddie over your shoulder," Julie said, reaching for another slice. "Luckily she knows how to ride!"

She was laughing. He had to shut his eyes. It wasn't clear Joe was even listening. "Well—ha—I mean, yeah, I couldn't see!"

The girls soon moved on to some other topic, but Tyler wouldn't let it go. "You were scared," he repeated a few moments later, and whether Joe was listening or not, this was Mitch's limit. This was more than enough.

"You think that's funny, Tyler?" Mitch barked.

Julie said his name. She wasn't laughing now.

"Let me ask you," he said, ignoring her, "was it funny when that girl broke her rib because you decided it'd be a good idea to drive drunk?"

Tyler's face was dead as a knife. As if to give them privacy, the girls turned up the volume on their conversation.

"No, it wasn't," Mitch answered for him. "Some things aren't funny. Was it funny when your mom had to have your stomach pumped? Was it funny when Tim got sick?"

Like a switch had been flipped, the whole table went silent. Mitch felt clumsy, and then he felt annoyed, like he did when someone fooled him in coverage, leaving him standing alone in the open field. He glanced at Tyler, who looked appropriately chastened, and then at Joe, who was finally done eating, his greased up napkin crumpled on his plate.

"Here," Mitch said to Joe, pulling out his phone. "I'll show you pictures." As though they'd never stopped talking about the snow. "It was the biggest storm since '09." If Joe was going to be with them, Mitch needed him with them; he needed to catch him up on the past.

Joe listened now for sure. He asked questions, but they were basic, questions that gave away how little he'd been paying attention in all their phone calls over the years. "When did you move in?" he asked, which he should've known: 2014. "And where'd you live before you built the house?" A Lynchburg townhouse. Should've known that, too.

Mitch looked at him, his face so much like Tim's that was gone. He was skinnier than Tim, though, so if anything, he most recalled Tim's worst face, the chemo face, the one Mitch would rather forget. The more he watched him, and he was watching everyone more closely these days, the more he understood that it was also a face in hiding. Eyes, nose, mouth, jaw: every feature in retreat. It was nothing like the voice Mitch knew from the phone, the voice that was so magically present. It seemed a waste to even have a face if this was how he was going to use it.

After gratuitous ice cream sundaes that left everyone clutching their guts, they drove back to the house to change into sweats and lay around on couches and floors until one by one they fell asleep. Except, of course, for Mitch. He was on the couch, his usual station, watching a nature show: two naked survivalists in the Amazon with nothing but a machete and a map. He had his vape, his own precious survival tool, and he had finally freed himself from his goggles for the day. Night was when his pain was the harshest, but it was also when he got to feel the most real.

He texted Hardy, out in Arizona. *Guess whos here?*

Who, the phone burbled forth.

My old man, he fired back.

DAZONK! A recent Hardy coinage. It meant "huge," or sometimes "check it out," or sometimes just "I'm here." *Srsly man no shit on accident?*

No cheesedick on purpose. I invited him

There was a pause and a pulsing ellipsis while Hardy thought about what to type. Mitch watched the female survivalist pull a scorpion off her partner's neck.

Proud of you man hows he been, Hardy said.

He's been an asshole

Lol fuck him

Yeah fuck him and his zen peace bullshit

Lol!

Death is part of life fuck you

He went on like that for a bit, brightening his mood with his thumbs. He scrolled back through their years-long conversation. There was Vicki cradling a platter of turkey. Still married, those two, married to marriage, if you asked Mitch. There was a beer Hardy was drinking. There was Hardy's gut. *DAZONK!* There was weird comfort in that gut, the white blurry mass of it that Hardy had been asserting on the world for fifty years. It had stretch marks like a historical record of jiggles. It had hair patterns no woman should ever have to see. It had a never-ending navel to nowhere, home to all manner of wax and lint. It was a goddamn thing of beauty, the fat lineman's stomach, and he hugged his own in solidarity.

After a while he was aware of another presence in the room and when he looked up Joe was standing by the screen. In the dark, with his ponytail, he managed to look simultaneously menacing and lost.

"Am I interrupting?" he asked.

"Hey," Mitch said. "No." He clicked the phone off and gestured at the many empty cushions on the couch. Joe chose one a reasonable distance away. They sat there until Mitch held out the vape, in sheepish atonement for his texts. "Want a hit?"

"Sure." Joe reached over and took his fix.

They stared at the screen, which was showing close-ups of the survivalists' bleeding mosquito bites.

"What's happening here?" Joe asked.

"They have three days to get to their rendezvous point."

"Think they'll make it?"

"I know they do. I've seen this one before. I've basically seen them all."

"That doesn't get boring?"

Mitch surprised himself by speaking emphatically. "I see something new every time. It's even better with the animal shows." He clicked over to Animal Planet, and they sat watching as a lion licked the berry red meat off an antelope, her tongue like a length of hunger-fixing tape. He'd never seen it that way before, though he'd seen this segment half a dozen times. Nor had he seen the giraffes turn one by one like dancers in a music video, a connected body wave of realizations that the lion huntress was near. Things didn't get old with repetition. They got more interesting. Especially when he was stoned.

"So," Mitch said, passing the vape back. "You don't drink, but you smoke."

Joe exhaled. "I know it's a contradiction for a lot of people. But I've been getting to know my body and my mind for a long time. One thing I've learned is that alcohol's a problem for me, grass isn't. Just the way I'm built."

"Were you built for long hair, too?"

Joe chuckled. "Were you?"

When Mitch glanced over, Joe's eyes were already there to meet his. "Nice to see your face," he said.

Mitch grunted a kind of thanks.

"It's a good face," Joe said.

"You're biased."

"Probably so. But it's also a treat for me. Even on TV all those years, you were mostly wearing your helmet. Thank God for that, don't get me wrong."

Joe had never made much of it, but at a certain point—*when?* Dr. Evans would want to know—Mitch had become aware that his dad was watching. It hadn't affected his play; in those days, he rarely thought about anything but the game in front of him. But from time to time, he thought about it afterwards, what his dad had seen, what his dad might think, and with nothing left to lose, he thought about it now: Joe driving to the nearest sports bar, Joe in a booth with the right TV in view, Joe ordering his food and soft drink, having given up booze for good.

Such devotion, from such a distance.

"You could've visited," Mitch said. He couldn't help it.

But Joe wasn't a guy you could rile. He'd done something to himself in the time since he'd gone west that had made him unwilling to argue. "I know," he said, without bitterness. "You're absolutely right about that."

Alyssa, Journey, and Cindy arrived the next morning. Mitch hugged his daughter as though nothing had changed. But while she kicked off her boots at the door he hung back and watched her, trying to decide if she looked more masculine. She was still slim, and wearing her dark hair long. She still had that face he wanted to please. But there was something possibly new in her posture: a swagger, a certain dominion over her space.

Journey's hair, meanwhile, was looking girlier than ever, a regular goldilocks. He introduced Mitch to his newest accessories—a smart watch he called a Star Wars tool, a stegosaurus he called Mike—before running off with them to the great room. "When do I get to meet Joan?" Mitch asked, once Journey was out of earshot.

Alyssa frowned, somehow hearing all of his half-heartedness

and none of his good intentions. "She has her own family, you know."

He bobbed his head eagerly. "Sure, sure, of course." He should've known better than to blitz her with support. "I just mean, you know, she's welcome. Tell her that."

"As welcome as Mom?"

"Your mother is always welcome."

This, she liked. She laughed. "Sorry she had to be the one to tell you the Age of Men is over." She arched her eyebrows, not unwomanishly, waiting for him to hear the quote. *The Return of the King!* His favorite movie of all time.

"Don't say that," he said. "That's an Orc talking. That's Gothmog."

She shrugged. "Sometimes I really sympathize with the Orcs. After all, I am no man."

"Now, Eowyn I can understand," he said, trying to sound scholarly enough for his daughter. "*That* makes a little more sense. Kill the Witch-King. Not me." Maybe they could all watch the movie again tonight, see new beauty in the death of an Orc.

"I'll think about it," she said. "Now where's my grandpa?"

They went into the kitchen where Cindy and Joe were already locked in conversation. He was happy to see that Cindy was actually taller than Joe, even in flats—everything good in him had always come from her, and it felt important that this not change—but he was less pleased with their easy rapport. Cindy's cheeks were flushed and she was smiling like a kid. Joe was giving her the full attention of his eyes, which Mitch couldn't help but register now as brown, the same as his. What about Tammy, Mitch found himself wondering? Joe was married, for Christ's sake.

"All right, you two, break it up," he said. "Journey! Get in here!" Everyone stood in suspension while they waited for the boy to show himself.

When he did, Mitch made the introductions.

"Great name," Joe said to Journey, apparently sincere.

"It's the trip, not the band," Alyssa said.

"I got that."

"Though the band's pretty awesome, too," Mitch told Journey.

And then they were out of ideas. Mitch adjusted his goggles. Cindy touched her hair. They all looked at Journey, who thankfully wasn't shy.

"I'm talking to myself in the future!" he said, holding out his watch.

"Oh good!" Joe said. "What's he like? What does he say?"

"He's on a cold planet," Journey answered. "He has hands. He says hi."

The rest of the day, Mitch found himself sticking close to his mom. He didn't want her to feel superseded just because Joe was in town. She was the real parent, the one who did the work, who brought them all into civilization. Journey seemed to have the same idea. He hung around at her feet while she prepped potatoes and Mitch sat at the kitchen island with a seltzer.

"Tell your future self I'd like to visit him on his cold planet," Cindy told Journey. "Do you think I'm wearing the right clothes?"

Journey evaluated her attire, a red apron over a white cable-knit sweater that made her chest and shoulders look even more assertive than usual. "You need a hood," he said. "And a Star Wars tool."

Cindy threw a red dishtowel over her head and selected a

balloon whisk from a caddy by the sink. "How's that?"

Journey giggled. "It's good."

"Not on this planet," Mitch said.

Cindy didn't care; she kept right on working. She was so present that it was hard to imagine a planet before her. But of course, like every person, she'd been born one day, in her case a day sixty-nine years in the past, and before that there were billions and billions of days on this planet in which she hadn't existed at all.

He looked at Journey. A second ago he was laughing and being adorable, and now he was leaning over his legs in a posture that suddenly struck Mitch as unbearably sad.

"What's wrong, Journey?" he asked.

"Nothing," Journey said to the floor.

"I don't want you to be sad," Mitch told him. Tyler had been sad in high school. It was why he acted so out of control. But why was Journey sad? Was it because his mother was dating a woman?

"Don't listen to Grandpa," Cindy said, an unnecessary caution, because Journey wasn't listening to anyone. He was looking at his wrist and talking nonsense to his future self. "You get to feel however you want."

"Childhood is supposed to be a happy time," Mitch said. "If he's not happy, something's wrong."

Cindy laughed, fluttering her dishtowel. "Stop reminding me how little you know about kids." He started to speak but she kept going. "Oh, you were so unhappy. Anytime you didn't get your way, which, I'll remind you, was most of the time."

"I wasn't *unhappy* though." He remembered running, green grass, catching football after football.

"Why do you think kids cry? All they want is independence,

and they can't have it. But that's childhood. It's normal. You have to learn how to be happy just like you have to learn to ride a bike."

She'd always had a dry, cynical streak, never really fitting in with other moms, but now he wondered how she'd survived in Virginia at all. "I would say you shouldn't be allowed near children," he said, "but then who would raise the kids?"

"Not Joe," she said, taking advantage of his sudden appearance in the kitchen.

"Not me what?"

"We were just riding you for being a dead-beat."

"Oh, is that all?" He pivoted to Mitch. "I think your ex-wife's here."

Mitch smelled Caryn before he saw her. After all these years she was still using her same almond-scented hair product. It was the same for him, with his ponytail. They both just were who they were.

"Grandma!" Journey cried, diving for her leg, apparently cured.

"Nice to smell you, Madame Marzipan," Mitch called from the safety of his island.

She was the one who'd taught him the word, but she wrinkled her nose like she had no idea what he was talking about. It was that haughtiness he'd fallen for at first. She was sexy, and she was entitled, a combination as irresistible at eighteen as it was at forty-eight. If only she hadn't lost her confidence in New England, he might still be with her.

"You have a beautiful house," she replied. She was technically middle-aged and it was technically winter, but the slowing of both seasons made her girlish outfit look reasonable. Her jacket was cropped at the ribs; her jeans were basically tights. "And this"—she looked at Joe with such possession—"this must be your dad."

Within an hour Caryn was organizing Joe, Julie, and the girls for an abbreviated yoga practice in the basement. "It's good to do before a big meal," she said. "We'll open up space in our bodies."

"No thanks," Mitch told her, jiggling his gut. "Mine has enough space as it is. You'll never get Tyler either."

Even so, he came down for a few minutes to watch as they all stood on their left legs, with their right legs stretched out behind them, like dead ends. Caryn and Alyssa's backs were flat as dinner tables. Joe's old hips kept twisting against themselves; both of his knees were bent. Journey sprawled at Maddie's foot and observed her biting her lip. As a balance trick, it must have worked; she wasn't wobbling at all.

"Make your body a line," Caryn said over Justin Bieber, who was singing about his body, too. "A line that extends in both directions forever, shooting out through your heel and your head, reaching to infinity! Feel rooted to the earth in that standing leg, feel the strength in that heel, *fire* up that belly—*reach* for China, *reach* for the far side of the world. Pull your belly in!" she shouted at Joe.

Mitch laughed. They all did, which made the lines wiggle and warp. Leave it to Caryn to use global conquest as a metaphor for personal health. No wonder they loved her in DC.

In the bathroom, with the door locked, Mitch attempted the maneuver himself. He bit his lip. He envisioned space inside. For some reason, it came to him as yellow. Through the walls, he heard them chant their final *om*, Caryn's clanging voice guiding the rest. She was a little off-key, more suited to karaoke than meditation, but that only made him admire her more.

Tim's girls, who were finally starting to look like a family without him, joined them for dinner. Afterwards, they all gathered around Mitch's Wal-Mart tree to open one gift each. Mitch's was from Joe.

"*The Book*," he said, holding it up.

"It's by Alan Watts," Joe said. "I sent you one of his YouTubes once. He's a philosopher, and he's written all kinds of things about anxiety and death. In this one he basically says our pain as human beings is all a result of this great hoax we've been believing for centuries."

Mitch tried not to look at *The Book* like it was dusted with anthrax. "Well, thanks, Joe. But you know, I'm not really into conspiracy theories."

"It's not a conspiracy theory. It's more of a conceptual framework. Instead of thinking of human beings as precious, separate egos born *into* the world, why not think of us—as we scientifically *are*—as part of the world, born *out of* it?"

Joe might've been sober, but his face was drunk with words. He had clearly given this speech many times. Perhaps he had even given the book to other unsuspecting egos. "It sounds interesting," Mitch said, even though it didn't.

"Think of it as a book of secrets!" Joe went on. "Stuff you've been waiting to hear all your life. I think you'll really appreciate it after all you've done—especially now that you're in therapy."

Mitch's anger flared in Joe's direction. "*Physical* therapy," he said to his kids, who were too preoccupied with Alyssa's magnetic tablet—a gift from Julie, for streaming shows or recipes on the refrigerator—to hear what anyone else was saying. "Anyway, it's been a long time since I've read a book. This will be good." He could hear the creak of reluctance in his voice. He needed to pep himself up. "You know what book they *should* write, though? My life story. Make that the book of secrets people give each other at Christmas. Anybody know any writers?"

Caryn looked up. "I have a yoga student at the *Washington Post*," she said. "And another one who writes children's books."

"Ask her," Mitch said. "Ask her if she'll do it." It would be the sum of all his triumphs, his journey from nowhere to the absolute top of the NFL. It was an extraordinary story, the kind you'd want to use to inspire kids. A man who'd done everything this world would permit, a basically happy person.

"Wait until you read this book, though," Joe said, jabbing the cover with his finger. Maybe he'd spent too much time alone out west, where there were even fewer people than in Virginia, because he clearly wasn't getting it. He wasn't hearing what Mitch really meant. "After you've read it," Joe said, "you're going to think of your story in a totally different way. You're going to think, what *is* my story? And you're going to realize it's no different from anyone else's. None of us exist without everything that surrounds us. Everything that was and is and will be."

He knew you couldn't argue with a person like Joe, but there was something soft about him, like a bruise on a fruit, that Mitch couldn't help wanting to poke. "It's a *little* different," he said. He was aware of Caryn listening. In her tight clothes, it wasn't immediately apparent whose side she was on. "I'm me," he declared. "I'm not anybody else."

"But that's just the ego talking," Joe persisted. "That's because you've convinced yourself you're a real person inside your bag of skin."

"Dad's ego is always talking." So Tyler had been listening, too.

Mitch, who had spent his whole life becoming a real person, did not appreciate Joe's cheap conclusion. Nor did he appreciate

Tyler's dig. He absolutely did live inside his skin. He felt its skinness every day, paining him, restraining him. The pain was what made him real. It was his daily proof of life, his proof of history, a regular ache that told him he had done things in the world, that his memories were not just laughs his brain was having at his expense.

"Watch it, Tyler," Mitch said with forced jollity. "Watch it or I'll whip your bag of skin."

"Hey Joe," Tyler said. "Grandma says you and Uncle Tim used to race."

Joe laughed. "That was a long time ago."

The rest of them had quieted down. Mitch felt his entire family look up from their gifts to become part of his conversation. "Oh, God," Tracy said. "I hope Tim won. He was impossible to live with when he lost." She still wore her little diamond ring, which long ago belonged to Tim's mom, and she seemed happy about this new memory of her husband. Good, Mitch thought. Let everyone just be happy for once.

"He won," Joe said. "Don't worry."

Mitch saw the asphalt straightaway outside his mom's old house, the green world fuzzy on either side. "I remember that race," he said. "I was in it. I was like, five. They smoked me. My whole life, NFL All-Pro, and I never beat my dad in a race."

"Boo-hoo," Julie said, and everyone laughed, including Mitch.

"It's not too late," Tyler said, that flash of anarchy again in his eyes.

"Oh, yes it is," Joe said.

"Are you kidding?" Mitch agreed. "His old bag of skin? He'd fall to pieces in a sprint. Whoops, there goes an arm. Oops, see ya, leg!"

"Hey now, I'm not *that* decrepit," Joe said, and as he said it, Mitch saw a brightness suffusing him from within, a conserved agility that belied his age. "I get my jogs in most mornings."

"I bet you do," Mitch said.

"Oh no," Cindy said. "I'm not driving anyone to the hospital tonight."

"He says he jogs!" Tyler said. "I smell a rematch."

"In your dreams, Tyler," Mitch said. "The turtle versus the walrus? No thank you."

"I'm just talking about a friendly competition. No heart attacks."

"Love you, too, son."

"Come on." Tyler was crumpling a sheet of discarded wrapping paper in his hands, packing it down like a metallic snowball. "You'd beat him."

"Obviously."

"Unless you're afraid you wouldn't."

The room filled with human sirens.

"All right, be serious y'all!" Cindy said, once the noise had died down. "Nobody's going to race."

But Mitch was, and she knew it. Everyone else knew it, too. In a football family, there was no such thing as turning down a challenge.

"I'm alive, aren't I?" Mitch said. He felt then that he was speaking for all the guys who couldn't. Tim and D and everyone else. "If I'm alive, I can run."

"Yes!" Tyler sprang up, firing his paper ball into an empty gift bag, having pulled off his great manipulation. "And I'm in, too. Ha!"

The noise of family started up again, half in protest, half in support. Mitch didn't even care that Tyler had finally tricked him into a race. What Mitch cared about, suddenly, was getting outside, on the grass, and beating Joe with his own philosophy: the motion he was, the action that was him.

Joe sat there in his bright old body, saying nothing, but declining all the same. He seemed to think there was another way to live, one that didn't involve competition. And maybe there was, but not in the world Mitch had always known, and not in the world he believed in.

"Why not?" Mitch said, getting to his feet. He threw all the force of his ego at his father. "Come on, Joe! It's a short move. It's a short move, Joe, let's go!"

It was already eleven o'clock, but it seemed much earlier. The darkness of Mitch's yard felt partial, just a passing affliction, held at bay by the floodlights from his deck. The entire family had gathered for the event, the thrilling night game, Alyssa and Journey with Tim's clan on the deck, Journey peering through the posts. At the foot of the stairs, Caryn defined alignment. Next to her Julie stood atop her strong, fighter's legs. He would sleep with Caryn again one day. On her legs there in his immortal Virginia, Julie probably already knew. She'd probably even forgive him.

He had taken a few good pulls from the vape throughout the night, enough to think a few necessary, radical thoughts, and to feel himself inside himself, goggle-free out in the dark. Mentally, he rolled on his tights, his skin's skin, which had always contained him on the field. What had to contain him now was family. Now everything he used to get from football, he had to get from them.

He looked ahead at the spot where Kaylie and Cindy had spread themselves, with their arms outstretched, awaiting the tag, which wasn't any particular distance from the starting line, but was generally about as far as he could see. Their limbs were visible. Their expressions were not, but his mother's was known to him all the same. It was a face that said, *When will it be enough!* (Never!) and a face that was already laughing at his response.

Maddie, who for some horsey reason owned a whistle, was ready as the ref at the start. His whole family, all his women, all of their voices and faces here with him now in the flesh. Finally big enough for a Suburban, finally big enough to stage a three-man race.

To his left, aiming for Kaylie's outside hand, was Tyler, tilting forward, wanting something he didn't seem to know he already had. To his right, aiming for Cindy, was Joe, compacted with age like a breathing stone. Here they were again, older, repeating a scene from the past. Because everything repeated, whether you wanted it to or not—but especially when you wanted it to, as a part of Mitch always did. A big part, maybe even a part as large as his body. Tyler had that part, too, but Joe, it seemed, did not. The part he had always declined to race—but then, somehow, always gave in. That was the pattern, anyway, when Mitch was watching. What were his patterns when Mitch was not watching? This, he couldn't know.

"It's a short move," Mitch told him, gazing straight ahead at his mom.

"Bastard," was Joe's cheeky response.

Mitch coughed in delight. "You would know!"

There were no false starts. Maddie gave the signal and they went. Mitch's body was the world and the world was Mitch running, his legs doing what he'd grown them to do. The darkness fled from him as he approached his mom, and her face came into sight. She seemed to be bracing herself for a collision, her eyes wide, her mouth small, her comprehension as layered as one of her silly pine cones. She feared him as much as ever. Because she'd given up love for him, a boy she'd lose one day, because he'd already begun his separation the moment he arrived in her womb. But she was ready, too. She was armored in all her self-grown scales and she was saying, *Hit me*. She was saying, *You maniac. You're all I've got.*

The cheering started before he reached the line. He went toward his mother; he tagged her hand.

12. SARAH, 2030

Mitch Wilkins' brain arrived in an insulated box marked Urgent Medical Shipment, like every other brain I've received. His was my ninety-first case, a fact that should've been neutral. But Mitch was from my hometown, the only brain in our bank to have attended my little Virginia high school, and though he was in college by the time I was born, I grew up a misfit and a football fan, in love with catches and contact and fascinated by the story of his success. If people like him could make it outside of Monacan, then surely I could, too. I was better at school than anyone else I knew; I had, bad joke, a brain. So when I finally met him, here, like this, in the midst of a bodily crisis of my own, it hit me pretty hard.

To cope, I assigned myself the gross exam, handled the sampling, stained the slides, something I'd normally pass on to the techs. It was a fairly healthy brain, at least as far as football brains went. Chronic Traumatic Encephalopathy, stage two, which matched our diagnosis while he was alive. He'd suffered headaches and mood swings and the occasional bout of explosivity. But that, he insisted in his 2025 assessment, just made him a football player; that was who he'd always been. Which is not to say the elevated biomarkers surprised him. "Play football, get CTE," he said in his follow-up. "I knew the risks, even though I didn't." He seemed determined to keep working, which was all he'd ever really known how to do. In that way, I could relate.

I watched those interviews, which predate my time, in preparation for my postmortem call with his family: partner Julie Matthews, mother Cindy Wilkins, and daughters Alyssa Wilkins and Madison Jones all side-by-side at the virtual table. They, too, were unsurprised. "Honestly," Julie said, without a drop of bitterness. "I wish he'd enrolled in a heart study instead. Not that he would've given up meat." Genial laughter all around.

Oh, how I loved those women, his earlier caretakers. There was something fearless about them, the way they offered up story after story, as though they'd really known who he was. The mother especially: a sturdy mom even older than mine, who was the last of the bunch to sign off. My mother knew him, too. She'd regaled me with stories of the famous Mitch Wilkins falling asleep in her English class, so many years ago, when Dad had taught at Briarwood and she at the high school, in that long middle stretch of their adulthood, the period of life that I'm in now. On their advice, I'd gotten out as soon as I could, picked a fancy college in New England that funneled me straight to New York, and eventually to Boston, where I'd finally settled down. But it wasn't like that for my parents. They remained outsiders in Virginia for the better part of their lives.

I was desperate to tell my mom about Mitch, but also a little afraid. What if she didn't remember him? Would it upset her? Would it upset me? She was only seventy-four but already battling dementia, while I was thirty-nine and swirling with hormones in a belated effort to have my own kid. The whole situation was delicate, demanding patience and clarity of thought. On my better days, I still had a bit of both.

I waited two weeks—two whole weeks!—until their next visit, which would overlap with my fourth embryo transfer, which I told them but otherwise didn't dwell on; they had enough to worry about as it was. They would be spreading the journey out over a few days, stopping with friends in New Jersey and Connecticut. The drive from DC, where they'd retired for the theater and museums, had always been trying, but this year it must have been worse. When they finally turned into my driveway, on Friday afternoon, they sat molded to their seats, visibly exhausted.

"I don't think we'll do this again," my dad said as we unloaded the car. I could see that it cost him to admit this, my dad the driver, who loved making excellent time. "It's hard on me," he said. He was seventy-six, two years ahead of her, though these days he seemed much younger. "It's hard on your mom."

I gripped her bag and looked at her. She was inspecting the tulips that Jonas maintained out front, paying no attention to us. Over the years she'd often withdrawn when someone had something embarrassing to say, but now I read all her behaviors differently, her aloofness most of all.

In the house I offered them seltzer with bitters, because Mom was no longer permitted alcohol. Jonas came in to greet them and we acted like everything was normal, but I could barely hold it together. My mother stood under the kitchen lights looking melted, her durable hair in its usual braid, her blue eyes watering reflexively. A month since I'd last seen her, and already, she had a different face.

"Mom," I said. "How are you feeling?"

"Fine," she said, brightly, as though these were pleasantries. "Happy to be here with you."

The next morning, Dad and Jonas and I had a strategy session while Mom slept in. She was finally on the latest cocktail of disease-modifying drugs, but the doctor warned it would take time to see any progress. In the meantime, her care team had suggested we fix her with a locater in case she wandered off. Dad was adamantly opposed. He was always with her, he said, and anyway, she was his wife; he wouldn't treat her like some cow. I understood but I also saw the value. We hadn't gotten much farther than that when Mom joined us, already dressed, her drapey blouse buttoned straight. She sat at the breakfast table, selected an orange from the centerpiece bowl, and tucked her fingernails into the peel. She looked alert, competent even. Maybe the cocktail was working.

We had a leisurely breakfast, talking about the usual things. My father's latest retirement project was a novel about his father, the cattle rancher, which in turn got us talking about the dairy at Briarwood, and all the related gear the college sold: Holstein-print t-shirts and baseball caps and mugs. We had loads of it; I even had a stuffed cow with eraser-pink udders. Looking back, I think we fetishized the cows for the same reason we fetishized football, because we were desperate to belong. We were dorks, godless city people. We didn't hunt or laugh at snakes or know how to operate heavy machinery; we rarely even swam in the lake. But we could admire Monacan's manmade patterns: cows grazing and resting, players covering one hundred yards of field. We showed up, like everyone else, to scream ourselves hoarse on Friday nights. It wasn't avant garde, Mom always said, but it was both ordinary and extreme, like flying in airplanes, and this alone made it worth our attention. Of course, the more attention we paid, the more interesting the sport became, a game of close and distant contact, of carefully managed personnel. A game built on the notion of forward progress, and measurements that everyone agreed were pretty arbitrary, but fun to hope for all the same. Most interesting of all, football was something Monacan did well, and we, good students that we were, had always been suckers for excellence.

"Why are cows ungulates?" Jonas asked, bringing me back to the moment.

"That just means they have hooves," Dad told him.

I quickly called up some cow facts. "But did you know they also have long memories? They can individually identify several dozen other herd members." I double-checked the number given. "Fifty. Fifty to seventy other herd members."

"Your memory's even longer," Jonas said. He'd been sucking up to me all week, and for good reason. The estrogen tablets had made me particularly edgy this go-around, and my breasts felt packed with heavy metal from the progesterone.

"I literally just looked that up," I told him.

"I mean you know a million people. But you also knew that without having to look it up."

"Fifty sounds like more than enough for me," said my father, who did not share my enthusiasm for groups. "I like cows because they ruminate."

"That part is disgusting," I said. "They basically eat their own vomit."

"You're thinking anthropocentrically. They take their time."

"You're the one thinking anthropocentrically. They're digesting. They aren't writing novels."

My mother liked cows, too, almost as much as she liked gardening and football, but this morning she said little. She seemed to need her headspace for breakfast.

"Hello," I said, waving my hand near her line of sight.

"Your mom's working on her orange," Dad said, redundantly, for it was obvious she was giving each section the same kind of meditative attention she used to give to student exams. Impatient for her company, I looked up more facts to rouse her.

"'Citrus trees belong to one superspecies, which is almost entirely infertile,'" I announced, already regretting my zeal for the topic. "Okay, right, they survive only through human cultivation."

"Mm," Jonas said. Could I hear him wincing on my behalf?

Whatever, I told myself, better to ignore the personal implication. "'The navel orange earned its name for the second, stunted, fruit at the base beneath its peel.'"

This got Mom's attention. "I thought it was because of the Navy and scurvy."

"That's N-A-V-A-L," my father intoned.

"Come on, Mom, you know that." I picked one of the remaining oranges from the bowl, clapped its grippy rind, and made as if to throw her a touchdown pass, with the second fruit leading the way. "They have belly buttons."

She laughed at the orange and at me, then darted her eyes somewhere lower. I don't think it was necessarily my belly, so I've decided to think it was not.

"Don't be silly, sweetie, I know that," she said. "I was making a pun. Like how everything was 'an utter delight' or 'utter madness' with the cows."

The cocktail was working. I had to believe it was.

I'd moved to Boston for my job, but mostly to get out of New York. I'd squandered years there in a panic of drunken cynicism, regularly falling into bed with aloof, charismatic men, pretending I didn't need them either. At work I was a gunner, winning grants, and I thought my friends were gunners, too, but then one by one they got married and pregnant, retreating from the old vigor of their lives. I felt uncomfortable watching them nurse, marooned in their photo-ready apartments, the city reduced to a rumor or a view. They were sleep-deprived and distracted and there was nothing to envy in their apologetic husbands, sudden grays, or billowy, spit-stained shirts. Even so, I felt threatened. I couldn't shake the thought that my friends were managing to expand their claims to life, their cells dividing and mattering more, while mine faded, unreplaced. I felt too good for motherhood and at the same time not good enough to care for someone else.

Once my tribe disbanded, I found myself wanting to be near my parents, but the right job hadn't come along. Meanwhile, football kept growing more lucrative, and more objectionable to certain sectors of the public, including, for a brief, exciting period, the offended players themselves. There were protests and articles and documentaries, and summits and symposia and sit-downs, and eventually the owners did a smart thing, endowing a brain center in perpetuity. Over the years, it had essentially saved the game, advising on rule and helmet changes, and very publicly researching a vaccine for active players; football, the implication was, would always take care of its own. Even so, when I was headhunted and eventually offered the directorship of the brain bank here, my Brooklyn friends were scandalized. They were, almost to a person, boycotters, and no amount of incremental progress was good enough for them. One of the nursers in particular campaigned zealously to keep me in New York, actually using the word collaborationist over an organic dinner I had cooked. But in the end, the money was too good, and I was too much in need of different company. If the game was still good enough for the players, it was good enough for me.

It must've been the right choice, because not even a month had passed before I met Jonas, the divorced historian. We were at the house of a mutual friend and he sat next to me on a couch, his leg barely brushing against mine. He was cheerful, nothing like the men I'd always fallen for in New York. We talked, and my skin felt elastic, I saw the human borders of his eyes, and it totally floored me because for the first time in my life I found myself wanting a child.

The desire dissipated almost immediately, but I accepted a date with him in the hopes of re-upping. We saw a special screening of the original *Blade Runner* in the old theater at Coolidge Corner, and he said all sorts of things I'd been on the verge of thinking myself. There it was again, that baby-hungry high. I felt an almost cultish desire to fuck him, which I did, the moment we got back to my place. Afterwards I looked in the bathroom mirror and almost cried. I felt as though I'd passed a life-saving test: I was not a sterile replicant, but a real irrational human after all.

I was lucky, because he turned out to be reliable, too. He drank a regular amount, just enough to give the appearance of being a regular man. He followed the news and showed up to work. I could see him, quite clearly, as a child, and this was something I liked very much. His one flaw might've been the volume of his voice, which was permanently set for the lecture hall. But most of the time, I hardly noticed that, because I liked the things he said.

Within six months I'd begun taking letrozole for ovulation induction, and he'd moved in and started a garden in my yard. From the kitchen I'd watch him hulk around in rubber clogs, transplanting tiny cabbages and kales, and it was hard not to think about the Briarwood groundskeepers I used to love, those strong men in mesh caps with color block t-shirt tans.

Not long after that we visited my parents. The Virginia Tech game was on, and we all watched it together, as we always had, and secretly still did, Mom on the chaise in her Hokie sweatshirt, Dad and Jonas in separate chairs, and me on the floor in various cow-faces and half-heroes to open up my hips. When it was over, Mom and Jonas went outside to check on some things in the garden, and it was at this point, with my right hip joint dropping audibly in figure-four, that Dad told me Mom was sick. Neither of them had the risk-factor gene, and even so, the moment he said it, I knew her condition was neurodegenerative. She often called me twice a day. She'd been repeating herself for years. I sat upright. Once I'd absorbed the news and stopped hating myself, I turned stone-cold scientific, interrogating him on every detail, stopping only when Mom came in, still wearing her bright yellow gloves.

"Mom," I cried, rushing to her.

"I know," she said, receiving the hug. "I know. Now where did Jonas go with that watering can?"

We wasted no more time. We went back to the fertility clinic the following week, to kick our treatments into the highest gear. Since then, it's been a year, three transfers, and still, still, no baby. Which seems to be the punishment I deserve for not wanting one when I was young.

Later that morning, I made the guest bed while Mom sat in the revolving desk chair, preparing her first dose of insulin. She loaded the cartridge into her nasal gun and fired it, straight to her brain.

"Did you get it all?" I asked, hugging a pillow against my breasts. She liked the little black device, which reminded her of taking drugs for fun. She said it made her feel young again. Though she said dementia did that, too.

"Yes," she said, turning the chair toward me. Her face was a little stunned, at that uncanny threshold between expressions. Not that different from a drunk face. Not that different from a baby's face either. But then it resolved into the specific face that I now recognized as hers.

I perched on the edge of the bed. "I've been meaning to ask…do you remember Mitch Wilkins, from Monacan? The NFL star?"

Excitement washed over her, but then she caught herself mid-smile. "Oh no," she said. "Don't tell me you have his brain."

"I'm afraid we do."

"Poor boy." She gripped the nasal gun in her hand.

"He had a heart attack at his dealership, a few months ago. One of his employees came in, they said he was an old friend, and apparently he was joking around for a while before he even realized. He thought Mitch was just napping at his desk."

There was a pause while my mother gathered whatever parts of herself were necessary for a response. "You kissed him," she finally said.

"Me? Oh no, he was twenty years older."

"You did. You loved older boys."

At this point, I had to marshal my patience. "We cheered for him on TV," I told her. "But I never met him. I only bring him up because I thought you might have some stories. Didn't you have him in class?"

My mother gave a private laugh. "He worked the grounds crew and he would come around and you would put on your scissor shorts and flirt."

When I was fourteen or fifteen, I did cut the legs off my old jeans and strut around in front of the college-aged groundskeepers. It was one her favorite stories about me. But Mitch was obviously not on the crew, nor did I ever succeed in getting one of them to kiss me. I dropped *y'all* and *ain't* like everyone else, but I read science fiction and refused to eat meat, which didn't make me very popular in Monacan. That was something Mom liked to forget, even before she starting losing her memory. To her, I had always been extraordinary. No wonder we became best friends.

"Not scissor shorts," I said. "Cut-offs."

"What?"

"The shorts. We called them cut-offs."

"I don't know what you're talking about." Her face went to its uncanny place again.

"The shorts, Mom. I used to wear cut-off shorts. But only on campus, where it was safe. I never had the courage to wear them anywhere else."

Now she was irritated. "*Stop* changing the subject," she insisted, as though she'd already commanded me once. "It's hard to follow and I don't appreciate it."

"It's the same subject, Mom—"

I stopped only when her face grew furious, like a hastily thwarted child's. She turned away, and with a wild pang, I wanted a do-over, and not just of this conversation. I wanted, in a way, to be pregnant with my unruined mom. I'd give again what I'd already given at the clinic: an oval of my most immortal skin, to be minced, and pumped with proteins, and reprogrammed into viable eggs. We'd fertilize them, we'd run all the tests, we'd make sure she got the best-chance brain. And then they'd implant her, and then she'd be born. She'd begin memory therapies long before symptoms presented, with mindfulness training from a very young age. This time she'd actually get to use her

Ph.D., finding fulfillment as a professor like my dad. They'd teach somewhere else—not Virginia—so she wouldn't have to drink through her prime. She'd keep her mind, she'd age in a normal way, and it would all unfold with a tactile slowness, this corrected, second-chance life. This mother who was actually my child and therefore not my mother at all.

A few days before my parents arrived we'd had the final blood test and scan to make sure my endometrium was ready. It looked like a tulip resting on its side, which meant it was thick enough, and the transfer could proceed, so we treated ourselves to a fancy dinner in Cambridge, at a new restaurant we'd read about online. Our meal was comprised entirely of small bites. One dish was literally just an egg in an oyster shell.

"To number four," Jonas said, which was how we referred to the embryo we'd selected from our surviving nine, in effect our fourth-round child. The first had perfect grades, but failed to implant immediately, your classic first-round bust. The second stopped growing within weeks. The third was a replay of the first.

"I'm not feeling good about it," I told him.

"You never feel good about it."

"That's because it's never worked. And the embryo quality decreases every time."

"But one day it will work," he said, uninterested in facts. "Irrespective of how you feel. We're manipulating things a bit, so it makes sense that it's all been a bit fragile. But we've talked about this; it's a numbers game. Eventually, the conditions will be right."

"Actually, studies have shown that reduced stress and positive visualizations can help."

"That's what I'm saying, you have to stop feeling bad about it."

I poked his airspace with my tiny fork. "That's *not* what you said. You said feeling good won't make a difference."

He laughed. "I know, I know. But what I meant was—well, okay, I did that wrong. Maybe what I meant was that you never feel good about it, and maybe that's a problem."

"That is literally the opposite of what you said. It's also not very nice."

Instead of talking, he slurped his oyster egg, a choice I found uncomfortable, because Jonas loved to talk. He almost never stopped, not even when he was eating.

"What?" I asked. "What?"

He frowned, and the lines that had been imprinting themselves on his forehead grew deeper. I was making him old. Every day with me was aging him.

"You just make it so hard," he said, and I felt a perverse flicker of satisfaction, because at least we were on the same page about that.

"Maybe this will be our silver lining," I said, suddenly annoyed with him for knowing me so well. "We tried. So when we fail, people will feel bad for us, instead of thinking we're child-loathing monsters."

"Who would think that? Not any of our friends."

He was so damn naive. You'd think he studied some forgotten period of history in which everyone had enough protein, and no one suffered pain of any kind, and civilization meant emotional fulfillment for every creature, not just Ivy League academics. But he didn't! He studied American capitalism.

"Maybe it's for the best," I said. "You see how stressed I am now? Imagine me with a baby! I'd be miserable. And the kid would hate me, too. Better to save us all that pain."

"That's ridiculous and you know it. For one thing, you're wonderful. Number two, in your scenario, there isn't even a kid to be saved. And c), the entire argument is specious, because who ever promised you a life without pain?"

"Be quiet. You're mixing your terms."

"When have I ever been quiet?" he boomed, triumphantly. People looked over from their boring dates, forcing me to shush him through my laughter.

He mimed a zipper across his lips, and I found myself wanting to kiss him. He really hadn't done anything so terrible. He'd only believed something would happen that hadn't.

"I just hate to see you tearing yourself down," he said, after we'd grown calm. It was one of his favorite laments: the self-sabotage of intelligent women. "You're a goddamn titan, and instead of using your strength to endure this, you're using it against yourself. Do you think your mom did that? No fucking way. She didn't have stem cells to manipulate or even IVF and she kept trying until she got you."

"This is not about me or my mother. It's about my toxic body."

I had him there. Or so I thought. "You're relentless," he said, shaking his head. "You're completely determined to fail."

"Well, lucky me, it's working!"

"All right," he said. "Maybe we should talk about your mother instead."

It was a cheap move and he knew it. But Jonas's bullishness was even more relentless than my despair. He barreled on, delightedly. "Look, obviously you know more about this than I do, but I've been reading about her treatment and the early studies are pretty optimistic. I think we're going to see some changes in her. I think she'll get to meet her grandkid."

I looked at my egg, which was gelatinous and perfectly filled its shell, a marvel, really, of cooking chemistry. You could put an egg in anything and it would spread as far as it could. If the vessel was small, like this one, it would cling. It took me a moment to realize I was unhappy with this idea, and with everything to do with eggs.

"Easy for you to say," I told him. "Your body's not the one on trial here. Your parents are obscenely healthy and young. Of course you think everything's going to be fine—because you're looking at all the wrong evidence!"

"Oh no," he said. "Don't cry. No, baby, I'm sorry, don't cry."

Saturday afternoon I got called into the lab to receive a fresh donation. As I logged it, I kept thinking about my mother's reaction to the news about Mitch. However sad it had made her, and however mixed her memory of who he was, at least his name had elicited some emotion.

In a way it was easier to be at the lab than it was to be with her, so before I left I spent some time at the microscope. My favorite slides in the Wilkins case number came from the amygdala. Stained purple, they featured only mild pathology: a single tau tangle lounging in the northwest corner like a wayward star on a national flag. Against my better judgment, I deactivated the locater on one and put it in a slide mailer. I thought Mom might like to see.

Sunday we awoke to a distraction. It had snowed overnight—in May. This was happening more often in recent years, especially in Boston: iced lilacs, graduation caps tossed with flurries. But rarely did it stick.

We decided not to let a few inches spoil our plans, which

involved a walk in the Mount Auburn Cemetery. Mom wore my old parka and her braid under earmuffs; if it weren't for her grays she would've looked like a teenager. Dad stayed back to write, probably relieved to have some time to himself. We'd be fine, we assured him, we'd be back in a couple of hours.

We visited the abolitionists, Harriet Jacobs, Julia Ward Howe, and a staggering number of stones labeled "Mother" and "Father." More than anyone else, more than senators, more than slaves or soldiers, even, this was who'd died in the nineteenth century: people's parents. It was heartbreaking. Even more heartbreaking was how often "Baby" died, too.

At Howe's stone, Mom began to hum "The Battle Hymn of the Republic." She was having a good day, her gray-blue eyes open wide, as though sampled from the post-storm sky.

We also saw newer graves. As recently as 2005, someone had buried the poet Robert Creeley. *Look at the light of this hour*, read the back of Creeley's modest headstone, each word on its own little line. We looked. It was noon, but the sun held itself back behind the trees, shyly, not wanting to overwhelm us.

"I suppose the meaning changes," Mom said. "Depending on the day."

After our cemetery walk, we headed to the old Middle Eastern bakery. It was crowded inside, with only a few places to sit, but we persevered, because I'd promised Mom rose-flavored cakes.

"Sit here," I told her, pointing to a little crevice between the spice racks where the bakery had stashed an extra stool.

"Such a boss, such a boss." Even on her good days, she had taken to repeating herself like a sportscaster, or the automated voice on trains. But she sat when I handed her my backpack. For so many years, she'd been the one to boss me, to sit me down with a bag or a pad of paper or a set of instructions for not moving while she went about her alluring and important adult life. I'd resented her then, semi-consciously, wondering why I couldn't be the one in charge and have her defer to me. What we were experiencing now was not quite the reversal I'd imagined, but that was mostly because she had become a new person, no longer the mom who'd bossed me. We'd each lost something and we'd each gained something, but nothing had been reversed.

I was only gone for a moment to give Jonas our order, and when I returned, she was not sitting where I'd left her. I had so expected to see her inquisitive new-person face, her braid pushed up in the hood of my parka, that I couldn't quite believe she wasn't there. I looked at the empty stool, and on the ground beside it, my backpack, somewhat longer than necessary.

"Jonas," I said, securing the backpack to my shoulders. "Jonas."

We had never lost her before. But I realized now that I'd been waiting for it to happen. It had almost been a fantasy of mine. And now that the inevitable had occurred, the world recalibrated itself. It was as though losing Mom was already our constant problem, and I saw how foolish my father had been to resist tagging her just because he had an ethical objection to treating her like a cow.

We ran out into the street, looking everywhere, and with each passing instant saw more of the map, but no flashing dot that was Mom. She had her untraceable magic, and we, mere mortals, were screwed. We would have to find her on foot.

We crisscrossed the neighborhood like children playing police. I checked yard after yard, popping through alleys, most of the time emerging to find no one, not even a resident who might've seen which way she'd gone. More often, I found Jonas instead.

"Maybe she went back to the cemetery!" I called after we intersected, clueless, for the third or fourth time. The afternoon cold was settling into my body and my toes were fusing into blocks.

"We can try," he told me. I'd never seen him so far from a laugh.

We took off together, the backpack bouncing on my shoulders, my fused feet landing sturdily on the road. Inside the cemetery gates, paths struck out in every direction—Clematis, Asclepias, Columbine—tormenting me with their poisonous suggestions. It was a labyrinth; the whole point was that you never got out. But our feet remembered the way and we soon found Mom at Robert Creeley's grave, just standing there, looking toward the sun, which was now a little further along on its course.

> *Look*
> *at*
> *the*
> *light*
> *of*
> *this*
> *hour.*

I had to stop for a moment, my hands on my knees, my breath in my throat, to make sure it was her, and not a ghost. Eventually she felt us there, and turned. She was shaking and clutching her braid in her fist.

"The meaning changes," her uncanny face said. "Depending on the day."

We drove her straight home, without collecting our rosewater cakes. She didn't even ask about them, having lapsed into one of her silences. Not a good day after all.

"I hear you had a little adventure," Dad said as we came inside. I stood there as he helped her out of her boots. She did not seem alert enough to be frightened, and that was a blessing, in a way. Now he would have to accept that we should tag her; she would definitely go missing again.

The slide, I thought. It might bring her back. I reached into my backpack for my hard shell glasses case, where I'd stowed it the day before.

Empty.

I closed it and opened it again.

Still empty.

The little mailer was not anywhere in my backpack. I put the bag down and went out to the car, but it was also not anywhere in the car. I sat in the backseat and tried, half-heartedly, to locate it, even though I knew I'd turned the locater off. I thought of my mom's blank face, of her existence that was no longer quite in my world, and suddenly I knew, in that dangerously unscientific way I sometimes know things, that she had Mitch. She had held my backpack for me in the café. She must have felt his significance—his familiar presence, the residual warmth from my hand—and wanted him for herself.

Too much time had passed and Jonas had noticed. He came out onto the steps in his clogs, squinting, and when he saw me, he joined me in the backseat.

"I've lost Mitch," I told him.

"What do you mean you've lost him? Who's Mitch?"

I told him everything, including my suspicions of my mom, but he didn't understand. "Can't you just make another slide? You still have the tissue."

"It's the principle." I was almost crying. "I fucked up. I

crossed the line."

"Well, why don't we ask her?" Jonas said. My partner, the non-scientist, who never met a problem he couldn't solve. Before I could argue, he'd gotten us out of the car and back into the house and was calling my mother by name.

"Laura?" he asked, "Laura." My heart was beating audibly. I stepped up behind him, using the right side of his body as a shield.

"Did you take a slide from Sarah's backpack?"

She blinked and he repeated the question. "It would have been in her glasses case. It's from one of her brains and she needs it. It belongs to her lab."

"Mitch Wilkins," I blurted. "Remember?"

"Mitch?" she cried, as though he'd come to see her after all these years. "You know Mitch?"

"Not exactly," I said.

"Did I ever tell you about him?" She was smiling now, and I was terrified of the nonsense she was about to spew. After all we'd been through that day, I didn't think I could handle any more.

"Yes, he was your student," I said. "That's why I wanted to show you."

"And in the summers he was a groundskeeper at the college," Mom went on. "With his uncle who was there for years, what was his name, Tim. I used to see them hauling branches around. Seemed like a big part of the job, actually, just collecting giant branches in their trucks."

"Really." I couldn't believe she had so much to say. Even though I now realized that this was exactly what I'd been hoping for: the famous person triggering memories where other interventions failed.

"And there was one day when I was driving in from town, and it must've been August because the students were starting to move back in. And at that first traffic circle, I see him on the front lawn of, you remember, that dorm by the first traffic circle, and he's standing there with a student and a giant purple sofa, one of those fainting couches, you know the kind. And they keep looking at the couch and then at the door, and it's clear they have a problem."

"What year was this?" I asked, but she wasn't listening. She was listening to her own brilliant memory. I could've killed myself for interrupting.

"When I drove by again," she said, "he was gone and she was gone and so was the couch. I decided he must've found a way." Her face was full color, and she was swaying a bit in her seat. "You remember his uncle, Tim? In the summers he was a groundskeeper at the college."

My heart sank. "Right, that's what you said."

"He was a groundskeeper. He tried to kiss me once."

"Mom!"

So much for sanity.

"He did." She made her cute, pouty face. "What, you don't believe me? You don't believe a big football player could ever want to kiss your little mom?"

"I believe it," Dad said.

"I told you that story," she insisted.

"I know you did," Dad said.

"There I was, this radical Yankee."

Now she was really sounding like her old self, the braggy, embarrassing one who'd had too much to drink.

"I'm sorry, guys, I have to—"

"He called me up a few years ago," she said.

"Who—Mitch?"

She nodded, and the motion was liquidy, her head bobbing like a buoy on her neck. "He was going through old things. And he said he found a paper he owed me. Can you imagine? He wanted to turn it in. I said, 'But Mitch, you already walked, remember? Graduation was forty years ago.' But he said, no, he was a man of his word. He had promised me a paper on *The Great Gatsby*, and he wanted me to have it."

"Come on, Mom, really?" I didn't believe her. She'd raised me to be rational, and I just didn't believe her.

"So he got in his car and he drove up here and he came to my desk and he gave me the paper. That was when he kissed me. He was so old. Oh, sweetie, he was wearing headgear to protect his eyes, like someone out of science fiction. He had rose-colored glasses, to protect his eyes."

Mitch had indeed worn migraine goggles for the last fifteen years of his life, a blind man look that was sort of disarming, at least on video. For his last decade, he'd also lived with an occipital implant. I wondered if Mom knew about that, too. She was looking at a middle distance between the wall and my face, her eyes filled with that reflexive water. Her voice kept cracking, as though through a bad connection, a voice from the past telling me about the future, or a voice from the future telling me about the past. Whichever it was, her information was incomplete, scattered, and partial—but that didn't mean it wasn't real.

I wiped my own eyes prophylactically. "It's just, I have to find Mitch. It's really important for my job. Do you have him?"

This tripped her up. She snapped out of her reverie and turned to look at me, at the place where I was actually standing. "Sweetie, are you sure *you* aren't sick? Didn't you say Mitch was dead?"

"The slide, Mom. From his amygdala. It was in my bag."

She shook her head the way she used to do when she caught me flirting with the groundskeepers. Amused. Composed. The older, wiser adult who'd watched me closely, and told me stories about who I was. "Are you sure you didn't leave it at work?"

I went to the mudroom. Before I'd even gotten one boot on, Jonas was there, blocking the door. "Where are you going?"

"Where do you think? The cemetery. I have to retrace my steps."

"Why don't we check the lab?"

It was an idiotic idea because I'd brought Mitch home. I knew that. I clearly remembered putting the slide mailer in my glasses case, and I knew for certain he was not in the lab. But Jonas could be so forceful sometimes, especially when I'd lost my cool.

The next thing I knew we were in the car and he was driving, which was a good thing because I was crying so hard I couldn't see. What had happened in my mother's life, really? What had happened to us all that afternoon? When my mother was gone, who would tell me about myself? How would I know I was real?

In the empty lab, we checked the cabinet where Mitch's case number lived; sure enough, one amygdala slide was missing. We checked adjacent cabinets and the drawers of everyone's bench. We even checked the freezers, opening boxes at random, digging among frozen slices of brain. The air swirled out at us like an overnight snowstorm in May.

"Where is he?" I wailed. "Where?"

I sank to the floor by my bench and leaned against the drawers, feeling the handles prod my aging back. I let them dig, wanting to hurt. Jonas closed the freezer he was searching and came to sit with me.

"I'll be fired," I told Jonas. "This is like embezzlement."

He pulled me into his lap and began to argue in his lecture hall voice that I was a titan and a lioness and frankly too likable to fire. I wasn't buying it, but I was soothed, because he was incapable of telling stories he didn't believe, and somehow he still believed in me. In a lot of ways, and this was one, he really was a lot like my mom.

I sat back to see him seeing me, bracing myself with a hand on the floor. It was slick from a recent washing and my hand slid back under the overhang of my bench. As it did, it brushed against a gap between the cabinet and the floor, and in that gap, a piece of matter. The material was plastic, and of the right shape and size.

"It's him!" I cried, finally, when the power of speech returned. "It's him, it's him, it's him!"

I got down on my belly and plucked him out into the open. He shot across the alley between the benches, ricocheting off the leg of a stool. I scrambled after him, falling on him just before he came to rest alongside the closest freezer. I had him. I had him in my possession. The slide mailer was filthy, completely covered in dust, having never even left the lab. But clasped inside it, he was safe, ready, still, to work.

Jonas collapsed against me. With my other hand I held his very tight and allowed myself to look into the future. Tomorrow, the embryology techs would thaw number four and within an hour it would be in my womb. We knew so much about it already. In addition to no serious early onset diseases, it had a good chance of above average intelligence, a low chance of being an athlete, light brown hair, blue eyes, a girl. In other words, our child. If it even made it that far.

I closed my eyes and tried to visualize that child, but for

obvious reasons all I saw was my mom: her real face, the one I remembered. And then I saw Mitch's face, which was more or less a fiction, since I'd never met him in person, and then I saw his mother, who I knew only through a screen but who'd lingered after the rest of the family had signed off to tell me a few more stories of her son: how he'd loved oranges, how he'd loved women more than he cared to admit, how he'd been his own person, a loaded weapon beyond her control. And then I saw my own mom again, but this time it was her current face, and then for a second, half a second maybe, but long enough that I'm going to count it, I saw my future child.

It seemed almost irrelevant that there were things that really happened in this world, and other things that didn't. The could've-happened were no less real than the really-happened, which vanished even with proper care.

When I was young, before I went boy-crazy, I liked to take a sketchbook to the campus pastures where I'd crouch by the fence and draw the cows. Briarwood was a women's college, so there were also horses everywhere, and plenty of campus dogs, not to mention cottontail bunnies, beavers, endless birds, and deer. But the animals I liked observing were the cows. I liked the broad pads of their noses, and the way they conspired to spend half the day lying down, each in her own quiet space. You had privacy as a cow, but you also had support. As a girl, I saw the power in that.

My mother encouraged my interest, buying me books about livestock, even arranging for me to go to the dairy to watch the cows get milked. It must've been an old-school place, because they still bred their cows with a bull, and one morning the dairy manager called my mom to tell her that several of the cows were in estrus that day.

She drove me out there, and we joined a few other observers outside a pen where a bored cow was harnessed for the bull. He licked her butt and we laughed, he rested his chin on her rump and we cooed, and then in a flash a thin penis flicked out from his abdomen at the same moment that he reared up on his legs. It was over in a matter of seconds, such a quick motion I barely saw it.

"Wait," I asked my mom, "was that it?"

"That was it." Back then her eyes watered with laughter.

It took the second and the third copulations to convince me that what we'd seen was real. I was horrified, and I seem to remember losing my interest in cows.

Time passed, we did other things, and then one day my mother reported that all three cows had calved. By that point my interest must have returned, because we visited the babies right away in the calf barn where they were wrapped in coats in individual dry beds and guarded by a white-footed cat. They groaned for milk, and while they waited, I got to let one suck on my hand.

I think of those cows more often than I ever thought I would. So harsh. Such an event. Such sudden, speedy life—

ACKNOWLEDGMENTS

Many generous people contributed to the writing of this book. Monica McGrath and Emily Piacenza led me to Ron Davis, Tre Johnson, and Doug Nettles, who shared football memories and stories. Terry Schuck and John Trojanowski schooled me on brain science. Bernie Caalim, Courtney Cass, Dick Cass, Lisa Dixon, Margot Stern, and Matt Stern provided access to NFL spaces.

I am indebted to the numerous scholars, journalists, and football players whose books helped me to see this story in context. They include Christian G. Appy, *Working-Class War: American Combat Soldiers and Vietnam*; Jefferson Cowie, *Stayin' Alive: The 1970s and the Last Days of the Working Class*; Nicholas Dawidoff, *Collision Low Crossers: Inside the Turbulent World of NFL Football*; Rich Eisen, *Total Access: A Journey to the Center of the NFL Universe*; Mark Fainaru-Wada and Steve Fainaru, *League of Denial: The NFL, Concussions and the Battle for Truth*; John Feinstein, *Next Man Up: A Year Behind the Lines in Today's NFL*; Henry T. Greely, *The End of Sex and the Future of Human Reproduction*; Nate Jackson, *Slow Getting Up: A Story of NFL Survival from the Bottom of the Pile*; T.M. Luhrmann, *When God Talks Back: Understanding the American Evangelical Relationship with God*; Greg O'Brien, *On Pluto: Inside the Mind of Alzheimer's*; Jeff Pearlman, *Boys Will Be Boys: The Glory Days and Party Nights of the Dallas Cowboys Dynasty*; Warren Sapp, *Sapp Attack: My*

Story, and Tony Siragusa, *Goose: The Outrageous Life and Times of a Football Guy.* I absorbed and borrowed a lot from these sources, and from ESPN's "30 for 30: The U," HBO's "The Alzheimer's Project," HBO's "Hard Knocks," PBS's "League of Denial," and especially Michael Robinson's irresistible YouTube show "The Real Rob Report."

My first readers—Jennifer Acker, Jonathan Corcoran, Brady Clegg, Elizabeth Farren, Hannah Gersen, Will Harper, John Hill, Freddi Karp, Matt Karp, Alice Mattison, Tom McAllister, Dave Scrivner, Ross Simonini, and Lauren Steffel—gave valuable feedback on early and late drafts.

Adelphi University, the Wertheim Study at the New York Public Library, the Virginia Center for the Creative Arts, the Wassaic Project, and the Corporation of Yaddo provided indispensable time and space to write.

Jim Rutman believed in my idiosyncratic vision from the start. I'll always be grateful to him for his unwavering faith and labor, and to Robert Lasner and Elizabeth Clementson, who ultimately brought this book into the world.

I couldn't write anything without the support of my friends and family—especially Matt Karp, my partner in spectatorship and everything else. This book has always been for him.

DATE DUE AUG 14 2020